W9-AHR-984

DIFFERENT PEOPLE

DIFFERENT PEOPLE

a novel

ORLAND OUTLAND

alyson books
los angeles | new york

ALL CHARACTERS IN THIS BOOK ARE FICTITIOUS. ANY RESEMBLANCE TO REAL INDIVIDUALS—EITHER LIVING OR DEAD—IS STRICTLY COINCIDENTAL.

© 2002 BY ORLAND OUTLAND. ALL RIGHTS RESERVED.

MANUFACTURED IN THE UNITED STATES OF AMERICA.

THIS HARDCOVER ORIGINAL IS PUBLISHED BY ALYSON PUBLICATIONS,
P.O. BOX 4371, LOS ANGELES, CALIFORNIA 90078-4371.
DISTRIBUTION IN THE UNITED KINGDOM BY TURNAROUND PUBLISHER SERVICES LTD.,
UNIT 3, OLYMPIA TRADING ESTATE, COBURG ROAD, WOOD GREEN,
LONDON N22 6TZ ENGLAND.

FIRST EDITION: OCTOBER 2002

02 03 04 05 06 a 10 9 8 7 6 5 4 3 2 1

ISBN 1-55583-763-8

LIBRARY OF CONGRESS CATALOGING-IN-PUBLICATION DATA
OUTLAND, ORLAND.
    DIFFERENT PEOPLE : A NOVEL / ORLAND OUTLAND.—1ST ED.
    ISBN 1-55583-763-8
    1. GAY MEN—FICTION. I. TITLE.
PS3565.U96 D54 2002
813'.54—DC21   2002071672

CREDITS
JACKET DESIGN BY MATT SAMS.
JACKET FRONT PHOTOGRAPH BY PHILIP PIROLO.

DIFFERENT PEOPLE

CHAPTER ONE
THE WORK OF LOVE

Having just packed off one of her rare visitors from her previous life, Emma Hamilton put on her gardening gloves and stepped out into her backyard, just as many a housewife in Reno, Nevada, was doing this June morning, before it got too hot to work outside. She was naturally a late riser, however, and it was already eleven o'clock, so she'd failed to steal a march on the shimmering dry heat. She wasn't surprised to see her son Eric already at work, hoeing vigorously in the garden.

"How's your water holding out?" she asked him, concerned to see him working shirtless in the hot sun.

"Fine, thanks!" Eric lied cheerfully. His water was gone, but he was in a groove, so to speak, and the last thing he wanted was to stop now. Next, he knew, she would ask about…

"Do you need some more sunblock?"

"No, Mom, but I could use some more SPF 4." He smiled without looking at her, knowing the cross look that would already be on her face.

She sighed, knowing the smile was there and the water was gone, or he wouldn't be tweaking her on the suntan thing to distract her. With his genes from his Greek father, she reflected, he was already tan year round, and the sun only bronzed him more. But skin cancer did not discriminate, she said to herself sternly, readjusting her hat unnecessarily.

"Are you tired yet?" she asked, already wiping her own brow. "You should get out of the sun for a while."

"Are you kidding?" he grinned impishly, looking at her over his shoulder. "Prime tanning hours have just begun!"

"Well, I'm going in," she said, deciding that gardening could wait till another, cooler day. "You want some lemonade?"

"No thanks. I'll take a Coke, though. If you can manage to touch one without pain," he needled her gently.

She rolled her eyes and threw her hands up as she went in. She'd tried to raise him with her own dislike for multinational corporations and the homogenization of cultures they brought with them, but her most passionate speeches had been no match for a boy's lust for yummy white sugar.

She poured him a Coke over ice (at least he'd get *some* water with all that sugar) and grabbed his SPF 4 but stopped on her way back out. Peeking out the window and seeing him oblivious to her, she uncapped the bottle and squeezed its contents into the sink with a noisy *squitch*, uncapped her own SPF 30 and filled his bottle with the sunblock before recapping it. "Small victories," she said to herself with a smile. Such victories were few and far between for her in Reno.

Rudolf had spent his entire visit clucking and chiding her over her choice of "this cultural wasteland, this dreary suburbia, this Yahoovia," much as he'd done on each of his visits over the last 20 years. He'd been one of the few real friends she'd had in New York City way back when, and each time he came he got all dramatic about how much he was willing to put up with by coming here in order to see her—and the boy, of course, he added abstractedly as if Emma hadn't noticed the effect Eric's looks had on him. But she never mentioned that, nor did she mention that Rudolf (whose birth name had been Ralph) might not have made the heroic cross-country effort had he not been as ardent an aficionado of Yahoovia's slot machines as he was of New York's cultural cornucopia. Ra—er, Rudolf never changed, that was for sure. It amused and amazed Emma that someone could go so many years without ever altering a whit. You'd think constant exposure to everything newly pronounced more fabulous than anything to come before would stimulate growth and change in a person, but not for him. On some level, Emma liked Rudolf's visits for precisely this reason: He reassured her that she wasn't missing any personal growth opportunities just because she lived in Reno.

"I like it here," Emma invariably replied. "And besides, this isn't suburbia," she said, indicating her neighborhood. "Suburbia is up the hill." It was true; the house on Arlington Street was in the city's Old Southwest district, where the houses were sturdy and well-aged, with enormous leafy trees and nicely sized lawns—a Thornton Wilder town, she often thought. All that was missing was a bandstand in the park. Reno had more than its share of boxy ugly suburban houses, but those developments were far from the valley floor, steadily consuming the Sierra foothills because such commanding views of the valley commanded the highest prices and therefore the highest profits to developers. As much as she liked the quaintness, however, she rarely admitted that she'd picked a house on Arlington, a busy four-lane street, because the one thing she really missed about the big city was the sound of traffic.

When she'd found herself a single mother in the mid 1960s, she'd grown sick of city life and wanted to give her son something he could never have had in the city. "A real old-fashioned American boyhood," she'd declared to the horror of her compatriots, "used properly, breeds confidence without arrogance and self-esteem without self-obsession. And I'm going to try and give my son one."

She'd picked Reno with care after months of travel; it was a real honest-to-God town, but with enough decadence in its history as a gambling, divorce, and prostitution Mecca to forestall the worst of backwards small-town prejudice. She liked the fact that on one side lay the green Sierras and Lake Tahoe (indisputably one of the most beautiful spots on earth) and on the other the forbidding desert. When she had chosen it, there were no documentaries on PBS detailing the complex ecosystems of the "living desert"; what lay to the east was, to her and most people, a whole lot of nothing. Only a few protested with bumper stickers saying NEVADA IS NOT A WASTELAND in response to politicians' efforts to ship nuclear waste to a state with only two members in the House of Representatives.

She had made a great concession by moving to Reno, not in leaving behind her liberal artistic friends, and most every form of culture, but because her politics were dear to her, as they had been dear to her mother, and she knew that there would be few signers in Reno for petitions to stop bombing Vietnam, stop building nuclear power plants, stop killing whales and dolphins and weird little fish who'd die if a dam was built. Emma had been a genuine "red diaper baby," named by her bohemian mother after Admiral Hamilton's famous mistress (only later his wife). Emma's mother had dramatically declared that she hoped her Emma, too, would make her mark on history.

But Emma had not chosen Reno as a place to make enemies, but as a place to raise a son. If villagers with torches appeared to ban a book from a school library, or drum a suspected homosexual teacher out of the school district, Emma could be found at the castle gate, denouncing the witch burners, trying—if nothing else worked—to shame them into doing the right thing. But years of watching her mother flit from cause to cause had taught Emma to choose her battles, and for the most part, her voice was raised in the bleachers at Little League games, cheering on Eric and his teammates, shouting out the opposing pitcher's weaknesses (which she had ruthlessly recorded in her scouting book from previous encounters). The dams and the fish were not to be saved in Reno, but perhaps her son could save them after he grew up strong and confident and safe—yes, safe: she had to admit that, even as liberal as she was, she had not felt safe as a woman alone in the city in 1966 when her son was born, and did not feel that he would be safe either. Maybe nothing moved or changed in Reno, but in most parts of town nothing jumped you in the dark either.

She poured herself a glass of iced tea and looked out the kitchen window at Eric. She couldn't help but think with a laugh of the proverbial hunky gardener—where was E. M. Forster to drool over the boy, or at least Colleen McCullough? He was a sight, no doubt of that. Eric Hamilton was 6 foot 2, blessed with his father's big shoulders (and his mother's big hips, too, though it would be some years before those would catch up with him). He'd broken 200 pounds by the time he was 18 and had a full mat of chest hair a year before that. In addition to inheriting his father's olive skin, he'd also gotten his dark curly locks and Greek beauty.

Like any mother, she was sad he'd turned out gay—but like a liberal mother, sad because he was going to have to face so much more gratuitous heartache in life than other people. She had reason to be sad: This was 1988, a very bad time to be anyone or anything off the dot. She'd never been embarrassed to talk about sex with her son, made a point of answering every question on the subject in both clinical and romantic terms. She'd raised him to believe sex was an expression of love between two people, even though she knew that with a young libido and his looks, love probably had little to do with what he was up to these days. Even before he'd come to realize he was gay, he knew from his mother that being gay was an expression of nature's plan, whether to reduce population or free certain people from child-rearing responsibilities, she couldn't say. Emma never believed people chose being gay any more than she believed other people chose being stupid enough to insist otherwise.

He'd had girlfriends in high school, and while she never asked for details, she knew he'd had an adequate heterosexual sex life, but she'd suspected he was gay—the way he'd inordinately idolized some of his friends in his early teens, and his lack of enthusiasm for any of the (for the most part) pretty, clever girls he'd dated. When he'd come home from his first year at Bennington and made the announcement that he was gay, she'd sighed with relief—just from not having to wonder anymore.

"There is nothing wrong with it, and never has been and never will be," she said during one of those speeches, the ones he knew were not about issues and politics but about people, the ones that would be as true tomorrow as today, the ones that somehow reached him the way the ones about politics never did, to her consternation. "But there are a lot of people out there who are really—I have to say it, there is no other word that will do—they are fucked up in the head about sex. And they will ignore every other good thing about you because they think this one thing is so bad."

Now Eric had made it through high school without getting any girls pregnant, and through college without getting any social diseases (that she knew about, she thought with a shudder; at least she knew he was HIV-negative). She knew he'd had boyfriends in school, young men he'd mentioned, but she also knew that she and her son were too close for him to have had a passionate connection with someone without informing her.

The doorbell rang and she went to it smiling, knowing that it was Carol Hewitt's boy Cal, come over to make some extra money helping out around the house. And it was partly because she knew her son was still unattached that when she'd run into Cal at Safeway by himself, she'd asked him for his relatively unnecessary help.

"Hello, Cal," she said with a smile. "Come out of the heat and have some lemonade."

Not that it was in her nature to play matchmaker, but she knew—even if Carol didn't (or wouldn't acknowledge)—that Cal was gay, too. He'd lived just down the street from the Hamiltons, but he'd never been a friend of Eric's; Eric had been an enthusiastic team sports player from the day he could crawl over and wrestle another baby, whereas Cal was the "studious" type, too quiet to be anything but a little afraid of Eric's raucous group of friends. Cal was fit, she'd noted, not having lost the appraising eye for men her mother had given her. She knew from Eric's yearbooks that Cal ran track and played tennis— played it well, too.

Not that she monitored all the young men in the neighborhood, or in Eric's life either. Most of them were happy puppies, some of them troubled by family problems but not seriously damaged. But Cal had always intrigued her—she couldn't put her finger on it. He was beautiful, for starters, but not effeminate or willowy. Slim and smooth, he had startling eyes, if only from the color, which she would swear was blue at some times and gray at others, depending on what he wore. There was a *directness* about him when he looked at you that could disconcert you if you were used to absent gazes. He was reading you, challenging you: *Interest me*, he demanded with the imperious of the talented and bored adolescent. If he'd been deliberately cooler, if he'd favored some sort of "rebel" pose, he would have been killingly sexy to his peers, but he sported a bland Gap look of jeans and khakis, T-shirts and polos and button downs, a sort of neutrality that projected disdain for even trying to look cool.

One day Emma had been out watering the front yard when she'd seen another neighborhood boy walking down the street behind Cal after school, who had suddenly and inexplicably (so it seemed to Emma) shouted, "Hey! Faggot!"

Cal had frozen in his tracks, and she'd instantly known from the look on his face that the taunt was true: *Caught!* was the look on his face. What had startled her most was not this confirmation of the truth, but the change in the boy. The cool imperious mien was gone; suddenly, he was a frightened little mouse, as if this one thing about him could knock the pillars out from under everything else.

"Afternoon, Cal," she'd said conversationally to break up the moment. The other boy looked at her sourly, for spoiling his fun. Cal, after all, was only a faggot and therefore OK to beat up, so his family and his world had told this boy. Perhaps the only thing that stopped him now was his surprise in seeing an adult looking at him as if he was about to do something, well, wrong.

Cal turned to her and made eye contact. It was one of those moments you can't readily sum up afterward in words, but don't have to: *Don't worry*, her eyes had said. *I won't tell. And it's all right.* She could see the fear in him, even though she had plainly intervened on his behalf; he was practically sniffing the air as if sensing a trap. He nodded back to her curtly, resumed his mask, and quickly cut across the street to his house and safety. Cal (and Eric) had been 16 at the time, and she had taken special notice of him ever after.

She'd noticed something else, too: Cal's cool melted whenever he saw Eric. "Hey, Cal," Eric would say when he saw him on the block (reserving a nod and a short, friendly, but almost silent "Hey" for hallway encounters at school), and Cal would whisper, "Hi..." Eric would coast by on the wind he'd just taken out of Cal's sails. It seemed to Emma that most adults must never look at children's faces; if they did, they'd know so much more about them. At that age, she thought, they can't hide it. Their emotions are right there on the surface, and the only way you can miss them is not to look.

Every time she saw their brief, slight interactions, she thanked God she wasn't a kid anymore, because she knew Cal's head like her own at those moments. It wasn't just Eric's beauty, enough to force anyone that age to stab themselves with their own hormones; it was his goodness, his kindness—not the fresh-faced student body president's calculated bonhomie but a genuine, fresh, good cheer he felt when he saw you, recognizing you as part of his sunny world. And Cal's world, she well knew, was darker than Eric's. Eric had everything you could want, he was everything you'd want to be, and he was so nice you couldn't hate him for it—what could hurt more?

Sometimes when Eric came home, Emma would be working out in the front yard, and something from across the street would would catch her eye. The Hewitts lived one house across and over from her, and the front of Emma's house was visible from Cal's bedroom window on the side of the Hewitt house. In fact, it got to be a habit with her at these times to peek up discreetly from under the brim of her sunbonnet and see if Cal was watching from his window, perhaps even waiting there to catch a sight of Eric coming home. Quite often he was.

Until this summer, she hadn't seen Cal in four years. She wasn't on speaking terms with the Hewitts and hadn't been for eight years. Once upon a time they'd been ignorable crackpots, but the rise of the Moral Majority had made them a real threat to everything she held dear. She and the Hewitts had been civil to each other as neighbors, until they'd helped run the Gay Rodeo out of town and made more than a legal amount of trouble for the local Planned Parenthood clinic. She'd always known Cal wasn't one of *them*, and his failure to come home for summers hadn't entirely surprised her. (She got her news of the Hewitts from a neighbor who remained neutral, more out of a keen desire to hear everyone's gossip than out of politics, and who Emma was sure passed as much information from one side of the street as she did to the other.)

This morning Cal smiled back at her greeting a little sheepishly and entered the house with a knot in his stomach. He was dreading the moment he was anticipating, the moment when he would be face-to-face with the one boy who had the power to hurt him. Adolescence is full of these moments where you are driven to do the one thing that is most likely to break your heart because you know it's going to hurt whether you do it or not; powerful longing paired with youthful, willful optimism force you toward your object of desire, even as painful shyness and self-abnegation push you away.

"Eric's out back," Emma said immediately, sensing his tension. "We'll leave him there for a bit while you cool down."

Cal *was* tense. He couldn't see Emma's face as she walked ahead of him to the kitchen and wondered if she knew. How could she? He'd never been here, she'd never seen him with Eric—hell, he'd never *been* with Eric, only crossed his path, except for their senior year of high school, when he'd had one class with him, an unavoidable science class in which Cal had kept a monastic silence. He'd gotten his only C that year, so intent had he been on simultaneously looking and trying not to look at Eric, seated alphabetically next to him. That year Cal had completely failed to grasp any laws of physics but he could tell you the exact position of every vein and hair on Eric Hamilton's right forearm. One hot summer day, Eric had broken the dress code and worn a tank top, and Cal had nearly died of fear that he'd be caught staring. That day he had turned to look at Eric full-on only when Eric spoke in class.

Cal could vouch for the theory that lust can give anyone a photographic memory.

Coming to this house today was the closest Cal had ever come to acting on his desires. They were allowed a certain range of motion inside his head where nobody could see them, but must otherwise be suppressed. *I can't be gay* vied in his head with *Nobody must ever know.* Today he forced himself to think that Eric had been away at college in some fraternity, drinking beer and getting fat. He would see less the golden boy he'd known than the complacently deteriorating bourgeois man all his other peers were becoming. This thought steeled him for the encounter. He had been horrified when she'd asked him at Safeway to come help her out, his first thought being that Eric would be there, and yet this was one of those moments where his desires exceeded their bounds, heedless of the punishment that might await. "Sure," they'd said for him while he was still in shock.

"I'm so glad you could come help," Emma chirped as she poured the lemonade. "Eric is taking care of the outdoor stuff, but there are things around the house that...well, he isn't...graceful, let's put it that way!" Which indeed Eric was not. For someone who could catch a football or a baseball with ease, he had a remarkable talent for knocking things over that he hadn't even seen until they were on pieces on the floor, as if vases were like catchers, meant to be smashed aside on your way to the plate.

"I'm glad to do it, Mrs. Hamilton."

"Emma, please. You're not a child."

Cal flushed a bit, pleased with the compliment but not sure he'd be able to get his mouth around her name so casually. *Eric isn't graceful, huh,* he thought. The idea of Eric fat and clumsy was a relief to him—it meant he wouldn't embarrass himself by drooling the way he thought he had in high school. Cal always wondered if Eric had noticed his attentions, if maybe that was why he was only passingly friendly.

Cal heard the sliding glass door open as he thirstily drank the last of his lemonade. "Mom, I could use that suntan lotion." His peripheral vision around the glass told him only that a large shape had entered the room. As he lowered the glass, he choked a bit on the last of the juice as Eric came fully into view.

Eric was not fat. Eric was unspeakably gorgeous. Cal drank in the sight of Eric in his khaki shorts and naught else but shoes with a greater thirst than he'd had for the lemonade. He had a hairy chest now, Cal noted, and his muscles were bigger—not Michelin man–bodybuilder muscles, but…well, *just right* for his frame. He was *resplendent.* Rare is the boy with such beauty who does not know that he is the Sun King, but Eric did not, discounting the value others placed on his physical gifts, as Emma had taught him to do. "Hey, Cal Hewitt, how are you?" Eric offered his hand to shake.

Cal took it, all sensors as he took Eric's—as Eric took his hand. Big, strong, meaty, sweaty palm, a brush of the hairs as Cal's thumb locked between Eric's thumb and forefinger, where Cal felt the softest, smoothest, warmest, well-hydrated skin. A firm press and a release that Cal was alert enough not to let cause his own hand to dangle there, tingling. "Hi, Eric." There had been more pleasure in the sensation of his thumb on Eric's skin than he had gotten from anything else in his entire life, and he was on fire with desire for more.

"So are you out of school, too?" Eric asked.

"Yeah, just had graduation last week."

"Where'd you go?"

Cal flushed, automatically launching into his explanation. "Well, I had to go where my parents would pay for me to go, which was American Christian College. It wasn't my choice," he insisted. "I mean, I could have gotten a scholarship somewhere else, maybe, but they wouldn't have paid my living expenses and—"

"A college degree is a college degree," Emma said, handing Cal his refilled glass. "Eric went to Bennington and got his in English Lit. And as far as I'm concerned, a degree from Bennington is about as good as the paper it's printed on." This was not really her opinion; secretly she'd been thrilled when Eric had chosen Bennington. For so many years he'd been on the "right track," that programmatic high school amalgam of sports, academics, and civic involvement that in many young people was part of a ruthlessly calculated design to get into the "right school." For Eric to chuck the expected outcome to go to a school where there was no track, where he would have to design his own way, had been a source of pride to her and he knew it, although they'd chosen to make a joke of her "disapproval."

Eric laughed. "She said I'd never be taken seriously with a degree from Bennington," he said, referring to the school's freewheeling atmosphere of self-directed education and student-selected curriculum. She had indeed said that, hoping that parental disapproval would reinforce a teenager's desire to do something wild and unexpected. But Eric had always known she wasn't reiterating her own views but only telling him what the rest of the world would say about his decision to jump off the "right track." "I'd never get a job. I told her, 'I'm going to get a B.A. in English Lit,—nobody's going to give me a job anyway!'"

"Well, that beats a business degree from ACC," Cal said. "Unless you want to become an accountant for Jerry Falwell." Emma and Eric laughed, and Cal had to smile along with them.

"Well, Cal, I'll get you started in a few minutes here. There's some cleaning supplies in the garage, but I want to get them. I know how to get to them without knocking anything over," she said, winking at Eric. Eric only sighed. "In the meantime," she said, handing Cal a feather duster, "why not take this and start dusting Eric's bookshelves—starting on *top* of the bookcase, which I'm sure is filthy—and I'll come get you in a few minutes."

"Mom," Eric registered his due course protest. "It's just dusty."

"'Just dusty.' Ugh," she said, handing off the duster to Cal and disappearing out the door to the garage.

Eric smiled. "Mom hates my lack of respect for spit and polish. Come on, I'll show you my room."

Nervous as a cat though he was, Cal had to laugh. "I'll show you my room" was so high school. *Appropriate, I guess*, he thought, *since I feel like a fucking teenager!* Eric was still shirtless, and as he walked behind him up the stairs to the bedroom, Cal's eyes couldn't decide whether to fix on his shoulders, his big waist, his big gorgeous muscular ass, or his veiny, hairy legs. Cal panicked as he realized he was developing a hard-on. "Think of England!" was what his sister Gina always said to calm herself down when a gorgeous man walked by; he laughed silently as the thought popped unbidden into his mind.

Eric's room was a surprise to Cal. He'd expected some of it—posters of sports stars, none of whom he recognized, the college banners (Notre Dame seemed the favorite; he didn't see one for Bennington and wondered if they even had a sports program), the trophies—but he hadn't been prepared for the books. Three bookcases, stuffed full! It was Cal's habit in any house to examine the books first, without even asking or commenting until after he'd "read" his host.

"You're a big reader," Cal said, praying that Eric wouldn't say they were his Mom's, stuffed in here for lack of room. And yet also praying that he would, because then he could put Eric in a box labeled "jock" and leave him there, where he couldn't torment Cal any more. Well, as much.

"Yeah, I'm a bookworm at heart. Don't tell anyone and spoil my big jock image."

Cal laughed and checked Eric's face. No sarcasm, just a playful smile, an acknowledgment of the inevitability of first impressions.

Eric had been a jock, but there had always been time for books, time enough for everything in his inexhaustible boy life—he'd worn his mother down every day long before wearing himself out. In the warm summer evenings, the other parents had called in their sons (and daughters: Eric had been sure to include girls in any games, for which they had worshiped him all the more than they already did), but Emma let Eric stay out as long as he wanted, knowing that the curfews of the other boys would act as his, too. When they were all in for the night, he would come in, grab a snack or even another dinner and head up to his room and read for hours, mostly fiction to her distress. (He wouldn't read *The Autobiography of Malcolm X*, now one of his favorite books, until college because it was one of the books his mother had tried to foist on him as a boy).

Cal scanned the books. A lot of science fiction, mostly the old stuff: Edgar Rice Burroughs's Tarzan and John Carter, Ray Bradbury's Martians and rocket men, Isaac Asimov's robots and foundations...tons of books on outer space, including Michener's *Space* and a new book Cal had heard about called *A Brief History of Time*, the joke about which was that everybody was buying it but nobody was smart enough to read it...all kinds of baseball books, everything baseball from box scores to biographies...three shelves of Oxford and Penguin Classics, mostly English lit, Cal noted, spanning 150 years from Richardson's *Pamela* (and a copy of the mammoth *Clarissa*, the spine well-cracked, Cal noted with awe) to Joyce's *Portrait of the Artist as a Young Man*. There were a handful of moderns, but not many.

"Did you read *Clarissa* for school?" Cal asked.

"No, for fun. It's a big book, I know, but it's not as intimidating as it looks," Eric explained.

Cal nodded. "The longest novel in the English language. I liked Harriet a lot better than Clarissa, of course."

Eric practically yelped with delight. "You read it! You really read it!"

Cal smiled. "'To *hope* for better days is half to *deserve* them. For who could hope for better who knew they did not deserve it? These are the thoughts with which I endeavor to support myself.'" He was paraphrasing, he knew, but he'd gotten the essence of it.

Eric wanted to hug Cal, he was so overcome with glee. "*Nobody* reads that book who doesn't have to."

It was Cal's turn to raise an eyebrow. "You did."

"You did too."

The look in Eric's eyes thrilled and frightened Cal. He had never seen it before in another person. One of the happiest moments in any life is this moment, the moment of the thrill of discovery of a fellow creature, the moment you realize an important part of you that you thought was yours alone, freaky and lonely, was a human part, belonging to another, too, and as such making you more a human being than you ever thought you were or could be.

Cal took the chair from Eric's desk and stood on it to reach the topmost shelf where *Clarissa* stood next to Fielding and Smollett and others Cal hadn't heard of—Maria Edgeworth, Susan Lennox, Fanny Burney.

Maybe Eric had already been primed for it by the *Clarissa* discovery; maybe the door would have opened anyway. Cal stood on the chair and reached up for the book, his untucked T-shirt rising over his midriff. It was the first picture of Cal that would strike Eric's own memory with the photographic force his body had had on Cal's—the young man's almost impossibly slim waist and well-ridged abdomen; the pelvic V shape that for some reason drove Eric crazy; the bubble butt that the khakis only outlined, Eric's imagination filling in the rest; Cal's tan and glowing skin (Eric had not been unaware of Cal's skin during their handshake)—the same perfect skin on his long, lean arm; the biceps revealed as he stretched, economical and wiry but by no means powerless—the profile, the graceful way the nose came straight down to a droplet at the end (a droplet Cal despised and wished he could have chopped off), and the slightly parted lips, the long graceful neck, all of which seemed to command Eric to kiss them.

When Cal saw Eric, he *thought*, he registered his hormones, and he registered the pain and worked to crack some joke or find some internal flaw that would shut the system down before he felt what he didn't want to feel, couldn't stand to feel, wasn't allowed to feel. Whereas Eric could just look at Cal and let it happen—let his heart break at the sight of something so beautiful that stood in complete ignorance of just how beautiful it was right now, let his heart break at the proximity of something he wanted to touch but wasn't touching. The pain that Cal ran from was sweet to Eric—it was a pain he'd never felt, a pain he instinctively knew meant that he was *alive, now, in this moment*. Rarely in a lifetime are we actually in the presence of what we truly desire, instead of only alone with our wishes and dreams for it. And it does hurt to be in its presence; in our dreams we always reach out and possess it, but in the world we rarely ever do, or if we do, we break it or chase it away. In this moment, Eric did not fear the pain as Cal did; his experience so far insisted that life was good, that it was good to feel all that life could give you to feel.

Cal stepped down off the chair, book in hand. He noticed the crust of dust on top of it and blew it off, coughing at the cloud. "And you haven't read it recently."

Eric regained his composure. Bennington had taught him much; perhaps most importantly, he'd learned from his peers how to be cool in these moments. "I read it in high school, actually. Did you know Mr. Weir? He taught Senior English? He said he wouldn't make us read it, but he begged us to."

"Same here. I had Mr. Werewolf second period."

"Wow, right after I did," Eric mused.

"Yeah," Cal said, remembering far better than Eric. The high hormonal point of his day had been when he'd gotten to Weir's class and found Eric still lingering, talking to the teacher. Cal had thought he was the only boy in the world who lived for a glimpse of forbidden fruit, never even daring to dream of tasting it, so overloaded by what he felt at just the glimpse of it; so much power had he invested in the object that, had he reached out to touch it, he would have been electrocuted.

Cal assumed a haughty demeanor, one hand over his heart and *Clarissa* in the air like a fundamentalist's Bible. " 'If you don't love this book,'" he intoned sonorously in perfect mimicry of the teacher.

" 'You have no soul!'" Eric joined him in conclusion. "Wait a minute—you called him 'Mr. Werewolf'?"

"That beard!" Cal said emphatically. "Remember how it grew up over his cheekbones? Like to right beneath his eyes? We called him Mr. Werewolf."

"I never heard that one."

God, Cal thought, *we really were in different worlds*. He'd thought everybody had called him that.

Eric turned the chair backwards and sat down, legs straddled around its back. "Sit down," he said, indicating the bed. Cal sat down on the side of the bed, a sudden sunny feeling coming over him as he unexpectedly relaxed. "So we just missed each other senior year," Eric said, and neither of them even registered that Eric had noted a regret at not having met Cal years before, for it was a regret they both felt. "What did you have first period?"

"Speech and debate. We'd sell doughnuts before school to raise money for trips to tournaments, and we'd eat the leftovers during first period."

"Oh, yeah," Eric chuckled. "I tried to stay away from the doughnuts, keep in shape. I would've liked debate. That would've been fun." Eric shrugged. "But there just wasn't enough time for everything, you know."

Cal didn't know; his own interests had been rather narrow. "You would've been good in oratory," he said, thinking how Eric's looks and demeanor alone would have convinced anyone he talked to directly for ten minutes. "But you would've been killed in debate."

Eric lifted an eyebrow. "Oh? Why's that?"

"You're too nice. No killer instinct. The kids who won in debate were the little sharks who were already on the law school track."

"As opposed to the B school track?" Eric asked, wondering what the difference was, if any.

Eric must have known Cal was going to B school next, and he looked at him for signs of sarcasm but saw none apparent. "Yeah. You go to law school to fuck over people. You go to B school to fuck over corporations."

Eric laughed harder than Cal expected, a surprised and delighted sound. "So what comes next for you?" Eric asked.

"I'm going to Stanford Business School for an MBA. I did better in the bullshit subjects in college than I did in high school, and got that all-important GPA." Cal had managed to conquer the "boring" subjects like math and science, but had been dismayed to discover just how much math business school would involve.

"And then what?"

"Make money," Cal said flatly. This, it must be stated, was his ambition, not his dream. Debate and public speaking and his flirtations with drama through his sister's heavy involvement in theater had given him a desire to be an actor, but actors starved, waited tables, had no power, and probably never made it.

"Yeah, I know a lot of people I went to school with who are going to B school or law school. They all realized this year that nobody was coming to campus to recruit us for jobs. But money's not that important to me, I guess." Throughout college, Eric had been content with a roof over his head, three squares, some money to party with on the weekends, and just enough money for used books and CDs. He knew his B.A. would probably lead to a job in a bookstore or work as a temp (corporations were desperate for administrative help who could spell and form complete sentences), but it didn't worry him.

"It's the most important thing in the world," Cal said, putting *Clarissa* down on the bed.

"Why?"

Cal looked at him incredulously. "Because money is power. Because with money nobody can stop you from doing what you want."

"Nobody can stop you from doing what you want anyway," Eric asserted.

"Yes, they can," Cal emphasized.

Eric shrugged. Genuinely happy people have a way of simply turning away from other people's bitter outbursts, letting the free-floating anger fly by without coloring their opinion of the person, as if it were a personality tic like cracking your knuckles that you could just ignore.

"And how about yourself?" Cal asked. "What's next for you?"

"I'm going to write," Eric said authoritatively. The way he said it surprised Cal. He'd heard people say "I want to be a famous novelist," or "I want to get a job at a big magazine," but Eric hadn't said what he wanted to do; he'd said what he was going to do.

"Nobody can stop you from doing that," Cal said poker-faced. He let Eric look at him for a second before he smiled slightly. Eric laughed, a new twinkle in his eye that said to Cal, *You surprise me.* The intimacy of it struck Cal in the gut; he swallowed and looked away. "I should get this dusting done," he said, getting up off the bed. He noted that Eric had a computer on his desk and examined it as critically as he'd examined the books. "386?"

"Huh?"

"Your computer. Is it a 386?"

"Umm…" Eric looked on the front of the machine. "It's a Leading Edge."

Cal laughed. "OK. WordPerfect or WordStar?"

"WordPerfect. Whew, glad I knew that one. So are you a nerd or something? No offense, you just seem to know a lot about computers."

"You should get a Mac."

"I should get an inheritance, too—then I could afford one."

Cal winced a bit. There was no arguing with either the Mac's superiority or its out-of-range price. "If you sign up for a class at some school, you can get a student discount on a Mac."

Eric shrugged. "I type on it, you know? The best computer in the world isn't going to get me to type any faster."

Cal laughed. "There are a lot of other things you can do with a computer."

"There are a lot of other things *you* can do with a computer," Eric smiled. "I'm a writer. Writers will never need a computer for anything other than typing."

"That's true enough," Cal admitted. "Can I have the chair again?"

Eric leapt up, eager to allow Cal to stand before him again, stretching to dust the top shelves. "Well, I can't say I endorse going to B school, but I'm glad you're going to Stanford. I'm moving to San Francisco myself, so maybe we can get together sometime…" Eric surprised himself with how hopefully he'd left the idea hanging there.

Just what is the biological reaction that causes that feeling, where your whole upper body from bowels to head turns to ice? Something like the moment when a roller coaster finishes its slow crawl to the tip of the first peak and the descent begins, small amounts of anticipation and dread suddenly combusting to produce exhilaration and terror.

"Yeah, sure," Cal said evenly, returning to dusting and

wondering if he was about to vomit up the suddenly sour lemonade in his stomach. A cascade of visions steamrolled through his head in a second, joyous and painful—he and Eric happy in bed in San Francisco, his parents finding out, having to drop out of school for lack of funds, being nothing and nobody and at the mercy of everyone. Maybe Eric could stand that kind of life, but not Cal. And Eric can't be gay—he can't be; Cal knew what gay people were—gay people were sissies. Eric was no sissy. *I'm an idiot*, he thought. *I'd make a pass at him and he'd tell. He'd tell because he'd be so disgusted...* "I'm not sure how much time I'll have once I'm in school. I think it's a pretty intense program."

"Yeah," Eric said, nodding. "I bet it is." He'd been startled by Cal's offhand...well, dismissal was what it felt like to Eric. *Let's do lunch sometime, my people will call your people*, he thought angrily. *I thought I made a friend, but I guess not.* Eric could not yet know that while, for him, desire was the overture to greater things, for Cal, it was the warning trumpet of doom.

"Well," Eric said, pulling on a Bennington T-shirt, "guess I'll go hit the yard again."

"OK. See you later."

"Sure."

Eric attacked the weeds out back with no less fury than Cal vanquished the dust from Eric's books. Eric, however, had the advantage of taking out his aggressions on ugly, spiky parasites whose removal was a service to the floral public, whereas Cal was only tormented further by still more intimate looks at Eric's book collection.

The sound of crunchy weeds meeting their fate came through the house (Eric had left the sliding glass door open), letting Cal know it was safe to slip a book or two off the shelf for further inspection. He could tell from the black thumb streak across the side of the pages of *A Brief History of Time* that Eric had actually read it. The next bookcase held little of interest, mostly textbooks from college classes, though he did find one shelf of contemporary fiction. None of the titles were familiar to him: *The Broom of the System, History: A Novel, Shikasta.* Then he saw a title that froze him as quickly as Eric's proposition had. *Dancer From the Dance.*

He's gay. He's gay! Cal sat down on the chair. He'd never forgotten a trip to San Francisco he'd taken with his parents when he was 17. They'd gone for some Republican political thing for his dad, and the family's expeditions in the Land of Sin had been narrowly confined to Union Square and vicinity. But Cal had been left to himself for a moment at TRO Harper Books on Powell Street while his parents, always bored in book-stores, took his sister to the jeans store across the street. Skimming the shelves, his eye had been caught by a book with a handsome shirtless young man on the cover, sweater tied across his shoulders, smiling in a friendly and inviting way. To Cal, the image wasn't a marketing ploy. He still had no idea how greedy he would be in coming years for friendly smiles from gorgeous men, but whoever approved it must have been a gay man, must have known how *different* it would feel to a gay man to have one of his own smile at him automatically, without even knowing if the object of the smile was young enough or cute enough to "deserve it." Cal picked it up and read the back cover's description of a life given over to pleasure, to the dance, to...sex with men.

Nothing in adulthood can ever command our totemic fasci-nation the way certain discoveries in adolescence can—especially the sexual totems. A first *Playboy* for some, a boy or girl in the neighborhood or at school for others, or, for a few, a book. Cal didn't think, he grabbed the book and raced to the front, some teen instinct telling him to grab several innocuous classics (including *Clarissa*), which he could produce from the bag at the requisite "What did you get?" question from his parents, books that would immediately bore them out of their need to pry. (If they'd known about the rape in *Clarissa*, though, they might have objected.)

Dancer was immediately packed in an inside pocket of his suitcase, where Cal imagined it slowly burned a hole through the nylon, like the Ark in *Raiders*, until his parents could see it. Back in Reno, the book went into the same drawer of his desk where he kept his cigarettes, and came out only after everyone's bedtime. As Eric sat up late with his lights blazing, reading anything that caught his fancy, down the street Cal read *Dancer* under the covers with a flashlight like a kid with a forbidden comic book he had to finish.

When he finished it near dawn, he turned off the flashlight and lay there stunned. The early morning sky was a J. Crew shade of blue and he felt as if he, too, had stumbled out of the noisy darkened club into the surprising light of a world where the day was beginning and not ending. He already had enough critical faculties to realize that there hadn't been a single sex scene in the book, and yet the whole book had been like eating some lush, overripe fruit that was a sensual experience better than most sex. All those men, drugging and dancing and fucking! *Living* to drug and dance and fuck! It was a world that had (Cal thought) been vaporized by AIDS. It tempted and repelled him and definitely frightened him—who had Malone been before New York, but Cal? Who had those Dutch sailors Malone had worshiped on Aruba been? Who had been those men walking dogs in the park, or the air traffic controllers, but Mr. Houk the gym teacher, all muscle and veins and blocky good looks; Sam the janitor, long and lean and projecting a sexuality that would get him transferred to an elementary school once the administration realized the depth of certain girls' attraction to him—who had all those objects of desire been but Eric, who was everything God and self-confidence could give a boy?

He felt sick, flat out on his bed waiting for the dawn. He had been raised far differently than Eric had, and while he had held fast to his basically rational core, despite all the onslaughts of his family, their friends, and his conservative education, there were some notions that had penetrated. Homosexuals are sick, they are child molesters, they recruit, they are miserable and drown their misery in sex and drugs (*Dancer* certainly confirmed that in his mind), and God had punished them with AIDS. Cal looked at the name on the book—Andrew Holleran—and the date of publication—1978. *He's dead*, Cal thought. *He's dead, he must be, they're all dead of AIDS.*

AIDS for Cal was what it was for most Americans—a skeletal figure in bed, days or (as in the infamous Benetton ad) even minutes before death: a Hieronymous Bosch painting brought to life, horrible purple sores all over your body. Even this Andrew Holleran had known it was coming, Cal thought—what was the fire at the Everard Baths, that all-consuming conflagration, but a metaphor for AIDS? Even though AIDS hadn't come down on them by the time of this book (well, it had; they were all infecting each other then, he reckoned), it was still a metaphor for something that would *have* to come and kill people who lived for nothing but pleasure. Wasn't it?

AIDS is God's punishment, AIDS is God's punishment rang in his ears. His crafty intellect had slipped through so many nooses slung around its neck over the years—only born again Christians would go to Heaven; Hell was full of secular humanists and papists; the Day of Judgment would occur exactly as predicted in the Book of Revelations and the Trilateral Commission would be consigned to eternal flames—but none of those things had been *about him.* He had always known there was something wrong with him; there had always been a voice inside him reminding him, *You're a faggot, you're a faggot, you're a faggot.*

"I'm..." he'd whispered to the ceiling. *No. I can't be.* He wouldn't say the words that had sealed Malone's fate. *I just can't be. I have enough problems already. I just can't.*

And he still just couldn't. He channeled his libido into dusting Eric's books as quickly as possible, careful to look only at the tops of them after that. "I'm done in there," he told Emma when he found her downstairs, "and I have to go."

Emma's eyebrows betrayed her. "Oh? Is there something wrong?"

"The dust. It's really got to me. Sorry."

"Oh, honey, that's no problem! I'm sorry, I should have thought of that. It's probably been years since Eric's touched some of those books." She looked around, lost for a moment, wondering what had really happened up there. "Just let me get my purse and I'll pay you."

"No, no, I couldn't ask you to pay me just for dusting," Cal said, waving a hand as he made for the front door.

"No," Emma said firmly, like a mother to an unruly child. Cal froze in his tracks. "I insist on paying you."

A key turned in his head. He was suddenly sure she knew about his attraction to Eric, suddenly and sickeningly realizing *she'd* set them up. Those shelves had gone undusted all those years; she didn't give a shit about dust! *She knows,* he thought. *She knows. Oh God...*

Emma fished a $20 bill from her purse. "It's not much these days, but it'll buy you some seditious literature," she finished with a wink. "I recommend H. L. Mencken."

Cal laughed weakly and nearly stumbled out of the house. *Oh God, oh God, I've made a mistake, she knows, she knows...* If she knew, it was real, it was true, it was obvious: he was lovesick for another man—everybody could see it. *They must all know every time they see me look at him....* He was young and still thought all adults basically alike in their perception; if one could see it, they could all see the truth.

I must never, ever go there again, he thought, resolved to fight it. *I can't, I can't, I can't stand it, I couldn't stand it, to be hated and get sick and die hated for being sick....*

Eric's house had a basement that Emma had converted to a "boy room." The house on Arlington was a big old house, loose and rambling for the most part, but the bedrooms had all been huddled together upstairs for protection by some uptight old Victorian to whom it never occurred that a boy would want to have enough privacy to whack off without his mother having to pass his room to get to the bathroom.

It had occurred to Emma, however, and she hadn't set foot in the basement for years. Down here Eric had their old couch, a TV and VCR he'd bought with high school job wages, some posters, some dirty magazines stuffed behind the couch, and a little fridge. Eric was one of those young men who can and must masturbate several times a day, and strenuous yard work only activated his hormones. He tried to concentrate on one of the guys in *Advocate Men*, but he couldn't get excited. He skirted around it for a second, resolving that he wouldn't beat off thinking about a rude asshole like Cal, but hormones have their own resolve, and moments after thinking of Cal's exposed stomach and trim waist...a waist he could probably almost put his hands around as he ground his dick up against Cal's perfect bubble butt... He exploded, vanquished by the boy he fantasized about conquering.

Eric hadn't read *Dancer* until college, under the tutelage of a Bennington professor—not of literature, but of anthropology, as an artifact from a lost civilization. The revolving diorama of sex and drugs had neither sickened nor appalled him; he'd only felt sorry for people who hadn't had what only Malone dared to say out loud was what they'd all really wanted—someone to love.

Eric had felt plenty of adulation heaped on him in his youth, more and more of it sexual in nature after he'd hit adolescence. Girls had worshiped him, and boys, too, though sometimes the boys didn't quite know themselves why. He'd taken all the sexual worship he'd received with a level head. From the day of his first nocturnal discharge, Emma had never flinched from telling him everything about sex—gay and straight—from telling him that it was all good, and also advising him that he was coming into an inheritance only God could mete out—a beauty that would bring him power over others without his even asking for it or seeking it. And he knew from her other lectures—the ones that really mattered, he tacitly understood, not like the Coca-Cola ones—that power was a responsibility, asked for or not....

Eric had never been molested, never had sex turned into something outside himself, which he could disconnect from while he used it to get what he needed. He had never been selfish enough to turn it into a vehicle for his own satisfaction that made his partner nothing but a hole, and he had never been used and thrown away by someone else that selfish. He'd had few partners, all of them boyfriends—all the sex he'd ever enjoyed had been a friendly exchange of pleasure.

And there was no way he could know why Cal gave him the brush-off. He didn't have many self-esteem issues, but nobody is without them. His Bennington B.A. was already turning into a chip in his shoulder; how could it not? Everybody was out there making money, and would keep on doing so under four more Republican presidential years; that much was obvious ever since Dukakis had stuck his little weenie head out of that tank. People laughed at him, even old high school friends who'd "wised up" and gotten engineering degrees or something that was already paying them bucks. "Oh, English Lit, huh? You went to college so you could drive a cab? Hey, maybe I can get you a job as my secretary!" Why should Cal be any different— he was off for an MBA, too, wasn't he? Money was everything to him, too, wasn't it?

Eric had the colors of a liberal, but he wasn't dyed-in-the-wool: There was something about the didacticism of people who told him what he *had* to think that he rebelled against. He'd gotten booed at school for doing a skit about an activist who had so much to stop now—stop apartheid now, stop bombing El Salvador, stop the slaughter of this, that, and the other animal— that he never got started on anything. But "everybody" had told him there were some people who only cared about money, and his experience since graduation had already confirmed that on this one point "everybody" was right. Some loser who was going to pull coffees in a café—when he wasn't sitting in one writing something about a bunch of queers that nobody would ever pay to read—wasn't someone whom a "winner" like Cal would want to associate with. *Shit*, he thought, *even the successful young writers these days were a bunch of assholes writing about hanging out with investment bankers and doing coke and fucking models in nightclubs.*

With those bitter thoughts, he resolved to purge Cal from his mind. Maybe nobody he'd ever dated had ever been half as much of a spark plug to his libido as Cal, but there were more important things in a person, he lectured his libido, that Cal was obviously lacking. *Not the kind of person I'd want to spend the rest of my life with*, he decided, easy in his decision with his orgasm only minutes behind him and testosterone's next onslaught on his will several hours away.

Home was the last place Cal wanted to be right now. Well, if he'd only felt at home there, he would have fled there gladly.

He prayed that his parents were gone when he returned so that he could avoid their inquiries.

American Christian College had not been the liberating experience most young people get when they go away to college; pot smoking, loud alternative music, sexual experimentation, and other forms of secular-humanist sin that for others were the very stuff of an education away from home were grounds for expulsion at ACC. But it had served its purpose (aside from giving him a degree) in that it had sent him far away from his parents' watchful eyes. During his freshman year, a history teacher had lectured on the horrors of life in East Germany: friends spying on friends, family members reporting on family members, microphones and cameras and informers ensuring an Orwellian blanket of surveillance on the guilty and innocent alike. "Sounds like my house," he'd cracked, and more than one of the students laughed out loud with the shock of recognition.

And when he had come home, a graduate and officially old enough for all of America's legal sins, he'd resolved to have a private life. "Where are you going?" his mother had asked him that morning.

"I'll be back later this afternoon," he'd responded.

Carol Hewitt simply hadn't known what to say to that. She was 44 years old and had in truth never needed a household Stasi; she asked her children and they readily confessed all. It was in the nature of things that they always had and therefore always would. For Cal to evade the question was a sure sign that he was going to do something she wouldn't approve of. When she didn't hear his car start, she parted the living room drapes (shut in all weather to keep anyone from seeing anything in the house they might want to envy, laugh at, steal, or gossip about) and watched in astonishment as Cal entered Emma Hamilton's house.

Mapp and Lucia couldn't have held a candle to the feud between Carol and Emma. To Emma, Carol was a busybody who had, as she put it to Eric over dinner more than once, "nothing better to do at night than lie awake, worrying about what other people were doing in *their* beds." Carol, Emma fumed, was a knee-jerk right-wing Phyllis Schlafly–soundalike who could always be found blocking entrances to abortion clinics or lobbying to have books removed from schools. She had earned Emma's undying enmity in the early 1980s when she'd been one of the leaders of the group that had persuaded Washoe County to refuse to allow the Reno Gay Rodeo to use the fairgrounds any longer, on the grounds that the event "promoted homosexuality" and brought AIDS and child molesters to Reno. The rodeo, which had been an annual event in Reno for years, brought millions of dollars into the city and promoted Reno as a year-round preferred vacation spot for gay men with plenty of disposable income. It would be fair to say that Emma hated Carol, not just as a person but as her own personal lightning rod for all she despised—ignorance, intolerance, subscription to a religion built solely on fear and hate and spite and anger and black satisfaction at the miseries of those who did not obey.

For Carol, the ill will was no less and just as well-backed by moral indignation. Emma's front garden was a riot of flowers (not daisies and carnations, either, but irises and lilies and gardenias), and while her house was an unobtrusive gray, the purple trim on the gables was clearly inappropriate—and defiant. Her son was some kind of sex machine (how Carol had arrived at this conclusion with no empirical evidence other than his oft-shirtless appearance must be left to the imagination). Emma's car had all those same bumper stickers Eric had mocked in his school skit, and every time Carol took up her biblical sword at the PTA or outside Planned Parenthood or at the Convention Authority or City Hall, there was Emma with her secular shield, prating about "rights." *"What rights do unborn babies have?"* Carol fumed. *"What rights do I have to shield my children from filth!?"* The far right was only just learning how to manipulate people outside its own corral; phrases like "special rights," which later would incite the neutral multitudes against homosexuals, were just being formulated, but Carol was ahead of the curve.

Carol was of a kind that is disappearing in our time, driven to the brink of extinction by an increasingly well-educated [and financially comfortable] populace, fewer and fewer of whom can be frightened by a bogeyman into a demagogue's corral. But in 1988, while we'll never know how many people really belonged to the Moral Majority, there were enough of them to make a lot of noise and be powerful because their noise made them sound powerful. Carol was not a crackpot; she was just one of her kind. They saw each other and heard each other—and nobody else— and what they saw and heard every day was normal, they believed, and everybody who was among not them was wrong, dangerous: the enemy. The frustration Emma felt toward Carol and her kind, the fear that the Hun was coming, Carol felt, too. *She* was right, *she* was frustrated, *she* was outnumbered by the Hun. This is the worldview of anyone who ardently desires to either overthrow the status quo or preserve it untouched, and always will be.

Carol sat in the living room and thought about what to do. She was not a woman without a sense of humor; however, she suppressed it as ardently as her son suppressed his sexuality. She had a wry vision of herself with rolling pin in hand, demanding to know why Cal had been at Emma's. When could she ask him about it? Not at dinner, not with her daughter and husband at the table. And when else did she ever see him, she thought with a small stab. He closed the door to his room now when he came home, and Carol had been raised as a child, and had it reinforced as a wife, that when a man closes a door, a woman doesn't knock and interfere with man's business, even if he's alone.

Why Emma Hamilton's house? What could possibly be there that could interest Cal? Who...

When a man is born, a cord is severed, but some believe that there is no severing the psychic cord between mother and child. Every mother knows in her heart what her child is, and yet it is her child, and must be what she wants it to be. The thought of Eric Hamilton was delivered up to Carol by her unconscious, the thought of what would interest Cal in Eric Hamilton was as clear as day to this part of her. But instructions for some antagonistic chemical process had been grooved into Carol's brain, instructions to some neurotransmitter not to make the connection that only waited for the signal to reveal the truth to her.

"Cognitive dissonance," psychologists call the process, though they cannot explain how it works on the chemical level. Someday it will be fascinating to discover what chemical denial releases—or forbids the release of—to enable a person not to know something they cannot stand to know.

It *must* be her, Carol thought, banishing Eric from her mind. She was poisoning Cal against them! It sounded far-fetched, but why else would he be closing his door? Why else would he be going out without telling his mother where? *Why else would he be going there?* (If the brain cannot make a natural connection, it *must* be provided with a detour.) "That bitch," she whispered, surprising herself with her own voice.

Then another surprise when Cal came home only half an hour later. Carol immediately grabbed a magazine and pretended to be reading; her son had never seen her sitting alone, lost in thought, for she rarely was in that state save when she was in bed, her husband asleep. "Back so soon?" she asked innocuously.

"Yeah, I was going to do some work around the house for Mrs. Hamilton, but it fell through."

Carol bit her lip. Why did it take half an hour to fall through, she wanted to ask. She could hear something in her son's voice, a sort of tense breeziness that belied whatever the truth was. "Sorry to hear it. You want some lunch?"

"No, I think I'll take a drive in a little bit, get a burger, see a movie."

"OK," Carol said, reflexively asking, "what are you going to go see?"

"*Die Hard,*" he lied, ruefully thinking she would never approve of *Beetlejuice*, his actual destination.

Carol put the magazine down after she heard Cal's door click shut. *Well*, she thought with satisfaction, *whatever happened over there didn't go well*. It didn't occur to her to wonder how her son might have been hurt by whatever had happened—that things had not gone well over there was all she needed or wanted to know.

The Hamiltons rarely ate their dinner early. Emma had become accustomed to a fashionably late dinner hour in the cities of her youth, and Eric's exuberant athletics schedule had dismayed him from large suppers before Little League games (though his metabolism and musculature kept him eating all the time anyway). They had a routine that set eight o'clock as dinner time, and both their bodies had kept to this schedule even after Eric had departed for Bennington. NPR accompanied their meals, always providing material when conversation flagged. (Of course, a dinner hour that did not care a fig for the prime-time television schedule was another Hamilton eccentricity that raised their neighbors' eyebrows.)

The heat started to dissipate around seven, and Eric often took a run around this time on a summer evening. Emma had to marvel at the stamina of someone who could hoe a garden, haul numerous 50-pound bags of fertilizer, mow the lawn, take an hour's rest and then decide to take a run. He'd wear a tank top and long, baggy shorts; he preferred to go shirtless in a pair of side-slit runner's shorts but had once, to his embarrassment, caused a traffic accident ascribable to gawking.

Running wasn't one of his school sports; he was a genuine "team player" and his run was his daily dose of outdoor cardio (he despised treadmills). Eric had taken it up to burn off excess energy, but had found that it provided him with much more—not just the endorphins released in continuous, strenuous activity, but a form of meditation. He need only watch out for cars, dogs and other pedestrians—labor that a small part of his mind performed automatically, while the rest was free to think, fret, fantasize, or go blank. And while Emma had structured their living arrangements to provide him with maximum privacy, there was still a difference between privacy and genuine "alone time"—time when you know nobody else is in the house, when you truly have your solitude.

Their house on Arlington wasn't too far from Virginia Lake, a beautiful spot in the southwestern part of Reno. The man-made lake had two paths around it, one dirt and one asphalt, exactly a mile around. Tall trees ringed the shore as well as the kind of expensive homes that immediately go up on waterfront property of any kind. Traffic was strictly kept to a 15-mph speed limit to guard the small children and waterfowl who often caromed heedlessly into the street. In the middle of the lake was a small island, originally the site of a fountain some visionary had ordered to be constructed out of Styrofoam—a fountain the geese had quickly eaten. Now the island was simply a heap of overgrown shrubbery which more adventurous teens would swim out to late at night because they could have sex or smoke dope unseen.

Eric trotted cautiously down Mount Rose and Lakeside till he reached the lake proper, but once he reached the dirt track (much easier on the shins than the asphalt path) his mind was cut loose from its moorings to drift. Anger was still the tide that swept it out to sea, as he thought about Cal and his kind. But as endorphins kicked in after his first pass round the lake, his thoughts hoisted sail and turned back on course. He'd graduated college and come back home knowing he was going "to write." Where, was the next question—not here, not only because it was no place for a young man with ambitions (especially not a young gay man), but because here equaled Mom, and it was time to break the cord; this was one of those socially accepted givens Eric didn't question. "Moving to San Francisco" had a romantic cast, certainly. He'd thought seriously about living in New York City, but in 1988 it was not an encouraging place. San Francisco's rents were cheaper by far (a crucial statistic in following through on a decision that would require writing "on spec" for an indeterminate number of years). In S.F., he was less likely to be mugged and/or murdered by some crackhead; and while he had avoided "the bug" thus far, there was no arguing that if he did get it, he would be far better off in S.F. than NYC. And of course it was a great place to be gay! He smiled to himself, feeling rapaciously horny.

He'd always wanted to write, ever since he could. Ideas had come and gone in his head since childhood, first conceiving of vast, ambitious science-fiction epics, under the influence of his early space-fiction reading, then dreaming of big triple-decker Victorians under the influence of high school teachers. College had pressed on him the necessity of writing cool, glassy, pointillistic sentences that put fragile sensibilities under a microscope for the duration of a slim collection of stories—were he to make a reputation as a "real" writer, that is. Eric had rejected this mandate, getting physically ill when he'd read David Leavitt's *Family Dancing*. How he'd raced out to get it, a fiction title from Knopf (which he had been taught to see as the glittering prize of a literary career, following close on the heels of publication in the *New Yorker*) from a gay writer nearly his own age. Every character had been depressed and flat in affect; nobody felt anything because they were so sensitive their delicate nerve endings had all been fried.

After he got over his dismay over what this meant to his future career, his natural optimism rebounded. That may be what *somebody* wants to read, but it's not what I want to read! "I'm going to write something *I'd* want to read," he'd said firmly, and any doubts as to his future career success were laid to rest. Even though now, as he used Reno and his mother's house as home base from which to find a place to live and a job in San Francisco, it was still not quite clear what he *would* write, he knew his young life hadn't enough experience to make a novel (though he'd been delighted with Bennington alumnus Donna Tartt's *The Secret History*—of course, he'd known her at the tiny school though her crowd had been a little "over" his own). But life in a big city would bring experience and plenty of subject matter, he knew.

At the end of a few laps, his unnatural disquiet was banished, and he walked home, cooling down, secure in the unconscious but ever-present knowledge that the fearless possess, that happiness comes to those who do what they *must* do in their hearts, not in the eyes of the world.

"Dinner's ready when you are," Emma called as Eric walked in the door.

"Quick shower," he telegraphed on his way up the stairs.

Emma's lasagna had been cooling a few minutes; she helped herself to a portion and covered the pan with foil, knowing that Eric had a way of losing track of time in the shower (she did not know that he often needed to masturbate after a workout, which easily distracted him from clocks). But this time Eric was indeed down in five, not at all hurt that

Emma had started eating without him. "There's some red wine if you want it."

Eric shook his head, shaking a few lingering droplets off his curls. "Nah, bad idea right after a run." He gulped spring water out of the huge tumbler Emma had filled and set at his place. "Smells great," he said, refilling his glass in the kitchen and helping himself to the lasagna.

"It came out well," she applauded herself. "I used a lot of basil. I can't remember if you like it that way or not."

"Basil is our friend," Eric assented. Emma rolled her eyes; Eric often responded to her chidings about excess dessert portions by claiming that "Sugar is our friend."

They ate in companionable silence while NPR related the latest dismal election-related news that an orderly transfer of power from Reagan to "his creature Bush," as Emma insisted on calling him, was all but inevitable. They exchanged their usual groans on the subject of the complete inability of the Democratic Party to provide a viable Presidential candidate for two elections in a row.

"Eric," Emma opened, giving her son fair warning that a serious question was coming. "Did anything unusual happen today when Cal was here?"

Eric stopped chewing for a moment while instinct decided how to answer. He swallowed first and grabbed his glass. "No, why?" he asked back, hiding his face behind the 32-ounce cup.

Emma gave her son what he knew was coming: The laser look. It was a look that demanded your attention, a look that called you on your shit. "He left here a lot more upset than he arrived," she said sternly.

Eric sighed, unable as always to avoid his mother's china blue eyes when they were on high beam. "It wasn't me, OK? I mean, I liked him," he said, too much the son to admit to his mother the rush of lust Cal had inspired. "He told me he was going to Stanford Business School, and I said I was moving to San Francisco, so let's get together, and he turned into some kind of fucking iceberg on me."

Emma didn't miss the emotion in Eric's words; quite possibly because he'd always been free to say any word he wanted, he reserved the more powerful ones for more powerful feelings. She heard the anger he stated, but also the hurt he expressed. "Why do you think he did that?"

"Because he's a proto-yuppie who's too good for the impoverished likes of me," Eric spat.

Emma laughed, to Eric's shock. "Is *that* what you think? Oh, Eric, you're blind."

"Blind to what?"

"Cal has a crush on you."

Eric glazed over for a moment, considering, rejecting. "That's a fine way to show it."

"He was terrified, Eric. You didn't see how he was looking at you when you came in? He practically inhaled his lemonade."

"I thought he was nervous, but I didn't..." Eric had been too well schooled by Emma to devalue his own beauty. "When we were in my room, it was like he'd hardly look me in the eye. He was looking everywhere but at...me."

Emma nodded as the light went on in Eric's head. "But I don't get it!" Eric appealed. "I thought he was hot—I mean, good-looking, too. Why would you be attracted to someone and then tell them to go to hell when they talk to you?"

"Well, for starters, Cal has grown up in the Hewitt household, and if he's accepted his own sexuality completely, I'd be as astonished as you were just a minute ago," Emma winked. Then her face changed, a little sadder. "Then again, sometimes the most terrifying thing in the world is the idea that you might get a chance at what you want. Because what if you fail? What if it isn't what you wanted after all? What then?"

"But that's what everyone wants: their big chance. At whatever." Eric shook his head. "That makes no sense. I don't get that at all."

Emma gave him a strange, sad smile. "I hope you never do."

Cal spent the rest of the day in his room, reading and listening to the radio. He'd resolved that Eric would *not* be thought of, and between his copy of *The Predator's Ball* and NPR, there was something to catch his attention when it wandered.

He scowled at the knock on the door. "It's Gina," his sister said. Relieved, he jumped off the bed and opened the door.

"Hey, what's with the closed door? Did Mrs. Hamilton pay you good? Did you tell Eric I want to have his baby? You look funny," Gina bombed him as she sailed past. She was a book-end for Cal, with his nearly blond hair and gray-green eyes belying the darkness within; she had brown eyes and dark straight hair but also apple cheeks and a sunny, almost blithe disposition.

Cal smiled. At 19, his younger sister was pretty much the girl she'd always been. Somehow "the Hewitt curse," as she called their parents' religious and political beliefs, had failed to fall on her. If Cal had rejected their strictures—at least, the ones they applied to other people—it had been because Gina had led the charge. She'd been the rebellious one, the one who came home drunk after curfew, who smoked pot in her room until the "incense" cover story was blown, who lost her virginity at 16 to a boy in the "Christian fellowship group" her parents had planted her in. She'd started school at the University of Nevada at Reno a year earlier (paying her own way after refusing to follow Cal to ACC) and had just moved in with her boyfriend, whom she'd known only since spring break. They were living cheerfully in a squalor that horrified Cal.

"What are you doing here," Cal asked her, "if you thought I was going to be gone? You and Mom going to paint some signs?"

She laughed at their inside joke; the two of them had made the pages of *Newsweek* as tots, drafted into the anti-abortion army and armed with tiny signs at various demonstrations in favor of unplanned parenthood.

"I was hoping to find you here. Can I borrow some money?"

Cal sighed. "*That's* why you wanted to know how much she paid me. How much do you need?" he asked resignedly.

"Just like 50 bucks, till Kevin gets paid."

"Till Kevin gets his *unemployment check*," Cal corrected.

"We decided to take the summer off," Gina shrugged. "It's still a check. You'll get your money back."

"How are you going to live? Pay the rent? Eat?"

"We're getting unemployment," she said, testily stating what she thought was obviously a sufficient answer. "We'll be fine."

Cal didn't ask when Kevin got "paid." Gina had always borrowed money from him and had never paid any of it back. His mother's voice rose up the stairs. "Dinnertime!"

"You staying for dinner?" Cal asked her, pulling 50 bucks out of his wallet.

She lowered her head and raised an eyebrow. "Do you want me to?"

"Pretty please with sugar on top," Cal begged. "Wait a minute! Why am I asking?" He waved the money around. "You want the money, you pay the price," he grinned.

"Oh, shit." She pretended to think. "You know, I don't think we need the money that bad."

"Oh, yes you do," Cal laughed. "Is it a deal?"

She sighed. "OK. But I book before dessert."

Both of them stopped in their tracks as they entered the dining room. Their father was at the table, at the regular dinner hour—a rarity usually reserved for momentous occasions like visitors for dinner. Moreover, he was not reading something, not watching the news or listening to the radio (he had the irritating habit of doing both at once, which made talking at the table nothing more than a disagreeable addition to the cacophony). The surprise was mutual; Calvin Hewitt hadn't seen his daughter at his dinner table since Christmas Eve. (A fight on Christmas Day had sent her running out of the house.)

"Who's coming to dinner?" Gina said by way of greeting to a man she hadn't seen in weeks.

"You are, I suppose," he countered with a hostility to which both children had accommodated themselves but never really become accustomed.

"Yes, Dad," Gina said tartly, flipping her hair and setting down in her childhood place at the table. "It's Patti and Ron. Didn't Mommy tell you we were coming?"

Cal had learned early to memorize Gina's remarks, to be chortled over later when they were alone. His father had never hit them, but sometimes a parent's bellow can hurt so much that a child prefers the belt. Downcast eyes and automatically fiddling with the napkin and water glass were Cal's preferred dinner-table modes of declaring Swiss citizenship.

Once upon a time, Gina's sarcasm would have received an officious retort—"You're mocking the man who's putting bread on this table"—but Cal Senior had learned long ago that this would only bring laughter from his daughter, who had openly despised him for years. It was clear to both sides in this unexpected skirmish that neither had expected to find the other on the same territory, and since both were unprepared for battle, it would be best to pretend each had failed to see the other and take circuitous routes around what would have been a pointlessly bloody field of combat.

Cal feared his father, disliked his father, and was ashamed of him. Cal Senior was a Navy brat, a 20-year veteran of the Navy—submarines—and had been raised like most men his age: to see themselves as the best and inevitable masters of whatever world they lived in. Beaten regularly by his own father, Cal Senior had allied with his fervently religious mother, taking her fanaticism about religion and his father's about politics in even doses. Cal Senior was proud that he'd never raised his hand against his own children; unfortunately, he felt that this accomplishment gave him license to treat them with an unmerciful harshness in other ways.

Out of the Navy in the mid '70s, with a wife and two kids to support and no real prospects for any kind of interesting work, Cal had found himself in Florida at loose ends. Then Anita Bryant had started her crusade against homosexuals, and like many other suddenly useless men of the Nixon-Ford recession, he was galvanized by her frantic appeal to save America's children from being recruited by homosexual teachers (presumably during recess when nobody was paying attention). After Vietnam, a recession, and an oil shortage—all events caused by America's sudden inability to dominate all decision making in the outside world—here was an enemy within who could be crushed. It was no coincidence that the same language used against Communists in the post–World War II era was being used against homosexuals, even down to the "recruiting" bit. But first, however, in the minds of Cal and others like him, it was necessary to turn a small and powerless minority into a monstrous threat so that the satisfaction of defeating it would be sufficient.

Cal Senior didn't have a job, but he had a mission, and nobody could disrespect a man on a mission. He circulated petitions, leafleted supermarket shoppers, knocked on doors, made phone calls—all the scut work of any political campaign. Then his organizational abilities were recognized and he started working on campaign logistics—charting the response rate from neighborhood to neighborhood, making sure there were enough bumper stickers and flyers for all the volunteers, and so forth. Even if he'd known it himself, he never could have admitted it. Some days, he never thought about homosexuals at all; some days, just the rush of being a part of something *big*, something that the whole world was watching, was enough. Anita called him Cal, knew him, and he knew her! Well enough to start confidently calling her "Anita" in front of everyone he knew or met.

Bryant's triumph galvanized two awesome political forces, but it would be her forces who would dominate the next decade. Cal had discovered that his natural talent for political work could pay, and as the Moral Majority took power over America, Cal's fortunes rose with it. Nevada had beckoned in the early '80s; its Republican politics were controlled by the ultraconservative wing of the party, but the Democrats put up enough of a challenge from time to time to make Cal's work interesting. Now he was the chairman of the Washoe County Republican Central Committee, an insignificant-sounding title, but he'd seen Senator Paul Laxalt's lapdog Frank Fahrenkopf rise from this same job to chairman of the Republican National Committee. When Fahrenkopf departed to a lobbyist job in a Washington law firm (the cornucopia that awaits all politicos who serve their masters well)—well, anything was possible.

Cal Senior was a family man, a traditionalist, a believer in family values. As proof of that, the picture on his office desk of his wife and children faced out at his visitors rather than inward toward his chair. But this family man had devoted little time to his family and had been a complete stranger to his children for the last decade. Cal Junior and Gina had gone to Reno High School, then the best school in town (the only private-school option was a Catholic school and that wouldn't have set well with his Protestant fundamentalist colleagues, to whom the pope was the Antichrist). Education about the wider world had taught Cal Junior and Gina that their father was a bad man. Cal Junior's extracurricular activities had been concentrated in public speaking and debate, Gina's in drama—two interlocking worlds that tended to attract the more liberal element of the student body. Their father being a constant presence on local television news, the very mention of their last name would provoke wrinkled noses from the more aggressively hip members of their circle. Gina would grin ruefully at his mention and tell a funny story about their appearance in *Newsweek,* but when Cal got the "Ew!" response, he would only shrug and say, "I'm not *his* father, I didn't raise *him* to believe that crap."

It might have been a thorn in Cal Senior's career that his children were so unwilling to appear at functions designed to display the party's "strong families," or that they completely refused to appear at *any* Young Republican function for any reason (or any amount of money), were this not the boat that many of his fellow party leaders were also in. No stones were thrown from glass houses on the subject of children's deviation from the party line; Reagan's cheery dismissal of his own liberal children from his life set the tone.

It had been Cal Senior and the men he worked with who had taught Cal Junior that money was power, that nothing could stop you from having your way if you were rich. He'd heard stories about their mistresses, even seen the way some of these men had looked at him, and on some level he had figured out that they were gay and were getting away with it because they had the power to get away with it. He couldn't know that the Republican Party was full of closeted gay men who were ensuring their own survival at the expense of the rest of their kind, but on some level he had absorbed the lesson—acquire money and power and then, and only then, you could do what you wanted. In a way, this was his bargain with his sexuality— it would leave him alone until he could act on it safely.

"Why don't you turn on the news?" Carol suggested to her

husband, knowing full well that there would be no other conversationalist at the dinner table. Cal thought of a hilarious book he'd read recently, Don DeLillo's *White Noise*, in which the TV seemed to be as much a character as anybody else in the novel's dysfunctional family. Cal Senior would flip between the three networks' evening newscasts, despising them all for their "liberal bias," yet well aware that it was essential for a man in power to know what all of them were saying. He allowed himself a small chuckle at an item about Dukakis, who had faltered when asked what his stance on crime and punishment would be if his wife had been raped. Dukakis had answered the question as if the person in question were anyone but his wife.

Gina groaned after seeing the clip. "Oh, my God, and I thought *Bush* was a wimp."

Her father was in too good a humor to rise to the bait. "That man is finished."

"He's toast," Cal agreed, hoping an indisputable but neutral statement would defuse a fight. "The Democrats will never win as long as they keep fielding party hacks who get the nomination in a backroom but don't have what it takes to win an election."

"You mean he's not telegenic," Gina accused. "He's too *short* to be president. Is that what you're saying, Cal?" Cal's attempts at peacemaking often irritated Gina—enough sometimes that she'd spar with him instead of the old crocodile, which suited Cal just fine. A fight with Gina could be made up for later, whereas a fight with his father always ended with the man shouting so loudly and cruelly that it raised his opponent's hairline an inch. "Napoleon was short, and he nearly conquered Europe."

"Napoleon never would have popped out of a tank looking like Beetle Bailey," Cal countered. It wasn't the world's best joke, but the rest of the family laughed anyway, and Cal smiled, relieved. Nobody would say anything much for the rest of dinner, too pleasantly surprised at having had a happy moment together to ruin it.

Cal and Eric had each resolved to forget the other, but each had found it easier said than done. Eric set aside his confusion over why Cal would run from what he wanted, and chosen to focus on what struck him as the only important fact: He wanted Cal and Cal wanted him. The question of their connecting was settled in his mind; it only needed the proper occasion to make things right.

For Cal, however, the opposite was settled—well, not quite. His decision to avoid Eric was settled, but his decision to stop thinking about him was far from it. It was his first encounter with a part of himself that had a will of its own. Masturbation for him had been a fitful thing, something to be hastily consummated when the pressure of an erection was too great to ignore. Cal was 22 years old, and he was a virgin with both sexes. As his mother marshaled her will to refuse to see what was in front of her eyes, Cal also marshaled substantial forces inside his head to suppress the same raging hormones that drove Eric whistling to the basement.

Cal loved to walk. Like many economically lean people, he was a limitless reservoir of kinetic energy. His favorite walk took him down Arlington, then up along the Truckee River, all the way up through Idlewild Park until the paths dead-ended in scrub, and then he'd turn around and walk back. The whole walk took a little over two hours at a brisk pace.

Reno was not a big city, nor were there many scenic walks—or runs. Arlington crossed the Truckee River at 1st Street, where the river split in two around an island that had become Wingfield Park. Cal loved the park; he used to sit in it and stare up at a four-story apartment building on 1st Street right over the river and across from the park, and fantasize about what it must be like to live in the top apartment, its balcony level with the tall trees and fully exposed to the sun. In the realm of Cal's experience, that apartment had the most beautiful view on earth.

He stopped at the park and sat on the grass near the river, where he could look up at that apartment and dream. Reno was a hateful place for him, a town full of fat, sullen white trash and a handful of fat, surly rich people. It was a good place to raise children and a good place to leave as soon as you were no longer a child. Industry consisted of warehouses and casinos, social life of country-western or heavy-metal bars, and politics of right-wing caricatures only Hunter S. Thompson and Ralph Steadman could have done justice in portraying. Cal would not accept his homosexuality, but he had accepted that he was different, however much he might hate that, and he knew it was suicide to be different in Reno in 1988 and not leave as soon as possible.

Still, there were these spots of beauty that made Reno tolerable; that was all Cal would allow. This park and Idlewild and the walk along the Truckee and Virginia Lake—and of course, Lake Tahoe with its Caribbean-clear waters and velvety beaches. Cal knew he wanted to live near water, if not right on it. If something forced him to stay here, he could do it—if he had *that* apartment. *Even a place on the Upper West Side of New York didn't have a river,* he smiled to himself.

He was not alone in his attraction to water. Eric had grown tired of his run around Virginia Lake and had modified his evening routine. Reno was a runner's paradise; the valley floor was almost uniformly flat. He ran in a trance, his mind wandering, puttering, toying with this and that—*I've got enough saved to live in the city for about six months without a job; should I just do that and write, or should I keep it banked and get a part time job...what am I going to do with that story Professor Haines liked so much; I should flesh it out and submit it, but how, but where?*—a flash of Cal's exposed waistline; big-boned Eric marveling at the other boy's slimness. *He must be only like six inches thick at the waist...like there's no room for all his organs...I could put my hands almost all the way around it...*

The stirrings of an erection came at the same time that Eric saw Cal sitting in the park, looking up abstractedly at the 1st Street apartment. He slowed, watching Cal's dreamily abstracted face, as lost in thought as Eric's had been only a moment before. Something fell inside Eric; he almost unconsciously swallowed as if his body was trying to convince itself that the two events had happened in the opposite, natural order. It was the first time he'd seen Cal with his guard down, his face open and unafraid and *young.* And Eric's initial attraction to Cal, the kindling of sexual urges and pleasantly surprised discovery of common threads, became something more in that moment. He would call it love and so would most people, for lack of any other word, and if it was not technically "love at first sight," certainly this seemed to Eric like his first real sight of Cal. Nobody who had lived through such a moment would be surprised to hear that Cal could sense something, some plucked string resonating in Eric, and turned to see Eric standing there, staring.

Cal's guard *was* down; he was at peace there by the river, listening to the water and thinking of the view from the apartment above. And it didn't go back up at the sight of Eric—Eric was already beyond it and it was too late, even if he'd wanted to bring it up. Eric sat down next to him on the grass as if they'd arranged to meet there.

"I used to work at the library downtown after school," Eric said. "But I didn't start until five o'clock. So when the weather was nice, I'd walk down the river and sit right over there," he pointed at a spot on the south side of the park, on the other side of the pathway, "and I'd read. I was in Honors Novel and Mrs. Mapplethorpe was the teacher."

Cal nodded. He'd had Mrs. M. for Senior Honors English.

"I went to Bennington convinced that a 'great novel' was one of those big old monsters she assigned. *Magic Mountain, Brothers Karamazov, Moby Dick.*"

"Talky novels," Cal agreed. "Talk, talk, talk."

"Bullshit, bullshit, bullshit," Eric laughed. "I got to college and they handed me *A Portrait of the Artist as a Young Man,* and I said, 'Cool! It's so short!'"

Cal laughed along with him. "And she worshiped the *New Yorker*—even though every story in it was the exact opposite of the books she taught."

"Yeah," Eric chuckled, in too good a mood to be bitter. "Glassy little present-tense stories in which nothing happens."

"In which nothing must *ever* happen until the end, when you get the tiny epiphany."

"The what?"

"You know, the tiny epiphany," Cal said with humorous

impatience. "Margaret goes to the mall. She feels nothing. She stares at the goods on display. *She does not know what she wants,* Cal italicized dramatically. "Then as she drives home— feeling nothing—a butterfly flies in the window of her car, she crashes, she's standing next to the car while the highway patrolman takes her license, and she watches the butterfly fly away— and for *one moment only,* her bruised, numbed, hypersensitive soul feels a flutter of emotion. The end."

"Brilliant. Excellent. Devastating."

"Luminous," Cal added. "The reviews of the short-story collection always say the 'prose' is 'luminous.'"

"Write by numbers," Eric scowled. "Bullshit."

"Not what you'll get up to, eh?" Cal smiled.

"Hell, no! I want to write about real people, not neurasthenics."

"Real people aren't neurasthenics?"

"No, only people with MFA's and teaching jobs, who've never left school their entire lives."

Cal idly pulled some grass from the lawn. "I think it's courageous—going out there and doing what you want to do, not being afraid."

"Not being afraid of what?"

"Of being poor. Of failing. I'm not saying you're going to fail," Cal appended hastily. "Just that, you know, if you just wanted to succeed financially you'd go get that MFA."

Eric thought of Cal's own plan to get an MBA but wisely decided to say nothing. "Thanks. I guess I'll wait tables or pull coffees or something while I starve in my garret," he smiled.

Cal laughed. "Be a bartender. You're…you could make some good tips," he said, his guard back up at last just before he told Eric he was more than good-looking enough for the job.

"And become an alcoholic," Eric added. "Like all great writers."

Cal laughed, relaxed. Bit his lip. "I'm sorry I was such an asshole the other day."

"Apology accepted," Eric said, startling Cal. He's expected to hear the usual American response, descended from its British roots, the slick, civil "Oh, no, no you weren't." Instead,

Eric had acknowledged Cal's bad behavior even as he forgave it. Cal flushed with embarrassment.

"I thought you were too good to associate with some loser with a B.A. who was gonna spend his life driving a cab," Eric admitted, seeing now after Cal's recent comment that such wasn't the case.

"No," Cal said hastily. "I just..." *What to say?* He was unprepared, had no cover story, never thought he'd need one, never thought he'd be sitting here with Eric, getting so...intimate again.

Eric put a hand on Cal's shoulder. "I know."

Man, Gurdjieff wrote, is asleep. Some awaken, most do not. A lucky few work their way into consciousness and stay there, but for most of us, the sensation of being truly alive is transitory. A mathematician who finds a solution to a key problem, a biologist who discovers the nature of a virus' behavior, a novelist who realizes suddenly where a character must go and what he must do, all experience a moment of ecstasy, a sense of being one with God and knowing the joy of seeing a piece of Creation in action. Or a young person who feels the touch of love for the first time in his life. We pine for our youth at heart not for the fun of it, the lack of responsibility, or even that smooth soft glowing skin we used to have, but because we lose the ability to feel the shocks of discovery with the joy and amazement and awe of youth, without the suspicion of what lies behind the too good to be true, without thinking how it's too good to last. Cal had felt moments of pride in accomplishment, mastering math problems or understanding the symbolism of a novel without being told, but all this was just making connections others had made, unnecessarily confirming results already proven by others. But nobody, nobody had ever felt what he felt now, this moment, and even if they had they never could have taught it to him.

For a moment everything was right in the world; Cal knew instinctively that this was the way life was supposed to be, Eric's hand on his shoulder, his warm kind brown eyes acknowledging everything inside Cal's heart and settling all debates with a silencing blanket of acceptance. Eric saw Cal's change, a neurochemical conversion going on in his head, pathways that had been blocked or routed around suddenly opened, dopamine and serotonin receptors opening like flowers bending to the light. Cal looked over the precipice at Eric on the other side of the canyon and for the first time thought he could jump and make it to the other side.

More experienced with these maneuvers than Cal, Eric sensed that now was the time to act. He leaned over toward Cal, for whom Eric's face took on the character of an annunciation. Eric closed his eyes as his lips approached Cal's, but Cal's eyes remained wide open, memorizing every degree of the angle of taper of Eric's eyebrows, counting the long lashes by the dozens, marveling at the heat radiating off Eric's glowing skin. But when their lips met, Cal's eyes closed, too, blocking out every sensory input that could distract from the electrochemical messages rushing across the hypersensitive tactile bridge Eric had thrown across the no longer extant gulf between them.

A car honked its horn on Arlington; a jacked-up truck with KC lights on its roll bar roared past; a fat young sullen face, contorted with rage, lurched out the window. "FAGGOTS!" he shouted, ineffectually hurling an empty beer can in their direction.

Cal's eyes flew open and the connection was shattered. Innumerable hearings of the word provoked conditioned response, adrenaline pumped and his flight instinct took over. He bolted up from the ground.

"Hey, it's all right," Eric said. "They're gone. Just some assholes."

Cal looked around the park, suddenly aware of everyone whom only a second ago hadn't existed. They were all potential attackers, norepinephrine convinced him. Eric was a goddamn fool to kiss him in public. "That was a stupid thing to do," Cal accused him. "We could have gotten the shit beat out of us."

Eric had lost the connection when Cal pulled away, but his conditioned response was more fight than flight. "I coulda beaten the shit outta that fat fuck," Eric countered. "He yelled at us because he was safe in his jacked-up 'big man' truck."

Cal shook his head. "OK, fine, then I was the stupid one for letting it happen."

Eric's face darkened with anger born of frustration. "Well, sorry I put you through such a terrible experience," he said with a sarcasm rare for him.

"No need to apologize," Cal said. "It was my fault."

"Well, by all means be more careful in the future," Eric raged, getting up and brushing grass off his shorts. Without waiting for Cal's response, he ran off, tension belying his natural easy gait.

Cal had been conditioned too well, and beasts like the one who had hurled his bile along with his beer knew it. What he had done was something to be punished, and the hate-filled pig had reminded him of that. Homosexuals recruited; they had to, didn't they, because who would choose to be one? They had sex in parks, in toilets, so that no neighbor or landlord could see them bringing a man home late at night, because they knew it was wrong. And they got AIDS and died, because AIDS was God's punishment, AIDS was God's punishment, AIDS was God's punishment. These and worse had been hammered into his head like nails, nails that only hurt when something deep inside him tried to push them out.

Cal walked home in shock. He was short-circuited. It was wrong, and yet it felt so good, so right. He wanted what he mustn't have, was what he mustn't be; as of this moment some part of him had been awakened, instructed, and would require that he pursue what another part of him had been made certain could only lead to his destruction. More gay teenagers commit suicide than any other group—this is why. Who but the strongest could endure such a dichotomy?

Only one thought came clear out of the fog: *I can't do this, I can't take this, not again.* There was no clear marker defining "it," for "it" was letting his guard down, kissing a man, experiencing so much joy and so much terror all now linked together in Pavlovian response in his mind. Wanting something so much that he forgot what it would cost, and, remembering the cost, shuddering in fear because he had just barely missed losing everything. What was "everything"? What it was to every man in America that year who feared his own desires—his place in the world, the love of his family, the company of his friends. *Everything. I can't, it's not worth it.*

He couldn't head home, not this time. He didn't have the strength for fronts now. He looked in vain for blocks for a pay phone, finally found one and called his sister. "Hello?"

It was Kevin, Gina's boyfriend. "Kevin, it's Cal. Is Gina there?"

"Um, sure, hold on." Kevin was used to a less curt greeting from Cal, who usually went out of his way to chat him up, being as he was the only family member to even halfheartedly approve of him.

"Cal, what's up?" Gina asked.

"I just need to come over. For a while. I just don't want to go home right now. Is that cool?"

"*Mi casa* et cetera, baby. Where are you? Do you need a ride?"

"No, I'm downtown. I'll be there in a few."

Nothing could be further from Cal's dream apartment on 1st Street than the place Gina and Kevin had found on Liberty Street, a few blocks east of the main library. An old one-story house had been chopped up into three apartments, Gina and Kevin's being the only one with a bedroom. It was the weirdest place Kevin had ever seen. The front room was depressing, completely paneled in wood so dark no light could escape farther than a few inches from the fixture before being swallowed up. A small corner of the room was given over to a sort of fold-out kitchenette, which consisted of a bathroom-sized sink (the bathroom didn't have a sink) and two hot plates. But the bedroom, which stuck off the back of the house and was obviously an addition, had windows around three sides and let in dizzying amounts of indirect light. They'd taken the place because Kevin was a painter and had loved the light in that room (oh, and because it was dirt cheap). He'd painted the whole room robin's egg blue with fluffy white clouds around and above, and added a moon and stars in glow-in-the-dark paint that was only visible with the lights out. So they'd solved the problem of the front room by turning it into the bedroom and the back room into their living space. Back there, two couches, a small TV, and an excellent stereo hugged the walls while Kevin's easel took center stage, canvases and sundry supplies covering all available space in the "bedroom."

Cal loved the place now as much as he'd hated it when they first moved in, even as he insisted to himself that he could never live in a hovel like that. Gina opened the door and the sound of The Smiths' "Louder Than Bombs" flew with morbid cheer out of the stereo. "Hey, baby, come on in." She hugged him immediately, seeing the wracked look on his face. She shepherded him back to the living room, snagging him a Coke out of the novelty-size refrigerator tucked under the "stove."

She handed him the Coke and picked up a bong. "The doctor is in," Gina announced. She handed it to Cal. "And this is doctor's orders."

Cal wasn't much for drugs or alcohol, but neither was he disinclined against him. Like many who'd been teenagers during the Reagan years, his elders had raised him to "Just Say No." Of course, the government had doomed its own campaign with the scope of its lies: insisting that experimenting with marijuana inevitably led to heroin overdose, when 20 years earlier *Consumer Reports* had issued a landmark report urging honesty about the effects of drugs. Cal took the bong as unhesitatingly as one of his elders would have reached for a bottle of Scotch after such a trying day as his.

He wouldn't smoke with just anybody. Marijuana, after all, lowers inhibitions, frees up those very pathways in our minds so many of us work so hard to keep closed. Only with Gina could Cal dare to get stoned and let gravity take its course, letting words flow freely down the pipes from mind to mouth. As the drug did for him what he couldn't do for himself, he found himself laughing hysterically as he sang along with The Smiths about how shyness could stop you. Gina joined him in the chorus and that was when Cal started to cry. Lost as she was in the little fluffy clouds in her own mind and on the ceiling, Gina laughed along with him until she looked over, intending to give him one of their flash glances of secret understanding, and realized she'd heard wrong.

She asked nothing, only moved to him and held his head against her breasts as he cried, rocking him to and fro. "OK, baby, OK. Let it out."

Which in turn only made him cry harder, a moan torn out of him. This pain he could let out with her—what was it but the result of something that must not come out, that wanted to be born and could not be allowed to?

"I'm so fucked, I'm so fucked, I'm so totally fucked."

"Uh oh. Was it Mom or Dad this time?"

Cal laughed. "I wish! Something I could handle." He detached from her, wiped his face free of snot and tears with his T-shirt before Gina could offer a tissue. "You're going to throw me out when you hear this, but you might as well be the first." He took a deep breath, sighed. He felt so relieved after his cry. Nothing could hurt him now. "I'm gay."

"Oh, I know *that*," she said. "Jesus Christ, Cal, give me some credit."

He looked at her, astonished. She had to laugh at the look on his face. "Come *on*! Drama club, no girlfriends, nose in a book, no team sports—it doesn't take a rocket scientist."

He shook his head. "I guess Mom and Dad know then, too."

She hooted. "Mom and Dad? They don't know what *time* it is. They think denial is a river in Egypt."

Cal laughed, never having heard that one before. "I mean," Gina continued, "they believe what they want to believe. They didn't think Kevin and I were having *sex* until I told them we were moving in together." She paused, locks tumbling in her mind. "Oh my god, you slept with Eric Hamilton!"

"I kissed him. Actually, he kissed me. Right in the middle of Wingfield-fucking-Park!"

Gina's bright brown eyes widened. "Wow! How romantic!"

"How *suicidal*," Cal countered. "Some fucking hillbillies threw a beer can at us. We were lucky they didn't stop and beat the shit out of us."

"I don't know, Eric's a pretty big hunk of beef. I remember when I was a sophomore and he was a senior, I used to masturbate thinking about him. Well, didn't *you*?" Gina asked matter-of-factly in reply to Cal's shocked look. "Of course, he wouldn't date me because I was a...well, a girl, never mind a sophomore!" she laughed. She bounced up and down on the floor, reaching for the bong. "And then what?"

"And then we had a fight. I told him it was stupid to do that. He got all pissed off at me. The end."

"What do you mean, the end?" Gina said through a small cloud. She'd just started pulling a big hit off the bong, expecting to have plenty of time as Cal told the rest of the story.

"The end. That's the second time we've been together, and the second time it's ended with both of us thinking the other was an asshole."

"Third time's a charm," Gina winked.

"Once a philosopher, twice a pervert, three times a total fucking idiot," Cal countered. "That's how it always ends, anyway."

"How what ends?"

"Gay stuff."

"Oh, *come on*, Cal! You sound like Dad. Oh, no, don't tell me you actually believe that 'hamma-sek-shuls is evil' shit," she finished, lapsing into a mock–Jesse Helms accent. "You know better than that!"

Cal smiled ruefully. "Do I? It sure hasn't brought me much happiness."

"Shit, Cal, you're a fucking virgin. You haven't even had sex with a man. How can you know whether or not it'll make you happy?" She thought of something she couldn't help asking. "I bet he was a good kisser."

Cal wordlessly stuck out his hands. She put the bong in one and the lighter in the other. He took a big hit, choked back his coughs, and this time released tears of ordinary physical pain as he exhaled enough smoke to fog the room. Thus fortified, he nodded. "It was like...Christmas morning."

Gina took a deep breath and sighed. "Wow." They sat there for a moment, thinking how apt that was for another experience they now had in common. "You should be a writer," Gina said.

"There's no money in it," Cal said automatically.

"You and money," she chided just as automatically. "Speaking of which," Gina said as she heard the front door open.

"Hey," Kevin said, not surprised to see Cal after the unusual call, but definitely surprised by the pot fog in the room. "Should you be doing that?" he asked Gina.

She sighed. "Kevin."

"No, don't Kevin me," he said with an anger that startled Cal. Kevin was a "big guy," the sort of body that was more muscle now than fat but on which the opposite would be the case in a few years. The easygoing young man's usual response to the sight of the bong would be to reach for it, but not today. "You shouldn't be smoking."

"Not now, Kev," she said. "Let me talk to Cal in private."

Kevin shook his head and left, the front door slamming behind him.

"What's going on?" Cal asked his sister.

"Well, you're not the only one with news today," she laughed grimly. "Cal, I'm pregnant."

"What! Don't you guys use rubbers?"

"Rubbers! I'm on the pill," Gina said scornfully.

"Are you kidding? You could get *AIDS*."

She rolled her eyes. "From Kevin? He's straight, he doesn't shoot up, and we both hate rubbers."

"Oh, Christ, Gina," Cal said, half in disbelief and half in sympathy. "How pregnant are you?"

"Two months. Still early enough to have an abortion."

The word triggered a world of associations in Cal's head. The picture in *Newsweek* of the two of them outside the abortion clinic, waving tiny signs; his mother's face contorted with rage outside a clinic, and how he'd shuddered at the famous picture of the white girl in Little Rock taunting the black girl on her way into school, the face so like her mother's on those days. "You're not going to have it."

"Are you crazy? Hell, no! Jesus, Cal, I'm 19. I'm in college. What am I going to do with a baby?"

"Kevin sounds like he thinks you're having it," Cal realized.

She got up. "Fuck. Fuck, fuck, fuck! He wants to get married and have the baby. And there's no way. No way. I mean, I like him, he's fun, I like living with him, we have good sex—obviously," she said, her black humor poking its head up. "But I'm not marrying him. And I'm not having his baby. I mean, my baby. Our baby. Whatever."

Good sex—and look what it got her! Cal thought, cementing his own resolve. *Consequences, consequences everywhere.* A moment of pleasure, as fleeting as a kiss, and then—AIDS, pregnancy, abortion or 18 years given over to someone else's life. A phrase he'd overheard once in the supermarket, two women in the next aisle thinking themselves alone, rang in his ears: "The fucking you get ain't worth the fucking you get," one had said, and they'd both laughed their heads off.

"What can I do?" Cal asked. "Are you going to tell Mom?" Telling Dad never crossed his mind; nobody told Dad anything. "I mean, if you want me to go with you…"

"To tell Mom? I'm not telling her shit."

"Well, I'd do that, but I meant, you know. To the…place."

"The *abortion clinic*, Cal. You can say it, they're not here."

He sighed. What a day. He picked up the bong. "Well, I need to get stoned again."

Gina laughed. "You and me both." She went to the stereo. "I need something *morbid* right now."

"No goth," Cal said assertively. "No Bauhaus, no Siouxsie, no Joy Division."

Gina ignored him and put on Depeche Mode's "Black Celebration."

"That works," Cal said morosely.

Gina went into the "kitchen" to cadge up some snacks. Cal crawled up onto the couch and flopped on his back, looking up at Kevin's "sky." He thought of what it would be like for a little baby to see that every morning, how wonderful it would be to wake up to blue skies every morning, to see his young, attractive parents beaming like twin suns above his crib, parents who would raise—would have raised—him with love, without hate. *The music was so sweet and painful at the same time,* he thought. *Life sucks, let's party. Poor little bastard, he'll never see this sky.* Tears rolled down Cal's face as he cried for more reasons, more deaths, than he knew.

Eric said nothing to his mother about his encounter in the park with Cal. He, too, had resolved to shut a door in his head and not open it again. He did not want his mother's generous, compassionate viewpoint, did not want to hear why poor Cal had been such a bastard this time. He had resolved to close his heart to Cal, and then his mother had shown him that it had been his very openness of heart that had frightened the other boy in the first place, and he'd dared to risk it again, the vision of Cal on the stepladder driving something more than his lusts, something that could only be called *longing.* Eric had never longed for anything in his life. He had set goals and worked to achieve them, and this was the first time he'd ever seen anything he wanted so badly and yet could find no way to attain.

The heat had swelled rather than dissipated in the late afternoon, promising a hot spell of several days' duration, possibly even breaking 100. It was nine in the evening (evening still, for the sun had barely set) before Eric could safely take his run.

Virginia Lake was deserted; the fishermen and sun-visored senior citizens who populated it during the day were safe at home, moving as little as possible to avoid taxing themselves in the heat. But Eric *had* to run tonight, had so much to burn off he couldn't bear it.

Eric had lost his virginity at 14 with another boy, and at 15 had had sex with a girl (once was enough of that), and had been a "serial monogamist" at Bennington, going through four casual boyfriends. Sex had been good for him, but not much better than a good run—energy was burned off, sweat purged toxins from the system, the whole thing ended with a release of opiates within the brain. Sex was fun, but it wasn't anything to get worked up about, pro or con. But something had happened when he kissed Cal; those electrochemical exchanges had been like the last ingredient eye-dropped into a beaker that suddenly makes the whole mixture smoke and bubble. Cal had stood on a precipice, and Eric had thrown the bridge across; they had met in the middle, and then Cal had run away. But the bridge was still there; he could walk away from it, too, but it was still there...

Here, alone, Eric's tears started to flow, the sweat from his brow concealing their origin. Like a child who had never known fire and put his finger in it for the first time, Eric felt the pain of love. He'd paid no attention to the songs that had advised him love hurts; he had been such a success at everything he'd put his mind to that he had taken it for granted that when he fell in love, he would succeed there, too—or that, like baseball, when he'd found that he wasn't the world's best pitcher, he could accept it and retrain himself, his bulk making him an excellent catcher, a position he enjoyed and played well. So why now could he not turn away from loving Cal, when there was no success to be had? Why now did he hurt so badly? Why now was he so miserable having failed? Why was he so full of rage at Cal and yet still so full of desire, not just lust but the *need to be with him,* just to see and touch him—touch him just to prove he really existed? The pain he had felt only days ago, looking up at Cal on the stepladder, had been so sweet—he had opened himself to it, so completely and trustingly, too young to know that there was *this* side to longing, too, that the pain was the knowledge that the beloved was there in that moment and then gone, that the longing fulfilled in that moment remained when its object did not, that the sweetness subsided but the pain did not.

Eric cried tears of frustration, tears of grief, tears of stunned amazement that he could not just turn away from the work of love and be happy again.

CHAPTER TWO
THE BURNING BUILDING

Emma waited at the airport gate for the arrival of Eric's flight from San Francisco. She had only seen him at Christmastime in the last two years, and only then as a command performance after paying for the ticket he couldn't afford. She'd raised him to be independent, and yet she felt a pang that he should be so independent as not to need her at all. She had practically jumped for joy when he'd called her and told her he needed to come over for a few days, rest up after his recent experiences, and could he bring a friend?

Eric could not have made more of a splash in the airport had he worn a dress than he did in his black leather jacket, decorated with more neon-colored stickers and slogan buttons than anyone would have time to read—or the inclination, once they'd gotten an eyeful of the green sticker with a rifle sight on it that exhorted all passersby, KILL JESSE HELMS, or the button that confessed, I GOT ARRESTED FIGHTING AIDS. All of which was crowned by two matching buttons that Eric had attached to the epaulets on his shoulders, round white buttons with a black rectangle in which was inscribed, in menacing all-caps Gill typeface, ACT UP.

A few weeks ago there wouldn't have been a person in the airport who would have reacted the same way they did today. A few weeks ago they would have thought he was some rock star or "punk rocker," dressing to shock a populace that had already seen it at the mall more than once, and maybe even bought an amusing postcard featuring his ilk. Today they looked at him with raw terror, for Eric was the symbol of a potent social force that had, to them, come out of nowhere in no time and dominated the American landscape for an entire week.

Worse, there were two of them; in the mob's instinct is the knowledge that the pack can hunt one down like prey, but two spell trouble. Eric's boyfriend Mikey made Eric look conservative; while underneath his jacket Eric sported a READ MY LIPS T-shirt, Mikey wore no shirt at all under his, his chiseled torso partially displayed—enough for anyone to see the biohazard symbol tattooed over his heart, and, should they be privileged with the right angle, to see the piercings in his nipples. Mikey wore baggy khaki shorts the waist of which fell below the elastic of his underwear, and his powerful calves were both decorated with "modern primitive" tats that trailed out of sight into his Doc Martens. Red Army soldiers parachuting in en masse could not have elicited more shock, fear, and rage.

"Hey, Mom," Eric said, embracing his mother. Emma knew Eric had become intensely involved in ACT UP, and like millions of others she had watched the proceedings of the Sixth International AIDS Conference as presented by Peter Jennings every night for a week. She'd even seen him on TV, being interviewed about the proceedings. And yet she found herself regarding him and his cohort now with a mixture of pride and fear—a fear of him she could not help but pick up from the herd around them, but more so a mother's fear *for* him, that he had chosen to make himself such a visible target for the rage and hatred consuming the country. "Mom, this is Mikey."

"Hey," Mikey said, shaking her hand. "Eric's told me a lot about you."

He's told me very little about you! Emma thought, smiling and thanking him, all the while sizing him up. Both boys had crew cuts, and she had to do some readjusting after 24 years of Eric's dark, curly locks. Eric noticed her gaze as they walked out into the August heat without a stop at baggage, both young men having already traveled around the country to enough conferences to know to pack everything into two carry-ons. "You like my new haircut?" he grinned, rubbing his hand over his head.

Emma smiled. "You always look handsome, Eric."

"Doesn't he?" Mikey asked, giving Eric a wicked look. Eric shot back a *Don't!* look in return.

"Wow, it's hot here," Eric said, taking off his jacket. Emma noticed the tattoo around one of his biceps: a twisted pair of barbed wires. *Dear God, I don't want to see his nipples if they're like the other one's!* she prayed silently. But as she registered the changes in Eric, she also sent a prayer of thanks for the things that *hadn't* changed. The large, glowing tan biceps assured her that Eric was still only "fighting AIDS" in the abstract.

When they got to the house, Mikey went to the bathroom. Eric had planned ahead; he casually said to Emma, "I told Mikey he could have the basement room, is that OK?"

Emma lifted an eyebrow. "Oh, I thought he'd be staying in your room. Of course, in this heat, the basement's much more comfortable."

Eric sighed. "Mom, don't make this hard on me."

"You're making it hard, dear, not I. Why don't you both sleep in the basement? Or are you saving yourself for marriage?" she finished, turning to the sink so he couldn't see her smile.

"I just didn't want to make you uncomfortable, that's all."

Emma regretted her teasing; she turned around. "I'm sorry, Eric. I didn't mean to make fun of you. I'm very proud of what you're doing right now, and I'm very flattered that you want to introduce Mikey to me."

"He's just a boyfriend," Eric said hastily. "I mean, we're not serious. Not super serious. I like him, but…"

She put a hand on his arm. "It's good that you have someone in your life. I'm happy you have some companionship no matter how un-super serious."

Eric laughed and relaxed. "Thanks, Mom."

Emma poured three well-sugared iced teas without asking and handed two to Eric. "So, why don't we all sit in the living room and you can tell me what's been going on."

In many ways, 1988 had been the best time to move to San Francisco, Eric had quickly decided. Yes, AIDS was rampaging through the gay community, and more than a few of the Castro District's residents scowled upon the ever-increasing number of heterosexual couples pushing their strollers down the street, having picked up a Victorian at fire-sale prices from a dying man. In the community there was a sense of helplessness, of doom even—but you had to be a member of that community to feel it, had to have been there to remember what it had been like not so many years before. Eric could not know what it had been like, could only feel what it was like *now* for a young, good-looking new arrival in the city.

And to be honest, for the likes of him, it was good. Rents were still cheap and apartments were plentiful, and he found a studio for $450 a month, an amount he could easily manage between his savings and a part-time job. The recession that was just beginning to loom over the East Coast had not yet crept across the country, and jobs were plentiful, especially for someone who knew how to use a computer. Best of all to Eric was the drought, a weather cycle that would require Californians to put bricks in their toilet and take five-minute showers, but that rewarded San Francisco in particular with real honest-to-God "California weather." For a few years, the city was warm and sunny from April to October, and like Eric, many who moved there during the drought had no idea this was far from the normal weather pattern, which encased the city under Soviet-gray skies most every day save a few in September and October.

No matter—that climatological misery was years away. Eric found work quickly as a temp, discovering he could command $14 an hour for his knowledge of WordPerfect. He'd modestly joked to Cal about his ineptitude with computers, but on his temp assignments he discovered that he knew far more about the systems than the people he was working with. On one plum assignment, instead of typing he'd spent his days patiently tutoring frightened secretaries in WordPerfect as they converted to PCs from their beloved Wang or DisplayWriter word processing systems. He even got a job offer from a law firm as a sort of in-house PC expert, which he was sorely tempted to take; it would have paid him $25,000 a year to start!

But he saw how the process worked in the firm, indeed, how it worked at most every place he worked: The workers produced far more work than they were really being paid to do, either flattered into it ("You're so good, I don't know what we'd do without you") or bullied ("This is a very important project, and we can't afford to have anybody who isn't 100% on board") or seduced ("I can't promise anything, but the word is there might be some big bonuses at the end of this"). This wouldn't be a job; it would be a career—and a career would mean no time or energy left for writing. "Oh, you write," more than one permanent employee had said wistfully. "I always wanted to do that..." *But instead*, Eric reflected, *they'd taken a job like this, slaving away at some bullshit job, driving their minivan back and forth between here and the suburbs.* Eric was a sweet boy, but he had all of ambitious youth's arrogance and disdain for all those who had come before and failed where he would not, and of course he didn't take the job.

He loved the freedom of temping; when he'd made enough money for the month, he simply stopped working, unless an agency entreated him with an interesting and well-paying job. But for the most part the work was not interesting. His facility with WordPerfect had landed him a string of jobs in engineering firms, where they needed someone who could handle footnotes, or automated paragraph numbering. It never ceased to amaze him how many people blubbered with gratitude to have a temp who could indent, let alone knew the key strokes for subscript and superscript needed to create printable mathematical formulas.

But the worst part of temping was not the work; it was the boredom that set in when the work was done. He would turn in something to be reviewed to someone who didn't have more work ready for him yet, and then he'd have to sit at the computer looking busy for the rest of the day. He'd learned the hard way not to ask for more work from other people, because if there wasn't any, he'd be led around the office until someone eagerly heaped a pile of filing on him. There were some firms where he worked for people who respected him, both for his computer talents and for his decision to make a go at a writing career, and they left him be. Where this meant hours, if not sometimes days, waiting for more work, he found himself in the enviable position of being able to get paid to write. He discovered that at most firms, people knew so little about computers that as long as he was staring intently at the screen and typing, he was assumed to be working.

At some firms there were busybody office managers who would discover Eric's slack time and put him to Xeroxing or shredding or filing. After a while, however, when Eric had realized the value of his skills, he would simply say no. Their eyebrows would rise and they would call the temp agency, who would call Eric, who would say calmly, "The reason I don't have anything to do is because I'm very good at what I do, and I'm not going to be punished for being good by doing the scut work they want to foist off on the temp." The agencies hated this; the placement people had developed an extreme servility toward their clients and expected the temps to follow suit. Eric would shrug and pack his backpack and go say goodbye to the manager for whom he actually worked. He would of course be asked why he was leaving, explain the situation, be immediately reinstated, and for the rest of his assignment the office manager would live in fear of him. This suited Eric fine.

The worst days were those where he had the time at work but couldn't write, or when he managed to crank out a few pages and found himself tapped out, with hours left to kill. A natural morning person, Eric hated the hours between three and five o'clock, which in themselves often seemed like eight hours. He thought it was pathetic there were people so incompetent that the only way they could measure their employees' productivity was by the clock. He was of course welcome to leave early sometimes, without being paid for those two hours, but for the most part his employers would rather have him around, willingly paying for his potential rather than actual usefulness.

The other thing besides the punch clocks that got him was the dress code. On the street anybody would have taken him for a mailroom clerk, so complete was his disdain for the pecking order that dictated a person's value to the company by what they wore. He wore Doc Martens, Ben Davis pants, and thrift-store shirts and ties, wearing the tie loose and never buttoning the top button of the shirt, not as a statement but because he felt literally strangled by the physical pressure if he did otherwise. In the more "advanced" companies, they had "casual Fridays," when the middle managers would dress as if they were going to play a weekend round of golf, not knowing what else to wear besides a suit around their peers. Eric wore jeans on Fridays when he was lucky enough to get an assignment that allowed it, and went as far out of his way to look good in them as he did to look bad in his "office drag." It was all an absurd farce—you could be a completely incompetent moron, but as long as you had a tie on you were, by magic, a "professional" who took his work "seriously."

His cheap rent left him with plenty of disposable income, but his job left him with nobody to spend it with. This, he was discovering, was the worst part of all about being a temp: Most people who move to the city make friends at work or school, but nobody makes friends at work with the temp, who will be gone before anyone gets to know him. Also, Eric had found there was a social food chain in large organizations; the temp figured barely higher than the mailroom clerk, no matter how he dressed.

Eric was lonely. He found himself on the phone with his Mom sometimes every day, not a normal situation for a young man footloose in the big city. He tried to make friends at some gay groups—one a gay computer users group, another a gay writers and artists group—but both of them turned him off. In both places, there was a snobbiness, a cliquey attitude that put him off. In any social group, especially those dedicated to intel-lectual pursuits, there will always be one person shoring up his own self-esteem by sneering at anyone who knows less than he does, and for some reason Eric found himself the one sneered at, for not knowing some obtuse point of MS-DOS at the computer group and for mispronouncing Proust's name at the writer's group. Eric hated that nose-in-the-air, groovier-than-thou behavior, and while he gave that as his reason for not going back to either group, there was also the unspoken hurt of a friendly puppy who'd been smacked on the nose with a newspaper for no good reason.

But something had to change. An only child who'd been comfortable by himself, he was also a team sports player, who didn't realize until now how much he needed other people in his life. He thought there was something wrong with him; he couldn't possibly know the city was full of people just like himself.

Bars were an easy place for him to *meet* people, because everybody wanted to have sex with him. It started to depress him; sooner or later everyone he talked to in a bar brought the subject around to how good-looking he was and how lucky any-body would be to go home with him, making sure he knew—as if he could possibly not!—that they wanted to be the lucky one to take home the prize. And if he ever complained about this cycle he was locked into, their faces would go sour and they'd say, "It's not easy being pretty, is it?" He stopped going to bars; despite AIDS, everyone still wanted to fuck first and ask questions later, and that wasn't his style.

He thought about Cal more than he liked. He'd never had a physical type before, but now found himself drawn to slim, smooth young men with impossibly small waists like Cal's. What sex he did have was usually with this type, though they always disappointed him outside of their bodies—they were too queeny, or too needy, or too *something*, it seemed to him, when of course, as everybody could have told him, it wasn't that they were too something but that what they were lacking was that they were not Cal. He often found himself fucking them and prompting his orgasm by fantasizing that the waist he had his hands around was Cal's, though he felt a little guilty about it, quite possibly because those were his best orgasms.

He even thought about moving home, mentioned it to his mom. "Well," she said, "you're more than welcome here. But if you thought it was going to be easy, I have news for you." Eric had moved gracefully through life until now; the good things he had set his sights on had been within his grasp. Now he was aiming higher and discovering that his reach exceeded his grasp, at least for now. He'd heard in the abstract about "struggling writers," but only now did he realize what it meant—moving someplace where he knew nobody, putting up with bullshit jobs, trying to gain "experience" while giving up the easy route to minivandom in exchange for the opportunity to remake the world in his own words.

No, it wasn't true; there was one thing he'd failed, one thing he'd wanted that he couldn't have. But this was not like loving Cal—this was not something that depended on anybody but himself; this was not work that required him to cause an echo of his heart in one other person. A hundred, a thousand people could reject his work, and he could press on because somehow, someday, he would find one person in the right place who could, would, open the road to a million others. He knew this with all the certainty of youth.

As the summer of 1989 rolled around, Eric made the decision to stop temping. He'd made a couple friends at one long-term temp assignment (two straight guys who worked—where else?—in the mailroom at a big company), but they didn't have much time to socialize with him, between their girlfriends and the band they were trying to make a go of. He took a job doing what he'd ruefully described himself doing back in school: pulling coffees. Only rather than a step down, Eric considered it a step up. Temping meant isolation, interaction with other people limited to a few minutes a day when he got work or turned it back. Temping meant staring at a cubicle wall, the only variation being between gray and tan. Temping meant listening to the blandishments of business over the hum of machines. Temping meant sitting at a desk, generating a pent-up nervous energy he had to run off at night.

Pulling coffees, on the other hand, meant forging a bond

with the people he worked with, as well as with the friendlier regulars. He pulled coffees in Spinelli, right at Castro and 18th, and got to see all kinds of people, sometimes even their dogs, going in and out—a constantly changing diorama. Pulling coffees meant cool tunes on the stereo, especially when it was his day of the week to select the tapes. And best of all, it was part assembly line and part show, calling the drinks if he was taking orders that day, or echoing the orders if he was making them up. He started work at five A.M. and was done at eleven, and while the hourly pay was about a third of what he'd made temping, there were the tips to be divided up, which bumped it up to about half. Best of all, when it was slow, he could *go*.

No, best of all, he was making friends—Sue and Tim and Neil and Jason, who all worked there; Rob and Patrick and Cecily and Rennie and Will and all the other regulars, who'd originally smirked at Eric's "perky" demeanor, until they realized it was real, that he loved being up at dawn, loved seeing people his whole work day, and loved drinking and serving—as they said all the time in the store, echoing everyone's favorite show, *Twin Peaks*, "Damn good coffee!" And his writing, which had been a hunt-and-peck smattering of attempts at stories, failed essays, and novel outline, took wing. He settled into a comfortable routine of working five days a week at Spinelli, getting home to his Panhandle studio around noon, eating something and writing for three hours. Then there was the gym, or a run, or a swim, and most nights he'd meet friends for dinner somewhere (*not* the Castro— there was hardly a place fit to eat down there) and then catch a movie or a concert at the Fillmore or the Great American Music Hall.

One night it just happened. He'd had a few beers—he couldn't remember how many—and he was standing outside GAMH, having just seen fIREHOSE, the band that had formed out of the remnants of the Minutemen. It had been a kick-ass show; he'd danced with Neil's girlfriend and then with Neil in one of those liberating "whatever" moments, and now he was standing in a crowd of talking, laughing people. And he started to cry as a door in his mind closed behind him; as he heard it click, he realized that he had walked into a life full of joy, that he wasn't alone anymore, that he was young and excited and talented and there was so much more joy ahead, and this was the way life was supposed to be.

Rob and Patrick were two of his favorite customers. Patrick was an interior designer just a little older than Eric, and the two of them shared an ironic sensibility that was yet to be officially designated as a hallmark of their generation. Patrick did a mean impression, in both senses, of Richard Simmons, a man he despised for being such a closet case. He laughed at the stereotype of the interior designer, even lapsing into an exaggerated version of it at times when discussing his work, a tactic he used to prevent himself from ever taking what he did seriously.

Rob was older than Patrick by about ten years, years that made the two of them practically people from separate planets. Rob was an old-style gay man—he had a large but rigorously manicured moustache and severely cropped hair, a well-paying job in a large company at which he was "discreet" to Patrick's ire, drove a Cadillac ("That's what these old queens consider 'classy,'" Patrick said one day, drawling the last word disdainfully), and preferred to vacation at the Russian River amongst other gay men. Patrick was "painfully blond" in his own words, "another blue-eyed chorus boy." He wore his hair in the new style inspired by *Maurice*, the movie gay men flocked to see, so rare was it to see their own kind on the silver screen (at least, as characters who didn't meet grisly fates because of it). Patrick drove an old BMW 2002 and preferred holidays in New York City, Amsterdam, or "anywhere tropical."

"Ever read the personals ads in the *Bay Times*?" Patrick asked Eric one day.

"The personals are like the *Enquirer*," Eric said. "Everybody reads it and nobody admits it."

"There are always these guys who use the phrase, 'Equally comfortable in jeans or a tux.' And they're always guys like Rob. They feel like they have to be butch for 'the cause'—and to get laid!—but really they want to be Ginger Rogers, not Fred Astaire."

"So what are you doing with him?" Eric asked.

Patrick shrugged. "He's a good person. Opposites attract, I guess. Oh, did I mention the sex?" he asked with an innocent mien.

Patrick invited Eric to dinner at their house, and Eric accepted, having decided not to turn down any social opportunity. Out of the public eye, he found Rob to be far from the brusque, cold mannequin he was in public. He could see the sparks between them and laughed at what had obviously become old routines between the two men, who'd been together for four years now. "That's 28 in straight years," Rob winked.

"He plucked me from the cradle," Patrick added. "Don't tell Jerry Falwell."

Sunday dinner became a ritual. Patrick introduced Eric to one-dish meals, gardening, and *Style with Elsa Klensch.* Rob introduced him to Billie Holiday, Ella Fitzgerald, and Dinah Washington, but Eric tenaciously resisted Rob's show tunes collection, as did Patrick, who was bold enough to declare out loud their common distaste for "that old drunken pinkie-ring queen music, that fucking *show people thing* Liza Minnelli does with that goddamn hand-flappin' thing of hers." Every generation of every modern culture needs to separate itself from the previous one, and Eric and Patrick's generation would steadfastly refuse to bow at the shrines of Judy and Barbra and Stephen Sondheim and "all that jazz." (Billie Holiday and the other old gals of song fell into another category altogether; there was nothing schmaltzy or Broadwayishly overdone about their timeless brilliance, and there was no crime in recognizing and appreciating it, no matter whether the tired old queens liked them as well or not.)

They also introduced Eric to good wine and great pot, "the classic San Francisco cocktail," according to Rob. From the '60s on, marijuana was to San Francisco what martinis had been to New York City in its golden days: an essential accessory. Eric loved the way grass reduced him to childlike delight at the flowers in the garden, which he could spend hours discussing with Patrick when stoned, while the late afternoon sun streamed into his friends' living room and Billie commanded her lover to "Do Your Duty" and chicken cacciatore simmered on the stovetop. "Life is good," he said out loud one day when they were all stoned, and the others nodded. It was too clichéd to say sober, but it was true and pot precludes sarcastic responses.

Eric didn't think much of it when Patrick came into Spinelli by himself, Rob sick at home. Patrick himself made light of it, calling it "that nagging cold" in the same tones used in the commercial. Eric expressed the usual concern when Patrick called and canceled Sunday dinner, and even more so when Patrick also stopped coming into the store. For weeks, his calls to the couple were received by the answering machine and not returned. One day after work he went over unannounced and rang the doorbell. Patrick answered the door, frighteningly drawn and pale.

"What is going on?" Eric demanded, trying to come in.

Patrick stopped him. "Rob has AIDS, Eric. He's dying."

"What?" Eric asked like an idiot. Recovering himself, he asked, "Why didn't you tell me?"

"We lost a lot of friends when they found out," Patrick said. "We didn't want to lose the rest."

"What do you mean? So you get rid of them before you can lose them? Let me in, damn it."

Eric had read about this kind of behavior: lovers who left when they found out their partner had HIV, friends who dropped friends. It was inconceivable to him for a number of reasons. First, his mother had instilled in him a highly developed sense of right and wrong, and abandoning friends in their time of need was *wrong*. In support of this, he also had youth's genetically programmed refusal to believe in its own death, a sense that AIDS wouldn't get *him*, which had been the downfall of more than a few young men, but in this case banished any fear of a sick or dying person's presence. Finally, there was his love for his friends, a love that was hurt since they had so underestimated it and assumed he, too, would abandon them. Bruised people come to expect the worst, once they have been bruised enough times by those they never thought would do it. Having been only rarely and lightly bruised, Eric could not understand the defense mechanism that had let Patrick and Rob to shut him out. But all of that could be put aside in a crisis, so he put it aside.

Patrick hugged him with more force than Eric had been prepared for. He could feel his friend clutching back tears. "Thank you. Come on in."

"Where's Rob? I want to say hi."

"He's upstairs in bed. But…just be prepared, OK?"

"For what?

"He doesn't look good."

He could not have possibly been prepared. Rob was so thin it scared him. It was *Death*, right there in front of him, and he felt a primal surge of adrenaline—*flight! flight!*—but he repressed it. Later, he would compare it to the film the soldiers took of people at Auschwitz just after the liberation, so thin no one could believe they could still really be alive—only their huge agonized eyes were moving and their arms were waving feebly and they were alive, just. He hugged Rob, who groaned slightly.

"What?" Eric asked, as Rob tried to say something.

"Don't hug him," Patrick said. "He's in constant pain everywhere in his body, and being hugged hurts too much."

That was when Eric started to cry, the horror of the whole epidemic dawning on him at last, all at once; after years of being untouched by it, he was devastated by a single realization: this was how it ended, and the end was so horrible it would even hurt to be loved.

He got the whole story out of Patrick: they were both HIV-positive. It might have seemed a dichotomy that Patrick would be so enraged by a closet case like Richard Simmons and yet be so closeted himself about his HIV status, but Eric had lived in the gay community long enough to understand the difference. Politicians had calmly spoken of containing the epidemic by tattooing infected people's buttocks with HIV+, presumably to prevent some "discreet" married man from fucking said buttocks and carrying the virus into the heterosexual population.

Conservatives had even proposed quarantining HIV-positive people in Manzanar-style camps where faggots and junkies could die horribly, out of the public eye. The rise of AIDS renewed tenfold the antigay frenzy that had quelled during the false bubble prosperity of junk bonds and deficit spending. Male homosexuals were no longer just recruiting young boys into their ranks; they were also carriers of the plague. A powerful senator from North Carolina repeatedly quashed efforts to educate Americans about the HIV virus and its transmission, and fear and ignorance incited people in Indiana to burn a young boy's home to the ground.

As Eric helped Patrick change Rob's IV-drip, he was learning learned a new acronym: TPN, meaning total parenteral nutrition, given intravenously to people whose bodies are no longer able to process solid or even liquid food—which within minutes they would either vomit up, probably weakly enough to choke on it, or shit out in a stream.

Eric had volunteered to help Patrick without ever saying a word. Patrick showed him what to do, how to roll Rob in such a way as to cause him a minimum of pain when they cleaned him up, how to pick him up so Patrick could change the sheets. "It's good to have a big strong man around the house," Patrick cracked with a gallows humor that startled and unnerved Eric until he realized it was a survival mechanism.

After Rob had drifted into a morphine patch–induced slumber, Eric and Patrick got drunk on the best wine in the house. "Do you want to know the worst part?" Patrick confessed around three A.M. "The worst part is—and you'll despise me for it, it's so selfish—the worst part is, I'm sitting there looking at him, and I'm thinking, this is me in a year or two. That long if I'm very lucky. I'm sitting there looking at him and I'm not seeing him. I'm seeing a truck that's coming at me—very, very slowly—and there is no way I can move. And nowhere I can look but right at that truck. And all I can do is stand there and wait for it to hit me."

Eric had spent over a year in San Francisco, half that time working in the heart of its gay community. But for all that,

AIDS hadn't really touched him. His friends were young and HIV-negative (or too scared to get tested), or HIV-positive and keeping it to themselves like Patrick. Living in San Francisco had made him well-educated about HIV: how to keep from getting it, how it can and can't be transmitted. The information on the subject was such a thick blizzard in that city that Eric had absorbed it by osmosis, without even trying to educate himself. And while he was a good-hearted person, he was also an artist, and as such a bit of an egotist. AIDS was a bad thing, and he was lucky to be living somewhere that people were doing something about it. Sure, it was unnerving to see a human skeleton with KS being wheeled down the street, but the part of that scene his sunny optimistic self retained was the goodness of the Shanti volunteer who was "doing something" by pushing that wheelchair. This freed him from having to do anything himself, which would have interfered with his writing or his socializing. And since the disease had not touched him personally, there had been nothing to shatter his complacency, until now.

He spent the next two weeks going to work from Rob and Patrick's house, and going back there after work. He tried to explain what was happening in his life to his friends, to people he thought he was close to. But he realized there was *no way* to explain what it was like to be nursing a terminally ill person you loved, to see them in so much pain and realize that he and his lover expected you to help him die when the time came. "Wow, gee," Eric's friends said, sounding like so many Andy Warhols, unmoved—and unable to admit it, even to themselves—by something so irrelevant to their own shining destinies.

Patrick had told him about the Seconals they'd been hoarding; Rob had hoped his family would come see him, but it had become apparent they were not coming, *AIDSAIDSAIDSAIDS* ringing in their ears like a fire alarm, a signal to evacuate, to save themselves and leave their loved one behind in the burning building.

Now it was time. As winter night fell early, the lights in the house were extinguished and replaced by a hundred candles.

Eric had filled Rob's room with vases full of color and scent; Patrick had moved the stereo into Rob's room and loaded the CD player with Billie and Dinah and Ella and Sarah. Eric wheeled Rob out on the hospital bed that had replaced his old bed, muscled the old bed back into the room, and moved Rob as gently as possible onto the mattress, onto Egyptian cotton sheets that in the morning would be shoved into the trash can marked BIOHAZARD. Patrick tucked Rob in under a white goose-down comforter.

Eric was surprised he wasn't crying during all this. It was as if he was too moved to cry; the whole ceremony was so full of grace. He hadn't been raised to be religious, and yet he felt like a priest preparing the way to the next life, even as he ensured the dying man the best of everything in this life before he went. *It's such a good way to die,* he thought, *here at home in your own bed, surrounded by the people and things you love.*

Patrick and Eric broke open the Seconals and mixed them into the yogurt in the kitchen. The doctor had told them this was the best way to administer it. They brought the bowl to Rob, who smiled. Eric was an empathetic creature, and while he still did not cry, he shuddered at the idea of a man so tormented that the sight of his bowl of hemlock made him smile in relief. Patrick fed it to Rob, stroking his hair, as Eric held Rob's hand on the other side. Eric had volunteered, but Patrick had insisted: "I have to be the one."

Billie broke into "Some Enchanted Evening," and Rob gave Patrick a hand signal they'd devised, indicating "Turn it up." His eyes stayed on Patrick for almost the whole of the song, then they closed. Patrick later said he knew—he could never explain how to anyone but Eric, who understood because he was there—when Rob was conscious and listening, when he was asleep, and when he was dead.

Patrick didn't cry either. The thought struck Eric that Patrick hadn't cried at all, ever—not that he'd seen. He seemed happy, relieved not only for Rob but for himself. He had seen the truck coming, Eric surmised, yet now he knew that when it hit, it wouldn't be so bad at the end. Wasn't that the real terror, not knowing just how bad it would be?

Patrick left town a week later. Rob's life insurance had left him well-off, and he decided to take a trip around the world "while I'm still ambulatory. And if needs be," he winked, squeezing Eric's biceps, "I'll get some hot, hunky nurse to push me around the rest of the world."

Eric missed Patrick, but was glad for him, too. But what amazed him was that life didn't go "back to normal" after his friends left his life. He had been baptized under fire and did not yet know how much this month had changed him, but others noticed it. His smile at work was still genuine pleasure at seeing people, especially people he liked, but there was knowledge there that had been impossible for him before—*You could be gone tomorrow*, some part of him thought as he looked at everyone he knew. The knowledge that he could be gone, too, he had not yet acquired. All things in time.

Twice in his life, Eric had been reduced to tears of helplessness. But this time there was something he could do—it had been too late to save Rob, but not too late to save Patrick, or anyone else he knew who might be HIV-positive. Eric inquired into becoming a Shanti volunteer, where he would do for a stranger all he'd done for Rob. But this business they had in the orientation, some kind of New Age thing where you did these movement exercises and breathing and all that chakra shit—it all reeked to him of helping people die, and he had already done that and wished never to do it again. The whole of AIDS charity work seemed to him to be about that, an acceptance of the inevitable and a "we can make you comfortable" mentality. He was too young to accept death, not only his own but anyone else's—he wanted to *fight AIDS*, not make dying from it easier.

One day he picked up one of the gay papers and read about a demonstration at St. Patrick's Cathedral in New York City. It sounded like something out of the French Revolution: Members of a radical AIDS activist group based in New York called ACT UP had shut down the church in response to Cardinal John O'Connor's vituperatively antigay rhetoric and the political influence he wielded in preventing the dissemination of safe-sex information in public schools. The story hadn't just made the gay papers; it had made the national news, although the media had focused not on the cardinal's homophobia but on a lone protester's desecration of a Communion wafer. *Never mind that*, Eric thought, having learned long ago from Emma that shock and horror make better copy than issues do. *Someone had fought back. Someone had decided not to sit back and let someone else make them comfortable. And something had happened.*

The paper had picked the story up from the AP wire but had added a comment from a member of ACT UP San Francisco. There was a branch of the group here, Eric realized. He, too, could help make something happen.

He asked customers at Spinelli the next day about ACT UP, and was astonished at the responses he got. Will's placid features darkened as he asked Eric angrily, "Why would you want to have anything to do with that bunch of punks? Interfering with religious ceremonies! They're going to get us all killed." And he'd left without another word. *How could anyone hate a group that was doing something?* Eric wondered. Then another regular came in, Keith, and Eric saw the ACT UP button on the lapel of his leather jacket. In fact, he realized the button had been there for months, a black-and-white key to his future that Eric had simply never seen before because it had never meant anything before.

Keith lit up when Eric asked him about the group. "Every Monday night at the Women's Building, rain or shine. If you come, bring a friend. We need more bodies!"

"Well," Eric said hesitantly, "I just want to check it out, see what it's like."

Keith nodded. "Don't let the General Body turn you off," Keith said, speaking activist shorthand for the main meeting. "It's a lot like congress—all bluster and blow. The *real* work goes on in committees. If you *really* want to get involved, join a committee. I'm on the Propaganda Committee," he said, handing Eric a sticker. "We do the visuals. Propaganda in New York made this one. It's from that demo in New York you read about."

Eric looked at the sticker. STOP THE CHURCH, it said in the same powerful typeface as the ACT UP logo, underneath a photo of Cardinal O'Connor. Then it gave the date, time, and place of the protest. Beneath that were exhortative slogans to fight the church's opposition to abortion and its murderous AIDS policy. TAKE DIRECT ACTION. TAKE CONTROL OF YOUR BODY.

Take direct action. That's what he wanted to do. Today was Friday—three days until he found out whether this was what he'd been looking for ever since Rob had died.

As Eric walked down 18th Street that Monday, there was no missing the Women's Building; hordes of people were gathered on the sidewalk out front. He went upstairs to the main room, where chairs were arranged in a huge circle. All the chairs were taken, even though more people were coming in all the time. Keith spotted him, and they sat on a table against the wall.

The meeting began with a demand for any law enforcement officials to identify themselves. "I type reports at the police department—does that count against me?" one woman asked to laughter. Minutes of the previous meeting were read, and members of the various committees asked for volunteers—Treatment, Insurance (Keith's group), City Hall, Women, Prisoners, and PISD, which Eric later found out stood for "People With Immune System Disorders," a committee originally open only to people with HIV, then expanded to include anything immune-related.

"OK," one of the two facilitators said, "the first order of business is the motion on racist behavior." Groans rose from half the group, who were hissed down by the other half. "Tommy?"

Tommy sat in the circle of chairs and referred to his notes. "OK, this is the new proposal. If you make a statement that someone else considers racist, and they call you on it, you are not allowed to respond, because we've all seen that degenerate into a shouting match that takes up the rest of the meeting. If you still think the following week that your comments were *not* racist, you can address the issue then."

Eric's brow furrowed. He raised his hand, but a half a dozen others shot up in the circle, each of them taking their turn to take positions that had already been aired the week before: "We're not here to fight racism, we're here to fight AIDS." "No, racism is a cause of AIDS: people of color are being left to die because of racism, and that has to come first." "There won't *be* any people of color left alive if we spend the rest of our lives talking about something that's existed in human society for thousands of years." "You're just a selfish gay white male who only wants to save his own ass." "You're goddamn right I want to save my own ass…"

Eric's hand stayed raised but ignored, until Keith raised his. The facilitator bypassed several people ahead of him who would have contributed nothing other than instant replay; Keith was obviously a leader in this "leaderless" group. "My friend Eric here has something to say," he said.

People turned around to see Eric, interested in what a stranger who had Keith's respect had to say—and of course pleased to get the opportunity to look at a hot boy. "I think your proposal is a lose-lose situation," Eric said. "I mean, if you're accused of being a racist, and you can't say anything in your own defense, then the only thing that stays in everyone's mind is the accusation. And if you come back a week later to say you're still angry about it, well, people will think, that just sounds like sour grapes—why are you still talking about *that*? So either you're a racist, or you're petty."

A rare moment of silence filled the room, and then applause and whoops burst out. Eric could see that those who had hissed previously had lost this battle; they sat with scowls and arms folded. In an instant he saw how divided this group was, that two irreconcilable sides had formed and he had just allied himself with one of them.

A few weeks later, Eric realized that ACT UP had become his life. He'd sampled nearly every committee save PISD, which he couldn't join, and Treatment and Data, which he couldn't understand. The problem with T&D, Eric thought, was that the people in it were too brilliant. Some of the members were lay people whose lives depended, literally, on their mastering the intricacies of chemistry and biology; others were Ph.D.s who had mastered the subjects before discovering that their own lives would become their new focus of study. T&D gave "educationals" at the General Body meeting, educationals that for most present went in one ear and out the other. The presenters knew so much that they simply forgot how little their audience knew, and while they were careful to start by talking down to their audience, as they needed to, they would get swept up in the subject and soon started tossing out new, unexplained words to an audience who had never heard of macrophages and microphages, let alone knew the difference between them.

Eric liked the ironically named Propaganda committee, which created the signs and stickers and buttons that were the icons of this new movement. Some of the members were professional graphic designers; one was a gay porn star turned porn director with a natural flair for visuals, others simply warm bodies willing to do the scut work of mounting posters suitable for framing on the foam core boards on which they would be displayed at the next demo.

Eventually, he settled on two committees—Media and Insurance. With an instinct nurtured in many of his generation raised on television, he turned his writing talents to the craft of the sound bite, the slogan, the press release. He'd joined the Insurance and Health Access committee, mostly because of Keith, but he soon realized IHA could be just as "sexy" a committee as Treatment. After all, it required one to be just as much of a brainiac to master the nuances of ERISA, or plow through Ted Kennedy's health care legislation and Claude Pepper's commission report, or create a list of demands (ACT UP did not make requests—it made demands) for California's newly created insurance commissioner (whose mandate from a public then apathetic about the health care system was to reform the overpriced auto insurance industry).

This was what he loved most about ACT UP—there was no bullshit hierarchy, no professional organization for whom volunteers were much like temps, condemned to stuffing envelopes or Xeroxing. If you could do it, *you did it*. You didn't apply to the Insurance committee and have to prove that you could understand health care legislation; you just *joined* and went to work. The majority of the people in ACT UP were young, under 30; they were the impatient ones. They wanted to be doing something *now*, they wanted to see change *now*. The young are right when they say there is no good reason to wait for things to get better; no good reason for things not to be better *now*; only the old at heart want to wait, their fear of failure or of making things worse arresting the evolution and progress of mankind. So many people all around them getting sick, waiting to get sick...all the members of ACT UP were young regardless of biological age, because they refused to believe in death.

Eric's first demonstration, the first demo sponsored by the Insurance Committee, was at the St. Francis Hotel right on Union Square, where George Bush's Director of Health and Human Services, Louis Sullivan, was speaking. The Insurance Committee had only four members, but warm bodies ready to protest and be arrested for it were always to be had at General Body. Dozens of ACT UP members waved signs with a photo of George Bush doing his trademark air-chopping hand gesture; the photo had been doctored in Photoshop into a Lichtenstein-like dotted cartoon, with a balloon coming out of Bush's mouth saying in cartoon letters, also in trademark telegraphic George Bush fashion, "People with AIDS? Let 'em die. Worked for Reagan. Stay the course."

"Is Louis Sullivan aware that *35 million people* in America do *not* have health insurance?" Eric shouted at the tourists who had gathered on the square, as he stood in front of the police who had cordoned off the entrance to the St. Francis. The cops were always at ACT UP events ahead of time—not because they had a spy in the ranks, but because ACT UP had a few friendly contacts in the department who were informed in advance of any demonstration. After all, if a line of police-men are required to protect a Cabinet member from a handful of young punks waving signs, it makes a great visual—and that was what ACT UP did best, made great visuals that attracted news cameras desperate for exciting content. (This was in the days before freeway chases and Court TV.) Eric eschewed the bullhorn; he may not have had time in school for drama or public speaking, but he was now discovering he had a gift for it. To him, a bullhorn was something old hippies used on college campuses, something people with painfully shrill voices used to make themselves even shriller. People turned away from bullhorns the way they plugged their ears at the sound of fire trucks racing by, yet they turned instinctively toward a compelling human voice.

"Louis Sullivan doesn't think we need a national health care system!" Eric stopped and looked around dramatically, making sure the cameras registered his pause—but not too long a pause, just enough to catch the attention of any TV viewer whose eye might have wandered— "But then, Louis Sullivan has the *best* health insurance *in the world!*"

It was perfect: the camera caught the laughter of the crowd of tourists at the punch line and the smiles of the cops behind him, men who might not approve of fags with AIDS, but were also blue-collar men who knew the score. (Actually, they loved the overtime they got for arresting the activists, who made a good deal of noise for the cameras as they were arrested but who ACTUALLY didn't resist much). And of course, the smiling and very photogenic Eric suddenly took his message into the breach his humor had created: "WHEN I WEIGH 95 POUNDS, WHEN I AM TOO WEAK TO BREATHE ON MY OWN ANYMORE, WHEN I AM BLIND FROM AIDS, WHEN I CAN NO LONGER EAT SOLID FOOD, WHEN I AM IN A DIAPER BECAUSE I CANNOT CONTROL MY BOWELS, I WILL NOT BE FLOWN TO BETHESDA! I WILL BE SENT HOME BY THE HOSPITAL TO DIE BECAUSE MY INSUR-ANCE HAS RUN OUT! *AND LOUIS SULLIVAN DOES NOT GIVE A DAMN, BECAUSE GEORGE BUSH ONLY HIRES PEO-PLE WHO DO NOT GIVE A DAMN ABOUT AIDS!*" It was a powerful vision of horror from someone so young and glowing and muscular. It said, *That's what's going to happen to me; that's what I'm going to be, if you don't do something.*

To ensure that the sound bite wasn't cut off after the punch line—which was the signal to storm the St. Francis, slowly but loudly—the activists joined hands and swept up the steps in waves worthy of (because inspired by) Eisenstein, only to be pushed back by the cops, who didn't enjoy this particular moment of close contact with people whom they presumed all had AIDS. The cops turned the protesters around and cuffed their wrists with plastic strips that could be easily cut off after a routine booking and release.

Once in the van and out of the camera's eye, the rage of most protesters dissipated. Some of the members of the group hated cops with a passion, often for good reason, but middle-class Eric chatted easily with them, charming them, startling them when they discovered he was HIV-negative. "You know, if you lose your job, you lose your insurance, too. You can pay for it yourself for a maximum of 18 months at the old premium price your employer pays, but after that you have to convert to an individual policy. And they can charge you anything they want for that, raise it every month if they want."

"Well, unless I shoot one of you guys, I don't think I'm losing my job anytime soon," one young, handsome cop joked. Eric caught the look the man gave him; he was coming to learn the type: a straight man curious about sex with men, a smart man curious about AIDS and the health care system, who in the presence of his straighter and more stupid compatriots needed to pepper his dialogue with the likes of Eric with hints of insult and violence.

"No, a civil service is a job for life, no matter what," Eric smiled. "But have you looked at your policy lately? Does it have a cap?"

"A what?" the cop asked.

"A cap. Say your policy has a $1 million lifetime cap. Your wife or your kids get sick. Real sick, cancer sick. Ever look at a hospital bill? They'll charge your insurance $10 for a Tylenol." The cops laughed, all of them having seen some relative's hospital bill if not their own. "Well, a serious illness will suck up $1 million real fast. And do you know what happens when that runs out?" His eyes swept the cops' eyes, checking to see if he had their attention. "Your wife or your kid won't be at the nice middle-class hospital anymore. They'll be transferred to San Francisco General. And you know what that's like." The cops twisted uneasily in their seats at the thought of their loved ones at the same hospital to which the poorest of the poor were diverted, to which they brought prisoners who'd been shot or stabbed or were in need of other medical care. General was the bowels of Hell, and they all knew it.

Eric moved in for the kill. "Nobody cares about this stuff until it affects them personally. That's why we're here, because it affects us personally. It affects the people I love. I'm seeing them die on a gurney in a hallway at San Francisco General because there are no rooms for them. Of course, the average AIDS case only costs about $100,000, but that's because people with AIDS die so fast."

He held the eyes of the handsome cop as he finished. Some things are telegraphed between people; there is no explaining it yet—some voice in our right brain capable of being as articulate in its way as our left brain is with our vocal chords, only using our eyes to send its urgent messages. Eric's eyes said, *This looks like theater, and it is—but it's not a game. We never thought we'd be here doing this. This could be you.*

Eric would have liked to skip General Body meetings altogether, but Keith begged him to attend. As constructive and exciting as the committee meetings were, General Body was destructive and draining. Eric had thought himself a liberal, or at least left of center, until ACT UP. He was not the only man in America, gay or straight, who was to be pushed right by a radical Left that had created the "white male boogeyman," responsible for every naughty thing in the universe since 1492 (the WMB being guiltless before that, since until then he only killed and oppressed other white people, who had presumably deserved it). His mother and Bennington had not raised a racist, but every time he spoke out against a proposal by one of the members of what he and others were calling the Red Army Faction, they stood up, purple with rage, tendons and veins trying to burst out of their skin to join their accusing finger in pointing at him and decrying his racism, which was his real reason for opposing some motion that would change the focus of ACT UP from AIDS to whatever Marxist pipe dream had yet to be proven a failure.

Every week, Eric was found guilty of trying to protect his "white male privilege." He laughed at this with Keith and the other GWMs during the break in the middle of the meeting. "I have no health insurance. I pull coffees part-time for a living. I have $1,000 in the bank, no property, no car, no nothing. So I want to know," he smiled, "where the hell *is* my white male privilege, because I could sure use some of it right now!"

They called it political correctness, and like many ideologies and formulations, it was designed not to change a wrong but to enable its proponents to seize power under the guise of changing a wrong. It was a stroke of genius; they took a moment in the mindscape of liberal Americans when it was considered bad to be racist, sexist, or homophobic, but not much could be done about any of these things, at least until the Washington political climate shifted. Americans had elected a Republican to the White House three times in a row, and there seemed little likelihood that the next hack to climb to the top of the ash heap of the Democratic party would make any more charismatic a challenger than Carter, Mondale, or Dukakis. For the Left, there was no real power to seize, and for people who lived for power, that situation was intolerable. They began to eat their own, to enact a party purge that would destroy the soft center and leave only the hard core, who would bully the rest of the body politic into doing its bidding by threatening to label them with the damning labels—*racist, sexist, homophobic*—and if you were guilty of one, you were guilty of them all, and if you were white, male, straight, or at least the first two out of three, you *were* guilty, no trial required.

One night at a particularly crowded meeting, Eric made his last speech on the subject, losing his temper completely in a way that is only possible for mild-mannered people in a political group setting.

"The next time somebody stands up and calls me a racist,

sexist homophobe, I will consider the conversation over and my point lost, because someone will have changed the subject to keep me from making it. You people sit there with a fucking *clipboard* and grade everybody on a curve, like a civil service test in reverse: minus five points for white, minus five for male, minus five for straight—if there were any straight men bold enough to come in here and endure this! You're grading us on a curve—you're so goddamn prejudiced yourself you can't even see it, but 'Oh, it's not prejudice, it's justice. You can't be prejudiced if you don't have power.' Well, that's *bullshit.* And I've got news for you: Jesse Fucking Helms isn't grading *any* of us on a curve. He's not giving me ten points for being a white male. An HIV-positive white male *faggot* is just the same to him as an HIV-positive black *dyke,* OK? He'll fucking kill all of us together, while we fight over whether or not my 'white male privilege' should let me go into the gas chamber first! And I must be the only person in this *room* who sees how *pathetic* it is for a bunch of college-educated *white boys* to stand around pointing fingers calling each other *racist!*"

That was how he met Mikey. Mikey was on the Propaganda Committee and a graphic designer by trade. They'd cruised each other a bit during meetings; for all the deadly earnest seriousness of the group, it was also a room full of hormonally charged gay men whose attention did not only wander around the room because a speaker had become strident, repetitive, and irritating. More than one hot boy had walked into his first meeting all prepped out in the fashionable Ralph Lauren-cum-*Maurice* look of the day, only to come back the next week with a shorn head, black leather jacket, Doc Martens, dog tags, and an ACT UP T-shirt bought at the table the group set up in the Castro every weekend—and all because he'd seen some hot guy at the last meeting who hadn't given him the time of day since he was sporting a look that had been superseded.

Mikey was attracted to him because Eric was not only good-looking but one of those men who look their best when they are righteously indignant, their brows furrowed a little deeper, their heads held a little higher, their voices commanding attention not with volume but with the conviction that steeled their tones.

Eric, to be honest, thought Mikey looked like hot sex. His previous sense that sex was something that went with relationships was being eroded by his environment. In ACT UP, there was a sense that sex was something to be had as much as possible (safely, of course—at least that was the public line, though not everybody adhered to it in private, especially if both partners were already HIV-positive), something that had to be preserved in the face of those who would extinguish it. There was a desire to keep lit the fire ignited in the gay community before AIDS, a sense that sex was something that bound people together, that jealousy and monogamy were chains to keep people down, that an army of lovers could not be defeated.

It seemed that practically the entire membership of the group showed up late Sunday nights at the EndUp for Club Uranus, a night that was created specifically for the subculture emerging from ACT UP—pro-sex, pro-drug (with a strong preference for hallucinogens and social drugs like X), computer savvy, their gay roots in the synthesizers of disco and New Wave moving in a darker direction appropriate to their circumstances, into "industrial" music, their generation's ironic distance translated into a cool inability to be shocked by anything.

The Sunday after Eric's outburst at General Body, Mikey approached him with a grin and pinned a button on him. A plethora of sloganeering buttons was an ACT UP must-have, another rebellion against the "whatever" spirit of their fellows. While New Wavers sported buttons full of sayings designed to shock the Protestant Ethic with their apathy, ACT UP members' buttons were meant to push buttons by saying, "I Mean Business": I GOT ARRESTED FIGHTING AIDS, or HIV-POSITIVE, or the legendary KILL JESSE HELMS sticker. Eric twisted his jacket around to read the button: ANOTHER RACIST SEXIST HOMOPHOBIC GAY WHITE MALE. He burst out laughing and resolved to Mikey and himself to wear it to General Body the next week. Mikey offered him a tab of acid. Eric took it, and barely had the presence of mind to invite Mikey home with him before they moved from simulated to actual sex right there on the pool table.

It was Eric's first experience with a "fuck buddy," as opposed to a boyfriend, a concept then unique and still predominantly gay. It was, simply put, the idea that you made friends with someone at the same time you had good sex with him, without the mantle of "relationship" descending on it. It was an idea of its time, born of multiple motives—first, the knowledge that sexual desire between two people almost always fades over time and that there was no reason to lose a friend because you lost the fire. Second, there was the basic urban trend to be "too busy" for a relationship, especially true among ACT UP members like Eric and Mikey for whom the group monopolized almost all time not spent working for a living.

Finally, for all the camaraderie of the group and the closeness the sex seemed to reinforce, there was the consciousness among its members that every relationship, friend or lover, was more of a risk than ever before. The person you let into your heart today was almost certain to be dead within a few years. For many in the group, Eric's experience with Ron had been repeated sometimes dozens of times, never hurting less the last than the first. There was, after all, a reason for all that "ironic distance" in their generation. A "fuck buddy" was someone, to be honest, who was not so valuable to you that you would die of the pain of losing him.

There was only one reason to keep going to weekly meetings, and that was the Sixth International AIDS Conference, to be held at Moscone Center in San Francisco in June. As the date drew closer, the Red Army Faction beat a strategic retreat on the subject of the membership's racism, sexism, and homophobia. It was suddenly becoming clear that this was to be ACT UP's D-Day, a week in which every issue anybody wanted to address could have its day. And just as the American armed forces suspended the purges of homosexuals during wartime, so did this AIDS army reschedule its purges, too, in order to acquire and retain every warm body.

General Body suddenly became an exciting, productive

place to be; it was where people were recruited to help with the prep, where committees told each other what they were planning. The schedule of protests and "strikes" was doctored to mirror the schedule of the conference; nearly as many posters were prepared for the events outside Moscone as were being presented inside. ACT UP had made its appearance at the last AIDS Conference in Montreal, but had made little impact—at least, not compared to the impact it could have here in America's AIDS capital, America's gay capital, where thousands instead of dozens would mass to protest, as organized a campaign as any military invasion.

The announcement was made in a meeting that the networks were going to anchor their evening broadcasts from the AIDS Conference *for the whole week*—the jubilation could be heard blocks away. The network eagle had landed, and an organization that had mastered on the small stage the art of media manipulation would now have its finest hour broadcast into tens of millions of American living rooms. ACT UP members from chapters around the world—for the group had spread to Paris and London—would be there in force, some members hocking everything they had in order to be there for what was going to be the event of a lifetime.

In the past, those who sought to change the world, and did, usually never lived to see the impact of their labors. They were ignored, laughed at, or, if their ideas were especially advanced, burned at the stake. It took a good deal of fortitude to stick to a belief that only you knew was true, that in your lifetime only you would see was true. It was a measure of how much had changed that Eric and the other ACT UP members could spend a day finding fault with the FDA's drug approval process, criticizing the government for its calculatedly slow response to an epidemic that was wiping out large sections of the population that did not and would never vote Republican, and then going home at night to see their targets thrust into defensive, reactive positions on the national news. It was one of those then-rare stellar conjunctions that provide a paradigm-shifting idea and its supporters with immediate gratification.

The world was changed in a week—at least, their world.

Scientists who had previously seen only a bug in a dish were faced with the human beings for whom their slow, non-tenure-endangering caution meant death. Americans for whom AIDS had been the face of a skeleton in a Benetton ad or dramatically enhancing a *Newsweek* article, suddenly saw a whole generation, a whole social movement, a whole way of dressing and thinking born of this virus, a group of people who were not dying gracefully but who had chosen to become resistance fighters against a government that had not brought on a holocaust but was well pleased to see it come.

The ACT UP message was visual, created by gay men with a sense of the visually striking, gay men whose culture had indoctrinated them in the paramount importance of visuals. Splashy graphics, zippy slogans, and perhaps most importantly a style of dress meant to strike terror in the hearts of middle America. The "new clone" look, as it was cheekily titled by an activist magazine, incorporated punk rock, storm trooper–chic, Tom of Finland motorcycle bad boy, "modern primitive" tattoos and piercings, mind-melded with the official gay look of exposed, chiseled, hairless muscle. The combination was sexy and dangerous, and even more terrifying when some shaven-headed punk opened his mouth on national television and brilliantly and ruthlessly detailed the reasons the FDA's drug approval process was so inefficient. America had been invaded not just by a virus but by an army born of its own apathy about that virus, an army comprised mostly of young, beautiful, and dying men who, although the group adhered almost religiously to the doctrine of nonviolent resistance, allowed their symbolism to belie that nonviolence and let the bourgeois world believe that these Nazi muscle punks had nothing left to lose and could be capable of anything.

The world changed in a week. Eric saw it—there was a new and awesome power in the world, as instantaneous in its impact as an A-Bomb. Hobbes was no longer correct: Political power no longer devolved solely out of the barrel of a gun; a good deal of it now resided in the eye of a camera.

Each night was a celebration; each one of the group's members who appeared on TV was cheered as if he or she had won an Oscar. Eric had been lonely once, then he had made friends and had a nice pleasant life, and it had been good until a bomb had blown up in his face and shattered his complacency. But it had been worth it to lose what he'd had before, because it was nothing compared to *this*, the most addictive feeling in his life, the feeling that he was a part of something that *was* changing the world—*now*. These friends were not just friends, but true comrades in the sense of what that word meant in the first days of every revolution.

He realized that almost accidentally he had stumbled into the very "experience" he had once vaguely been taught would be a requirement of his writing career, and which he had just as vaguely known life in a big city would provide. For his generation there was no other great cause, no other life-or-death movement (for ACT UP was about nothing less than life or death). This, he realized, was his Spanish Civil War, his Lincoln Brigade, the defining moment of this decade. He honestly and without arrogance pitied all those who had only stood by and watched this parade pass, too well-convinced of their own powerlessness against a Moral Majority zeitgeist to believe that they could have done the same, felt the same, died now or later but at least died having known they'd tried.

But Eric had come back to Reno not so much to rest from the group's triumph as from the harrowing that had followed in that triumph's wake. ACT UP's success had been seen by all the right people—and all the wrong people, too. All manner of radical leftist groups who had spent the last 20 years being completely ignored suddenly became eager to seize upon ACT UP's brand identity and reforge its message in their own image, communism and capitalism not dissimilar in the end. A rumor that could not be confirmed, yet seemed as plain as day, was that the most divisive members of the group were plants from a Chicago-based Marxist group called Prairie Fire. The intentions of these new members of the group were made clear the night one of them, frustrated in his attempt to steer the group toward a protest of something completely unrelated to HIV, shouted at Keith, "Fuck you and fuck your AIDS!"

Behind the scenes plans were being made in secret; people were talking about splitting off into a new chapter. The beauty of ACT UP, after all, was that there was no organization. Anyone was free to start a chapter anywhere and call it ACT UP. "Why shouldn't there be two chapters here?" people started to ask, putting out feelers. One group for AIDS and one for...everything else.

Eric was ready to quit the group if the new chapter didn't come to pass. Success had spoiled ACT UP, and the carpetbaggers that success had brought in were hell-bent on either dominating or destroying the group. One of the major insanities that was draining the spirit out of the group was its "consensus" policy, in which all the members had to vote to approve an action before it was taken. One dissenting vote was enough to stop any action; one could be community-minded and abstain, a measure by which you could indicate your disagreement but your unwillingness to obstruct. The Prairie Fire plants were geniuses at parliamentary maneuver, and they would never abstain when they didn't get their way. Consensus was one thing in a room with 30 people who knew each other reasonably well and had the same goals—quite another in a room of 300 people, many of whom would have rejoiced to see their enemies across that room die horribly.

Eric saw the consequences every week; people would come to General Body enthused about what they'd seen on TV or read in the paper, then they would watch this worm devour itself for hours on end—and they'd never return. He had joined the group so that AIDS could no longer fill him with powerless rage, and now he found himself again filled with powerless rage as he watched the smug hateful faces of people who really, truly, did not give a flying fuck about anything but power and how this group could give it to them.

Worse, he had found himself forging friendships with people who had died, sometimes quite abruptly. One day he was laughing and joking with someone, then it seemed like the next day he was at a memorial service for that same person. "Activism keeps you alive," many people with AIDS in the group asserted, and there was no disputing that, though perhaps it wasn't AIDS activism in particular but rather having a reason to live, any reason. But in the face of this virus, that was not enough to keep you alive for as long as you were supposed to live. Eric had a young person's perspective on age, and while 35 seemed eons away, nonetheless it was a constant shock to see that age in the obituary column again and again. Every demonstration was a battle won for him and the group, but every friend's death was a war lost for that person.

When he had joined the group, rage had seemed simply telegenic, something like the frenzy he'd whipped himself into for intramural sports to get the blood going. But now his rage was real, uncalculated for the cameras, something that without ACT UP would have turned homicidal.

Members of this group wore stickers that said KILL JESSE HELMS. And Jesse Helms should get down on his knees every night and thank God for ACT UP, because without it the rage felt by many who had nothing left to lose would have been expended in incalculable congressional bloodshed.

Mikey was not an early riser, whereas Eric was by nature, his habit reinforced by his hours at Spinelli. This gave Eric several hours in the morning to read, write, think, and best of all, talk to Emma, who had been there and done all that years ago.

"I want you to read something," she said one morning after he'd finished pouring out his frustrations. "Well, a few some-things, actually." She pulled some books off one of her shelves and handed them to Eric. He perused the titles: Doris Lessing's *A Ripple From The Storm* and *The Sentimental Agents* and George Orwell's *Homage to Catalonia*.

"Political correctness is nothing new," she told him gently. "Only the name of it. And group dynamics are nothing new, either. People behave the same way time in and time out."

A Ripple was slow going, but he saw why she'd given it to him to read. The story of Lessing's own involvement with the Communist Party in Rhodesia was the story of Eric in ACT UP/San Francisco: the same infighting, the same backstabbing. Orwell's *Catalonia* told the same story of life in Spain during the Civil War, only it was the Stalinists doing to Orwell's faction what Prairie Fire later did to ACT UP. As for *The Sentimental Agents*, Eric found Lessing's satire of political correctness right on the mark. He knew only too well what she meant by colonial agents who fall victim to the device of "undulant rhetoric." Eric had seen that happen to many, including himself, in General Body meetings. He eagerly devoured all three books in three days.

He was eager to discuss the books with Emma. "So if this has been going on for years, if people have written and known about this for *50 years*, why is it still happening? Why does it happen over and over again?"

"Because people behave the same way over and over again. You have an advantage, having read these books—you can see it now, for what it is: a pattern. You can't break a pattern—"

"Until you can see it," Eric finished, smiling. The aphorism was one of Emma's favorite exhortations.

"And it always ends the same," Eric sighed. "All these people allegedly on the side of what's right destroy each other without any help from the side in power."

Emma knew that political correctness had pushed her son further to the right than he ever would have gone otherwise, but she also knew ACT UP was a powerful social force, the likes of which might not be seen again for a long time. Many of her sympathies still lay with those on the other side from Eric, and she knew her son had come to be an important person in the group. "I don't think splitting the group in two is a wise idea. It tells the other side that you're divided and that you can be divided further. There's an old proverb, 'Only two fools fight in a burning building.' Not that you're a fool," she added impishly.

"Wow, that's a good one. Who said that?"

She shrugged. "I don't know who said it first. I heard a Klingon say it on *Star Trek* once."

Eric laughed, a good hard laugh for the first time in a long time, the first laugh that had not been generated in anger and bitterness.

"I'll conceal the source when I use that at a meeting. Unless Klingons count as oppressed people of color, then it would have more authority!"

Emma smiled, perturbed by the reflexive scorn Eric seemed to have acquired toward the people his enemies were using as straw men in their march to power. But now was not the time to try and "correct" him. There was a bigger fish to put on his plate, and she'd been waiting for the right time to do it. Three days after his arrival, he seemed relaxed and ready to hear it.

"I've been meaning to mention to you. Cal Hewitt is home right now, too."

Eric surprised her by shrugging. "So?" During his first months in San Francisco, at least once a day, he'd thought of Cal. But since he'd made friends, especially since ACT UP, Cal was just a disagreeable memory, someone who now lived on the *other planet*, that place where other gay people lived in apathy or fear or shame.

"Well," she continued, "it's just that he's home because his father is dying. And from what I've seen of his mother, she's not doing too well either, at least not mentally."

Eric bit his lip. A Cal gone to business school and well established in some comfortable yuppie job was a nonperson, another one of the smooth, pressed faces he'd temped for downtown; but a Cal with a dying father on his hands pushed several buttons in Eric. He'd accepted his own father's absence, understood that his mother's long-ago fling with a man in a photograph would never have produced a stable family, and he'd found his own father figures in friends' fathers, coaches, teachers, anywhere he could, and he had adjusted remarkably well for a fatherless boy. Nonetheless there was that unavoidable pang whenever other boys' fathers ruffled their hair or gave them a hug, and Emma always saw it with a bit of guilt.

Eric well knew that the advantage to not having a father was not losing one, especially a good one. He didn't think Cal Senior had been a good one, based on what he'd seen of Cal, but still… Moreover, after so many experiences with dying friends, Eric could not help but feel for anyone who was going through "having someone die on them," as he put it with an almost childlike despondency.

"Well, I'm sorry to hear *that*," he said with an odd emphasis on the last word.

"I'm planning to go over there tomorrow, bring her a casserole."

"That's nice of you."

"I thought it would be nice if we both went over, in case she needs some heavy lifting done or something."

Eric got up to take his glass into the kitchen. "Well, I'm right down the street. If you need me, just call."

Emma sighed. "OK, I'll fess up." Eric sat back down. "I saw Cal the other day, and he looks terrible, Eric. I think he might be sick himself."

Eric felt nauseous at the news. The picture of Cal that he carried in his head was always and forever the same: Cal standing on the chair and reaching up to the top shelf—that memory was so glowing and alluring. Whatever else he thought of Cal, the thought of him dying of AIDS brought back so much to life in him. Real love can be pruned back, even cut down to the stump, but unlike a tree real love cannot be killed unless the soil it roots in is poisoned. It was only in this moment that Eric realized he had not uprooted Cal, nor had what Cal done been so unforgivable as to poison that soil. His helpless anger overtook him again, not just in the face of death but in the face of feelings he had dismissed from service and commanded never to darken his door again.

"So what should I do about that?" Eric asked.

Emma was truly taken aback now. "Eric! I thought you were doing what you're doing in ACT UP because you were a compassionate human being. Was I wrong?"

Eric shriveled under the rare and therefore all the more powerful tongue-lashing. Emma immediately regretted her words. "Eric, what did he do to you that makes you hate him so much?"

He remembered Patrick talking about the truck that you waited for when you had HIV, that truck that would hit you and there was nothing you could do but wait for it. He couldn't help changing that metaphor, for a truck that hits a man often stops, but a truck gathers flies on its windscreen unconscious that there is any tragedy. He did not realize that in the life of a real AIDS activist, *this* was the moment of initiation into the innermost circle, this moment where it's all too much, when the straw breaks the camel's back, when you wake as if from a dream and realize that this is all for nothing: we're all going to die anyway.

"I'll go," Eric said numbly.

"You don't have to come," Cal's mother had told him on the phone. "Your father knows you're just starting your job. He practically insists you don't mess that up."

"No," Cal said, "I'll come."

He couldn't yet say how he felt about going home; all he knew was that here at last was the one viable reason he could present to get away from work. It sounds horrible to say that Cal welcomed the news of his father's imminent death, but his was not the worst reaction a son could have. He didn't think of what he might inherit; he didn't gloat over a son's final victory over his father, namely that of longevity; he wasn't going home to spill all the poison built up in him into his father's ear while he still had a chance to force the old man to listen. All he wanted was to get the hell out of New York City and away from this job.

Our minds are full of channels, streams—call them what you will. Some scientists say we are not one person at all but a cacophony of competing desires and fears, our "I" only the shell that regulates them (if it is a strong "I," that is). Such a theory would explain many human behaviors. That day in the park with Eric, Cal had dammed up his libido, redirecting its energy into other channels, channels of endeavor where he could succeed, where he could be in charge and powerful instead of weak and afraid of louts in trucks.

Cal was a strong person, too strong to consciously accept that he was really afraid of hicks calling him "faggot," afraid of being cut off from what little trickle of love he could eke out of his parents by pretending to be what they wanted him to be. But his sister's experience of getting pregnant and having an abortion, combined with a fear of AIDS he whipped up in himself to suitably hysteric proportions, allowed him to convince himself that he avoided his sexuality not because of the shame that was so clearly irrational, but because of the caution that was so clearly rational.

The closet is a hell on earth. Cal would have felt shame at being weak enough to "cave in" to his socially unacceptable desires, yet he could feel no pride at going home alone every night, after a night out with his fellow freshly minted investment bankers—nights right out of those trendy novels Eric despised, full of cigars and cocaine and cognac and fashion models draped across louts in suits who bellowed with fraternal heartiness at all manner of fag and AIDS jokes, jokes at which Cal smiled weakly, sick with himself for engaging in that complicity with their boorish hate "necessary" to hide his own bulls-eye at the heart of their target. No matter that his smile was weak and his laughter nonexistent at these jokes; Cal rarely laughed at anything anyway because there was no joy in him.

He had moved through Stanford as if he were a computer program executing instructions gracelessly but efficiently. He had participated in the intellectual extracurricular activities that would look good on his résumé, he had kept a sterling GPA, and he had made no friends. His mother occasionally asked him on the phone what he'd done over the weekend, and originally he'd told her he didn't have time for friends. After a while he realized with a pang that, for all her faults, Carol was concerned about him, bothered by the thought of her son alone and friendless. So he started making up stories about what he'd done over the weekend, modeled on what people in his classes had said they were going to do or on upcoming events he'd read about in the school paper. He went to the movies alone and would tell her afterward how much he'd loved/hated the film and how his imaginary friends had agreed or disagreed, depending on how much Cal's own opinion varied from the general consensus.

Cal had put aside his loneliness—of mind, of heart, of genitals—only by reinforcing and widening that channel that Eric had initially interpreted as an insult to himself, that channel that said, *All this is tolerable because in the end you will have money and power and nobody will question you.* Perhaps on some level Cal had made a bargain with himself, that all his desires would be fulfilled one day, including his desire for men, but not until he was so powerful that the unveiling of those desires would be as ineffective in unmanning him as that unveiling would be to David Geffen, Barry Diller, Malcolm Forbes, Merv Griffin...Roy Cohn...

He hadn't been as heavily recruited as he'd thought he would be, as he would have been only two years earlier when he started B School. The Reagan/Bush recession had just begun on the East Coast, and mergers and acquisitions and junk bonds were suddenly no longer "sexy." All the same, being as he was near the top of his class, he had several opportunities to choose from. Cal had also developed a coldness that his potential employers identified with and admired.

But no young heart, however cold, can fail to leap with excitement at the prospect of advance and change. And Cal's first sight of New York City brought him a measure of joy, if only anticipated joy. His new home was the story narrated by Gershwin, Ayn Rand, Woody Allen—a great thrumming machine that initially astonished him. Whenever he finally left work, some nights well after midnight, there were always plenty of places to eat still open, even bars, and it seemed there were as many people on the streets at four A.M. as there were on the streets at home at noon. And these weren't just the skaggy people one saw out at four A.M. in Reno, loitering around its 24-hour casinos and bars—no, these were *all kinds* of people, well-dressed and well-fed, thinking nothing of getting home at dawn.

But this was also 1990, and there was fear, too. The sound of gunfire was never far away, save when he was down at the bottom of the island in the Wall Street area, where murder and robbery were carried out more discreetly. He stepped over legions of homeless people day and night—they were everywhere, mentally ill persons or crackheads or both—some of whom would jump up and start screaming and terrify him. And of course, there was AIDS; though he kept well clear of the Villages east and west, his building on the Upper West Side had its share of gay men with AIDS, some of whom could be seen on weekends being taken out for a glimpse of the sun by a friend or a volunteer. (Volunteering, which in employers' eyes had been so sterling a thing to do in college, was now frowned upon as a waste of time better spent making money—write a check if you must, take an evening off if your wife insists on going to a benefit, but by no means commit any of your time on a regular basis to anybody but us.)

Cal's anticipation of joy turned sour quickly. He hated his coworkers, failed jocks who compensated for their shame at not being good enough for the pros by being even more jock-like than the pros, chomping on cigars, shouting at the TV during games, pretending that their paper shuffling was a sexy, dangerous sport at which they could "win," even high-fiving each other at the end of deals and chanting, "We're number one!" It would be years before Cal would realize that they were just as miserable as he was, as full of rage that they'd had to redirect their lives away from something they loved into something they didn't; as full of shame as Cal, because they hadn't been good enough to realize boyhood dreams of championship rings. They played hyper-aggressive individual sports like squash or racquetball, or pickup games of basketball where fouling was part of the fun. Cal got called a "sissy" for avoiding the rugby-like pickup games, but he'd played tennis through college and quickly became a ruthlessly good squash player, which prevented him from being eaten by the rest of the pack.

And he hated the work. During his first week, Cal got his first taste of real-life economics, as opposed to the theoretical and algebraic bullshit they'd fed him in school, his first week of work. He'd expected to be put onto analyzing a company's performance, working on SEC filings, going over financials. But as "fresh meat" he found himself—even though he'd been near the top of his class at Stanford Business School—spending 12 to 16 hours a day making copies. Huge numbers of documents needed to be copied, and Cal asked one of his fellow MBA drudges why temps weren't hired for this scut work.

The other young man chuckled derisively, the only advantage keeping him from the very bottom of the food chain being that he knew the score. "It's like this. Temps are paid like $9 an hour just to stand around and copy. That means you're paying the agency $18 an hour—$18 times eight? Except say you're keeping that temp 12 hours. That's four hours of overtime. $27 an hour...?"

Cal knew this, too, was part of the macho contest; he had to do the math in his head and fast. "One forty four. Plus 27 times four, that's 108. So that's 252..."

"Times six or even seven days a week, like we work, that's— let's call it $2,000 a week, times 52, is around $100,000 bucks. If," he raised a warning finger, "if you hire somebody by the hour. Are *you* making $100,000 a year? No, you are not," he concluded, for a moment forgetting that neither was he. "So they hire you at 50 grand, salaried not hourly, and save 50 grand a year. And a year from now, if you're lucky, you might get to do something interesting."

Cal felt sick. He was 24 years old, and a year at 24 is ten times what it is at 34, a hundred times what it is at 44. Fifty grand a year in New York was nothing, just enough to get by, especially when part of this competitive sport he had been drafted into involved keeping up appearances in the form of expensive suits and ties and shoes, and, of course, forking out your share of $100 bills you could ill afford to spend on those "wild" nights out.

A year before he could even begin to do anything for which he could be recognized, rewarded, promoted! A year of *this*, of monotonous, mind-numbing assembly-line "work." And that night, after his teammate had told him the score, he saw a man jump or pushed onto the tracks and run over by a subway car. During the next week, he passed three cordoned-off crime scenes, at one of which a body was covered by a tarp.

The other guys started asking him why he didn't pick up girls on their outings at Nell's or Odeon or wherever (those places were all the same), and he produced his sister's picture and told them she was his fiancée "back home," the gay man's classic tool for deflecting curiosity about his inactive sex life. It was Cal's little joke at their expense, a way of asserting a superiority over them that meant something to him but nothing to them, and a far more dangerous game than any they boasted of playing so well.

Had any of them been paying attention to the world of books, they would have recognized Gina's picture. Around the same time Cal had moved to New York, Gina's book about growing up in an ultraconservative family and the fallout from her own abortion, a slim memoir at turns hilarious and harrowing, had made her literary reputation. She'd never intended to write about it, but time and again she'd left Cal on the floor with horrified laughter as she described going into the abortion clinic, through the back-alley entrance no less, so that the protesters outside wouldn't recognize her as Carol Hewitt's daughter, or how the employees inside had treated her when they recognized her from her childhood of enforced protests (generally, they had been compassionate though several had been unable to hide their smug internal triumph over Carol as they aborted her grandchild).

Cal had told her she had to write it all down, and she had. The book had gained celebrity not just because of Gina's gift for description of absurd situations, but because of its graphic portrayal of what it was like, physically and psychologically, to have an abortion, and because it mocked the political cant of both the pro-choice and pro-life sides, leaving it clear that "either choice left someone either dead or wishing they were," as Gina put it. While Cal had encouraged her to write the book, he had also begged her not to include his own confession of sexuality, and critics noted that the book's one failing was that while Gina claimed to have a close relationship with her brother, he came off as "a cipher." Cal was grateful for her discretion, but reading the book he also realized that in the service of discretion she'd turned him into a straw man. It made him sick with himself that he had stolen part of Gina's story from her out of fear for himself, and her dedication to him for making the book happen was not a balm to him.

It was more of a "relationship" than the other men could claim; nobody had time for a girlfriend, but on these evenings the guys could pick up chicks and convince themselves they really were the "masters of the universe," irresistible studs of finance whose phallic tower of net worth would one day dwarf any real jock's. And the women would convince themselves that they had hooked a "powerful man" whom they might also net and turn into their own personal ticket to social status. They were all like gay men just before AIDS descended on that world, blissfully unaware that their own world was also about to be swept away, that the "losers" they'd mocked so smugly were about to inherit their earth from under them and be their masters now.

Power is addictive in that once addicted, you can never get enough. Cal's crowd got a taste of it in the deals the senior partners made, a thrill at dawn when they saw the headline on their way home that announced with shock and terror the latest agglomeration they had slaved away on; the recognition in a girl's face when they named their employer, Kohlberg Kravis Roberts or Goldman Sachs or some other powerhouse firm more in the public eye than any corporation that actually made something; the way they could strut past velvet ropes at the "right" clubs, cigars clenched in young, handsome jaws, eager to look as frog-like and soured as their bosses as quickly as possible. And yet they knew they were not Caesar but only Caesar's army, and reflected glory was not the name of this game.

Sex with "supermodels" was part of the spoils of war; so were the absurdly expensive wines and Cuban cigars. But most of all there was cocaine: a vastly expensive substance one could never get enough of, a substance that made one feel all-powerful, blazingly sexual, and—most critical in their 24/7 work weeks—inexhaustible. Cal had shied away from this last temptation of yuppiedom, for his 50 grand a year could have ill afforded it. Nevertheless, the night came when he tried it.

It was too good. That was Cal's initial feeling—that of course this was illegal, feeling this good *had* to be illegal. Lonely, bored, depressed, exhausted—and all this eliminated in the space of moments. Did it really matter how, after all this time? Did it really matter that it was expensive, illegal, bad for you, blah-blah-blah? He had resigned himself to his Sisyphean doom in this world, there being no other where he could even hope to take power and be free of the rule of others. Now suddenly the stone was gone—he was teleported to the hilltop, and all that desolate landscape he'd been inching up was spread out beneath him, no matter its desolation now that he was its king.

Life went from unbearable to fabulous. Cal was happy, confident, full of brilliant ideas. He was still naïve enough to be surprised to discover half the other bankers at work were coked out, too, and that several of the bicycle messengers he saw every day used their legit line of work as cover for their far more lucrative jobs.

There was only one problem with coke—it made him horny as fuck. He could look around a club, or even around a table, and have the hormonal equivalent of a seizure as he envisioned another man naked, taking him with drug-accelerated force. He beat off as often as he could get hard and still couldn't get sex off his mind.

One night one of the guys told a funny story about how he and his date had accidentally wandered into a gay bar off Times Square one night after the theater. Not only was it a gay bar, it was a hustler bar, and even Cal had laughed at the story about how some guy had struck up a conversation with the couple, which had abruptly turned when he'd asked if the girl-friend wanted to join in or just watch. But all Cal took away from the story was the name of the bar, which he repeated again and again in his head to burn it in.

Cal really was naïve; he still thought a male hustler was only to be found while cruising the streets in a car, and only in the form of a teenage runaway. That he could walk into a bar, where the hustlers at least look to be of drinking age, and pick one up without anyone seeing anything other than his hasty dash from doorway to cab, was an awakening to him.

He left his coworkers early, one A.M., and took a cab to the bar. He hadn't really known what he expected until he got something else entirely. Something out of *American Gigolo* had been what he'd had in mind, but with different lighting this could have been a hardware store: a false ceiling with fluorescent lights that would be switched on at cleanup time, a handful of indirect colored spotlights that would look more at home in a fake grotto with fake plants in some tiki lounge, a pool table where the objects of affection could show off their forms under the hanging lamp, and discreet booths for discreet transactions.

Cal ordered a $5 beer and took a booth, wondering if there was anywhere he could do a toot in here. Probably no doors on the stalls, he thought with a momentarily sober flash of humor; otherwise, some of the transactions might take place on the premises. He surprised himself with his own savvy, avoiding the eyes of anyone who didn't appeal. A moment's hesitation in looking away, he knew, and someone in whom he had no interest would be at his table.

It wasn't long before he saw someone he couldn't have broken eye contact with if he'd wanted. He didn't have Eric's face, but he had Eric's features—his coloring, his dark curly hair, his big build. There was nothing of Eric's friendliness in him; he was broadcasting on one channel, and Cal was on that same channel. The young man nodded, Cal nodded back, and Cal felt his genitals contract as he approached, sliding smoothly into the booth as if their meeting had been planned.

They exchanged names (Ken) and a few quick pleasantries. A cocktail waiter immediately appeared, as if to ensure that the bar got its cut of any imminent sales, and Cal forked over 15 bucks for two drinks.

"So you do know what kind of place this is, right?" Ken asked him.

Cal nodded. "Yeah."

"Cool. So what are you looking for tonight?"

Cal hesitated, afraid to name his desire for fear he'd shake his head and walk away—another no-go. "Just some company, some fun."

"Are you a cop?"

Cal shook his head. "No, are you?"

"Nah, I didn't think you were. You look pretty lit. You partying?"

"Huh?"

"Are you high?"

"Oh, yeah, I've got some coke," he added eagerly, feeling like Ken needed to be enticed with more than just money.

Ken's eyes lit up. "Yeah? Fuckin' A! Let's go, man."

"I don't have anywhere to go," Cal admitted.

Ken shrugged. "That's cool, I've got a room."

They took a cab to Ken's by-the-week room (Cal paid a $10 visitor privilege, the house's cut of the trade). Once the door shut, Ken turned to him coldly and said, "It's $150."

Cal fumbled with his wallet and put the money in Ken's hand. Ken resumed his relaxed demeanor and started stripping. Cal eagerly poured a pile of coke on the faux-lacquer dresser. "Help yourself," he said, offering a straw to Ken, who was down to a pair of underpants gray with age. He had taken his own giant snort and watched as Ken held his nose, refusing to sneeze out any of the fat line he'd done. He thought of how much this young man looked like Eric, if you just didn't look too close.

"Can we turn the lights down?" Cal asked.

"No, I like to be able to see what's going on, in case somebody pulls some shit, you know?"

"OK," Cal said, disappointed and not a little petulant that he couldn't have his way in the matter in exchange for $150 and twice that much in drugs.

He didn't know what to do next, but he didn't need to. Ken pulled his underpants off and stood at the edge of the bed. He had a beautiful cock, not the first Cal had ever seen but the first he'd touched. He wanted to hold it in his hand for a minute, to feel the heft of it, the softness, but Ken shoved it in his mouth and made him suck. Cal almost choked, more with panic and unfamiliarity than anything else, but the coke kicked in and he opened up. It was like being raped, he thought distantly, like being taken.. *You deserve it*, another voice said. *Fucking faggot closet case, how else should you get it?*

He looked up to see Ken's face, waited for him to acknowledge Cal's look, but Ken looked anywhere but at Cal while he held his head and hammered his mouth. Cal pulled away for a second, long enough to beg him, "Fuck me!"

Ken stepped back. "I don't get into that, man. I don't fuck ass."

Cal felt enraged, cheated, frustrated, desperate. "I'll pay you double."

Ken appeared to think about it for a moment. "Lemme see the money."

Cal leapt off the bed and opened his wallet, counted out eight twenties. "Here." He shoved the money at Ken.

"You got a rubber? I won't fuck a guy without a rubber, and I don't carry 'em on me, see, 'cause it's evidence if I get arrested."

Cal wanted to cry. "I'll go to the corner and get some. Please!"

Ken shrugged. "OK, if you want it that bad. But you better be clean. If your ass is full of shit, I'll beat the crap out of you, you hear?"

Cal wanted to vomit with excitement. He put his clothes on and ran down to the corner market, bought rubbers and raced back. He went back to the hotel and waited for the man behind the glass to buzz him in. "I was just here," he protested. "I just went to the store! If you want another ten dollars..."

The desk clerk pressed the intercom button. "He go right after you go. He not here anymore."

Cal walked back out onto the street, temples pounding with rage. "Fuck! FUCK! FUCKER! YOU FUCKING ASS-HOLE!" he screamed down the street, and nobody paid him any mind in this part of town. He'd paid good money to be humiliated, and had been humiliated, more humiliated than he could stand. He had $20 left in his wallet, with which he took a cab home, where he couldn't sleep and ended up staring at the ceiling all coked up while listening to his roommate fuck some girl. He beat off halfheartedly, unable to get it up until he thought of seeing Ken again, getting Ken to take him and smack him and rob him and rape him, and these thoughts got him rock-hard, and he came more explosively than he ever had.

He was in hell, and the call came, saying, "come home." And home had been a hell of sorts, too, but nothing like this, nothing at all like this... In Reno it was quiet; the traffic on

Arlington was nothing compared to the traffic anywhere in New York, and late at night or early in the morning there was real silence, and he found himself more grateful for that than he could have imagined.

Gina was home, too, in a sense. She hadn't left Reno after the success of her book; publishing's crafty compensation scheme being as it was, she had a bestseller but had yet to see a dime of her royalties; if she wanted money now, she would have to sign a contract for another book and at the moment she had no idea what if anything to write next. She still had the place on Liberty Street after all this time, though she had lived there alone since the abortion. Cal went to see her as soon as his sleep patterns had leveled out.

"So how bad is he?" she asked, handing him a joint.

"The official diagnosis is congestive heart failure. It's not good."

"They can't do anything for him?"

"Yeah, well, they said he could go on the list for a heart transplant, and he turned it down."

"Why?"

Cal shrugged. "I don't know. I mean, he's got connections. He could get one. But he doesn't want to do it."

Gina pulled hard on the joint. "I'm stoned all the time these days. Cal, I feel so fucking guilty."

"For the…?"

She shook her head vehemently, holding in her toke. "No, for the book. Fucking Kevin hates me. I didn't use his real name in the book, but all our friends know our whole personal life now. And every time I've called home since the book, *she* hangs up on me. It's like it's cost me everything."

Cal smiled, accepting the joint gratefully, even knowing it would probably make him pass out on her floor. "You still have me."

She hugged him impulsively, surprising him; he hugged her with one arm and tried not to light her on fire with the joint. "I would be crazy if I didn't still have you."

"I don't think the book caused his heart attacks, if that's what you're thinking." The fact was, some people said it was his daughter's book that was killing him, for he had become famous on the national stage after all, but only as the villain in her piece, the man who trumpeted family values even as he neglected his own family for other values. "Our old man has smoked and drank and eaten red meat all his life, and men his age pay for that with prostate cancer or heart failure. It's a 'lifestyle choice,'" he concluded with a smile, knowing Gina would get the joke; conservatives were always calling AIDS the result of that very same thing.

"Yeah, but tell that to Mom."

"Oh, she doesn't blame you for ruining *his* life," Cal corrected her. "She blames you for ruining *hers.*"

He'd quickly realized when he got home that it had been a good thing to come, not just for him, but for his parents. His mother was cracking up, he saw immediately. Gina's book may or may not have had an effect on Cal Senior, but it had ruined Carol's life. Not only had her own daughter had an abortion and written about it, she had written with rueful black humor about her family and her mother—and made Carol look like a sad dupe and a brazen idiot. She became afraid to go to the store, afraid both her friends and her enemies would point at her and say, "There she is, did you read it?"

The truth was that most of Carol's foes had read the book, but none of her friends. If she had held her head up like Anne Boleyn on her way to the block, the whole thing would have blown over, but her inner queen had failed her and she had been dragged to the block sobbing and screaming. Her trips to the store for herself and Cal Senior were organized like midnight raids, literally—she'd frequent the 24-hour supermarkets, never the same one twice in a row, late at night, where nobody could see her. Cal was moved to pity and disgust by the gratitude on her face when he'd volunteered to do the shopping, and Carol had retired to her room.

"Cal, I really want to see him. I mean, you know, before he goes. Are you guys talking, could you, you know, ask him?"

"We're...well, *I'm* talking," Cal said, not sure how to describe it. "I'll see if there's a...moment, an opening, you know?"

Gina nodded sadly. "Just try."

Cal and Cal Senior had been awkward together at first. Cal had come home to escape his life, but how would it look, how would it feel, if he came to his father's figurative but not literal bedside? That first day, Cal Senior had asked his son to read the paper to him, since he couldn't really hold it up or focus for long. This led to magazine articles, and within a week, Cal was reading *Middlemarch* to his father. He'd remembered reading it himself long ago, and thought the old man might like it. But he'd forgotten about Causabon, dying with his "great" work unfinished and no loss to the world that he hadn't, and wondered if Cal Senior would think he'd picked the story to rub it in. But he'd chosen not to mention it, in case the similarity had gone by his father. *What the hell*, he thought. It seemed every relationship in *Middlemarch* called something to the fore within himself.

Who was Cal, in that book with all of life in it? Not Fred Vincy, content to idle if only someone else would pay for it; not Dr. Lydgate, bent on scientific discovery—he wondered how Eric was doing when he read scenes with Lydgate, who could "no more help be dressed right…" Maybe Will Ladislaw, knocking about for something that would be the right work for him… It was clear to Cal that he had no stomach for the world he had set himself upon, that his self-hatred and despair could only grow the longer he stayed there.

One day about a week after he'd seen Gina, he was reading the passage where Dorothea finds Causabon dead before he could extract a promise from her that she would throw her life away on his useless work. There was something so compelling to him about the scene, such a sense of relief that Dorothea's commitment to futility had ended, that there was no avoiding its resonance in his own life. He thought of himself standing in front of a copy machine, endlessly Xeroxing financials for SEC filings, petty pointless bullshit work as useless to the world as Causabon's "Key to All Mythologies." He made no concrete connections, did not equate Causabon with his father; all he could feel was enormous relief as he realized *something* was dead, that he was free of *this* at least. He knew it with certainty: "I'm not going back."

In the space of a second, it felt as if dark skies parted over Cal. The sheer physical relief he felt in that moment was almost like collapse. He didn't have to go back, not if he was bent on chucking that whole life. For what? It seemed not to matter; it seemed to matter only that it was over, this awful existence he'd had as a cog in a dark, greasy, smoky machine that made nothing and existed only to be fed and grow stronger. He almost sobbed with relief as he closed the chapter, leaving Dorothea insensible, hurling promises across the divide between the living and the dead that she no longer had to keep.

Something in the story had affected his father, too, some sense of relief that death had come and taken away the obligation to do what needn't be done. Father and son locked eyes for a moment, and Cal thought later of that moment in the park with Eric, where another bridge had been thrown across; this time he knew he had to walk across, to ask while he could, "Dad, why didn't you get on the list for a transplant?"

Cal Senior looked away for a moment. "I'm tired, son."

For a moment, Cal thought his father was avoiding the question. Then he realized that was his father's answer. Was this how he would feel, he wondered with horror, 30 years from now? Would he also be tired of fighting someone else's fight when all it had brought him in his own life was grief? His momentary flight of freedom was cut short—*It's not enough*, he realized. *There's something more you have to turn away from, and more than that, something you have to turn toward...* Cal couldn't face that now, he wasn't ready, he got up and busied himself with sickbed tasks and told himself that it was enough, that he wasn't going back to that life, and that would have to be enough.

To say that nothing could have surprised Cal at this point was pretty close to the mark, even when Eric and Emma Hamilton appeared at the front door.

"Cal," Emma said, reaching out and hugging him instinctively. He did look bad, she thought—tired, drawn. Eric took his measure as well, came to the same conclusion, but realized with a surprising drain of tension that Cal wasn't sick. Eric had developed a sense that anyone of any sensitivity acquires who spends any amount of time with the terminally ill: a knowledge of who was going, a sense that the eyes of the person before you were too bright, their life force glowing too intensely for someone so frail, a consumptive vitality like spontaneous combustion. Cal just looked tired, Eric sighed, at once selfishly glad that death hadn't buddied him on this retreat and selflessly glad that Cal was all right.

"Thanks for coming," Cal said impetuously, realizing that aside from people at the store and the pharmacy, this was the first human contact he'd had outside his family in the two weeks he'd been here.

Emma was good in a crisis, and she let herself in without further ado. "I brought you some food," she said, indicating a casserole dish in her hands and a container of lasagna in Eric's. "We'll just put these in the fridge and you won't have to worry about cooking."

"Thanks," Cal repeated, regarding Eric dully. *Oh, yes,* Cal mused to himself, *there's another crisis: he's still hot.*

Eric was surprised at Cal's apathy upon seeing him. Eric's vanity registered hurt feelings until his better self took hold and reminded him that Cal had other things to think about right now. "How are you doing?" he asked Cal while Emma busied herself in the kitchen, setting herself to washing a pile of dishes Cal had neglected for a few days.

Cal shrugged. "I'm all right, how about yourself?" Eric's crew cut looked good, Cal decided. Tactfully, Eric had left his READ MY LIPS T-shirt at home and worn something simpler.

"I've been better," Eric admitted, suddenly feeling as tired as Cal. He found himself wanting to let Cal know that he, too, was seeing hard times. "I've been involved in ACT UP in San Francisco. It's been good, but it's been hard. I've seen a lot of good people die…" he blurted.

This well-intentioned speech raised Cal's hackles. Eric seemed to be his same glowing gorgeous self; there was no fatigue about him, no cause for pity. "And a lot more people are going to die," Cal said, "thanks to ACT UP."

"What do you mean?"

"Well, let's see," Cal said sarcastically, his anger at everything coalescing at this one perfect lightning rod. He had seen ACT UP close up in New York, and even been one of the unwitting victims of its ire during a Wall Street protest when a man had screamed at him so rabidly (being as he was part of the capitalist profiteering apparatus that was killing people) that he'd sprayed his saliva in Cal's face. In his shock and terror after that episode, Cal had been ready to agree with what other people in his building were saying about ACT UP. "Here's a group of terrorists who say things like 'Kill Jesse Helms,' who shut down federal government offices, who go into St. Patrick's Cathedral and desecrate the host—"

"That was a lone member of the group who had a lot of issues with the Church—"

"And," Cal cut him off sharply, "who are making the *handful* of people in this country with any pity for people with AIDS *despise* everything and everyone with HIV, every gay person. They're setting the stage for the big roundup—"

"That's what we're trying to prevent!" Eric shouted.

"Eric!" Emma came out of the kitchen.

"You don't give a shit, Eric. You all want to be on TV and that's it. If you gave a shit, you wouldn't be fucking up the works and making things worse."

Eric purpled. "You know who makes things worse? *You* make things worse, you fucking closet case!"

"ERIC!" Emma shouted, but for the first time in his life he ignored her.

"You make it OK for them to walk on us, because you tell them they're right and we're wrong—we deserve to die, we're such fucking chickens."

"Everybody has to do it your way, don't they, Eric?" Cal asked. "Anybody who doesn't see it your way is an idiot or a chicken, isn't that right? Anybody with a grain of sense in their head, who knows better than to threaten a United States senator..."

"Or kiss in a public park," Eric said, the evil on him now, sure this would be the knife in Cal's heart.

Instead Cal only nodded darkly. "Or kiss in a public park, anybody with any caution or common sense is a fool because they're not Eric Hamilton, who does what he wants because everybody applauds no matter what he does. Who never stops to give a shit whether other people might do the same thing and get smacked for it, not applauded."

Eric withered, shamed. Here he was in Cal's house, his mother nuts, his father dying, the whole burden on Cal. And what would it have done to the Hewitts, if Cal had confessed his sexuality, as Gina had confessed her abortion? "I'm sorry, Cal, I'm really sorry."

Cal wouldn't look at him. He slammed every door inside himself and let himself feel nothing but the hot furious wind racing down the corridors of his mind. "Please go."

"Cal…" Emma said, reaching out to him, but Cal sharply pulled back his arm, like a child refusing false affection.

"Please just go."

Cal shut the door behind them and Eric put his face in his hands. "Oh, shit, oh, shit. Mom, I really fucked up."

"Yes, you did," she said, taking his hand. "And there's nothing you can do about it. Now let's go home."

Emma took the unusual step of giving Eric a sedative out of her Xanax stash and took it upon herself to entertain Mikey for the afternoon. As Eric lay on the bed, sliding gently into unconsciousness, a thought stole in on him like a last ray of light: *Cal had talked about what would happen to gay people as if he were one.* Eric kicked himself for his tendency to see things only after the fact, to be blind in the moment of transmission and decoding the messages too late. Two years since he'd seen Cal, and then this, this fraction of a second with him in which he'd managed to fuck it up…and yet even as he kicked himself, a part of him jumped for joy, as much as any part of him could jump out of the tender grip of a benzodiazepine: *Cal is gay. He hates living with it, but he's accepted it, and that means someday, someday…*

This is how I want to be forever, Cal thought, sitting in the darkened living room where his mother had once sat, wondering what dark alchemy Emma Hamilton was working on him down the street. He was completely numb, and amazed at how darkly satisfying it could be to hurt another person, to exchange hurt for hurt and be compensated on the spot, leaving nothing behind to feel afterward. He had made Eric cry, he knew, and he was glad. He had absolutely no idea how many times Eric had cried over him, only that Eric had made him cry and at last he'd been avenged.

He thought of the *New Yorker*–type stories he and Eric had belittled, how little they'd had to do with real life. *Margaret goes to the mall,* he thought with some still darkly comic part of himself. *She feels nothing. The lucky bitch.*

CHAPTER THREE
THE AGE OF ARROGANCE

Eric's first glimpse of New York City was as full of joy and anticipation as Cal's had been, and his desires were not so different from those Cal had felt at the same sight. He, too, had been invited by one of the engineers of the massive machine to enter into its work of generation. Whether Eric would be as disappointed as Cal had been remained to be seen, but he knew damn well that there were plenty of 26-year-olds who would kill for the chance to meet with an editor at Weatherall Press, and he was here to discuss the book he had just been contracted to write.

Eric hadn't joined ACT UP for "the experience" he'd need as a writer, but he'd quickly realized that it would provide experience, and copy, in spades. Shortly after he'd returned from his vacation at Emma's, the group had—well, some said "imploded," others said "exploded." Like everything else about the movement, it would be argued over endlessly. The fact was, success had spoiled ACT UP, and the factions competing to harness its power in their own interests had killed the proverbial goose. Quietly, behind the scenes, the more conservative, AIDS-focused members engineered a split that created a new chapter, ACT UP/ Golden Gate. Eric had to shake his head at the thought that the AIDS Coalition to Unleash Power lost its best and brightest because they were too "AIDS-focused."

Eric didn't hesitate to go with the new group, which experienced a surge of energy as people who had been turned off by the old ACT UP model gave the new group a chance. A two-thirds majority vote replaced "consensus," and *things got done.* Even people who weren't getting their way on a regular basis had to admit that incompletely correct action was better than the old group's politically correct stasis.

But ACT UP/Golden Gate exploded, too, the combination of external and internal pressures too great for it to survive in any vigorous form. Saddam Hussein's invasion of Kuwait was allowed to take place by George Herbert Walker Bush, who hired the publicity firm of Hill and Knowlton, who provided the daughter of Kuwait's ambassador to the United States to testify before Congress. She pretended to be a refugee from "the terror" of Saddam's army, members of which, she fabricated, were taking babies out of respirators and throwing them onto hospital floors and wheeling the equipment back into the "Evil Empire." College kids unscathed by war and untouched by AIDS and longing for a cause, any cause, marched the streets of San Francisco and other cities, beating drums, their painted faces shouting "No War!"—although they were without any clue or concern as to whether there might be cause for such a war or not. Hippies had been against war, and college campuses had been boring since the hippies had imploded; now there was a war and they were in college, so obviously the thing to do was to be against it.

George Herbert Walker Bush encouraged the people of Iraq to rise up against Saddam, and sent one million American troops to the Gulf in the middle of the worst recession America had seen in 20 years. Saddam's Republican Guard was pulverized in a matter of weeks, and Bush, newly minted in his own mind while the greatest statesman of his age and with the Bismarckian poisons of Henry Kissinger poured into his ears fresh each day, chose to lose the war by not removing Saddam in order to maintain "geopolitical stability." In the process, Bush blithely left the

Iraqis he had incited to rebel to die as horribly as the people with AIDS he had just as blithely ignored at home.

CNN was America's eye and everyone shuddered at the sight of jets taking off to pound Baghdad with bombs, the sound of missiles landing in Tel Aviv, the knowledge that in this day, any war was a scenario that could escalate into world war. And in ACT UP Golden Gate meetings, leftist members who had departed the old group out of frustration with its inactivity showed their colors, demanding that the group "take a stand against the war, declare our politics."

Eric fought against any stand being taken at all. "Don't you see this is the *whole point* of this war, to take our minds off what's happening at home? If we start devoting our energies to protesting a war, he gets what he wants!" He, of course, was George Herbert Walker Bush, an oil man for whom the occupation of a tiny country that just happened to be oil rich was an atrocity not to be brooked.

Bush won his war at home if not abroad; flags were waved in the streets of Dallas and Kuwait, his popularity soared and the Republican National Committee broke out the cigars. Alas, he had won too early. By election time, Saddam was still a thorn in America's side, massive resources were still being devoted to containing him within his own country, and people remembered that they'd had time to wave flags in the streets because they were unemployed. The entire thing, so dramatic at the time, was soon afterward dismissed by the bumper sticker that cost George Herbert Walker Bush his Presidency: SADDAM HUSSEIN STILL HAS A JOB—DO YOU?

ACT UP/Golden Gate continued to exist, but it became more an effective ombudsman for drug companies and the FDA than any sort of social force. Eric returned to coffee pulling and started writing about his experience in the group. He thanked his mother a thousand times over for having given him the accounts by Doris Lessing and George Orwell of what had been essentially the same experience. He wrote and rewrote a piece about the two dissolutions of the group. It struck him that ACT UP had been one of those rare occasions in American life where all class boundaries had—momentarily—been crossed. He drew profiles of two of the most effective people in the group, both of whom had given over their lives full-time to AIDS activism. One of them was a speed freak on welfare, who lived for the protests and the arrests and the expenditure of his formerly powerless rage in a way that made him feel powerful; the other was a trust fund baby, a member of a New York diamond merchant family, who had left the family business to become essentially a biologist without the diploma. Both men were HIV-positive, each as likely in that day to die of the virus as the other; that one would die more comfortably was the only difference. They would have never met—and Eric would never have met them—if it had not been for that moment in time.

He worked all through 1991 on the piece, expecting that someone else, probably someone from the "more important" ACT UP/New York, would soon produce a memoir that would make his own irrelevant. But there was nothing. He wondered about it for a while, then realized that anyone with anything to say—or even any axe to grind—was just not up to bringing the whole thing up again. Any view from any perspective would be assailed as vituperatively as it had been assailed before, with choruses of "That's not how it was!" ringing from every side. Who had the energy to live through all that again?

Eric thought he did, if necessary. There are moments in each writer's life where he finishes something, puts it down, and comes back to it a few weeks or months or even years later and says, "My God, who wrote this?" Of course, the sense of wonder comes from knowing all along that *I did*, the realization that usually comes only for those who live with the record of words, the record that says, you are a different person now, who you were before that moment could never have said this. In the best writers, this moment comes only once for each piece; time passes, and you reread the same thing and say, "My God, please let this go out of print!" But it's a moment that can come in a lifetime devoted to growth again and again. Eric had been raised with confidence, a well-regulated supply of dopamine and serotonin that in youth can withstand any criticism, deserved or not. But after having finished this piece and set it aside and then come back to it, Eric realized it was not just youthful optimism that would carry him forward from now on. He was *good*; his work was not perfect, but it bubbled with potential that each serious effort would actuate further.

He knew the rules of the orderly march to success: take an MFA, write in the style of the day, get published in the "little magazines," get a teaching job, aim at the *New Yorker*. His sojourn at Bennington had shown him other ways to succeed, and his time in ACT UP had shown him that orderly marching sometimes only led off the edge of a cliff. Waiting patiently for your turn and doing what you were told could put you in the grave without your ever having touched the things you really wanted.

He'd heard that an openly gay man, Andrew Sullivan, had taken over the editorial helm of *The New Republic*. He picked up a few issues and was bowled over by the sudden influx of wit into the article titles, unaware that Sullivan was only carrying *The Economist*'s cheeky style over from his native U.K. He sent the article off, with only the briefest cover letter—brief as he had no credits to flaunt in it; the piece would have to speak for itself.

It did. "A Burning House" was a cover article and the making of Eric. It was well researched, grimly humorous—"What would Tom Wolfe have made of this? People milled about idly, smoking and chatting, then, suddenly, a signal for rage to erupt! Lights! Cameras! Activism!"), and of course reignited the debate among all the participants in what Eric had called the "Lincoln Brigade of the '90s" as to who was at fault for what. The magazine was as gratified at the attention as Eric, who to his surprise found himself being interviewed about his piece by his now fellow members of the media (this in the days when the self-conscious, self-referential media behemoth we take for granted today was still in its infancy).

Now what to do? He had leapt from no résumé to a cover think piece for a "hot book." But Eric had learned more than one trick from ACT UP; he knew his *New Republic* article was as much an opportunity for him to blow his wad as to succeed. It didn't matter if you were Tama Janowitz or The Knack or Eric Hamilton: You could be a one-hit wonder if you weren't careful.

It was his first glimpse at the inherent laziness of journalism, its stubborn unwillingness to let you evade being pegged. While making follow-up calls about his proposals, Eric found out that he was already seen as "the AIDS writer" or "the gay guy." It would be crucial for him to write next about something that had nothing to do with either and yet to produce as winning a piece as the last.

Fortunately, Eric least required the asset he had the least of: patience. Seemingly out of nowhere the issues he had once fought for on the fringe were out front and center. Maybe he and others had reached the likes of that policeman in the van after all; it certainly seemed that way when Pennsylvania elected a United States senator solely on his promise to reform the health care system. The whole massive engine of the presidential election campaign turned on a dime; suddenly health care was a key issue. As he saw Bill Clinton rise from the ashes of the bimbo eruptions, Eric realized he had been fortunate—twice in a lifetime he could be present at the fundamental alteration of the world. His *New Republic* piece was his press credential, and he joined the Clinton campaign for the duration of the ride.

He soon realized he'd made a mistake—correctable, but a mistake. Ever since Kennedy, reporters had sought to make a name for themselves by writing a book about the making of each president, and practically every writer on the bus had a contract for the same book idea Eric had thought himself clever in pursuing. Moreover, by writing about politics far more conventional than those of ACT UP, he had stumbled into territory he was not prepared for. He found himself grudgingly included as a "young pup" in the bullshit sessions of the older reporters. He was allowed to listen to them hold forth on the Republic, and the Process, and the Status Quo. He immediately saw that they *were* the status quo. He saw that the mainstream media wrote off third-party candidates, not because the candidates weren't viable but because they meant 50% more work for the reporters, who in return for disabling upstart campaigns were rewarded with inside access to the conventional ones. (In 1992, Ross Perot would do them the favor of ably disabling his own campaign.)

While Eric was permitted to ride in the backseat of the media caravan, the old pros running the show reserved access to any real information for the old pros writing it up. He might get a few minutes with Clinton by himself one day, but it would be like a Hollywood press junket where every reporter gets a 30-second clip, guaranteed inclusion in a group shot of everyone nodding as the star repeats what is repeated to every other media hack.

Eric knew from ACT UP that success came not from doing the same thing everyone else did and hoping yours was the voice people listened to; success came from saying and doing something that nobody else was saying and doing, but that people needed to hear and would listen to, if it was different enough not to get lost in the static. One afternoon when the campaign bus stopped at the Little Rock campaign headquarters, Eric accepted a doughnut from Dorothy, a sweet little old lady whose husband had recently died. "I've never volunteered on a campaign before," she said in her Arkansas accent. "I've never even voted according to my own conscience before. I always voted the way my husband told me to. And I like Bill Clinton. He reminds me of Kennedy, he's out to help people."

Eric had to ask. "You know, he just had a fund-raiser in California, and the audience was mostly gay people." She didn't blink so he went on. "And he told them that we need every person to make the future, that he would include them in his vision of the future. What do you think of that?"

"Oh, I know that, hon," she smiled. "That's why I said that to a nice gay boy like you. About Clinton helping people."

Eric spent hours in conversation with Dorothy, drawing out her amazing story. She'd had three sons, one of whom had died in Vietnam; another had of died of AIDS, and the third was alive, but estranged from her—over what she didn't immediately volunteer, and Eric, nice gay boy that he was, didn't pry.

Writing is a craft, but it is also an instinct, and what Eric smelled that day was *drama*—a story: how all the things in this woman's life had brought her to the Clinton campaign. He realized immediately that it was time to get off the bus, to let everybody else tell the same story, each version slightly different as each one fought successfully for a different crumb of it. He was going to stay right here and write about these people who, like the members of ACT UP, never would have joined anything, never would have met each other, if it hadn't been for William Jefferson Clinton.

He took a room at Dorothy's house for a few months. She confessed she had boarders less out of need for money than out of loneliness. She had corralled more than a few of them into volunteering on the campaign, and did her best with Eric, too, but he told her he was "an impartial observer."

Eric had decided he didn't want to be a "professional" writer, the kind who goes looking for something topical to write about and then researches it, either becoming interested in the topic along the way or faking it come time for the book tour. Twice now, events had grabbed his life and shaken it up. He had written about them because he had known them, felt them, lived them. He'd gone with the Clinton campaign in the first place in search of a story, and now he had one.

As a consequence of not being a pro with a career plan, he didn't know quite what he'd write. He asked Dorothy for permission to write her story first, and made an immediate sale of it to *The New Republic.* He told Andrew Sullivan he planned to write more pieces about more people on the campaign, and Sullivan encouraged him to do a book proposal. "How do I do that?" Eric asked; his editor laughed but sent him a sample to show him how it was done.

His success at *The New Republic* and the topicality of the idea spared Eric the attendant bullshit of book publishing's Stone Age pace, in which months or even years can pass before a thumbs-up or thumbs-down is given to an idea. The piece in *TNR* was considered proposal enough, and Eric found himself suddenly in possession of a $50,000 advance on a book. Now he did have one of the professional writer's burdens—he had to come up with copy whether or not there were any more people as interesting as Dorothy on the campaign. Fortunately, there were. Eric found himself flush with cash, not just from the advance but from the secondary income he got from selling each piece of the book as a *TNR* article.

His spadework ended the first Tuesday in November in Little Rock at Clinton's victory celebration. He knew this was the end of this story, this party where thousands of disbelievingly happy people celebrated something indefinite and yet certain at once—no way to say quite what was to come, only that power had been transferred from one generation to another, that the generation that inherited it was more inclined to grant others equal membership in humanity regardless of difference, that 12 years of Moral Majority stranglehold on the bully pulpit was over. For gay people especially, it was a day of rejoicing; for people with HIV, Clinton was Moses, come to deliver them from Republican pharaohs who had sent them to their deaths en masse.

And now, New York City. He had come to meet with his new agent, with his book editor to discuss shaping the book, unifying the articles into a single piece of work, to meet with magazine editors and pick up work. He strode the streets—yes, he did, he was too successful now to merely *walk*—and he was one of them, the handsome, the sophisticated, the successful, the ones on every inside track. As quite often happens to young people who gain an enormous amount of success at a young age, Eric had started to acquire a veneer of arrogance. One met people like oneself at this level, and it was taken for granted that it would have been impossible for one to be at any other level. There was no luck involved, no good timing, no fortuitous connections—no, it was manifest destiny, a self-fulfilling self-referential belief: if we have all this, it must be because we deserve it; therefore, having it is proof we deserve it—good dinners over expensive wine, the scent of Aveda in the air, and the sheen of Kenneth Cole leather jackets under soft tasteful lighting, the gentle brush of an ultra-thin Banana Republic wool pullover as your dinner companion excuses herself to go to the powder room and attend to her meticulously high-glossed pineapple blond hair in a coolly lit mirror over a marble counter top and exchange rumors about your net worth with a friend…the good life.

Eric's editor took him to such dinners; Eric's new high-powered agent introduced him to her other clients, also respected nonfiction writers. Within days, Eric had been initiated, incorporated into Rolodexes, and signed up for meetings with magazine editors to discuss whatever work he had in mind to do next, no question that he was officially a member of the "dollar-a-word club." He felt honored, special, singled out, had no idea that he was the gorgeous young flavor of the month, that he had an insider's celebrity of the sort that went on the cover to sell *Vanity Fair* to other insiders (or wanna-bes): "ERIC HEWITT on the First Hundred Days," his handsome mug as much a ticket to the "About Our Contributors" pages as his talent.

Emma had been happy for him but had warned him from her own experience. "There's a lot of pressure involved in New York Success," she'd said in a tone that had capitalized the letters for him. "It's as if there's this communal set of folded arms and not quite impressed faces always asking, 'All well and good, but what are you going to do *next*?'"

In fact, "What are you going to do next?" was what Nathan Quail, editor of *Pendennis*, was asking him now. Eric sat in the slingback metal and leather chair across from the editor's glass desk, trying to remember what the chair's style was called. Breuer chair? Bauhaus chair? He needn't have worried; Quail would simply assume a *Pendennis* writer would know what kind of chair it was, and would never bother to quiz him about such a detail.

Eric shifted in his chair and wondered himself what he'd do next. "Well, I'm kicking around a few ideas," he said, playing for time.

"Let's hear 'em," Quail said to Eric's dismay. Eric didn't actually have any ideas, which he was already savvy enough to realize was not something to ever admit; he had been anointed as clever and was expected to be full of fresh ideas all the time.

He thought back to the campaign, which had been practically his life for the last few months. *Nah, I told all the good stories there*, he thought. *Well, what about the not-so-good stories?* a voice suggested. Everybody was going to want articles on Clinton's people, who by then it seemed were going to hold key positions in the new administration. He remembered an incident with James Carville, a man he disliked intensely after having seen him in action on the campaign trail. There was an image in his mind he'd never forget: Carville at an airport, pushing a short old woman aside to get to his suitcase, not an hour after telling the world on national television how much Clinton cared about "the little guy."

"How about James Carville?" Eric asked, only to play for time, sure that this already overexposed subject would be turned down.

"Hmm. We haven't done anything on him yet. Why don't you give me 20,000 words on him; I'll have Contracts draw something up."

Eric couldn't quite believe it. A casual comment and just like that, a contract for a lucrative piece in one of America's premier upper-middlebrow magazines. "Great," he said as offhandedly as he could, as if he picked up work like this all the time.

"Oh, and the magazine's throwing a party tonight you need to go to. There'll be some people there it'll be really good for you to meet."

"Sure, great," Eric said again, still sort of numb. Next thing he knew, he was up and out of the office and on the street.

He'd purchased a laptop computer, as much a rarity in 1992 as a cell phone—and about as trustworthy. It had cost him plenty, but he also had an accountant now. ("My tax guy" was the proper imperiously casual way of referring to this specimen in the new circle he'd developed in only a week's time, and he was a quick study.) Tax guy encouraged him to spend as much as possible on tax-deductible items. Eric had worked with computers too long to trust them completely, and days of notes from meetings with editors were best transferred to disk and taken to a service bureau and printed on good old reliable paper.

It was a brisk November night, and Eric walked down Broadway with a disk in his pocket and frets on his mind. He'd just signed a contract for a 20,000-word piece on James Carville, someone he didn't really want to write about because he disliked him heartily. For a moment he felt a hiccup of hilarity: *I should lead off the piece with that scene at the airport!* But then he felt a twinge—was that what the editor wanted? Why hadn't he told the editor how much he loathed the man? *Because 20,000 words is $20,000!* he admitted to himself, and he hadn't wanted to queer the deal. *Pendennis* was a magazine that would want an "objective" piece—i.e., Eric could destroy the man, but only by quoting other people's words.

He found a copy shop that offered PC rentals and went inside, not realizing how cold it was outside until the warm blanket of air inside enveloped him. There was only one person working there, his back to Eric as he made color copies on a machine behind the counter. Eric waited a few seconds and then cleared his throat. "I'll be with you in a second," the clerk said without turning around.

Regardless of central heating, Eric went into a mild shock. He actually looked at the clerk for the first time and realized, yes, it was Cal. Even from the back he could tell, especially with the voice. After shock came astonishment—what the hell was he doing working in a copy shop!

Cal turned his head to check one of the copies coming out, and Eric at first could only tell that Cal looked different—still gorgeous, but somehow...different.

Cal turned around. "Can I help...you!" He laughed like a happy baby when he saw Eric, the look of shock on Eric's face would have set anyone off, it was so priceless, but especially so since Cal was stoned to his gills.

Eric smiled, too, relieved that Cal felt no enmity toward him over their last encounter. "Cal, what are you doing here?"

Cal arched an eyebrow. "Here?" He raised his arms mock-majestically. "This is my kingdom."

"You own it?"

Cal laughed harder. "Hell, no. Just a peon." He checked Eric out. "You look good. Successful. Fat and happy."

"Thanks, I guess. I'm doing all right." The preposterousness of having this conversation with the only man who'd ever touched his heart—over a copy shop counter, under fluorescent lights—was too much for him. "I guess we have a lot of catching up to do. I mean, I didn't expect to—"

"See me here?" Cal grinned, and Eric nodded, his startlement over Cal's very presence replaced as it subsided with amazement at Cal's...looseness seemed to be the only word for it. "Well, that's a story."

"I'd like to hear it. I mean if you..." Eric trailed off.

"Sure, I'll tell you yours if you tell me mine," Cal said. Eric looked at him for a moment and Cal realized what he'd said and started giggling. "I mean you mine and...you know what I mean!"

Eric smiled tentatively, the way you do when you're not laughing but don't want to blink dumbly at someone. "Sure, great, when's good for you? What time do you get off work?"

"Oh, I'll just close now. Nick was supposed to be back from dinner half an hour ago, so fuck him. Ah, speak of the devil," he said as a young man with a goatee wearing an old gas station attendant's shirt walked in the door, bag in hand. "You're late. This is Eric. I'm going, see ya."

Nick didn't miss a beat. "That's not good business practice, Calvin Coolidge."

Cal laughed. "That's *my* business, Old Scratch. See you later." He grabbed his jacket and they were out the door.

"Why'd he call you Calvin Coolidge?"

"Oh, that. When the other guys found out I had an MBA and used to work at Goldman Sachs, they started calling me Calvin Coolidge. You know, 'The business of—'"

"'Of America is business,'" Eric finished the quote with him. "You don't mind?"

"Hell, no! I just call Nick Old Scratch—that pale skin, those dark eyes, that goatee—he's a sexy devil. He's straight—all the guys there are straight, but they get off on it. They play the game."

"Huh," Eric responded neutrally, still processing information that was so massively contradictory to what he knew. Eric couldn't believe he was talking to Cal Hewitt. The boy who had sat on his bed so stiffly, who had lashed out at him with such fury on their last encounter—that wasn't this Cal. This Cal was...relaxed. Openly gay, obviously—the young man who'd been afraid to kiss Eric in public was flirting with straight boys!

"So do you live here now?" Cal asked him.

"Uh, no, I'm just visiting on business."

"Business? So you gave up on the writing thing, huh?"

"No, actually, that's my business. I write for a living now." Eric was embarrassed. He'd wanted—expected—to hear Cal mention at least in passing that he was aware of Eric's new place on the national radar.

"Ah," Cal said. At this news, his glaze cracked a bit. Over the last two years he had discovered that his generation's ironic pose in the face of defeat suited him well. *Time* magazine had named it "Generation X" in 1988, although ten years later its boomer editors would strip them of this title and award it to their own children, inherently more interesting because they were their own. The boomers had had everything—the sex, the drugs, the rock and roll—then they'd turned to their younger brothers and sisters and said sternly, "We've had our fun, and we've had yours, too." There was nothing left to do but set up shop selling black-humored frustration and hang out your sign in air quotes.

When he'd seen Eric well-dressed, his mantle of self-assurance a little more brick-like and, well, stiffer than his former happy puppy-like innocent trust in the benevolent future, he'd assumed that the rules were in operation and Eric had given up on his dream and settled for something hollow and well-paying.

"So what do you do? Advertising, P.R.?"

"No, I write magazine articles. I wrote one about ACT UP for *The New Republic*, and it snowballed from there. I just signed a contract for my first book."

Cal nodded. "That's good," he said softly. *So someone's plan had worked out.* Why did it hurt that it had turned out so well for Eric? "So where are we going?"

"Oh," Eric said, realizing they were walking aimlessly, assuming Cal the resident was leading him somewhere. "Well, there's a good bar in my hotel. It's not far."

"No piano, is there?"

Eric laughed. "No, no piano."

"Then off we go."

Cal and Eric surprised each other by ordering nonalcoholic drinks. "You're so pure," Cal noted.

"So are you."

"No, I'm stoned. Alcohol does not go well with pot."

"Ah," Eric said neutrally, thinking he'd discovered what accounted for Cal's newfound mellowness. "You get stoned before you go to work?"

"What do you mean before?" Cal grinned. "We're all stoners there. That's one of the job requirements. You don't really think it's humanly possible to make copies all day without being high, do you?"

"Oh," Eric said, feeling stupid as he said it. *I'm trying so hard to be polite. I should just say what's on my mind!* "I don't understand, Cal. You were so set on making money, you can't possibly make any at that job."

"I don't," Cal admitted cheerily. "But I don't need to. My dad died, you know." Eric nodded. "And he left me a surprising amount of money. A couple hundred thou, not enough to buy a yacht or anything, but enough that I don't have to work."

"So why do you?"

Cal shrugged. "I wouldn't know what to do with myself otherwise. I came back to New York and quit my job and thought, 'Well, now what?' There was no point in moving back to Reno, so I got my own place and decorated it and then I didn't have the faintest idea what to do next. I'm not much of a shopper. I've got a cheap apartment, thanks to the recession for *that*, anyway." He smiled ruefully. "And frankly, the only thing I ever learned how to do at Goldman was make copies. I drifted in there one day to do my résumé, because I decided to look for some kind of job because I'd gotten so bored sitting around. I started talking with Nick and the other guys. They got me stoned in the stockroom, and I was hired."

"But what are you going to *do*?" Eric asked with an earnestness that made Cal laugh.

"Smoke dope, take it easy, see if the recession ever ends and if I ever find something I want to do with my life. I *was* set on making money, and then I didn't make any, and then I didn't have to. Kinda takes the wind out of your sails, being a trustafarian."

"A what?"

"A trustafarian. Like a Rastafarian, only white, with a trust fund."

Eric laughed. "Ey, mon, how's da portfolio?"

Cal gave this a stoned giggle. "Yup." He paused, realizing he ought to ask Eric about his career, but he also wished he could smoke the joint in his pocket. "So do you get stoned?"

"Sure, sometimes. Not as much as I used to at Bennington!"

"Well, what say we go up to your room? I've got a joint."

Eric's stomach knotted at the idea of going up to his room with Cal. He felt as much the teenager at the thought as Cal had four years earlier. "Sure, why not?"

Cal smiled, their first time alone together also on his mind. He had been so scared! More scared of his own desires than of anything that might have—could possibly have—happened before, with Emma downstairs.

Eric was right; Cal had accepted his own sexuality—he was not happy with it, and he still hadn't told his mother. He'd told the guys at work that first day because he was stoned and he wanted to see what they'd say about it. Some burst of anger inside him said, *We'll just see now how cool they really are.* And the fact was, they really were cool. Nick had labeled himself "disgusted but curious" and the others had assented to that. Cal later realized he'd taken the job more because it was the first moment in his life that he'd felt himself accepted. In a way these straight boys were his first real friends. They were *guys*, they worked there to support themselves while they played in bands or because they had a knack for computers, for which there was as of yet no great market, and working there beat working in tech support at some fucking black iceberg downtown where you couldn't dress in rags, let alone play the boom box, never mind get stoned in the back when there was nothing to do (or when there was, no hurry).

They had made it clear to Cal that there would be no political correctness, that he would have to give as good as he could take and he would have to take plenty of comments about Hershey highways and fudge packers. He responded in kind about how straight guys loved straight porn because it was the only place in the world where guys so fat and ugly could make women so hot scream so loud. He hated the work, but he loved his job.

When Cal took the copy shop job, almost a year ago now, he hadn't even attempted sex since his episode with the hustler. The guys ribbed him when they described their own sexual exploits, real or imagined, and he would say truthfully that he had none to report. "I told you, I'm disgusted but curious," Nick insisted, "so I wanna hear some details." Cal didn't insult them by inventing any, but he realized he might as well try and get some.

New York is a sexual city. People look each other in the eye—and not from half a block away—before deciding to ignore you once they're in your space. Women evaluate you, gay men evaluate you, straight boys challenge you to size them up, knowing from growing up in the city that contrary to the belief of most straight men in the hinterlands, gay men do not desire all men, any man, however gross, but have the most exacting standards; if a gay man cruises you, you're hot. Cal had let go of much when his father had died. It had dawned on him slowly that what he had considered necessary to please the world was really what was necessary to please his father, that the world—at least, New York—didn't care whom he slept with. But sex was still compartmentalized, something "to be dealt with later." His father was dead, and Cal had money, if not the billions of dollars he'd once associated with freedom. All the same, sex still meant danger: AIDS, thuggish fag bashers. It was something to be dealt with later...someday. Not today.

But men cruised him as they walked past, and he cruised them; he might not have had the effect on anybody else that he'd had on Eric, but they often turned around hoping he would turn around, too. He never did.

Finally, he'd gone out with someone he met at the copy shop, a regular—and only then because the guy kept asking him out. Each time he'd declined, Nick and Andy and Neil would wait until the door closed behind the customer and shout, "What the fuck is wrong with you?"

There was nothing wrong with this guy—Cal couldn't even remember his name now, partly because of his pot habit but also partly because, well, because there was nothing wrong with him. He was well-mannered and well-groomed, 30-ish, obviously a successful entrepreneur, slightly and politely but never devastatingly witty. "Any of you guys have sisters?" Cal asked them one day during his ritual ribbing over the guy. "And she would come home from a date with a guy who didn't impress her, and she'd say, 'He was nice.' Nothing wrong with him," Cal said, raising his hands as if under arrest for a crime he hadn't committed, "but nothing to write home about him, let alone not come home at all for him."

Eventually, he had gone out with the guy, more so that he could say afterward, "I'll call you," and never call him, and get the guy to find another service bureau. And to get the gang off his back. The guy took him to a nice dinner, paid for everything, treated him like a prince, came up with a valid reason for inviting him home, smoked a joint with him, and made love to him.

The sex bored Cal. *Here I am*, he thought, *losing my virginity at 26, and I guess it's true: the first time is always the worst.* The guy was so considerate, so tender, that it rang false to Cal. *He doesn't even know me, and he's treating me like a china doll.* It was all about intellectual messages: *I respect you, I will treat you well.* Where was the passion? He'd seen some gay porn, plenty actually, and he'd found frequent masturbation to be an effective deterrent to having actual sex. And sex was supposed to be...*hotter* than this. His only prior sexual experience had been Eric's kiss, which had more in it of...*desire, need, lust*; there was something about a man taking something he needed from you that gave you what you wanted and needed. At least that was how Cal saw it.

He'd talked about it a bit with Nick, who'd cheerfully admitted he liked rough sex, but it was hard to find girls who were into it—or at least girls who'd admit it. In Nick's experience, everyone liked rough sex whether they'd admit it or not. Cal had nodded. "Ayn Rand sex." Nick burst out laughing and Cal smiled; it was nice to be around people who got your jokes.

"You should have told him," Nick said. "You should have said, 'Harder!' "

"I did," Cal admitted. "And he did it for like a minute, and then he was out of breath. And really, he just did it faster, not harder. More effort, no aggression."

"I oughta fuck you," Nick said, half flirting and half kidding.

"I think you should," Cal challenged him. "How about tonight?"

Nick flushed, then laughed. "Oh, you," he said, retreating behind a sissy façade.

It was a watershed moment for Cal. He'd been so attracted to these young men, their easy familiarity with all the things Cal had believed spelled danger. But for the first time in his life, Cal had looked over a chasm, fully prepared to jump and fall with the man on the other side, and the man on the other side had blinked. He didn't process his transformation intellectually, only smirked a bit and called Nick a "chickenshit" and let it go. But he felt a surge of triumph—he was unafraid now to go places others wouldn't go. And the places that lured him were not sunny parks where innocent kisses were exchanged, but darker, unknown places where the whole purpose of putting your hand in the flame was to get burned.

And so he was amused as he and Eric entered the hotel room, amused at their change in position and amused at the thought of what Eric would find this time if he tried to kiss Cal again. The room was not cheap, Cal noted; it had the stiff, uncomfortable, Court of Versailles–style furniture that people with money still associated with elegance.

Eric took off his jacket, and Cal admired him openly. Eric's T-shirt was a tight black Lycra thing that along with his black wool slacks (nipped at the waist to show off his thighs and draped in the back just enough to accent his cheeks) bespoke a whole way of living and being for a certain sort of gay man— expensive, tasteful, and barely discreet in advertising the essential wares of chest, biceps and ass. Cal noted that the little tuft of hair that had once poked out the back of Eric's T-shirt had been waxed off. But Cal's admiration was more of the "I have to hand it to you" variety than it was of lust—Eric had become a product, or at least the sort of man recruited to sell products...and buy them. He imagined that sex with Eric would be something like his virgin experience with Mr. Nice, not the dark and wild encounter he had been so willing to have with Nick.

Eric was as nervous as a cat; the two men's co-owned knowledge of the previous sparks between them was as much at the forefront of his mind as it was of Cal's. Eric wanted to make some joke about it, a reference to bring it out in the open, but as he realized that he was the awkward, unsure one, he bit his tongue, having rapidly learned in his new world that displaying the chinks in one's armor was generally an opportunity to get stabbed.

Eric's own sex life over the past few years had adhered to his lifelong pattern of serial monogamy: sex was something you had with your boyfriend. While ACT UP's freewheeling climate had loosened him up about sex on the first date, he still didn't go to bars by himself, and when he went out with friends, he only cruised other guys as a diversion, something to do while the others were getting fresh drinks or taking a piss. And while Cal's speculation about what sex with Eric would be like could only be confirmed or denied in practice, it was true that Eric dated men not unlike Cal's nameless first-time partner. This was not to say that Eric found such sex irresistible, only that he had found through experience that sex was "nice," but that was about it.

Cal fired up the joint and handed it to Eric. "So," Cal croaked through a lungful, "how's your love life?"

Eric smiled, relieved. Cal had cracked the ice on the subject far more smoothly than he could have. He used his hit off the joint and several seconds of lung retention to put himself into a casual banter groove (the pot helped with this quickly).

"I told myself I wanted to start seeing other people," Eric said, "that I still really cared about me, but that I just wasn't satisfying my needs anymore."

Cal nodded. "How did you take the news?"

Eric shrugged. "All right. I wasn't happy about me leaving myself alone on Friday nights, but I got over it. How about you?"

"Right now I'm dating pretty much the whole active stable of Colt Studios," Cal said.

Eric nodded, wondering why he was happy that Cal had just told him his current sex life consisted of whacking off to gay porn. "I've been seeing quite a bit of the guys from Jocks and Mustang," he lobbed back.

"Ah, young, slim, and smooth still your thing, eh?"

Eric blushed. "Yep. Big and beefy still yours, obviously."

"Whatever happened to that punk rock guy you brought home that time?"

"Huh? Oh," he laughed in recognition. "You mean Mikey." He shrugged. "It was nothing serious." Like so many people in ACT UP, after the group's collapse they'd drifted apart. "How do you like the pot?"

Eric was amazed that he was already stoned. "It's fucking awesome."

"I bought it in San Francisco at the Pot Club. There's a magazine story for you," Cal nodded.

"How so?"

Cal's eyes bugged. "Oh my God, you're kidding! You don't know about the Cannabis Buyers' Club?"

"Oh, yeah, I've heard of it. It's a place for people with AIDS to get marijuana."

"Oh, it's way more than that!" Cal jumped up, excited, waving the joint around. "It's this building on Market Street, and it's three or four stories high, and it's chock full of stoners every day. You can get a membership with the lamest medical excuse, and it's just like Amsterdam—you go up to the glass case, and they have different grades of pot, and you can smell it before you buy it…"

"Wow," Eric said, picking up on Cal's excitement. "And they haven't shut it down."

"No. It's *totally brazen*, and the cops are like, 'So what? it keeps people off the street.' It's like…well, it's just this amazing place. You've got gay men with HIV, and you've got street people who are using it as, like, their daytime homeless shelter, and you've got these college kids who work there and are signing up *everybody* to go out and collect signatures for a medical marijuana initiative on the California state ballot, and they're making so fucking much money from the pot that they're paying people 50 cents for every signature they collect…"

Eric's radar was pinging madly. "So there's like all these

people there who wouldn't socialize any other way?"

"Yeah! I mean there are these black guys from the Fillmore, total homies in their puffy, baggy rapper clothes, and they're being like totally cool about all the fags, which they'd never do on the street, and everybody is just *stoned*, and they're playing Pink Floyd and shit like that, and they give out stoner snacks for sugar crashes, baskets of oranges under the ficus trees next to the ratty old couches..."

"That sounds so cool," Eric said, doubly stoked over a great story and how Cal was just as enthused about such an environment as Eric would be. "That's why I picked ACT UP to write about in my first article, because it was like that, people who'd never have anything to do with each other except that something happened where they *had* to."

"That's right, you wrote about ACT UP," Cal said, half sitting and half bouncing up and down on the bed. "I'd love to read that."

Eric recalled their last encounter, the lash of Cal's tongue on him over this very subject. *Could he have forgotten?* Eric wondered. In fact, Cal had offered up this interest in the article as a subtle apology, but Eric missed it. Cal, however, considered the apology accepted when Eric retrieved a copy of *TNR* from his suitcase. "Here, I have a copy. Not because I force it on people or anything, but because it's like my résumé and I need to have it on me." He handed Cal a copy.

"Holy shit, this was a cover story! 'A Burning House: The Rise and Fall of ACT UP by Eric Hamilton.' Wow, Eric, this is great. Congratulations. Do you mind if I read it now?"

Eric was as thrilled as a child bringing his first drawing with an "A" on it home to mommy. "No, no, it's kinda long but go ahead."

"Does this place have room service? I'm starved. I'll pay, of course," Cal smiled.

"Actually," Eric said, his heart squeezing a bit at Cal's smile, "I have a party to go to tonight—catered food, open bar. You wanna come along?"

Cal laughed and swept his hand over himself. "I don't think I'm dressed for it."

Eric felt a twinge of shame as he realized he agreed. Cal was wearing a nice white button-down oxford, presumably left over from his Wall Street days, but tucked haphazardly into a pair of Ben Davis work pants that lapped over a pair of Doc Martens. *Fuck it,* he thought. *He's my friend and this is New York City, and for all they know, he's an eccentric artist of some kind.* "You look fine."

Cal shrugged. "Sure. Why not?" Then he gave Eric an impish grin. "Let's party."

They decided to walk—well, Cal decided to walk. "Aren't you cold?" Eric asked.

"Yeah, but I'm also stoned, and I couldn't handle the subway right now."

"That's what cabs are for."

Cal laughed. "Spoken like a New Yorker. No, let's walk."

"OK," Eric acquiesced. His own plush, drapey fabrics were guarantee enough against the cold, but he feared for Cal in his windbreaker. Eric had to laugh; Cal's windbreaker was actually a dark-gray gas station attendant's jacket—a facsimile so accurate it even had a white oval patch with "Cal" sewn on it in scrolly red letters. That aggressively downscale look had just caught on with presumably upwardly mobile college students as a reaction to the Bush recession. It was a look that said, *No matter what I do, this is the best job I can expect to get.* It was ironic enough that these jackets were sold dearly at Urban Outfitters for what a gas station attendant made in a week; and to Eric, the idea of Cal in this look, with his MBA and his recent inheritance, seemed even funnier.

Cal's reason for wanting to walk was partly THC-related anxiety but, more importantly, a desire to spend a little more time with Eric. Cal knew the mechanics of this engine called New York, knew that parties like this were not for relaxing and having fun but for seeing and being seen, meeting the right people and pitching yourself. Once they arrived at the party, Eric would be sucked into its maw and Cal would be by himself. (For the stoned, parties were not as threatening as subways, because you weren't trapped in place and you could feed on munchies ad nauseam.) For all that had happened—or more to the point, not happened—between them, Cal felt a twinge of sorrow. *If only I hadn't been so fucked up then,* he thought, *I wouldn't be so fucked up now.*

His automatic chuckle at the thought brought him Eric's attention. "What's so funny?"

"Oh, just thinking about life, how things turn out."

"So you're happy? With your life?" For Eric, laughing was what you did when you were happy. It would be some years before he would learn that laughing was also what you did when you weren't happy and couldn't do much about it.

Cal shrugged. "I manage." That was true enough: He had his job, his work friends, who were pleasant, agreeable company; he had his apartment and his cable TV and his weed; he had no money worries, which he well knew from his childhood during the last recession was a blessing in itself. Staying stoned meant feeling agreeable or numb or drowsy; it also enabled him to watch porn, get excited and get off without feeling, as he had when he'd watched porn without pot, when at the moment of climax he'd felt that somehow, somehow he had to reach out and touch that, make it real, that he would just die of frustration if all he ever did was beat off for the rest of his life. Pot has a way of changing the subject on you, whether you want it to or not; it disallows any extended focus on any one idea. Which was fine with Cal.

"You deserve to be happy," Eric said, having already realized that Cal wasn't.

Cal raised an eyebrow. "Do I? How do you know?"

"Everyone does."

Cal thought about that and decided not to disagree.

It was Eric's turn to chuckle and, when he didn't, explain to Cal what had struck his funny bone. " 'To hope for better days is half to deserve them,' " he quoted. "Do you remember?"

Cal laughed, pleasantly surprised. "Yeah, I do. But you know, you can hope for better days *and* deserve them, but just because you deserve something doesn't always mean you get it." He surprised himself with this observation.

Eric decided not to answer that. What could he say? He

was walking to a party with a beautiful stranger, someone whose life had been full of disappointment and pain and fear. His own life had had its pains, but they had all been small and useful, nothing to level his vaulting ambition and confidence. It was Eric the journalist who looked at Cal now and thought dispassionately, *What did we ever have in common?* In his room it had been like a magic spell, like they were two kids alone in his room again, only this time he had been the nervously lustful one... And now poof!—his lust had gone out like a light as he saw what he took to be Cal's general negativity. Eric was a naturally positive person, but unlike earlier days when Cal's darker side had rolled off him like water off a duck, this was more like oil and it felt...icky. Whatever passion there had been was gone; he could tell because even as he looked at Cal some part of him was thinking there was an article in this whole gas station–chic thing...

Although it didn't look it to Eric, Cal's reaction was less dispassionate. The problem with deep emotional observations that take you by surprise is that they often loosen the rocks that keep other observations tucked well out of sight. *Nothing I want has really come to me*, Cal thought with shock. He looked at Eric now and saw the resignation, knew Eric's feelings for him were gone. And he in turn no longer saw the iconic jock of teenage fantasy but rather a "nice man," like the one with whom he'd had his one sexual encounter. Some dark element within him, enraged at being awakened from its enforced slumber, whispered in his mind, *Don't you just wish you could shove a stick of dynamite up life's ass and blow it to smithereens?* Yes, he did, he wished there was some way of just saying FUCK IT on such a massive scale that everything changed forever, that all his fears and frustrations could be smashed like so many scarecrows in a hurricane, and he swore then and there that next time God fucked up and something good came Cal's way he wouldn't run away.

The party they arrived at in relative silence was the sort of affair *Pendennis* threw all the time, and as Cal assumed, it was all business. As usual, one of New York's restaurants du jour hosted it in exchange for the free publicity and cachet acquired through the presence of several major and numerous minor celebrities—celebrities herded to the party at the direction of their publicists so as to earn the goodwill of *Pendennis* and perhaps become cover fodder. (While covers would be reserved for movie stars, trendy—and photogenic—novelists and artists were recruited to decorate couches in magazine feature spreads, and their handlers encouraged them to audition.) *Pendennis* thus displayed its awesome power and rank in the mediacracy through its ability to marshal said hot restaurant and celebrities at its beck and call; which in turn lured advertisers to underwrite the costs of the event, advertisers who were in turn repaid when the magazine used scads of pictures of beautiful people, with the advertisers' logos prominently plastered in the background. The more people considered "now" and "hot" who attended, the more successful the party would be for all concerned.

Eric introduced Cal to Nathan, his editor, who acknowledged him politely (unless they were already famous and applauded for being rude, people were always terribly polite at these parties; one never knew in New York when the nobody you were shaking hands with would turn out to be the somebody who could do so much for you) and then detached Eric to "meet some people." Cal was glad to be on his own and left Eric not feeling like a bad person for abandoning him. Cal made his way to the buffet table, from which only a few were eating only a little, and began to help himself with all the enthusiasm low blood sugar can muster for toast points and caviar.

"Listen," Eric said to Nathan, "I've got an idea for another article."

"Great," Nathan said, one ear on Eric, another tuned for nearby gossip, and both eyes scanning the room. "Let's hear it."

"There's this medical marijuana club in San Francisco," he started, and he quickly relayed all that Cal had told him about it. "And I'd really like to do this piece," he ended.

At last Nathan gave him both eyes. "Well, I really don't think it sounds like that's for us." Eric, having had nothing but success in his career so far, was therefore completely unacquainted with the cold finality and utter disinterest that was contained in the words "not for us."

"But it's a really great story…" he reattempted the battlements.

"I'm sure it is. Why don't you try *Details*? It sounds like the kind of, you know, funky downscale thing they might like. Howard!" he shouted at a man just cut loose from another slipstream of conversation. "Howard!"

Of course, Eric thought, mentally slapping himself, some remnant of his old ACT UP self reemerging, needing to mock Quail. *All those sick poor people on a drug that isn't cocaine— how dull.* He resolved he *would* send the article to *Details*, damn it. *Pendennis* wasn't the only magazine in the world, and with his credits he could sell it somewhere, he was sure. That *Details* also paid a dollar a word was not lost on him.

"Howard Marx, I'd like you to meet Eric Hamilton," Nathan said. "Eric, Howard's done some work for us and he's been dying to meet you."

Howard Marx blushed a bit, ducking his head. "Well, Nathan, you make me sound like a teenage girl, squeaking at her first sight of Marky Mark."

Eric laughed. Howard was a funny-looking guy, Eric thought. Tall and…well, lean would have been the polite word for it. His head was a little large for his neck, though he had reduced it in size by shaving his head. He wore large black spectacles in the days when large black spectacles on a beautiful fashion model were considered a "commentary" on beauty, but when large black spectacles on someone like Howard simply marked one out as a geek—these also being the days before the geeks inherited the earth. Eric had seen the self-consciously mocking look's debut back in San Francisco; ancillary to ACT UP had been a subculture full of nerds and geeks who wasted their time playing with computers and had chosen to emphasize rather than minimize their freakiness with tattoos and piercings and shaved heads and anything else that marked them even further off from society than society had deemed that nature already had.

For many, the pose was haughty and, to Eric, sexually a

turnoff, at least when the whole thing was a pose, a statement of the "groovier than thou" variety. But in some, the genuinely freaky who were tuning and turning their oddness to their advantage, Eric sometimes found a distinct allure. Howard, he already knew, was of the latter type. Eric could already see in his eyes a fierce intelligence and wit; he had been letting Eric know he was by no means a blushing schoolgirl, and there was something in his voice, deep in measure but light and playful in tone, that Eric liked.

"I imagine Marky is probably at this party somewhere," he replied, smiling.

Nathan laughed. "I know we invited him. Oh, there's Norman. I'd better go say hello." And with that the editor left them.

The main purpose of this party was of course to enhance the glory of *Pendennis,* but there was something else, too. Men like Nathan are too intelligent to serve merely as apparatchiks to the cult of celebrity; they could not live with themselves if they could not list any higher motives for their actions. So these parties also functioned as a sort of salon, where the bright and talented could meet their fellows, and Nathan had risen to his position because he had an eagle eye for the sort of people who would click. He was thus able to gratify his intellectual need to be doing something to forward the culture while at the same time gratifying his need for first-class foreign travel and Meissen porcelain. New York is full of people who would die if they could not fulfill both desires.

"So you're going to be writing for Nathan," Howard opened.

Eric nodded. "Yeah, this thing on James Carville, which isn't really what I want to be doing right now."

"Why not?"

Eric made Howard laugh by telling him the airport story, then told him about the pot club. "Yeah, I live in S.F. I've been there. That's a great story."

"You do!" Eric cried with delighted surprise. He had not yet spent enough time traveling the world to discover how small it was. "So do I!"

Howard gave him a winningly wicked smile. "Well, I have a

membership card, and they're rather lax about guests. When you get back home, I'll take you if you like."

Eric nodded vigorously, weed and champagne and youthful enthusiasm getting the best of him. "Yeah, that would be great, yeah. So what are you doing in New York?"

"Meeting with my editor at Viking. I'm working on a book on the failure of sentimental humanism."

"What do you mean?"

"Well, the first example I use—because everyone's so familiar with it—is the 'tree hugger.' The environmental movement in this country, when it got started, had a very small base, and that base failed to grow because its roots were in sentimental humanism. You remember the type, the proverbial tree-hugging hippie who would literally hug trees, dance around them, bang a drum, enact pagan rituals...basically build a culture antithetical to anything in the dominant culture and then turn around and become *enraged* when everybody they met didn't see that the rain forest should be saved. Trees falling and drums banging didn't sweep the rest off their feet, because they weren't hard-core sentimental humanists."

"Well," Eric pointed out, "that *did* work when the sentiment crossed the boards. Like with the baby seals, for example. Everybody wanted to save the baby seals because they were so cute."

"That's a good point," Howard said. "Then think how enraged environmentalists got because people would cry for baby seals but wouldn't cry for, say, snail darters. And there was no such thing as a cute cuddly tree."

"Unless you were a tree hugger."

Howard laughed and Eric smiled. When was the last time he'd had a conversation like this? After navigating the minefields of rhetoric in ACT UP, Eric had become an adept at seeing what people did or didn't say. Howard hadn't said, defensively, "I've already thought of that"; instead he had given Eric credit for leaping ahead and seeing it without explanation.

"So my thesis is basically that several movements have been held back because they've been spearheaded ideologically by sentimental humanists rather than pragmatists—in the

William James sense," he clarified, and Eric nodded. "Only now have environmentalists come to see that the way to save the rain forests is to talk about the potentially life-saving drugs coming out of there, rather than about Gaia or some such thing, that the way to preserve indigenous peoples is not by fetishizing their primitivism and knocking Western culture as inferior to theirs, but by appealing to Western culture's tradition of individualism and independence to let them live unmolested. But those were intellectual arguments, and always therefore inferior to emotional appeal, and those who were unswayed by heart over head were to be scorned and despised as inferior. And anyone who didn't conform to their sentimental, overemotional world view was someone to be worked against, not with. Crackpots, basically, but I need a better phrase."

"Orwell called them 'fruit-juice drinkers,'" Eric supplied helpfully.

Howard laughed. "Where did he say that?"

"I can't remember, but I'll look it up and get it to you." He could see a flash of understanding in Howard's eyes. This was flirtation, only where in usual circumstances people talked about loaning CDs to newfound friends to indicate some hope of permanence in the connection, they were talking about trading literary references. Eric couldn't quite believe it, but he was finding himself getting sexually excited by Howard. He wasn't really such a funny duck after all when you looked at him right, he thought. And he had such a soft, beautiful, mellow speaking voice…

"Listen," Howard said, his head cocked in a way that said, *This is a crazy idea but…* "Would you like to go get a cup of coffee somewhere? I keep getting elbowed and jostled and…"

"Yeah, me too," Eric said, his "me too" more a confirmation of mutual interest than anything to do with elbows, though Howard was right, the party was obscenely crowded. "I just have to find a friend and say goodbye."

Cal's mellowness increased as his appetite reached satiety. A spot on a couch was not hard to find, since most people at the party seemed to prefer constant motion (only the most august grandees or those with reputations for extreme languor to preserve remained stationary). Cal dusted off the last of his shrimp puffs and began to examine the picture hung over the couch with ardent interest. At first it had appeared to be a blown-up photograph, but as he looked more closely at the corner nearest him he could see the dents and ridges of actual paint. He got up to look at it from a distance, then closely. Photorealism in painting was still something of a novelty then, after so many years of abstraction; it was still considered the sort of thing one did for walls in hotel rooms rather than walls in salons. But it was the subject that plainly saved it from relegation to the dust bin of art history—it was a perfect representation of a country crossroads at dusk, an almost Hopperesque glare coming off the land everywhere, save where the Wal-Mart billboard threw shade. Cal had to chuckle, it was like a *New Yorker* story writ in oils, where all you needed to prove your subtle grasp of irony was to toss in a reference to trash culture.

"Do you like it?"

Cal turned to the speaker, a young man he would have presumed to be a fashion model were it not for the wicked glint in his eyes. Suddenly, he realized this was the painter; he recognized him from a photo blown up and mounted in the lobby. *Pendennis* had just run a series of photographs of young artists and their work, and this bad boy had posed, shirtless, slouching and smoking before one of his paintings. Images like the photo in the lobby can exert tidal pulls on gay men, and it had subtly crossed Cal's mind, as he and Eric walked past it, that there was the sort of boy who could get you in trouble...

Cal knew it was now his place to say, "Oh, yes!" and when the mask was torn off to gasp and gush, but he wouldn't fall for that. "You missed a spot," he said, pointing to a corner.

"What!" the artist said indignantly, rushing forward with manic intensity. Only when he heard Cal laugh did he turn around, his anger morphing into a terse smile.

Cal looked at the tag on the wall, read the name, and extended his hand. "Pleased to meet you, Neil. I'm Cal."

Neil took the proffered hand. "So you got me fishing for compliments. I had it coming."

"You deserved it. But you also deserve the compliment. It's a very nice picture. Or am I not suppose to say it's 'nice'?"

"No, you're supposed to say it's 'bold' or 'daring' or 'expressive.' It's too bourgeois to be 'nice,' you see."

"You don't look very bourgeois in that photo in the lobby."

Neil was genuinely puzzled for a moment, then laughed. "Oh, right. Kinda spoils the element of surprise, doesn't it?"

"Well, when you pose for a photo that draws that much attention..."

Neil raised an eyebrow. "Did it draw yours?"

Cal had been functioning perfectly well till now; light flirtation was his stock in trade at the copy shop, but this was something else. Here was the bridge—would he cross it? If there was one thing Neil didn't look, it was "nice" in the sexual sense. And hadn't Cal just sworn that the next time something came his way he would grab it?

"Very much so."

Neil smiled. "I'm surprised. You look like such a good boy."

"I'm tired of being a good boy," Cal said in a harsh tone. He could see that Neil was at first taken aback but then smiled; there was, Cal saw, no need to modify his tone.

"What are you going to do about that?" Neil asked. He was, Cal could see, no novice at the art of cruising, but there was something in Cal that plainly scared him. Cal thought of Nick backing off and thought, *Let's go.* Some door was opening and it was dark beyond it and he wanted to go in. *Come on, somebody, let's go...*

Cal took Neil's hand. "I'm going to take your hand, and you're going to guide me out of here, and you're going to take me home and show me your etchings."

It was sheer coincidence that Eric ran into Cal as he was on his way out; Cal had forgotten about Eric, and marijuana could not be blamed for his thoughtlessness. "Hey!" Eric said as he stopped Cal and his companion. "I'm glad I found you. I, uh, I've got to spend some time talking with someone about a project, and I just wondered if you'd be all right on your own?" Even as he said it, Eric thought he could kick himself. Why couldn't he tell Cal he'd met someone? There was nothing between them, so why did he lie?

Cal smiled. "No problem, I've met some interesting people myself tonight." Then Eric noticed Neil and kicked himself again. Damn, this guy was good-looking. Was this Cal's type, someone just as lean and dangerous as himself? *Maybe I never had a chance anyway*, he thought absurdly, wondering why he cared.

Eric managed a polite smile for the stranger. "Well, listen, I'll be in town for a few days. Call me at the hotel, OK?"

Cal nodded. "Sure." Then, impulsively, he gave Eric a quick hug. "Thanks for inviting me."

Strangely moved by the hug, Eric nodded. "Sure, my pleasure." Then Cal and his new friend were gone.

Eric felt disoriented suddenly, as if something had changed. But it took him only a moment, as he found Howard again and got his smile, almost shy but more like that of a boy who's found buried treasure in the field round back and can't believe his luck. Eric smiled back, suddenly relieved and even a little giddy. *Everything is coming right*, he thought, *for all of us*, and he was glad for Cal, and as Howard extended his elbow in a courtly gesture, Eric laughed freely and put his arm through Howard's and walked out with him.

At any age, there is something about an immediate and powerful attraction to another person that makes you giddy, a sense that you've known this person all your life and several of your previous lives, too. And when you're still young, as Eric was, and have yet to learn that what you see is not always what you get, the feeling is even giddier. As he walked down the street with Howard, Eric's circuits were firing on so many levels. First and most surprising to him was the physical attraction he found himself feeling for Howard—the first time in his life that such an attraction had not had its initial roots in basic sexual chemistry. There was something about Howard's intelligence, his self-confidence, that appealed to Eric; and the fact that Howard was also a talented and successful writer who respected Eric's work in turn was an aphrodisiac to the ego not to be denied. Eric had also come of age in an era of acute self-consciousness, in which it was impossible for a bright young man with a sense of history not to be noting momentous moments in the biography of the Great Man that might well be written of him. With Howard, Eric found himself feeling that all the skeins of potential were being gathered up and placed in his hands.

Eric mentioned his idea for the pot club story and Nathan's lack of interest in it. Howard chuckled. "No, that's not a *Pendennis* kind of story. Your Carville piece is more up their alley."

"But I don't really want to write that piece," Eric said, surprising himself. "I don't like the man."

"You don't need to like him to write a good piece. I've written plenty of articles on things that didn't fascinate me. One has to eat, you know."

Eric shook his head. "I'd rather starve." Then, hastily, he added, "I don't mean that you're doing anything wrong..."

Howard brushed Eric's sleeve with his hand. "No, no offense taken." Eric was pleased with the intimacy of the gesture, and impressed with the light and casual way Howard made it. "You're young and arrogant." He arched an eyebrow impishly. "Not that there's anything wrong with that."

Eric laughed. "I guess I am. ACT UP made me dogmatic, I guess. How old are you?"

"Me? I'm 40."

"No!" Eric said, genuinely surprised. Now that the revelation impelled closer inspection, he could see Howard's stubbly receding hairline, although Howard had done the wisest thing a balding man could do by shaving his head. The blocky black frames of his glasses drew attention away from the creases around his eyes. But the signs of age only made Howard more attractive to Eric. Perhaps much hay could be made out of the lack of a father in Eric's life, but then much the same could be inferred from him not having older brother or, more broadly, most young artists' desire for a mentor.

"I must say"—Howard shifted away from the subject of his age, which made him feel a little more conscious of the difference in physical gifts between himself and Eric,—"there are certain advantages to being selective in your assignments. It's rather shameful to be too prolific, you know. Think of great artists who are underrated because of it: Haydn, Trollop—"

"Joyce Carol Oates," Eric added.

Howard turned a delighted smile on him. He'd done well so far hiding the light of his attraction to Eric under a bushel, refusing to let Eric's beauty overwhelm him when the likelihood (he insisted to himself) was that the younger man only wished to talk with someone successful in his field. There are certain advantages to age and disappointment, foremost of which is the ability to keep certain of your hopes down, a skill which after a certain age can save you a lot of grief. Still, Howard was now having a hard time suppressing said hopes. Beauty alone can be discounted after enough experience, but beauty and brains is hard to resist at any age.

Eric caught the tenor of Howard's smile and flushed, pleased and excited. He hadn't lacked for sexual outlets in the last few years, but he hadn't really felt this *tug* since...well, he had to admit, since Cal.

As they walked into Big Cup in Chelsea, laughing and talking, heads turned to cruise the new additions to the mix, and expert eyes could not be faulted if they thought that here was a young, happy couple who'd known each other much longer than a few hours.

Neil and Cal had taken a cab back to Neil's apartment in Hell's Kitchen. Inside, Cal was momentarily disoriented. The floor seemed to be—was, he realized, rather dramatically slanted. "Don't worry," Neil said, dropping his jacket on the floor, "you're not high—yet," he grinned. "The foundation's settling on one side of the building faster than on the other. The place should probably be condemned, but, you know..."

Cal nodded. "Yeah, it's New York and we need the apartments."

Their cab ride had been as giddy an experience for Cal as Eric's walk had been for him. *I'm going home with this guy. We're going to fuck, and I don't care, I'm free.* "So what do you get into?" Neil had asked him in the cab.

"I don't know," Cal answered truthfully. "I'm not very experienced."

"Ohh, a virgin, huh?" Neil had asked sardonically, thinking Cal was role playing. Like those who were even now seeing Eric and Howard together, he could not be faulted for his error. Neil was experienced enough to know a hot fuck when he saw one, and there was no doubt of the heat rising off Cal.

"Practically," Cal sighed, and Neil realized he wasn't kidding.

"Well then, you've got a lot to learn."

"I'm ready," Cal said darkly, staring out the window, and even a sexually seasoned if not jaded man like Neil had to be a little afraid—in a good way—of how far Cal was ready to go.

Cal sat down on the couch and watched Neil busy himself in the kitchen uphill. "You like to party?" Neil asked.

"Sure," Cal said. He thought of his days on coke at Goldman, of that one abortive sexual encounter. "Coke?" he asked.

"Nah," Neil said, coming out with a glass pipe. "Crystal. You ever smoke it?"

"I've never done it."

"Oh, man," Neil said, in the admiring tones of a man bent low by the pleasure-delivering power of what was in front of him. "You're in for a wild night."

"I'm ready," Cal repeated. "Show me."

Big Cup was a rare place in those days, before Starbucks nationalized the idea of sipping coffee to contempo tunes while slouched in big chairs and couches. Certainly, it was a funkier, less made-to-order atmosphere; unlike Starbucks, the colors clashed and, surely deliberately, none of the furniture matched. "I love this place," Howard enthused. "It's so nice to go somewhere gay that's not a bar."

"It's still pretty cruisy," Eric said, noticing elements in the crowd that wouldn't have been out of place in San Francisco's Café Flore during the ACT UP's heyday—ostentatiously reading the tome du jour or biting pens and frowning over their own words with far more furrows in their brows than would have been plowed in private. Eric looked around and was regarded in turn, and for a moment Howard felt foolish for thinking Eric might have found him attractive. He wondered about the place of that young man at the party in Eric's life and asked him, "Who was that guy you said goodbye to at the party?"

"Oh, that was Cal. We were..." *We were what?* he asked himself. Friends? No, they hardly knew each other. "We knew each other back in Reno, where I grew up, and we ran into each other today in town and I invited him along to the party."

"Ah." Howard noticed the perturbation on Eric's face at the subject of Cal. Eric realized that he had given Cal more weight on his mind than he'd intended to show to Howard, and the only thing for it now would be to explain in full.

"I was very attracted to him when we were younger," he said, still young enough to think of four years earlier as an aeon ago. "But it didn't go anywhere. He was very closeted, came from this family of...right-wing kooks, basically. His sister wrote this really funny book about the family, after she'd had an abortion."

"Gina Hewitt," Howard supplied. "I met her on her book tour."

Eric yelped. "You're kidding! That's amazing!"

Howard shrugged. "Not really. It's a small world. I recall her mentioning her brother in passing, not too much detail—how they used to have to wave signs outside abortion clinics with huge gory color photos of dead babies on them. I suppose that would fuck anybody up."

"Well, it fucked him up. And it's too bad. He's smart, he's got a great sense of humor, he's—" Eric stopped himself before he could say Cal was gorgeous. "I'm sorry. That's rude, talking about someone else like that—someone who's not even my ex. I mean, it's still rude, you know. It's like talking about your ex on your first date with someone else..." He sighed, realizing he'd made a jumble of it. "I should just shut up."

Howard raised an eyebrow. "But we're not on a first date, are we?"

"Well," Eric said, flushing. "Kinda maybe?" He felt stupid all of a sudden, like an awkward teenager, little realizing how charming that can be to an older man who hasn't yet tired of always having to lead.

"You're a gorgeous, brilliant young man, Eric, and anybody would be lucky to be your friend, let alone something more." Howard was pleased with himself at that; he'd expressed interest without expressing hope, therefore maintaining his dignity. The young, he well knew, were fickle; they could be wildly enthusiastic about an idea—or a person—one day and the next be completely apathetic, having made a snap decision that they didn't like that anymore. Their communication skills were often lacking, and they often couldn't tell you why you weren't it today when you had been so very much it yesterday. Sometimes this was because all they really knew was that they'd found something else they didn't want (you), one more step in the process of elimination before they found, if lucky, what they did want.

Eric blushed. "Well, I like you. And I find you attractive." *There*, he thought, *the bridge was thrown across.* He couldn't help but recall that moment in the park with Cal and feel a moment of dread as Howard looked away as if, like Cal, he had remembered, too, something that made it impossible to walk across.

"Inhale slowly and steadily," Neil said. "Don't suck on it like a pot pipe. Suck just like you're taking a long breath." Cal put his lips on the pipe as Neil applied the torch, watching the white crystals in the bowl turn to amber liquid. "OK, now." Cal began to inhale. There was no irritation, no cough to suppress as there was with weed. The bowl of the pipe swirled and bubbled like a crystal ball in a movie, coming to life to show the future. When Cal's lungs were full, he nodded, and Neil let the torch go out and took the pipe away, sucking the rest of the vapors out of the pipe as the drug recrystallized in the bowl.

Cal held the hit as long as he could, then blew out a huge cloud. "Whoa, you got a good hit," Neil said without breathing.

"Did...I?" Cal failed to finish the question as the drug flooded his brain. The first thing he felt was this sense of amazement, of wonder, followed by a thrumming in his groin like the afterglow of the best orgasm he'd ever had. "Oh, my God," he said involuntarily. He was ignorant of the chemical processes at work, would have been ignorant of them even if he'd understood them, because intellect was suspended by a wave of pure pleasure. He had felt a good deal of pleasure on coke, but he'd always snorted it. That sort of pleasure had always crawled up on him; it had never been enough to wipe away the rage and pain and hate and boredom and frustration and everything else that had just now been banished from his life, never knocked him upside the head like *this*.

Then Neil touched him and he gasped. It was just a finger along his forearm, but Neil knew that was more than enough at this point. "Fuck. Oh fuck." Cal was beyond words. This was happiness, this was what made people smile. Everything was all right, everything felt *so fucking good.* This was what his parents and their preachers had meant when they described heaven, a place with no pain or sorrow, only joy. Where everything was white fluffy clouds, just like the ones he and Neil were blowing out of their lungs.

Neil was slipping out of his clothes and pulling Cal's off him. Even the feeling of his shirt coming over his head, brushing every tiny filament of hair on his body, was orgasmic. And then, as Neil began to kiss him and his lips exploded, as his torso pressed against Neil's, he truly knew what he had been missing, but there were no recriminations, no sorrows, no ways to dwell on regret and pain because now was all there was and now felt *so good* and nothing mattered outside his skin except what touched it to give it pleasure.

"There's something I need to tell you," Howard said. "Before we go any further."

Eric raced ahead. "You're HIV-positive."

Howard was surprised. "Yes."

"I figured that out when you told me about your pot club membership."

Howard blushed and quickly calculated; had all Eric's earnest protestations of interest in Howard come before or after that? After, came the sum, to his surprise.

"I don't care. I mean, I really don't care. And I know what I'm talking about, Howard. I was in ACT UP, I know how to have safe sex. I've had HIV-positive boyfriends. It really doesn't matter at all."

This, Howard had to admit, wasn't the voice of a boy ignorant of the dangers. Eric was mature, intelligent, sexually aware. Howard knew the difference in tone between a young man who didn't want to think about the danger if it interfered with his pleasure (and besides, he was going to live forever anyway) and a man like Eric—yes, a man, not a boy, though still so young and beautiful.

"And," Eric added boldly, "I'd really like to go home with you tonight. Not that I sleep with everyone I meet the first time," he added, but Howard brushed that away; they were gay men and didn't judge anyone on their hormonal behavior. "I mean, if you find me attractive, too..." Eric added, remembering Emma's words about beauty being in the eye of the beholder.

Howard smiled, touched that Eric allowed that someone might not find him attractive. "I do. But I have a rule, one that's worked for me for a long time. You sleep on that decision to sleep with me. If you still want to get together next time, then that'll be a different story."

"Why does that work for you?" Eric asked. "I'm not arguing, I'm just curious."

Howard sighed. "I've just found in many cases when you tell someone...I tell someone," he modified, remembering to make it first person, "that I'm HIV-positive, and he says, 'Oh, that doesn't matter'—because nobody is ever going to say to your face, 'That's terrible, get away.' But then he doesn't call you, or lets the machine pick up when you call him, because it does matter." He shrugged. "Because why should you date someone who's going to die, when you can date someone who isn't?"

"We're all going to die," Eric said, feeling an empathetic pain for Howard. He remembered how Patrick had refused to tell people he was HIV-positive because it was like crossing over a line, beyond which in the eyes of so many people you weren't a person any more; you were already dead, to be buried and forgotten.

"Some of us sooner than later," Howard said, giving Eric a direct look. Eric knew what it implied here, now, in 1992: Love me, watch me die.

"We're all going to die," Eric repeated, and Howard smiled.

That there could be circles of Heaven, Cal would no longer doubt. He had thought, as the first hit off the pipe did its work, that there could be no greater joy, and yet there was, each hit he took giving wider range to his capacity for pleasure. Neil was adept at this sort of thing, and Cal found himself discovering just what was possible, and pleasurable, between two men. That there was pleasure in pain, he'd had an inkling of from the porn flicks he'd watched, but here was confirmation. Neil bit his nipples, smacked his ass, smacked his cock and balls, and all of it was oh-my-God so good. "You like that, don't you bitch?" Neil asked, and there was no comedy in it. Yes, yes, he did, and he wanted to be a bitch, a dog, a punk, to be taken and used and abused. He was being punished for his pleasure, as surely as he'd been raised to believe he would be, and that made it all right, made it all the better.

As Neil shoved him onto the bed facedown, some dark door opened in Cal, some black-winged beast took flight. Neil's tongue, his fingers, then his cock entered Cal's ass, and there was no conversation, no intermission to discuss the Issue, there was only this ring of pain and then, deeper in, a searing pressure that met with a response from his brain that was even more pleasure. It was skin on skin, hard and fast and rough, and the glass had been broken, the border had been crossed, and all that he had seen and desired and refused was his—and who in their right mind would do anything that might interrupt this, anything that might stem the pleasure even a fraction? Neil was deep within him, he was a virgin no more, the drugs saturated his brain, and there was nothing but now, and Jesus Christ, now felt so good, he was in Heaven.

Eric and Howard walked down the street together, pleasantly stunned by their conversation. "I feel like I'm in a Henry

James novel," Howard said. "One of those moments when the characters realize something momentous has happened. *The Golden Bowl*, maybe."

"Bah," Eric said. "Early Henry James was better. Before his sentences became those long, endlessly curly wrought-iron thickets that went on for pages until someone finally says out loud, 'That's how it is, isn't it,' and the other one says, 'Yes, it is,' and by then you don't know what the hell what is or how it is or who's talking. Edith Wharton could say in 200 pages what Henry James never said in 600."

Howard laughed. "He is an acquired taste." Nonetheless, it was clear Eric knew exactly what he was talking about, however much he disapproved of the author. There was something very comforting to both men in being with someone with whom they could talk like this—and so casually, Howard marveled; he'd had satisfying intellectual relationships with boyfriends before, but this—this irreverent fun that Eric was capable of—this was new. The others had always been declaiming for an exam committee, showing off their erudition; Eric's blunt, cruel dismissal of James would never have flown in academe, would never have come from the mouths of any of the clever, learned men Howard had known before. And he couldn't in good conscience fail to admit, none of them had ever been as, well, hot as Eric.

Eric could feel it, too; this sense of something being built, each of them in turn supplying a beam for the framework, a brick for the fireplace, both marveling how well each piece fit. And he had a feeling that the sex would be fun; experience had given Eric, like Neil, a sense of chemistry, a foreknowledge of fun. Safe sex wouldn't be a limit because they were both too brainy for the experience to be purely physical in the first place; it would require finesse to introduce the condom at the right time in the right way. Done right, it would make the other smile and improve the experience. Each was sexually mature enough to know that abandon could be scheduled at the proper time and that this was not a contradiction in terms.

Tomorrow, Eric thought, feeling a heady sense of anticipation.

He smiled at Howard, and got the same smile in return. There was something to look forward to now, if not tomorrow then someday soon, and again after that if all went well. After all, miraculously to Eric, they both lived in San Francisco. There was all the time in the world.

CHAPTER FOUR
PARIS IS BURNING

It didn't used to be like this, Eric thought stubbornly, looking out the window of his mother's room at the St. Francis. Union Square might have looked shimmery to the tourist's eye, but to Eric's the rain only made the filthy square look sticky as he thought of what the water had rehydrated: bum piss, gum, pigeon shit. It had been raining since Emma's arrival, and every afternoon the weather had thwarted their plans to do something. Eric offered to rent a car, but Emma told him not to. It wasn't the money, he knew; she would spend every penny she had on this trip if she could. In some way he thought she was actually glad for the rain, glad for the excuse to sit and rest and watch and talk. It was Eric who thought he'd go crazy if he sat still another moment.

There was truth in his thought: It hadn't been like this. Well, it had, but not since he'd lived here. He knew that he'd moved here during the drought, that he'd gotten lucky, that normal weather patterns were resuming or, due to various Ninas and Ninos he didn't understand, getting worse. What he meant, of course, was that life hadn't been like this before—life had been summer for two years now, and all of a sudden it wasn't summer anymore and never would be again. Perpetually inclement weather is the worst environment for the depressed, as Eric was discovering.

"Would you hand me the phone?" Emma asked, and Eric rushed to bring it to her. She smiled. "Want anything from room service?"

He shook his head. "No thanks."

She nodded. "I'll order you a club sandwich."

Eric didn't argue. He tried not to look at his mother's arm as she dialed, tried to concentrate on being happy that she felt like eating. It was the first time in his life he'd had to try to be happy, and he sucked at it.

Emma ordered enough food for six hungry people and then dialed what Eric knew was his and Howard's number. "He's already on his way," Eric said. "He has to stop at the pot store." Emma had called Howard earlier and asked him to perform this favor, but she'd forgotten.

She looked abashed, in truth more for Eric's sake than her own. She'd gotten accustomed to her loss of short-term memory, a product of the weed in association with the legal medications, but she knew it was painful to Eric.

Then she smiled and pulled the pipe out of her caftan. "Well, I think I have a resin hit in here. Do you mind?"

The first day in the doctor's office, she'd known, and she'd made her decisions then and stuck to them since. And one of those decisions was that she wouldn't suffer in any fashion. Eric would suffer when she was gone, and there was nothing she could do about that; all that was left was to take this time and enjoy it. Emma liked being alive, enjoyed it, and she'd like to live some more but chances were not good and that's life, too.

She hadn't smoked pot in years, but she took it back up the day of her first chemo treatment. As Cal had found years earlier, THC coats life with a sugary glaze, and at this moment she needed to be glazed.

Eric shook his head, "No, of course not. Go ahead." Emma had not been the only one to take up habitual pot smoking recently. Eric had started again some months before the news of his mother's cancer, but he hadn't let her know that because she would have wanted to know why. The last few years he'd barely touched a glass of wine, he'd been so committed to his health and fitness, and as to why he'd taken up weed with a vengeance recently, well, he must never tell her, and she must never know.

Things always went wrong, but for a while it had been the things that hadn't mattered. Sure, there was a recession, and people in publishing were even more hesitant than ever to commit to anything, but how could stupid things like a recession get you down when you were in love? And Eric was in love for the first time, really—the way adults fall in love, not kids.

Howard had been surprised when Eric had called him the next day, Eric could tell. It pissed Eric off to think that people could be that fucking shallow, that they would throw someone like Howard out of their lives because he had HIV. He himself was determined to make a friend of Howard even if the sex didn't go anywhere—and, it had to be admitted, to Eric if the sex hadn't gone anywhere there wouldn't have been anywhere for the rest of the relationship to go. But that hadn't been a problem. Howard had been more nervous than he had during their first night together, constantly breaking off in embarrassed laughter after a particularly passionate attack on some part of Eric. "I'm sorry," he laughed.

"For what?" Eric asked.

"For being so greedy, for eating you like a peach."

Eric smiled and offered up his peaches for consumption. He was in his physical prime at that moment and knew it. For anyone who liked his type, he was a dream come true. Some dewy drops of youth still clung to his face; maturity had hardened his jawline and given his eyes a firmer set, but the skin over that jaw still glowed and the eyes still shone. Rigorous gym work had framed off his shoulders and chest, which he showed off in conformity to gay law by shaving it (Howard would put a stop to that). The ridges of his abs were infomercial-ready and his wide square hips were still minimized by a plunging V into his crotch. Best of all to Howard, there was nothing stiff about Eric; it was obvious this body *belonged* to him, it was not something that looked forced upon him. For ten years now, gay America had plunged into bodybuilding, as if accumulating sheer mass was at least a psychic bulwark against AIDS, and the streets were full of men whose bodies had lost their natural shape and charm in pursuit of "more." Eric still walked with grace despite his size, fluid and loose and natural; there were for Howard's taste too many men walking the streets with broomsticks up their asses, arms nearly T'd out by overdeveloped lats, all made even worse by the frowns on their faces, as if they ever unpursed their lips all the air would come rushing out and they'd slump over, spent and exhausted and empty.

Howard was one of those men, Eric had discovered, who look better out of clothes than in. This was partly because his wardrobe was so deliberately nerdy; had it been better cut his assets would have been obvious. Many a slender man has laid claim in a personals ad to a "swimmer's build," but—minus the powerful shoulders—this was what Howard had. His muscles weren't large, but they were defined, and he had surprisingly smooth skin for a 40-year-old. (Howard told Eric that first night he was just lucky, but later Eric would discover Howard's skin-care products, chuckle, and say nothing.) Without his glasses, Howard had a boyish quality that Eric had always and would always find irresistible. Both men were sufficiently endowed and both were versatile, though it took Howard a while to feel psychologically comfortable while physically dominating Eric. In short, the sexual attractions and the sex were both plentiful.

Back in San Francisco, they had kept seeing plenty of each other, but not too much. Howard had a work ethic about his writing that Eric both admired and emulated. They would go to the gym in the morning to work out, spotting each other and encouraging each other to push the limits a little further, a regimen that because of its physical benefits and male bonding quality enriched all their interactions sexually and conversationally. Then both would disappear into their projects for the day, usually meeting again in the evening.

Egging each other on to new things, in and out of bed, became an exciting game. Howard defied his fear of heights through skydiving with Eric, and Eric overcame his fear of sushi at Isobune, and both of them helped each other through rough patches in their work, suggesting avenues out of quandaries. Howard once started a stimulating conversation by suggesting that the risks they took were a replacement for the risk they weren't taking in bed, seeing as how they scrupulously observed safe sex. Eric needed to be hastily reassured that the sex was definitely exciting, that Howard's point was that maybe risk was part of life and if it had to be avoided in bed, it could be found and shared elsewhere. They could talk about things like that for hours; there were times when Howard was talking and Eric just wanted to throw him down and fuck him—he was so damn sexy when he was on fire like that, just reaching out and spinning these webs and that lovely soft voice of his...

They quickly became one of those couples people talk about with a note of envy. Gay men to whom Eric embodied the magazine ideal were always surprised to see him with Howard, and the two of them so plainly keyed into each other physically. Both successful writers, people would ask them when they planned to collaborate, and they'd look at each other and laugh. Consult each other, yes, constantly, but collaborate, no, never—each was too possessive of the final outcome to allow someone else to alter that. Most people loved them, and the few who hated them, hated them in that way of people who see what they themselves want and think they can never have.

And their lives together had been perfect. "I'm waiting," Howard said one night after Eric had expressed his happiness.

"For what?"

"The punishment."

"For what?"

"For being this happy."

Eric had laughed. "People don't get punished just for being happy. People are supposed to be happy." To his surprise, Howard had not continued the conversation. Later he would put the pieces together and realize that by this time Howard's health had already begun its decline.

Now, Eric thought, looking out the window so he wouldn't have to look at his mother and cry. *Now the punishment is here.* "It didn't used to be like this," he'd say of the weather now, and people who had been here longer than he had said, "Oh, yes, it used to be like this all the time. This is the way it normally is. What you experienced was the freak incident."

Howard arrived from the Cannabis Buyer's Club, and all three of them got stoned on T2, the best shit available. Already determined to smile, Emma's now became even broader, Howard nodded with an epicure's satisfaction with the quality, and Eric was merely content to watch the lines of time blur. Cal had discovered that THC could keep him from dwelling on sex for too long and was thus able to delay his sexual awakening for several years; Eric was now using the gift of a short attention span to avoid thinking about the Truck—Patrick's metaphor for, well, all of it. He'd told Howard about the Truck back when everything had been perfect. But no matter how much he thought about the Truck these days, he couldn't ever mention it to Howard again; he had to remember that the Truck was too awful to talk about now.

Howard wasn't the only one dying. Eric had gotten to the point where he couldn't look at the gay paper anymore, because he knew he'd see a picture in the obituaries of someone he'd known. No, nobody he loved, nobody he really cared about, just all the people he knew, had ever known, exiting his life vertically, the fabric of his life unraveling around him. Those obituaries were part of the Truck, too; he couldn't avoid it hitting him, but he didn't have to stare into its headlights every second either.

"This is worth every penny," Emma said, eating some more ice cream, having timed her room-service order to Howard's arrival with perfection. Eric and Howard nodded wordlessly, even Eric momentarily lifted up out of the ditch. "This," they knew, meant not the pricey pot, the expensive hotel suite, or the exorbitantly priced room-service ice cream, but any and all of the above, this moment of peace and calm and contentment.

Emma had walked out of her doctor's office and driven straight to the airport. There was no way she would tell her son over the phone, nor would she even tell him she was coming without explaining—nothing to provoke anxiety without knowing its cause. She herself had been in such a situation once and had never had a worse day in her life. Fortunately, the flight from Reno to San Francisco was short, and she knew that Eric and Howard kept Calvinist work schedules and she wouldn't find herself on the doorstep of an empty house on her arrival.

Eric had been stunned to answer the door and find Emma. "Mom!" Initially delighted, he'd turned for a moment to shout out for Howard when Emma had grabbed his arm and said, "Eric, let's talk in private a moment."

News like Emma's cracks your skull open like an egg and the brain, suddenly freed of its casing, expands, axons reach out to now distant dendrites as nothing rushes in to fill the void, a great silent nothing that renders thought impossible. There had been little cracks, sure, each time Howard had come home from the doctor more unwilling to discuss his latest T-cell count, or each time a few more prophylactic prescriptions had to be filled. Eric had felt useful then; his work in ACT UP had familiarized him with the AIDS Drug Assistance Project, which provided meds to those too middle-class for MediCal but not rich enough to pay for their own pills, and he had attacked Howard's paperwork with zest, glad to be a patient advocate again. And truth be told, Howard had needed one; Eric felt himself fighting his lover's fatalism each time things got worse, screaming at Howard once and only once: in face of the need to sign up at the San Francisco AIDS Foundation Howard had given him what Eric called "one of your goddamn shrugs."

The San Francisco AIDS Foundation had been the first dark tunnel of Eric's new life. This was an institution whose only real goal was self-perpetuation and whose essential service was keeping graphic designers employed by generating safe-sex "materials." The AIDS Foundation would swallow buckets of money to produce posters full of hot men urging other hot men to be safe. Criticism of the foundation's use of hot young chiseled white men in its campaigns led them to begin also using hot young chiseled African-American, Latino, and Asian men. ("The unhot," Howard had noted tartly, "can drop dead for all anyone cares.") Posters were plastered around town, estimates were made of how many people walked past and checked out the hot boys, and smug press releases were issued announcing how many at-risk individuals had been reached. This bureaucratic toadstool acted as the gatekeeper for AIDS services in San Francisco; a good number of social workers were paid to register people like Howard so that he could register all over again at other smaller agencies that actually provided direct services.

After San Francisco AIDS Foundation had fucked up Howard's Social Security Disability application by handing it to a trainee, Eric joined what over the years would become a rising chorus of community loathing for the foundation, a chorus that would do nothing to change things because the foundation's executive director was an uptown socialite. Her chums on the board represented all the major media outlets, who ensured that their reporters never wrote anything negative about the trough the foundation had become for the director. (She had become director by heading up a search committee to find a new director, only to end up selecting herself and her hand-picked cadre.)

Eric had in fact been so enraged that he'd contemplated rejoining ACT UP, but he didn't have the heart for it, didn't have the heart to be fighting so much wickedness at the same time he'd have to deal with ACT UP's internal struggles. Howard was his struggle now, and that was all he could manage. Besides, ACT UP was becoming a joke, a bunch of crackpots who said HIV did not cause AIDS and that the answer lay in laetrile, orgone therapy, drinking your own pee—a thousand absurd miracle cures.

But he had been able to manage; while navigating the sticky sea of paper and appointments and approvals, he'd also found many good people as horrified and concerned and committed as he was (none of them ever worked very long for the AIDS Foundation). Eric continued to make sure Howard had everything he needed and never let himself sink down into the lassitude that was softly enfolding Howard. "I'm just tired," Howard would say on his worst days, and had Cal been there he would have felt a chill; it was same tone his father had used in his last days.

Emma had sat Eric down and explained everything. It was breast cancer, advanced, and it had spread to the liver. There would be radiation and chemotherapy and a radical mastectomy, but because it had gone to the liver, because it was spreading so hard and fast, her chances for long-term survival were not good.

She then laid out for him in detail what she had done to prepare. Eric's days in ACT UP had not been for nothing, she insisted, because he had taught her what happens to the sick in America to a depth of knowledge she'd never considered acquiring and never thought she'd need to know. Several years earlier, she had quitclaimed the house to him—it was and had for some years been his sole property; Medicare and Medicaid would not be able to take it to pay her bills. She had been paying him a modest rent of $400 a month on the house for a number of years, depositing the funds in a savings account he'd opened as a teenager and forgotten to close. It now contained about $25,000, and that and the house would be all she could leave him.

She would, and did, attempt all medical means, but after six months she was still terminal, six months to live, and she was now going to spend the rest of her money enjoying what was left of her life, and she hoped he would help her spend it and not resent her decision.

Of course Eric was in no condition to utter the formal polite disclaimers. He sat there and could handle only one thought: *This is the end of everything, this is too much, there's nothing, it's over.*

They'd been stoned for about a half an hour, but even stoned, Emma could pick up her son's mood as the high dipped from its initial saturation point and Eric got quiet and distant again. "Do you know what I'd love to have right now?" she asked.

Eric looked up, his eagerness to please still unaffected by all that was happening. "No, what?"

"Fruit comfits. French candied fruit. Little plums and apricots and cherries. I haven't had those since I lived in Paris. I'd kill for some fruit comfits."

"They have them at Real Foods," Howard said. "Out on Polk."

Eric grabbed his jacket. "I'll be back."

"Let me give you some money," Emma said, but Eric shook his head and repeated, "I'll be back."

The door shut behind him and Emma and Howard looked at each other. "I'm worried about him," Emma said.

"So am I," Howard assented. They looked at each other for a moment and burst out laughing at the same time. Nothing is quite as fun as two people getting stoned when they both already have a sense of the absurd. Emma wasn't supposed to know about Howard; Howard knew this from Eric's strict injunctions, and Emma knew it from the pale look of terror on Eric's face when Emma enquired Howard about his health, about which his words lied better than his complexion. But they both knew where they were and where they were going and because of that they could laugh about it. Eric couldn't, and they couldn't around him, because being in the absurd moment and watching someone you love experiencing absurdity are two very different states of being.

"I'm sorry I can't leave him more money, but at this point it's either spend it on my hospital bill, or on weed and fruit comfits." She shrugged. "That's America."

"We're fine financially," Howard lied, because he lived in America, too. Soon he would be needing more care, and that would mean MediCal, and that would mean draining his assets to the bottom of the barrel. He was now collecting Social Security and California State Disability; because he'd paid into the system for so long, the combined checks provided him with about $2,000 a month. However, when he went on MediCal, the state would expect him to pay what was called a "share of cost," which would mean every penny he received that put him above the poverty level.

"How the fuck does anybody expect you to live on $630 a month in San Francisco!" Eric had raged. "It's just an organized way to *kill off* sick poor people without looking like you're doing it!" Howard almost shrugged but chose to cough instead, because that wouldn't get him in trouble. The money would be needed as he got sicker, and he, too, was paying Eric "rent" on their flat in the Castro so that there would be something left later. When the state disability checks would run out, he'd have $1,100 a month from SSDI and would have to pay "only" $500 a month for his medical care. Until that time, he'd take what care was available at the public clinic at San Francisco General. Hieronymous Bosch would have had a wealth of material to sketch there, a clinic where a patient as likely to catch TB as be cured of anything. And when the state money would run out, Howard could afford to go to a real doctor's office—if he could find one who'd take MediCal.

Emma fixed her wide china-blue eyes on Howard. "I'm sure you are," she said and Howard had to look away; Emma's firm gaze was not one many liars could stand up to. "I just wonder how he's going to cope when…"

She left it hanging, but Howard was keen of mind and could spot a judicious ambivalence when it was dangled before him. Howard very much wanted to talk to Emma about what she was going through, about how she was managing to be so cheerful, even though the ice was breaking up all around her and the river would soon be sweeping her away. He wanted to know for his own sake, and he got the feeling she, too, wanted to talk about death—hers and his. But he'd promised Eric he wouldn't mention his health status to her; she knew he was HIV-positive, and having see him regularly ever since Eric had proudly brought him home, the first man since Mikey to have had that privilege, she could see the difference in him.

Howard admired Emma's intellect; that was partly why he so wanted to talk about all this with her, to get her insights as he only could in a two-way conversation—but Eric had blocked his way. He loved Eric, and Emma was Eric's mother, not his; the decision had to be Eric's.

"Eric is young and strong and resilient," Howard said. "He'll manage. It'll be terrible for a while but isn't it always?"

Emma nodded. "Yes, it is." Diplomatically, she ensured the subject would be soon forgotten by holding the pipe out. "Would you be a dear and refill this?"

The rain stopped while Eric was walking up Geary to Polk, but a chill wet wind came up and made for miserable travel. San

Francisco is a small walkable city, especially for somebody with legs like Eric's, and the public transportation is so terrible that it's often faster to walk—certainly more comfortable. By the time the 38 Geary buses come (they travel in packs of four or five), the first ones would be jam-packed with wet people—and you have to get on the first ones because so often the last, totally empty ones would pass you by no matter how frantically you waved. This was the sort of thing about the city Eric dwelt on now, hating it for having betrayed him.

"It" is of course an example of anthropomorphism; cities do not have emotions or intents. But this city had been sold on the open market for years as the city over the rainbow, the Happiest Place on Earth, the place that made everything better. But, for Eric, it was a city of the dead and the petty and the irrelevant. Everything had gone to pieces here all at once, and it had felt as if nobody cared, nobody wanted to hear it, nobody wanted to think about it. Eyes closed and heads down, San Franciscans went on pretending little cable cars climbed halfway to the stars; they threw out one mayor because he was John Major–gray and replaced him with a new one who had "style." Everyone agreed that San Francisco needed a mayor with style! "Hooray! Look at his hat! We're saved!" Never mind that the new mayor was a political hack who'd spent his life working for the tobacco lobby in Sacramento and would do little if anything about the city's crumbling infrastructure—no! He had *style*, just like the colorful old rogues of the Barbary Coast, and when, lo and behold, San Franciscans discovered he had more in common with those rogues than just charm, they were shocked, shocked. The ones who lived for the myth, who refused to acknowledge everything that was killing that myth, infuriated Eric to no end.

He'd gotten a writing gig easily enough at one of the local gay papers, was in fact handed a column within weeks of handing in his first freelance piece. There he would discover that the public face of the gay community was as much a mask as any public face, that there was just as much rivalry and greed and pettiness, only all of it had to be swept under the rug. We all had to hold hands and sing like Whos in Whoville because it was the only way to save ourselves from Jesse. And in his column Eric had made the mistake of calling people in the gay community on their shit, such as the independent film director whose whole crew had worked on spec. Rather than paying them, he'd taken the money and used it to send himself for several years to the Berlin Film Festival, where he could be adored—"They love me in Germany!" And when Eric wrote about this—indeed, when he wrote about any malfeasance in the community—the ones caught with their hands in the honeypot would always bray, "It's so terrible that you wrote that! It's so hurtful to the community!" He hated the way these vampires hid behind "the community," as if being gay meant nobody else gay could say anything bad about you—"Think of what it would do to the community!" Eric wasn't a shit stirrer; he just had a (perhaps too) finely honed sense of outrage and absolutely no appetite for dropping names and kissing ass instead of naming names and kicking ass, tasks for which he was eminently well suited.

Then, recently, there had been the death of a famous gay author, and Eric had lost his job because he had refused to join in the beatification process of a man he felt had hated being gay, hated the gay community, and despised all the freedoms Eric had learned to cherish. And Eric's crime had been to say that during the beatification (which had become all the more important thanks to the presence of some cracker preacher who traveled around the country to funerals of AIDS victims just so he could hold up a sign to inform the departed's grieving relatives that GOD HATES FAGS). It wasn't a matter of speaking ill of the dead; it was a matter of having a platform where you had to say something and what you had to say was against the grain. It hadn't helped that ever since Eric had gotten the column he'd had an enemy at the paper, a man who worked in the production department and had wanted the column for himself when it had come open but hadn't gotten it. Later, Eric discovered that this man often scribbled tart, sour, bitchy little notes on the preliminary layout of his column in blue pencil, notes the publisher would see whenever he approved the paper before it went to bed. So of course, when the shit came down and the publisher had to decide what to do about Eric, there was Jim in production, whispering in his ear. It was some small satisfaction to him to discover later that the arts editor informed this person that he may have lost Eric the column, but he hadn't and would never gain it for himself. *O but we must never talk about that in public,* Eric thought. *Whos in Whoville, we all hold hands and sing and love each other to death.*

It was as well he lost the column; when he'd started it, he'd been popular—funny, clever, a reason to turn to the second page of the arts section. Of course, when he'd started it, he'd been happy, his career going well and his love life a pop song. But as Howard's health went downhill, Eric's rage mounted and his column changed, went from funny to angry without the scalpel edge his humor had had at first. By the time he lost the gig (which only paid $35 a week but was worth gold in exposure) he had also found himself in his first instance of writer's block. And when the column was gone, something that at least forced 900 words a week out of him, there was nothing left to make him write. The recession had put the kibosh on any more book deals; houses were terrified of buying anything less than a sure blockbuster. Most of his will had been directed into ensuring Howard's well-being, and the walls he had to throw himself against on Howard's behalf left little for the bruising and humiliating process of hustling freelance article proposals.

A hustler on Polk asked Eric for a light and he gave it to him. His first instinct had been to say "Don't smoke," but that was no longer true. Eric had taken up pot smoking with a vengeance when Howard had; initially he'd loved the way pot allowed him to generate ideas and fancies without ever having to do anything with them, about them, without having to market them or promote them. His hips were now starting to thicken as he fell victim to the dietary habits that come with continuous low blood sugar. Howard didn't miss the V of his crotch or the six pack abs; in fact, for the first time in his life he found the presence of a—slight, he was a gay man after all—padding of fat on his lover to be strangely reassuring.

A year earlier Eric had the privilege of interviewing Anne Rice, one of his favorite writers. He'd had to fight his editor (an opera queen who'd give endless column inches to the San Francisco Opera, even though they looked down on the paper so utterly that they wouldn't give him press tickets) to get as much as the interview into the paper as he did, about a third of the original text. The Anne Rice interview soon proved to be the one thing people mentioned to him most often at parties, envious that he'd been able to sit in a hotel room alone with Herself. Rice had lived in San Francisco for years, and her daughter had died of leukemia there. He remembered how she'd talked about how hard it is to be unhappy in the Happiest Place on Earth, how death here is not to be "dwelt on": you're supposed to buy the notion that a white light takes the dead, and they're happy so why aren't you?—because if you're unhappy here, there's something wrong with you. If you're miserable, you know, you're just spoiling the view for the rest of us. After her daughter's death, Rice had moved back to New Orleans.

Eric knew how she must have felt as he wandered through Real Foods. The people in here were happy—prosperous, at least, or they wouldn't be shopping here. Eric had once temped for a woman who'd taken him at the last minute as her replacement date to a pro tennis match at Stanford. She had driven, and he asked her if on the way back they could stop at the grocery store. Sure, she'd replied, and he'd found himself for the first time at Real Foods. Shocked by the prices, he'd spent $30 on the makings for a chicken dinner (he'd planned to spend $10 at Safeway). "It's awfully expensive in there," he said afterward.

"Oh, it's so worth it to get good quality, though," she said, shaking her expensive pineapple-blond hair. "Organic food is so much better for you."

Some of us, Eric thought, can't afford what's so much better for us, but he knew she was wealthy and had no idea that for some people, including Eric, better quality food wasn't an affordable option. "California! Where the living is easy!" the bank commercial had proclaimed when he'd moved here, a montage of golden joggers jogging against golden bridges and golden sunsets, the summit of joy attained via a cable car ride, smiling faces everywhere. It was easy for women like that; it was the nicest place in the world to be rich. Sure, they cared about AIDS, threw their money down that black hole, the AIDS Foundation, because it was run by people like them.

Charity was what people of that sort did best, right?

He'd always had a good time in here with Howard, who loved to watch what he called "the Alex Katz people, all ponytails and Cabriolets." Eric had had to go to the library and find a book of Katz paintings to find out what Howard was talking about. Katz's women: serene, prosperous, slim, wide-eyed earth mothers in nice simple dresses with glasses of wine in hand, enjoying another beautiful California day, every day, forever.

He knew prosperity was no guarantee of happiness; he and Howard had discussed that, too, in muted tones back at the meat counter, cruising the cute boy who was deboning their chicken for them. "But their kind of unhappiness is that Iris Murdoch kind, you know," Howard said. "The crises of over-educated rich people. 'How can we be good? What is good? Oh dear!—the turtle's in the swimming pool, or the bird's flown in the window, or the dog's swum out to sea. Suddenly it's all clear, oh dear.'" Eric had laughed hugely and freely, but now the memory of laughter was pain in itself.

He found himself in line behind a reasonably attractive man in his early 40s, still fit and trim and tan. He had a House of Blues baseball cap on, and Eric invented a life for him that probably wasn't too far off the mark: he worked in a skyscraper, in one of the sort of finance cowboy jobs that Cal had once thought himself destined for, he made six—no, seven figures, quite possibly a good deal of it going to a first wife. He had an expensive sports car sitting outside, Eric wagered, and had a tendency to play rather loudly the sort of music that would make people think he was cool—reggae, grunge, the blues indicated by his hat—the sort of music that had nothing to do with his life, not really, but because he hadn't really suffered, he didn't know the difference between suffering and neurosis. He used to live in the suburbs with the wife and kids but had moved back into the city for his second childhood. He was buying fruit, and some wine. Eric speculated that the man didn't cook; certainly, he could afford to eat out *in perpetuum.*

Eric had never been raised a child of privilege, though Emma could have afforded to do so. Instead, she had deliberately raised him as a middle-class boy, equipped to earn his way in the world, his only sense of entitlement that which came with his physical and mental gifts. He and Howard had had another good laugh over the way money was handled (or, more often, avoided as filthy and unmentionable) in fiction; after Howard had made him read *The Ambassadors*, Eric announced he would be writing a doctoral thesis on "Unspeakable Toilet Fortunes in Henry James." UTFs had become a running gag, even though Eric as an adult now knew that his mother had herself been heiress to a relatively small UTF.

With a sudden flash of insight he was truly grateful to his mother. What if he'd been raised a floppy-haired cool-eyed scion of privilege? What would he do now in the face of death and destruction? How well would he handle the loss of everything that had ever mattered? He'd always felt happiness was a right, but never an entitlement due him in his station.

The man in front of Eric caught him looking and gave him a nod. Jarred, Eric nodded back; suddenly, he could see himself in this line and had his own absurd moment. *I look.like one of them*, he thought. *I'm young and handsome and certainly not starving, and I have a bottle of wine and some fruit comfits in my hand, not so unlike the man in front of me, I look like one of them, and there isn't a one of them who knows there's been a mistake. I shouldn't be here, buying wine and comfits like there's nothing wrong, like the world isn't coming to an end.*

Cal sat on the BART train on his way back into town and tried not to move. He wore wraparound sunglasses even though it was raining outside, partly because the fluorescent light on the train was painfully bright but mostly to avoid eye contact. These were the uncomfortable moments, when the drugs were still pumping through his system but he was forced into inactivity. He could have tapped his foot or messed with his "overnight" bag, but that's what tweakers did and everybody knew it—better to sit perfectly still, gritting your teeth, waiting for your station.

It was a work day, and the train was full of commuters on their way into the city. Cal was on his way home, after a night at the baths in Berkeley that had passed in the blink of an eye, it seemed. Funny how you could just lose track of 16 hours in a place that was always dark and, like the factory floor it had once been, had very few clocks on view. Funny how you could get fucked so well by so many men and still not feel quite satisfied. A couple of adequate guys had wanted to take him home, but he'd deferred since he'd felt on fire, sure there was someone better waiting for him if he could just hold out a few more minutes, another hour at most...

He probably could have stayed and reregistered for another eight hours, being on good terms with the staff, but there was something depressing about the baths in the morning, with the light leaking through the old skylights and the attendants vacuuming the halls and the showers closed for a thorough sterilization. Besides, there was nobody left worth fucking around with, so he left.

It was on the way home that he remembered that no, he couldn't have reregistered, he didn't have any money left. He'd bought an eight-ball yesterday and spent the rest of his money on the baths and a round-trip BART ticket. Rather than depressing him, this fired him into action. A plan! He needed a plan. But it wasn't urgent; he had enough drugs to last a while, and that was what mattered. Still, what if he wanted to hit the bookstore? Even that had cost $3 in tokens. *A plan, a plan*, he thought.

His apartment on the edge of the Tenderloin wasn't close to a BART station, and he didn't have bus fare (and hadn't thought to buy a bus pass when he'd had the money—there had only been so much to go around), so he had to walk from Civic Center station. Despite the rain, there were still people on the street, mostly hookers with little chance of scoring now but out there because they needed to score *now*. Posters for long-ago concerts that had been stuck on boarded-up windows peeled and tore in the rain and refastened themselves to the sidewalks. Cars and buses treated pedestrians like so many orange cones, to be avoided if possible but if not, oh well. Cal swept through it like a man on a mission, unremarkable in this part of town. He looked like he belonged; he had a tattered denim coat and old sneakers and a look on his face in tune with the faces he passed, all of them enduring some form of hunger or another.

His studio apartment on O'Farrell Street wasn't the worst place in the world; the rent was under $500 a month, and his block, just on the other side of Polk, was quiet. The building had once been home to showgirls way back when Geary Street had plenty of theaters with something other than Broadway's second-best showing in them, but whether it ever had been like *Stage Door*, with girls running up and down the halls visiting each other, that wasn't the case now. The building was full of queers and old people, all of whom kept to themselves; the heat worked and the windows opened, and all of that suited Cal fine.

In the mail was a red notice from the cable company, which he disregarded. Cable was something he'd nobly told Gina he could live without, if she'd just pay his phone bill, he couldn't live without a phone. Besides, all he watched on TV now were porno videos anyway. He checked his answering machine; there was one message. He hit play and heard "Hi, Cal, this is Gina. I'm calling to see how you're feeling…" He hit stop, and the machine briskly beeped at him. He'd call her later; right now he didn't feel like dealing with it.

OK. It was time to scare up some cash. CDs were always the best bet for money—nobody paid shit for books. Yesterday he'd scored big when two of his Armani suits from his previous life had gone on concession at a shop on Upper Polk for $500, after the store's cut. That had paid for the eight-ball and the trip to the baths, but today was a new day, a new struggle. He looked at the CDs he had left, only about 20 of them now out of a collection of several hundred. The music of his youth, mostly: New Order and Depeche Mode and Pet Shop Boys—not the music of the new youth, who favored "authentic" music, meaning guitars and low, droning, soulful male vocals; no electronics at all, never mind a bunch of old all-synth bands. But the new youth were the main consumers at Amoeba out at the end of Haight—a long way to go but they paid more there.

Memories of Gina and him in the cloud-dappled room, listening to this very music, made him feel sad, and there was only one thing for that. He reached up onto the top shelf of the kitchen cabinet and brought down a stone box. Inside were still plenty of quarter grams of crystal meth, individually portioned out in small plastic jeweler's bags; this batch of bags had smiley faces on them, but Cal liked the ones with the blue dolphins best. He pulled his Pyrex pipe and his torch out of the bag of sex essentials he'd taken to the baths, and adroitly tucked the stem of the pipe into the bag, pouring the contents down into the bowl without losing a crumb. Then he started warming the bowl with the torch. The torch had been his one expensive purchase, at $50, but the cheap $12 ones kept breaking and if you were going to put your money into anything, everyone said, a good torch was a good investment. The crystal melted like sugar and began to vaporize, at which point Cal put the stem in his mouth and started to suck, just as Neil had taught him. Since that time he'd gotten better at it, now able to expertly apply and withdraw the torch to ensure a bong-size hit. Then he pulled the pipe out of his mouth and capped the end of the stem with his finger to prevent the vapor in the bowl from escaping. He swirled the crystal around in the pipe to recrystalize it and set it down on the lid of the stone box, exhaling a huge cloud of meth. He took another breath, and it hit him where it always did, in the groin, pulling on his insides so hard he bent over a little, involuntarily doing a crunch. He grunted, another involuntary motion. Then awe and wonder and relief and so much pleasure and no worries, no pain, only stillness in his head as his heart pumped harder and his hand moved to his groin and for a few minutes there was no thought of money, of Gina, of anything at all.

Several things had amazed Cal about speed. First, how many gay men were doing it. He'd seen guys walking down the street looking so hungry, so hunted by their own lust, and only now did it occur to him that this was why: they were high as fucking kites. And was it any wonder, Cal thought, after a few nights like the first with Neil, then with friends of his, finally with men he'd meet in the bars he was no longer afraid to go into. Cal had been afraid and had hoped for a shield and been handed a sword. Crystal lets you sweep into any room and know that it was all good, that the boys and the bass were there to make you thrum and hum—and why not? Why ever not do something that felt this good? Inhibitions were passé, darling. Have a bump. Fabulous, fabulous, everything and everyone glittered and shimmered, and the greatest thing was that none of it was behind glass any longer, or if it was, it didn't matter because Cal was no longer on that side of the glass. His body was still lean and beautiful and his skin still soft and glowing, and when he took off his shirt on the dance floor he was desired.

He thought of *Dancer From the Dance* often then, and thought of rereading it, but there was no time for books anymore. Besides, why read it when you're living it? One might answer that the novel was a precautionary tale, but Cal in this moment would not have cared if you'd told him the roof would fall in tomorrow, for he was alive at last and there was no tomorrow; there was only now, this perfect moment that felt so exquisite, and even better, a perfect moment to last all night, and all tomorrow meant was the chance for another perfect moment where there was no thought because there was nothing to think about. There was so much pleasure, it couldn't be processed normally; normal pathways of thought had to be bypassed, and for Cal, there was nothing that pleased him more than that. That was his second discovery.

His third was that it could be surprisingly expensive to live in the moment. He'd do a line if offered, but why did people bother when it was so much better to smoke it? It felt so much better, and you stayed harder and you didn't have to stand around wiping your nose in public. Cal would make jokes about money going literally "up in smoke," but it was true. Of course, at a certain point one realized it was silly to buy a quarter or two at a time when you'd just need another tomorrow, and so much cheaper in bulk. Cal bought teens, eight-balls, quarter-ounces, and he offered hits up eagerly to the men he wanted, eager to close the deal. For even though he was desired, he had a hard time believing it—the magazines, the ads, told him what was required and he didn't have it, the muscles and the ridges. Men would tell him how much they liked his "boyish" body, but he didn't believe them. He craved the icons in the ads for the dance parties he went to, with "pecs like sauté pans," as Jesse

Green once famously put it. He would have liked them hairy, too, but the magazines dictated hairlessness on the dance floor and few disobeyed. He wasn't stupid; he knew they reminded him of Eric, big and blocky and handsome, and the more they looked like Eric, the better. In his last weed-soaked encounter, Cal had dismissed Eric from his life, but not from his libido; that desire was imprinted in adolescence with all the fires repressed passion can muster and would last him a lifetime. Blonds, universally adjudged beauties, would confidently dance into Cal's line of sight, never of course making eye contact but making themselves available for examination with a casual glance his way if they were sure he wasn't looking…to be completely disregarded like so much wallpaper. He knew what he wanted, and he thought it would be hard to get, but there was always speed to clinch the deal. He would never know how many of the men who went home with him rarely, if ever, did speed but did it with him because he offered and they didn't want to say no to him.

His job was a memory; too many sick days and late entrances and no shows and even Nick, who was fully prepared to tolerate a certain amount of partying, had to draw the line. And his bank account was getting perilously low—no surprise when your income disappears and your expenditure goes from take-out food, a few videos, and some weed to an exorbitant drug bill and other necessities of life on the gilded pleasure barge like shiny mylar pants worn only once or plane and hotel fare even for just the "essential" circuit parties. A trip to one of these parties in San Francisco showed him that rent (and drugs and cover charges and everything else that mattered) was much cheaper there, and he moved one day with two trunks of clothes and CDs and a few other things worth saving without saying many emotional goodbyes to many people; speed is not conducive to deep emotional bonds in the first place, and most of the men who might miss him would probably see him "on the circuit" anyway. He liked the thought of moving that way, just up and packing and being gone, no attachments that could keep him anywhere if he felt like leaving. There were no duties to perform, tasks to complete, obligations to fulfill—he was free to live for pleasure, without fear, without guilt, without shame.

If you'd sat him down and grilled him, Cal could have told you when he'd started lying. He'd told Gina the truth when he'd told her he'd left New York for San Francisco because it was less expensive; but he'd also told her it would be better for his health, which was a lie. By the time he left New York, he hadn't seen her in over a year, the longest they'd ever gone without any face time. Gina had not left Reno, and her phenomenal success had not been repeated. After telling her family's story she'd found herself blocked for a number of reasons—nagging guilt that the book had contributed to her father's death and her mother's breakdown and a nagging insecurity that she only had one story in her. The book remained in print and the money continued to come in, the flood now a stream, but she would never have to work again, "which is kind of a curse in itself," she sighed. She knew Cal had broken free of their upbringing at last but had no idea how he'd gone about doing so; she had an idea there were drugs involved, but it didn't occur to her that it would was any more than a little "tweekending." A serious drug problem rarely looks that way as long as the addict can afford it, and by the time he landed in S.F., Cal still had about $25,000 in the bank.

He'd been lucky in his choice of apartments, which had been cheap and plentiful on his arrival thanks to the recession. He'd picked it because of its centrality, right off Polk Street (which he knew his New York buddies would find enchantingly sleazy) and within easy walking distance of both the Castro and Folsom. It had entertained him, this low-rent affair, a perfect tweak'n'fuck apartment. When the money was all gone, however, he'd been relieved he hadn't opted for anything grander because he would've had to move.

Gina wanted to visit him, but he'd put her off several times, even actually scheduling a trip when she'd put her foot down and then canceling due to "illness" at the last minute. She'd wanted a nice long visit, and Cal frankly didn't want to have to crash and dry out before her arrival and stay dry for a whole fucking week. Two years earlier it would have occurred to him that Gina needed this visit for her own mental health, but that was when he wasn't on speed. The selfishness that speed builds like a fortress was not yet monstrous in Cal, but it was significant, a selfishness that simply puts its foot down and says, *It's impossible, I can't do that, I can't handle that, it can't be done, I won't.* He thought about it, realized that he couldn't accommodate her by going without sex and drugs that long, and that was that.

Cal had a hard time accounting for the money he'd had in the bank—there'd been so much, and when he sat down with bank statements while only slightly high he saw that most of it had been cash withdrawals at the ATM. He'd taken to going out less and less as time went by; he got nervous standing around in bars now, and when he looked in the mirror he knew he didn't look as good as he had. He didn't have much flesh to spare and he wasn't sparing it. More and more often he convinced himself that he could have just as good a time at home with a bottom-less bag of meth, a few Titan videos, and some sex toys, and when that got him too worked, there were always the escorts in the back of the gay paper Eric wrote for (Cal turned straight to the sex ads and never even knew Eric had a column), some of whom were glad to party with Cal when he offered, which he always did. A night like that could cost $500, between the escort and the drugs, and regularly raiding that much out of the horde in the bank, never mind the boring practical bills to be paid, made short work of $25,000.

The first time he'd really told a whopper had been only two months ago. The money was gone. Cal had watched the bank balance plummet and had made what economies he could, like foregoing the hustlers and buying those four-hour loop tapes for $10 instead of renting better films for $5 a pop. He'd finally run flat out of money and thought, well, that's it. It didn't bother him because there was nothing he could do about it, and yet at the same time he held on to an absolute conviction that "something would happen" to make everything all right. He slept 16 hours a day for two weeks while his body tried to recalibrate and repair. When he was awake he was tired; a triple espresso could rouse him enough to get out the door and sell some suits or CDs, but that was it. He hustled up enough cash to pay the rent and marveled how $475 could suddenly seem like so much money.

Gina had called a few times, and he'd told her he was sleeping, sick—anything to get her off the phone. He'd taken her calls while on speed because the drug let him be "on," so entertaining that she would think everything was all right—"Cal's doing great, I can tell." Eric had been through much the same attention-diverting experience with Patrick years before; it is an art practiced to perfection by all kinds of people who wish to keep their hells private. Finally, after the second week she'd asked him, "Cal, are you all right? I mean, are you sick? I mean..."

He knew what she meant, and suddenly a thought occurred to him. It was true, wasn't it? He *was* sick. "Yes, I am," he said. "I'm HIV-positive."

There had been no condom that first night with Neil, and the day after, the sex over and Cal back home and a nap under his belt, the terror had hit him, the unique modern terror that he might have just killed himself with sex. *AIDS is God's punishment* no longer rang in his ears the way it had years before, partly because many of those who had most vociferously declaimed this certainty had lost their bully pulpits to congregations that had punished them for their own financial and sexual sins, and partly because a state of terror as complete as Cal's had been cannot be sustained forever. And there had been no denying that the pleasure of that night had been anything but punishment to Cal. And obviously, in the midst of wild, drug-soaked, hot nasty sex, there was no appropriate moment for sober reflection and consideration and discussion; *fuck, yeah* was a state of mind that Cal had achieved for hours on end, and in that state he wished everything that could dim its incandescence to stay far away, unthought, unsaid. The drugs inside him, a man's cock inside him, no barriers anymore between him and pleasure, damn it—and damned if he'd go find another after all this time, all this wasted time...

It had only taken a few hours for Cal to come to this conclusion, to decide that just as he had once simply willed himself not to think of sex in order to achieve his desires, now he would apply that same willpower to refusing to think about HIV. Besides, it was probably already too late; Neil was a nasty fucker and obviously experienced and probably HIV-positive, and therefore Cal was now, too. The dark beast that had ruffled its wings deep within him the night he'd met Neil now rose up in the sky and dwelt only on the joy of flight, of the hunt, of the moment.

Cal had not taken the test, but in his mind "being positive" simplified things enormously. The great barrier to pleasure had been crossed and now there were no more barriers, nothing left to fear. As he retreated more and more into his apartment, he found a whole world of men like himself online, ironically enough on America Online, its wholesome family image belying the fact that in San Francisco, its M4M rooms were full of men describing themselves as "poz party pigs," which meant kinky bareback sex while taking drugs. Cal found it was easier to get laid with another tweaker if you said you were poz, too, so he did, and presumably by this point he was. It never ceased to amaze him, the men he met, anesthesiologists and social workers and shrinks (*lots* of people in the helping professions, he discovered), smart and talented and well-off and none of it enough, was it?—not without pleasure, not without this pleasure, this intensity of constantly renewed desire and constantly frustrated fulfillment, just a little more, just a little longer, just another guy to join us, just let me watch that scene in the video one more time, just one more hit, just fuck me like that again, just don't stop…

So in Cal's mind, he wasn't lying to Gina when he'd said he was sick. Wasn't addiction an illness, after all? He'd tried to stop, hadn't he? And look at him, he couldn't even get out of bed without speed. Speed over time shuts off higher brain functions, and it could be argued that the moral center is one of the highest brain functions of all—also the one most likely to interfere with one's random self-gratification. Speed redirects power to the rationalizing centers, where fatality and self-pity combine to deflect criticism from inside and out. The more these centers are shut off, the more consciousness centers on the primitive brain, which know only pleasure and pain and fear.

"Oh, my God, Cal. What can I do?" Gina asked, and no part of Cal's soul was touched. Only that lizard brain stirred, its eyelids flickering and its tongue darting, sensing food in the air.

"Nothing, really," Cal said. "I'll be all right."

"No, you won't," she said firmly. Gina could not hear the self-pity, only the fatality, a common error among those with little experience of being worked. Like Eric faced with Emma and Howard, Gina burned with a need to *do something*. She'd known for some time that something was wrong, but drugs hadn't crossed her mind, and AIDS had only darted around the edges of possibility, knowing Cal's horror of it as well as she had.

"Are you OK financially?" she asked.

"Well, I've had a lot of expenses," he said elliptically. To the rationalizing mind, this was not a lie, and that made it OK. At this point in Cal's mind, stealing was still wrong, as was lying; that was what desperate lowly homeless skaggy drug addicts did. His moral center's ability to make finer distinctions now suspended, Cal was satisfied that he was not lying now. He *had* had a lot of expenses lately.

"I'll send you some money," Gina said, and Cal bit back the urge to ask her to wire it today, afraid of tipping his hand. "No, I'll *bring* you some money," and he didn't argue. The problem of crashing and burning before her arrival was solved at the moment, so she might as well come now…

She'd come, checkbook in hand, and at her first sight of him she'd started crying. He'd always been slender, but curves had become hollows and the body that had spoken of a dancer's agility now told only of a frightening fragility. Food had been occasionally necessary, even on speed, but Cal found that he had little appetite for anything other than sugar, maybe a little pasta; his body would now rebel against anything more substantial. At a certain point during his sleepathon he'd started getting hungry again, ravenously so, but that had gone away after a few days.

Gina took charge, shopping for him, feeding him, insisting he go to the clinic and get checked out. Nothing shocked Cal more than when he began weeping copiously every time Gina started crying. He started to eat, prodigiously, and to sleep only

12 hours a night instead of 16. They went to the clinic together, where Cal was given his report—he had 460 T cells, not in the danger range for illness but within the parameters to begin some kind of treatment. Cal said nothing as Gina cried, fearful of giving away the secret that his infection had not been officially acknowledged before now.

They offered him AZT, and he declined. Gina had seen the other men in the clinic, men whom Cal told her truthfully *were* on AZT; that and not HIV was why they looked so terrible, their skin so papery and their hair so thin, every strand of protein in their bodies being destroyed by the drug. Life on AZT was worse than death, he insisted, and having seen it with her own eyes, she didn't argue. Besides, under her care Cal was beginning to look better, his weight rebounding, his mood improving, a bit.

They would reminisce and hug and cry. Cal realized he wasn't crying out of anything other than a deep emptiness inside that he couldn't explain, an emptiness caused by meth's systematic strip mining of the pleasure centers of his brain. There was no ordinary pleasure left in ordinary life, but it must be acknowledged that Cal had rarely felt that ordinary pleasure in his life anyway, which was the reason speed had been so alluring, so soothing, so exciting all at once. For Cal, doing speed was self-medicating his emotions; without any outside direction in another more constructive path, few other options were open, and once he'd gotten a taste of meth, no other options mattered.

After three weeks, Gina was ready to go home. More to the point, Cal was ready for her to go. His physical health had been restored, but not his mental health. When Gina went off to sleep in a sleeping bag on the floor at Cal's feet, he was free to dream, to lie in bed and dream of meth, to dream of the pipe and the rush and the explosion inside, the heat of which dried all tears. Renewed vigor, a sister's love, that's nice, but what is that to the Rapture? Wasn't this, after all, what his father had spoken of with such emotion, what the people in church had screamed and fainted over, this moment when the whole world around was in flames—and hey! They could go to hell as far as you were concerned, for you were saved, alight. This was it, the all-encompassing flood of joy that takes you up and never lets you down; this was it, and that you were saved was all that mattered.

Gina left him with a few thousand dollars and the promise of a regular supplement to that; Cal was not yet able to apply for Social Security Disability since his health had not failed sufficiently to meet federal guidelines for establishing imminent doom. He took the BART with her to the airport, saw her off, went back to town to see his connection, and ran home like a greedy fat child with a box of baked goods. This money must last, he told himself firmly, and that meant no escorts, no baths, no movies, no toys, only essentials. He nodded with resolve as he filled the pipe and began to tremble.

That money had gone, it seemed, just as fast as it had before, when he was throwing it all over the place. Sure, he'd gotten back online and met guys, and they'd come over and he'd gotten them high, but really, how was it possible to go through an eight-ball in just a few days? But there it was: it was gone, again, and again the problem of how to replace it, and again.

What to sell, what to sell, Cal thought. He scooped up his CDs and headed out the door but didn't get far. Eyes were on him—*How did they know? Don't know, but they do, they know.* He turned around and went home, shaky, the only thing for it being another hit off the pipe. Then he got online, just to see who was around, what was going on. There was this one guy he'd kept blocking but who kept changing his screen name and messaging Cal again. "I'll pay you," he'd once desperately messaged, and Cal had disgustedly blocked him again. Now here he was again, messaging him. *Hmmm,* thought the lizard brain, stirring, hunting, hungry.

Emma grabbed Eric's hand. "Now I know you're *hungry,*" she chided him, and he chuckled nervously, "but I want you to *savor* this. Eat it *slowly.*" Eric took a small glossy apricot from the box and took a small bite.

"Mmm," he said. "Mmm!" The comfit was delicious, and he was for the moment in the mood to savor it. Probably the long walk had helped his mood; he hadn't been to the gym in weeks, which was probably the longest he'd gone without some form of strenuous exercise in his life. It had also helped that the sun had come out for a cameo appearance, and the city looked better in the hard Pacific light after a vigorous rinse. And he'd returned to find Emma and Howard enjoying themselves immensely, stoned to the gills and sharing funny stories—Eric trusted his lover but was always steeling himself to return to the two of them to find that the secret was out.

Howard ate one of the cherries and gurgled agreeably. "I've had this very same brand," he said. "In Paris."

"Type, darling," Emma chided him, "not brand. Brands are mass-produced, these are anything but. That's where I had them first, too."

"Really?" Howard asked. "When were you there?"

Emma looked at Eric. "Oh, long ago. I lived in Paris for a while."

"You never told me that," Howard playfully accused Eric. "I bet you've got all kinds of great stories you've never told me about your mom."

"Well," Eric said hesitantly, looking at Emma. "There's not that much to tell. About that, I mean."

Emma sensed that Eric didn't want her to tell Howard about "that," but he read her gaze and contradicted her. "I just thought you might not want to talk about it, that's all."

"Actually," Emma said, "I wouldn't mind. If you don't."

"I just thought it would be unpleasant for you to tell a stranger."

"Oh no, it wasn't unpleasant at all," she said emphatically, and Howard giggled. "And Howard's hardly a stranger, is he?"

Eric laughed, feeling the fool, but in an OK way.

"Actually," Emma continued, "I think I'd like to talk about Paris right now, if you don't mind, dear?" Eric shook his head.

Emma was pretty relaxed, she realized, which was partly the weed and partly the Fentanyl patch and partly the company and partly that she hadn't had those comfits since way back when.

"And you've bit the Madeleine," Howard ruled. "Now you *have* to tell."

"Fuck Proust, that boring old closet queen," Emma said, and they laughed.

"I don't know how much Eric's told you about his grandmother," Emma began, "but I suppose you know she named me after Emma Hamilton, hoping I'd grow up to become some famous man's legendary mistress, or some such." Howard did know this much, and nodded her on. "She's in several books on the old days, you know—Paris between the wars and all that. Quite the character. Unfortunately, characters are usually not very good parents, especially back then, when the bohemian Left saw stability as a personality defect.

"She had me well-educated, I'll give her that," Emma nodded. "Swiss boarding schools and then Barnard College, even if she only did it to keep me out of the way—hard to lie convincingly about one's age with a teenage daughter lolling about. I'm not bitter," she said, and Howard and Eric believed her; there was only a matter-of-factness to her recollections. "I just knew I wasn't her first priority."

"Who was *your* father?" Howard asked.

She shrugged. "Who knows? Some British actor with a pencil moustache? Some choleric Russian exile with breath like cigarettes and coffee grounds? It could have been any number of men, none of whom would have been keen to rush forward and claim responsibility. I'm surprised she had me at all; sometimes I think she had a baby out of wedlock because it was the only thing *more* shocking in her circle than an abortion, and she was desperate to one-up the rest of them!

"Anyways, I managed well enough as long as I had the structure of school. It was after that when I started having problems. I don't know if Eric's told you about the family fortune, such as was left of it when I got it." Howard nodded, and he and Eric smiled, both thinking of UTFs. "It was enough I didn't have to work, but not enough I could live some Doris Duke splendid isolation from the rest of the world. I knocked around New York City for a while in the early '60s, doing what well-bred young women did while they waited for husbands—worked in an art gallery, some light modeling, that sort of thing. Young Jackie O. shit. The problem was, I didn't want to get married—I didn't want to end up like my mother," she empha- sized, "but I didn't want to end up like my grandmother either! It wasn't an appropriate time to be young. I don't know how else to put it. It was too late to be a beatnik, too early to be a hippie, I know people my age rattle on about events like Kennedy's assassination, but really, it was a terrible thing. It made us all wonder if there was any point in trying. I was born in 1938, one of those generations that falls between the cracks of two really interesting times.

"Anyway. Back then every smart girl knew French—you had to know it, especially after Jackie—and when a secretarial job opened up in Paris working for this friend of the family, I took it. I wasn't really qualified to be an executive assistant, but his wife wanted him to bring a presumably wholesome American specimen along, rather than having him employ some French girl who'd use her foreign wiles on him.

"Well. Have you ever been to Paris?" Emma asked Howard, who nodded his head. "Then you know," she said, with the secret nod of Americans who have visited another planet. "It opened my eyes. My God, everything was beautiful, everyone was beautiful, everything was delicious. People put so much effort into enjoying life. Everybody looked at each other on the streets, not hard and lustful, just...appraising. Interested, maybe, wondering if you had potential. I can't...well, I can, but it'll sound silly to you, Eric, so bear with me. It's just as if there was this *message* in people's eyes, like they were all say- ing to me, 'Of course, silly, didn't you know. Where have you been?' Every conversation you had you had to put out, I mean just that everyone was capable of talking about ideas, and after they got over their anti-American prejudice and discov- ered you were capable, too, well, it was amazing. Every day was amazing. I'd go to some nondescript boulangerie in the morning and order a chocolate croissant to wolf down on my way to work, like I would in New York, and I'd *stop* on the sidewalk—just *stop* and *taste* it, it was *so good*, it would have been a crime to shovel it down. And work wasn't anything, you know, much—it usually isn't—but after work, a drink and some wonderfully contentious conversation with some young

French people from the office, and a lecture, and a dinner that was better than most sex you'll ever have, and then a café, all these beautiful people looking at each other and taking it for granted, that yes, *this* is how life is supposed to be, and I'd been so bored for so long and never knew that there was anywhere you could go and live and *not* be bored, I was so grateful some nights I just wept for joy in my bed...

"Anyway. Of course it didn't take me long to meet a man. Not in Paris! I wasn't bad-looking when I was that age, and blond, too—yes, naturally. He was of Greek origin, but Frenchified. He'd been raised in France and had mostly French ways, except for... well, never mind that!" She sighed, suddenly eager to finish the story. "Anyway, we fell in love, at least I did, I got pregnant, and he took it for granted I'd have an abortion—I was young and I had money and I wasn't Catholic so why not..."

Howard waited through a decent interval of silence before asking, "So why not?"

Emma pursed her lips. "It's hard to explain. I didn't think it would be right. Not because I was opposed to abortion or anything like that, but I was opposed to it for me, there, then. I mean, there was so much *beauty* all around me. There was so much to live for, and if I'd gotten an abortion then, how could I ever have thought of all that without thinking, *I killed a child so I could keep all this to myself?* I know some babies are better off never being born, if they're unwanted, but I wanted this child; I wanted it from the moment I knew I was pregnant. I'd been reborn in Paris—how could I deny my child the possibility of all that?

"Anyway. I made the most of my time between knowing and showing, so to speak, because I knew I'd get shipped back home—no way the Three Initial Corporation was going to leave an unwed American girl 'in trouble' abroad in their employ. I ate that time up, enjoyed every second of it, relished it..."

"But you didn't have enough money to stay there on your own?" Howard asked.

"Well, it wasn't just that," Emma sighed. "France under de Gaulle didn't feel like a very free place, and its educational system was underfunded and overcrowded—that's why the riots started in May 1968, you know. Funny the little things you start thinking about when you're about to have a child. Beauty and intellectual stimulation and culinary delight are all well and good for adults, but children need other things, like safety—you never knew when Soviet tanks would start rolling over borders, back then.

"And I wanted Eric to have *roots*, I wanted him to grow up anchored and safe and free, one of those American boys with their unbounded self-confidence," she smiled at him. Eric smiled weakly in return, his own self-confidence having taken a pounding recently. "French boys were smart and cute and clever, but there was this *shadow* over them, this *gloom* people get in old civilizations that have been conquered more than once. I didn't want my child to have that shadow."

This was too much for Eric, who burst into tears. Emma took him in her arms, expecting this. She'd spoken of beauty and joy, knowing Eric was blind just now to both. "It's not fair!" he shouted. "It's not fair!"

"What's not fair?" she asked him gently.

"All of that—you lost all of that for me, and now it's all for nothing!"

"No, it's not. It's not."

"But you're going to die…" he said, unable to restrain himself. It was the first time it had been said out loud, by anyone.

Emma nodded. "So I am."

"And so is Howard!" he cried. "Howard's going to die, too. Then I'll be all alone! And why? Why the fuck was I ever born, if just to end up all alone? You lost everything so we could all be miserable!"

Emma looked at Howard, who had been sitting there helplessly, wanting to comfort his lover but not wanting to interfere between mother and son. On his face she saw relief; keeping the secret had been a burden he was glad to be rid of.

"Oh, my God," Eric said, sitting up, looking at them both, suddenly ashen. "Oh, my God, that was so selfish of me. I'm so sorry…"

Emma shook her head. "It's the place of the living to be selfish. The dead don't need anyone's concern."

"But you're not dead yet."

Emma laughed. "No, I am not! And neither is Howard. And neither are you."

"It's just…it's just so awful," Eric said, groping for words. "And it's not just the two of you, it's, it's *all this death*, all these dead people I know, all these lost chances and all these things that'll never get done and there's nothing anyone can do about it. It's like the world is ending, but I'm the only one—I'm the only one who can see it. All these other motherfuckers out there are still dancing and partying and laughing and fucking, and they *don't care.* They know, but they *won't see it…*" He trailed off, exhausted.

"Look at history," Emma said. "Look at the Black Death, the Holocaust, things that looked like the end of the world, and yet someone always survived. There hasn't been a plague yet that could have taken us all out."

Eric looked into her eyes and she shuddered at what was there. "Don't you understand?" he asked. "That's what I'm afraid of. That *I'll live, all alone.* And that's worse than death."

Emma was stunned. She had no words of consolation for Eric, no way to tell him that life would go on, that people's parents die every day, because that wasn't enough. She hadn't seen it till now with perfect acuity and horror, that it wasn't just her or even just her and Howard. To Eric it was the whole world, all the people he knew, loved, gone or going. Perversely, she thought of Hitler ordering Paris burned and one Francophile general staying the order, one man saving a world of beauty and joy. But for Eric, Paris was burning and there was nothing he or she or maybe anybody could do about it.

Eric pulled himself together. This was wrong. He was the healthy one, it was wrong to be selfish, he must be strong. "I'm sorry."

"Don't be sorry," Emma said, taking his hand. "Eric, let me tell you something. The day we can't talk, the day we can't open our hearts to each other, no matter how it hurts—*that's* the day we're dead."

Cal had been rude and dismissive to his online importuner, which had only made the man want Cal all the more. "Last time we talked"—Cal typed with his pulse racing even more from

nauseous excitement than from speed—"you said you'd pay..."
His own abruptness startled him.

His breathing got shallow as he waited for the answer.
Hustling had never occurred to him as a source of income; it
seemed impossible that anybody save the most repulsive troll
would pay him for sex—Cal had as little regard for his own
beauty as Eric had for his, albeit for very different reasons. "One
hundred," came back the crisp answer.

"One fifty," Cal typed impulsively.

The man astonished him by sending back his room number
at the St. Francis. Cal logged off the computer, dizzy with
excitement and fear. I don't even know what he wants! But then
he thought of what he himself had always wanted from
escorts—could he give it to another in his turn? Getting hard on
speed was no problem for him, as long as he was turned on—
could he get hard for some old geez?

He took a solid hit off the pipe before leaving the house
(afraid to carry it with him); he exhaled and waited for the rush
but instead a picture of Ken popped into his head. Ken, his first
"sex," the hustler who'd sucked up his coke and left him high
and dry. At the time Cal had been enraged: how *dare* he! He took
my money and my drugs and gave me *nothing!* With an empa-
thy rare on speed, Cal suddenly understood Ken, understood how
little Cal *mattered*, how little any considerations mattered when
you were *hungry*, when all that mattered was getting yours.

He walked the short downhill distance to the St. Francis,
tensing as he went through the lobby, speed paranoia plucking
at his nerves. Did they know this guy was hiring hustlers?
Could they tap into his keystrokes? Did they know a hustler
was coming who liked to "party"? Would security be waiting
for him in the lobby? Would the police? The lobby was, as
usual, teeming with people and Cal was unremarkable-look-
ing; in his current state he couldn't know that only the most
disheveled street person would be stopped, if noticed in time.
All he knew was that he had to hurry through the gauntlet,
and he heaved a sigh of relief in the elevator. *Were there cameras in here?* he wondered. He pushed the button and tried to
look casual.

To Cal's astonishment, the door of the suite was opened by a beautiful young man. "Hey, you must be Cal."

"Uh, yeah…but…"

"Oh, you thought Jim was going to answer the door," he laughed. A little shorter than Cal, dressed like a preppy in a long-sleeve polo shirt and baggy jeans. "He's in the bedroom, tweakin' on the computer, trying to see how many guys he can get over here." He turned away, leaving Cal at the door unsure, then suddenly turned around and smiled at Cal. "Oh, hey, I'm Luke."

Cal was smitten. Luke looked young, 20 at most, with dirty-blond hair, blue eyes and the softest, most luminous skin Cal had ever seen. His blue eyes were bright in color but dark as only the most knowing eyes can be; he reminded Cal of Neil, only more… something. Cal was taken with his beauty, but also with his élan, the casual way he seemed to be taking this whole scene. Here was no low-class hustler like Ken, Cal felt sure, but someone like himself, someone maybe in his own boat.

Luke sat down on the couch, in front of a coffee table littered with syringes and spoons and cotton balls, and began fiddling with a small brown lump, breaking it up into one of the spoons, suddenly oblivious to Cal's existence. Cal peeked into the bedroom and saw a heavyset man in his jockey shorts sitting in the dark, tapping furiously on a laptop. "Hello?"

Jim looked up. "Oh, hi. Make yourself comfortable, I'll be out in a bit."

Luke chuckled without looking up from his spoon. "He's been in there for three fucking hours,. You might as well sit down. Your money's on the desk."

"Oh. OK." Cal took the envelope off the desk, peeked inside to satisfy himself that there was probably $150 in there, then sat down on the couch. He watched Luke working assiduously, the tip of his tongue sticking out of the corner of his mouth. He knew heroin when he saw it. He had an absurd vision of Luke passed out on the couch, the old man hooked on the computer, and himself sitting here twiddling his thumbs. Luke looked up and saw Cal watching him. "You shoot?"

"Um, no, I just do speed, thanks."

Luke gave him a sardonic smile and Cal flushed at the idiocy of what he'd just said. "Heroin's a lot better for you than speed, you know," Luke said.

"I'm sure," Cal said, matching Luke's smile with his own lightly sarcastic words.

Luke laughed, handing Cal a syringe. "Go on then, do your hit. Jim's paying." He indicated a baggie of meth on the table that must have had an eight-ball in it. Cal watched Luke put the torn-up chunk of heroin into a spoon and add water, put a lighter to the bottom of the spoon until it was cooked to his satisfaction, then taking a pinch of the meth and adding it to the mix before dropping his cotton in and drawing up the hit.

"I've never shot myself up," Cal said. *Why didn't I say I don't shoot up?* Cal thought. He was afraid of sounding supercilious again. The fact of the matter was that he'd been around "slammers" before, back on the circuit, but even the most decadent pleasure barges have their rules, and among the well-off professionals on the circuit, shooting up was what lower-class people did. It was nice to snort, social to smoke, nasty to boot (stick the drugs up your ass), but icky to shoot. Of course, Cal thought, all this was a hierarchy of folly; doing speed is doing speed, but for many users as long as there's no needle involved, there's no "drug problem."

"You want me to hit you?" That sounded funny, Cal thought. Luke wasn't talking about slapping him across the face; he was talking about sticking a needle in his arm. He thought back to the few people he'd known on the circuit who'd admitted to slamming and told him about it. "It's indescribable," one said. Another, a man invariably and incandescently flip, had looked at him seriously and said, "Don't ever do it. If you love crystal, once you slam it, you can never do it any other way." One of his dealers, who had made an iron law for years about only snorting it and stuck to it, only shrugged and said, "You'll go to hell. The ride is great, but you don't get off till you're in hell."

"Yeah," Cal said now. Truth be told, smoking it had started to lose its effect. There had been proof enough of that tonight, when he'd done a mighty hit off the pipe and nevertheless been able to clearly and uncomfortably recall his Ken episode. Once not so long ago, cognitive thought, never mind unpleasant memories, would have been impossible when he was high, but no longer. And all his previous opportunities to shoot up had been in environments full of dire warnings—even those who were themselves shooters usually hiding it. Here tonight was a gorgeous young man who seemed to be suffering no ill effects from his own injection drug use—Cal had yet to learn how heroin can give junkies a flush of good health belying the cellular changes within—and was matter-of-factly offering to shoot him up as if there was nothing to it. He was suddenly seized with the giddy happiness of the addict in those moments when there is nothing between them and pleasure, when the world's problems are solved even before the drug is taken and they are possessed of the knowledge that the drug will only make them happier. Such moments are rare, but so clear and ringing and fresh that those who feel them will pursue such moments for years if not forever, refusing to believe they were ever fortuitous accidents never to be repeated. Cal was in such a moment. *Why not?* he thought. He was sitting in a plush suite with money in his pocket, anything he wanted either on the table or a phone call away. He would probably end up fucking with this cute boy and not the old thing in the bedroom—*everything was going right tonight, why not?* He might have found all kinds of reasons why, had he looked for them, but in his relaxed state of denial none of them were currently tugging at his sleeve, and therefore they didn't exist.

Luke looked at him narrowly. "But you *have* shot up before, right?"

"Oh, yeah. I've just never done myself." Cal knew this was an essential lie. Believe it or not, most of those who have found themselves on "the point" have been able to save only one small shred of their souls by insisting that they will never, ever introduce someone else to the point. To lose yourself and your soul and your life as you knew it, is your right, but to help someone else to achieve the same fate...they *know* there is no turning back from the point and the ritual of preparation and the rush. "I can handle it, I'm just curious," those who have never done it will say, but when their curiosity is satisfied, their ability to handle it is gone with their curiosity. Cal had come powerfully close one night, during one of those intense sexathons, when his partner had revealed himself as a slammer but had backed off the idea quickly when he'd found out Cal was a virgin to the needle. This time, Cal knew, it would be best to lie; only by deceptively easing Luke's conscience could he get what he wanted.

"You want any chiba with it?" Luke asked.

"Any what?"

"Chiba. You *no habla español,* man?" Luke grinned.

"Oh. Heroin. No, thanks." That, in Cal's rationale, was drug addiction; you could always walk away from speed without withdrawal, he was sure. All drug addicts do this: hold out one last extreme to which they have not yet gone to prove that they are still in control.

Luke capped his own point and set it aside, picking up another spoon and putting it into the eight-ball bag, measuring by sight. Cal irrationally thought how beautiful the room-service spoon was as Luke drew some spring water out of a bottle into a syringe. The water hissed and spit as he shot it into the crystals in the spoon. Then he flipped the point over and started mashing the water and drugs together, using the flat of the plunger like a pestle. Then he drew them up together into the syringe, holding it up to the light and smacking it to remove air bubbles.

Cal watched all this with benign fascination. How could something that demanded such precision and care be so wrong? Luke rubbed his arm with an alcohol swab. "Don't you need a tourniquet or something?" Cal asked nervously, finally afraid of how much trust he was putting in a stranger's hands.

"You've got great veins," Luke said, and Cal watched with clinical interest as he slid the needle ever so slightly into Cal's flesh. Cal almost moved out of surprise when Luke pulled back slightly on the plunger and a few drops of blood billowed into the barrel of the syringe. Then Luke pressed and Cal watched the drug enter his system, watched Luke pull the point out and cap it, then smoothly hit the carpet with it at a 180-degree angle, snapping the point off.

"So how long before…" Cal was cut off by a cough that seized his lungs, all the air forced out, and then just as suddenly all his airways free to take a huge gasp. He felt as if he'd just been startled, and yet the astonishment grew rather than diminished, he gasped for air as if he was a fish out of water and yet each gasp was life, fueling rather than extinguishing the light in his head. He felt as if it was too much pleasure to stand, and yet each moment brought still more and he couldn't stand it, it was too much, it had to stop, but nevertheless there was still more than that.

"Oh my God," he repeated over and over. What did he think? He didn't, he couldn't, thought was no longer possible, his consciousness severed from the higher brain, fully present now only in the limbic system, that knows only pleasure and pain and fear, and there was no pain or fear now, only every single dopamine production site in his brain exhausting itself like stages of a rocket propelling the capsule ever higher, ever faster, ever farther away from gravity and mankind. There was no thought, and it is this state, the Rush, that for minds in hell is the reason there is no turning back from the point, from this perfect moment, from a rapture that such minds are sure can never be attained otherwise, and *why bother to try otherwise* when there is this perfection so easily attained, only a few dollars and a push away?

In the world outside Cal, life went on, for all that mattered to him. Luke smiled knowingly and went to the bathroom, where it would take him nearly an hour to do his own hit, his veins exhausted save for the huge deep ones at his groin and collarbones, spots marked by star-shaped puckers, one of which he always kept open and bandaged and which was still a trial to hit. Jim, the man in the bedroom, consumed by a vision of ever more young, hot guys, ignored the two already present in the excitement of the unknown, the hunt. Luke grunted and swore in the bathroom, and the man in the bedroom feebly stroked his flaccid penis as he cruised the Net frantically, and only Cal was at peace in that room in that moment, with no need of sex or drugs or money or anything because he'd found it at last, the end of the journey, the raison d'être, Shangri La, *this* was the real thing, *this* was the Rapture.

That night Cal crossed the border between recreational and occupational drug use. He had been approaching this border for some time, yet until now some strands of practicality had anchored him to earth. He had taken some enjoyment in his daily hunt for money, a perverse pride in his ability to wring one more dollar out of what possessions he had left; he had enjoyed the rough hot sex marathons for which speed had been the fuel. Now nothing of the outside world mattered at all. Every moment outside the Rapture was unbearably dreary, and the pleasure of sex seemed inconsequential next to the pleasure of the rush—in fact, he soon found, sex after slamming was almost a letdown, a distraction from the paradise in his head. While the rush was peaking, the sexual fantasies he devised were more exquisite and satisfying than the real thing ever would be again, all the more so because in the real world, people so often failed to stick to the script, to maintain the level of intensity he thrilled to in his fantasies. People had the disappointing tendency—especially if they were also high—to get paranoid or leave the room and become obsessed with some item in the next room for hours, or their dicks would get ever softer and smaller the more they got anxious about their shrinkage. Cal would feel the rush, and his fantasies like the thousand-and-one nights would come upon him, and the adrenaline that accompanied the dopamine would *insist* that he do *anything* to get *fucked, now,* yet the adrenaline also triggered anxiety, an inability get to a bar and stand still long enough to play the game. So he would shoot, and rush, and masturbate until the frenzy was on him, then he'd dress and leave the house but only to walk the streets, never stopping in a bar, never even relaxed enough to make eye contact on the street, until finally it was so late nobody walked the streets but the dregs of the earth and he came home. And that was the pattern, enough to make any rational person engaged in any rational pursuit abandon it in frustration, enough to make him say, "Fuck this!" An hour of pleasure followed by a night and a day of fruitless pursuit of an unobtainable goal. But for Cal, for most slammers, the scale was weighted in favor of the hour, and of all the impressions of the night, none was yet so terrible that it outweighed the asteroidal impact of the rush, the awesome all-obliterating explosion of pleasure that made the cloud of dust encompassing Cal's world for a seeming ice age afterward all worth it.

Luke had taught him how to slam, directed him to the local needle exchange, in exchange for time in Cal's apartment. To Cal's surprise, the handsome well-presenting young man was homeless, a hustler meeting his needs by working Polk Street. Luke was not 20 as Cal had thought, but 25, and gave Cal an elaborate biology lecture on how heroin altered you on the cellular level, keeping your body in a constant state of teardown and rebuild, as if you were still an adolescent (thus the warm, soft, glowing skin of heroin addicts still in the first decade of their addiction). Luke did well on Polk; older men accepted his lie that he was 18 and were pleased to have a "date" with such impeccable middle-class manners, nice clean clothes, and none of the thieving ways of the more desperate and short-sighted young hustlers on Polk. But then Luke had his eye on the long view and rarely killed geese who laid golden eggs; these older men were more than happy to have intelligent as well as beautiful companionship in their homes for a few days, which enabled Luke to stay clean and tidy. A heroin addiction in such a nice boy was seen as a tragedy; that was the only reason he lived on the streets, a tragedy that enabled them to take pity on him, which in turn gave them the feelings of doing good for the deserving and of having the upper hand over the needy. Some older men occasionally offered him a pass to complete redemption in the form of full funding at any rehab center he'd choose, but Luke never accepted, demurring that treatment centers weren't structured in ways that he could cope with. The fact of the matter was that heroin felt too good to stop, but Luke would admit this only to himself.

Luke worked the days and evenings on Polk, pretty much every day—heroin is a harsh financial mistress. At Cal's, he would lock himself in the bathroom, sometimes for hours, trying to get his hit. Cal would worry, all the more so because the speed he was shooting was such an obsession-building drug, but his worry wasn't unfounded: there was a heroin addict in his bathroom, and how was he to know when the day would come that Luke would finally fuck up and O.D.? Luke would pull up his pant leg and blithely detail how a missed hit of speed had turned into an abscess that had turned into the gaping crater on his leg, so painful even on chiba that he would limp around the apartment. Or Cal would see a constellation of little bruises on the inside of Luke's otherwise soft, creamy white arm, like a negative image of distant galaxies in a photo taken by an observatory telescope, failed attempts to find a vein he hadn't blown yet. And yet Cal was not looking at a picture of ten million years ago, but at a picture of not too many years from now, a picture of his own fate if he kept shooting—Luke had started at 17, but Cal had started at 28; Luke still had the asset of youth on his side, whereas Cal's assets in that department, as in all others, were running low. All the same, still even these horrors were not enough weight on the other side of the scale, all of *that* later meant nothing while you could feel *this* now.

Luke's presence was a blessing and a curse. With Luke there, Cal was less likely to go mad spinning his wheels; Luke could hold an intelligent conversation, and his opiated serenity counterweighted Cal's amphetamine-fueled Catherine wheel of ideas and notions and digressions. But it was also a curse; there were moments when Luke came out of the bathroom dripping wet from a long shower with only a towel around his waist, moments of astonished clarity when Cal thought there might be something better than speed. This beautiful sparely sculpted smooth, soft-skinned body was so unlike what Cal had used to desire.

He yearned just to touch Luke, but Luke didn't like to be touched (a common side effect of work in the sex industry); he wanted Luke to fuck him, but Luke was still HIV-negative and didn't want to risk it (heroin's calm providing him with enough presence of mind to use rubbers with dates and San Francisco's needle-exchange program providing him with clean works, he was one of very, very few hustler-addicts to avoid the bug).

Moreover, heroin gradually sapped away all of one's interest in sex (and the little interest left in him had to be marshaled in the interest of gain).

"You just want me because you can't have me," Luke would half-playfully accuse, and Cal would flush. There was truth in his words that Cal wouldn't see: what was Luke's lithe young body but the last pleasure in the world denied him? How could he not yearn for the last piece of forbidden fruit? But it was more complicated than that, too, Cal knew. Luke did have a *something*. He was special; he was smart and good to be with and sometimes even surprisingly kind. But Luke would never believe that Cal had more than one reason for wanting him, and that the reason was the simplest and most venal he could think of. Luke had an absolute certainty in simple conclusions that was endemic to heroin addicts; the opiated state is a state of serene highness in which everything appears clear and plain, the mind stripped of all madly flapping wings that might cause it to veer away from unpleasant truths. Heroin takes away the curvature of the earth that makes other parts unknown; it makes the world flat, easily mapped, clear to the eye to all four corners. It is a condition of Olympian disdain for lesser states of mind and those who dwell in them, and Cal's earnest silent protestations of genuine desire were so much dross to the mind free of the needs for self-deceit and desire. Yet, as it is also a state of Olympian pleasure, it allows a small forgiving chuckle for the emotional needs of mere mortals below—in the end it was this that hurt Cal more than anything, the idea that his huge yawning yearning for Luke might seem to the other man such a ludicrous little pothole, to be stepped over in an easy giant stride and left behind without a thought.

Emma too rarely left her sanctuary, and she had visitors who brought her drugs and solace, but the comparison ended there. She and Eric and Howard had become a mutual aid society, and the pleasant buffleheadedness brought on by THC was neither as overwhelming nor as irresistible as Cal's or Luke's drug of choice.

Emma was seeing a lot of Howard, the two of them alone, these days. After Eric's outburst in which the Henry Jamesian

"Unmentionable" had finally been mentioned, Emma and Howard were finally as free in each other's company as both had long wished to be. Death was on the table for discussion now, to the relief of both of them. Eric had seen this and rather than being glad for them had flagellated himself even more for having selfishly deprived them of the pleasure for so long. "You were trying to spare me," Emma said kindly, "and I appreciate it," but Eric only flinched as if so much undeserved kindness was worse than the lash.

This day Emma and Howard were alone. Eric was at home trying to push out a piece he'd managed to get a contract for, a humor piece about gay versus straight fashion, and how, as a friend of his had put it, "They beat us up for wearing what they'll be wearing two years from now." But he couldn't get the tone right; he knew what it should be—breezy and winking and all in the spirit that it doesn't really matter what you wear—but the more he tried to be funny the harder it got to write. Eric had always been one of those writers who would stare into space for a moment, formulate his thought, type out the sentence, go back and add or change a word, and move on. Never in his life had 1,200 measly words seemed as impossible as a lay epic. He'd always had good work habits, and even after taking up the pipe had forbore to get stoned until after his day's work was done, but now that was out the window as he loaded up in the hopes that somewhere in those first giddy moments would come the easy humor he needed. But instead he'd find himself distracted by the little fluffy clouds in his head; the ease the weed brought urged him to lay down his burden and relax. Maybe then it would come to him, so he'd drift until nap time stole up on him, then wake up with a dry mouth and a blank page.

Emma and Howard were feeling more productive this day. They fiddled around the "stoner channels"—Discovery, PBS, AMC, A&E, et al—until a show on reincarnation caught and held their attention. During a commercial break, Howard asked Emma, "What do you want to be in your next life?"

"An alien," Emma answered promptly, having already given this some thought.

"Huh?"

"Well, what makes you think we have to come back on this planet? If your soul can travel from here to China for your next life, then distance is no object, and if it's not, then what rule says you have to be reborn as a human being? Why wouldn't you be able to reincarnate into any sentient being in the universe?"

"So you're saying you wouldn't want to be a human being again?"

"Not that I'm prejudiced against the human race or anything," Emma demurred, "but there's got to be a way to learn something that's not so...painful? Difficult? Maybe not. Maybe it's just as bad on any other planet."

"Or worse," Howard offered. "What if humanity has the best deal? I mean, not in everything, but say in sensory perception. Say nothing you eat will ever taste as good to you as it will to you as a human, or sex will never feel as good, or music will never sound as good..."

"Well, acute appreciation of pleasure is what makes everything else so painful, doesn't it? I mean, the more you know of pleasure, the less you're willing to put up with pain. Maybe if you don't know how good the good things can feel, you're more prepared to endure the bad, and maybe you learn more that way. I don't know. We're all just guessing. I had—have—this neighbor, a fundamentalist Christian. I envy her sometimes; she never guesses, she knows it all."

"Oh!" Howard exclaimed. "I almost forgot to tell you. She called."

"Who?"

"Your next-door neighbor. Carol something." Watching the look of amazement on Emma's face, Howard apologized. "I'm sorry, was it important? I thought she was just a neighbor, maybe a sympathy call. I wrote it down. I would have remembered when I got home."

Emma granted his appeal. "It's no big deal. I'm just...well, she's the last person I'd expect to ring up with a sympathy call. She was my worst enemy all through Eric's childhood." And Cal's, she thought, wondering whatever had happened to the boy, of whom she'd heard nothing since Eric had reported their New York encounter.

"I'll call Eric. Get her number, I wrote it on the pad," Howard said as he reached for the phone.

"No, don't interrupt him. He's working," she said. Howard didn't look at her, which she knew from their experience with the Unspeakable meant that Eric probably wasn't writing much. She thought of all the times she'd had words with Carol over one issue or another. "I think I know the number."

But Emma didn't pick up the phone right off. Instinct and experience dictated that she only speak to Carol when straight. She stopped smoking, sent Howard home at four—the scheduled end of Eric's work day—had some coffee sent up from room service, and then made the call.

"Hello?"

"Carol, it's Emma." Brisk and businesslike, as she'd always been with her adversary.

"Emma," Carol said with a relief that startled Emma. "Thank you for calling me back. Oh," she said, clearly distracted. "I'm so sorry to hear about your illness. How are you feeling?"

"I'm feeling pretty good today," Emma answered honestly. Some days were good and some weren't, but that was enough information for this call.

"I'm glad." A pause. "Emma, I'm calling to ask you a favor." Emma's painted-on eyebrows lifted but she said nothing. "It's Cal. We…well, I haven't heard from him in years, but Gina's kept in touch with him. He lives in San Francisco, but lately he's stopped answering her phone calls, and she got worried. He didn't answer the door when she drove over there to see what was going on, and the landlord wouldn't tell her anything except that he was alive, and she staked out the building for a day but didn't see him…" She caught herself short. "Emma, Cal has AIDS and we're worried about him."

Emma's breathing stopped. Her first thought was for Eric, for what the news would do to him, how it would confirm his belief that everyone who ever mattered was dead or dying but him. "HIV, Mom," Emma heard a voice in the background she recognized as Gina's scolding Carol. "He has HIV, not AIDS. Yet."

"As far as we know," Carol shot back with that short stinging voice Emma recognized from so many duels at the PTA. "And we were wondering if you or Eric had heard from him."

"No, I don't think so. I mean, I haven't. Eric probably would have mentioned it." *Then again, he might not have,* she thought. *Better call and ask.*

"How's Eric…?" Carol asked hesitantly, and Emma read her meaning. She suddenly wanted to cry, for everybody's sake.

"He's fine. He's taking my illness hard. And his partner has AIDS, so it's doubly hard on him right now." She'd hesitated only a moment before saying it—fuck her, she thought, if she doesn't like it.

"I'm sorry to hear that," Carol said with what Emma could only take as sincerity. Amazing how so many years of anger at a person could just *go away* when you found them in your own boat. "Is there…can you think of any way we could find him? I mean, short of hiring a detective. Which I'll do if I have to, but…I just don't want some stranger telling him to call home, I don't know…" Carol broke off helplessly.

Emma nodded. "I can put Eric and Howard on the case. They know a lot of people. We'll see what we can find out."

"Oh, God, thank you," Carol said with a relief that was almost plaintive.

"See, I told you," Emma heard Gina say.

Carol laughed. "It's funny, isn't it? Cal Senior spent all those years fighting for 'family values,' and look at our family."

Emma did start to cry now, silently. *I'm so blessed,* she thought, thinking of Eric and of Howard, too. *I'm so lucky to have this family.*

"You have Gina," Emma offered, "and you'll have Cal again, too."

Carol snorted. "It's funny. Gina and I haven't spoken in years either. It's taken this to get her to talk to me." Emma heard Carol start crying, breaking down, and a rustle as the phone was taken by Gina.

"Thanks, Emma," Gina said. "Anything you can do to get him to just call us, let us know he's alive."

"Gina," Emma said impulsively, "let me talk to Carol again." She heard Carol pull herself together and take the phone. "Carol, I'm dying. And Eric's lover is dying. He's not going to have anybody, but he's going to have my house. He'll need friends. And good neighbors."

Perversely, memory brought back to Carol the day she'd been so furious that Cal had gone to Emma's house, so afraid of this woman's potential power over her son, and she was ashamed of herself. "I'll do everything I can," she promised. "And, Emma?"

"Yes?"

"I'm so sorry."

Emma was moved. She knew what Carol meant: *I'm so sorry for all these years, all this foolishness. These are the things that matter, and I never saw it till now.*

"So am I," she said, meaning it.

Emma had summoned Eric and Howard and told them about Carol's call. She'd been afraid of fresh tears from Eric when she'd revealed that Cal was HIV-positive, but he'd only nodded numbly as she confirmed what he already knew—everybody was dead or dying but him. Emma recounted everything Gina had told her about Cal's life until his disappearance, enough to make Howard nod and say, "I know some people who might be able to help."

If Eric had been confronted recently with all that was wrong with San Francisco, he still would have readily admitted that Howard was the incarnation of all that was right with the city. Howard had a tolerance for every kind of person that was genuine, not adopted out of political conformity, an open-mindedness about other people's beliefs and behaviors made of outer-directed curiosity. Over the years he'd made friends high and low with little regard for their status in the city's various sexual, economic, and intellectual food chains; like any good writer, his primary qualification for an acquaintance was that they be interesting: "good copy" whether they ever graced his pages or not. His gay circle included A-list gays, Democratic party hacks, toilers in AIDS, Inc., Radical Faeries, circuit boys and more. People liked Howard because he was a good listener, that is to say, someone who kept listening because he was paying attention and not waiting for his own opportunity to say something—and when he did say something, it was usually something you remembered.

Gina had filled them in on Cal's recent past, and based on what she'd said about Cal's circuit party experiences, Howard called a boy he knew who lived on the pleasure barge, doing a little escorting, a little drug dealing, nothing full-time, just enough to fund busy days spent tanning, working out, shopping, dancing, always "in training" for White or Black or Morning parties, a life of pleasantly oblivious hedonism available for a few years to the happy few.

"Oh, sure, Crystal Cal," Shane had drawled. "I know him."

"Why do they call him Crystal Cal?"

"Because nobody's ever seen him off crystal! It's like the second thing he says to anyone he meets: 'Do you like to party?' I mean, everybody likes to party, but please. He dropped off the circuit. He lives here in town, but nobody sees him anymore." Howard had to smile at Shane's "nobody," blithely blanketing every human being not on the circuit.

"Do you know where I could find him?"

"At one of the tweaker bars, I'm sure."

"'One of the'? How many are there?!"

"Hmm, let's see. There's the Watering Hole on Folsom. That's more an old leather crowd. Castro Station on Castro, ditto. Very icky. Or Cocktails on Mission at Ninth. Though of course everybody ends up at the EndUp sooner or later."

Howard had heard of or passed all these bars, even been in a few, but with the exception of the long-lived and universally notorious EndUp he'd never known any of them to be tweaker bars, let alone all of them. *What was it about gay men and speed?* He wondered, thinking that would make a good piece someday.

"Though if I were you, I'd watch out for him," Shane added darkly.

"Why's that?"

"I hear he slams now, and those people are *evil*," he added with the absolute assurance of someone who would never ever do *that*.

Howard knew perfectly well what slamming was, and hesitated to pursue things any further. While he couldn't or wouldn't state with Shane's authority that Cal had become the devil's own the minute the first needle had entered his vein, it had been his experience that slammers were, if not the devil's own, certainly lost souls, anchored to this world only by the physical body that was still necessary to transfer the drug from the world to their consciousness. Slammers were often crazy, almost always sociopathic in the pursuit of their own agenda. Indeed, a bar, a public place, would be the only place Howard would be willing to confront one of that ilk.

He duly reported this information to Emma, along with his opinion on the type. Emma was surprised; for Howard to be urging her not to pursue contact with someone was very serious indeed. But this matter couldn't be dropped now, and honestly, she thought and said aloud with a twinkle, what did she have to be afraid of—that Cal would kill her? Howard laughed at her gallows humor as only he could and continued the search.

The bars were a rarity for Cal now; the deeply addicted have little use for people, save inasmuch as they were useful tools at the moment. Cal lived in his home, in the whirling galaxy inside his head, Luke his only conduit to the outside world and a shaky one at that. Heroin grants serenity in the world within, but irritability with the imperfect world without, and Cal's high-strung tweakiness would pluck Luke's nerves some nights. Luke could say the cruelest things about Cal's pathetic state, and Cal would only cringe, knowing Luke was right. It was pathetic, to be so taken with drugs at his age, to be living for pleasure, to be all the more smitten with Luke, the more scornful Luke was to him. Luke seemed to Cal like the possessor of a dark knowledge, a blithe ability to skate across the frozen wastelands of other people's stunted desires, satisfying a bit of one here, a bit of one there, in exchange— always in exchange—for something he needed. Cal's pain, his increasing speed-fueled terror of the world and its people, his mounting guilt as Luke berated him for having had all manner of opportunities and making a hash of them, were all so much fodder for Luke's scorn, and yet on some level he must have wanted it, must have been taking some black satisfaction in it, God's punishment at last, why else would he continue to have Luke over? The fact of the matter was that Cal needed pain now, needed pain to justify what he knew in his heart was *too much pleasure.* If life was painful enough, there was always reason enough to medicate it with pleasure, and if there wasn't enough pain in his life to justify that much pleasure, he'd go out and find some.

Even so, some nights Luke's scorn would drive him out of his own apartment, as if Luke were more worthy of peace and quiet than Cal, that Cal was depriving him of it through his ever-increasing edginess and fear. To the objective mind this appears absurd, the idea that anyone would let a homeless junkie hustler kick you out of your own home. To anyone who has been through emotional abuse, asked for or not, it makes perfect sense. Luke was good and Cal was bad, and Cal was lying when he said he loved Luke, because if he did, he wouldn't treat him this way, that way, so rudely. Speed did make Cal rude, it was true; he'd rush to complete Luke's sentences for him as if to show him, *See, I understand you, I'm listening,* but all he did by cutting him off was irritate Luke even more. All he got for his attempts were withering looks of scorn that only drove him further into himself, only made him flagellate himself for fucking up again. Never mind all that he gave Luke, in terms of physical comfort, all that he could, perhaps all of love that he could in his addled state, none of it meant anything in the face of his glaring faults, faults that were all that mattered in the end.

And so one night he'd fled his own house and this situation of his own devising, as if it were not in his control, and he went to a bar. Not just any bar, though, but the dank deep recesses of Cocktails. It had the typical San Francisco bar setup; it was on the ground floor of a three-story building (the two stories above comprising a sleazy by-the-week hotel), but its tweaker allure was in its basement dance floor, a perfect subterranean hideout from sunlight, creditors, and personal demons. Cal was hardly the only person to come through the bar's front door and walk as quickly as possible, head down, toward the sanctuary of a basement so dimly lit only cats and tweakers could have navigated it with assurance.

Downstairs a DJ played music with a frenetic beat, and a girl's high squeaky voice in a musical form called Hi-NRG. This genre, completely unlistenable to anyone who had heard anything better, was bread and milk to tweakers like the DJ, who hadn't left this dungeon or one like it for the last 20 years and never *had* heard anything they liked better. It was ideal music for dancing if you felt the need to "dance" at a pace that would eventually cause you to turn into butter.

"I feel your love in me, that's where I want your love to be," squeaked some nameless chipmunk as Howard winced. He may have found most people somehow tolerable or forgivable, but there were some works of "art" that were neither and would never be, and this crowd-pleasing buzz saw was one of them. He wondered if the music was any kind of approximation to the beats per minute inside a tweaker's head, and sighed, knocking back another cocktail to dull his sensibilities. Eric would have squawked, had he seen Howard mistreating his body with hard liquor, but then Eric wasn't here.

The first time Cal walked past him, Howard didn't recognize him. He'd been given photos of Cal, family photos from his college graduation and his high school senior yearbook picture since that was the only head shot available. But it was mighty dark in the Cocktails basement, and only after Cal was leaning over the bar to order his drink did Howard recognize him.

He went over to the fidgety man who still resembled his old photos, in the flattering orange light illuminating the bottles of booze. "Cal?"

Cal jumped; Howard's tones had been kindly inquiring but hearing his own name was beginning to give him a start. There were nights when he was alone in his apartment, and he could swear he heard his name being sung in the distance—*CAL-vin HEW-itt, CAL-vin HEW-itt...* Teasingly, as if tempting him to come to the window and see who was there. But there was nobody there, only a few people traversing his block who, if they chanced to look up and saw him staring down at them, looking for the singer, would be just as startled as Cal was.

"Yeah?" Cal said, sizing up Howard sexually and dismissing him without a thought. Men were either tricks or threats, and Howard was no trick.

"I'm Howard," he said, offering his hand, which Cal took desultorily. "I'm Eric Hamilton's boyfriend, and I've been sent by Emma Hamilton to find you."

Fingers of dread gently brushed his spine. "Why?"

"Your family's very worried about you. They haven't heard from you in a while."

Cal knocked back his drink, the CNS-depressing alcohol barely making a dent in his amplitude. He hadn't called Gina in a while, it was true. Not since the night he'd overheard his upstairs neighbors talking about him—he didn't know how he heard them. He'd never heard a word from up there before, but he heard them this night—talking about how he used his sister for money for drugs, how he lied to her about being sick, "When really he's just a fucking tweaker," the girl had said to the guy.

Cal had been terrified. How had they known? How had they been able to hear what had gone on down here? What else had they heard? But they had, hadn't they, just as clearly as he'd just heard them... He'd been ashamed, mortified to have been discovered, to know that his neighbors were listening, despising him, and why shouldn't they? it was despicable, wasn't it? That night he'd still slammed, but first he'd hooked his VCR up to his stereo and plugged in a pair of headphones so he could watch porno and they wouldn't hear him upstairs.

Now they'd sent someone for him; he hadn't thought they would, hadn't thought about them much at all lately. Life without Gina's subsidy was harder, but at least now he was providing for his own habit. Once he'd said of his addiction that at least he wasn't a liar and a thief, and now he was both, but every addict holds onto something that makes it all right, that preserves their "integrity" such as it is and allows them to go on, and for Cal this something was that at least he wasn't stealing from his family. At least he wasn't bringing them any grief—never knowing how much grief and pain and fear his silence was capable of.

"I don't want to talk to them," Cal said curtly.

"You don't have to," Howard said. "Just come with me and talk to Emma so she can tell them you're all right."

Cal laughed, his fine mind not so gone that he couldn't appreciate irony. "Am I?"

Howard raised an eyebrow, appraising him. Obviously, the poor lost soul was not all right, but that wasn't Howard's business. He'd long ago learned not to try and rescue little boys lost; they tended to come to you to get their knees bandaged only so they could go get lost again.

"Emma's at the St. Francis. She's dying of cancer and she'd like to see you." This was a cheap shot, but Howard's nerves were fraying, and he wanted to finish this business; tweakers transmit their frantic pingings on the widest possible bandwidth, and between picking up on Cal's edginess and this goddamn shitty music, Howard had about had enough.

This news stunned Cal, brought an honest horror to a mind increasingly horrified only by its own imaginings. Unbidden, the picture came to his mind of Emma outside her house, saying "Morning, Cal," saving him from a bully's beating. For a moment he was awake, here, looking at himself in this dingy basement bar, chock full of speed, and awareness of himself allowed awareness of the rest of the world to come back to him: Gina, frantic, wondering what had happened to him.

"Asshole," came a voice from next to him, but he turned and there was nobody there. He was scared and guilty and tired, and he latched irrationally onto the idea that somehow Emma could make everything all right.

It was late, but Emma was up. Her chemotherapy had included a drug called methotrexate, the "meth" in its name no coincidence she thought, so sleepless nights were not only Cal's province these days. The weed allowed her to pass out sometimes, but it was getting harder to smoke it; she was coughing more, and more painfully. Baked goods from the pot store were a godsend but more and more often now it was hard to keep food down. She tried not to puke when Eric was around, but that was getting harder. Fortunately, the pot store also sold THC tinctures, green drops half honey and half bitter, and she exceeded the recommended dose of these with gusto when sleeplessness became exhaustion so complete she couldn't speak a complete sentence.

Tonight wasn't bad. She'd slept a good deal of the afternoon, and now the only thing bringing her down was loneliness and the paucity of decent late-night television. She remembered the days when insomniacs had it good, and three A.M. would provide some juicy tear-jerking "women's picture" from the '30s— but all those had been yanked from the local-station libraries to coin money once again, this time on video. Now all that TV had to offer in the night's longest hours were infomercials, amazing ways to tone a body she'd never have again or cook a meal she'd never make again, or make a fortune with no money down (*Now*, that *I could use*, she thought).

She could look out the window, but she couldn't open it; she grumbled frequently that a luxury hotel room where you couldn't get fresh air was no luxury. In truth it wasn't the air she missed (the nights were too damn cold for much of that) so much as the sounds. She'd been alive in New York; she'd been alive in Paris, even in Reno when Arlington Avenue was abuzz, because there had been the sound of life outside: people and cars and music. She hated this window because it was separating her from all that, and this was her last chance to sit in a window in a city and feel alive.

The phone rang, and she knew it had to be Howard. Eric didn't call in the middle of the night, afraid that the one time he did she'd be asleep and he'd have deprived her of a precious moment of rest. She wished he would, whether she was asleep or not—these loneliest hours of the night were the only times she couldn't prevent herself from being depressed. He was probably awake right now, she knew from Howard—he would get stoned and try to write and fail and get more stoned and cry and stuff himself and pass out at seven and wake up at three, right about now, and lie there in bed pretending to be asleep so as not to disturb Howard, who knew he was awake, could feel him wake up when he stopped twisting and turning and dreaming awful dreams that made him murmur in distress. *It is ridiculous*, she thought, *all this pretending we're*

still doing, even now, all pretending something to save some-
one else's feelings.

"I found him. I think I can get him there now, but I would-
n't bet on catching him again."

"You make him sound like a greased pig," Emma smiled.

"More like a frightened rabbit. He's out of his mind on
crystal."

"Do you think he's dangerous?"

Howard thought about it, looked back from the pay phone
at Cal, sitting on the curb at the corner of 9th and Mission, the
gas station's phosphorescent lamps illuminating a hunched,
tired figure. "No, not really."

"Then bring him here, please. I'm up."

It would be hard to say who was more shocked at the sight
of the other, Emma or Cal. The plump, wide-eyed earth mother
of Cal's childhood had diminished to this scrawny yellow
woman in a turban—only the eyes were the same, and he read
her shock at the sight of him with a surprise she couldn't feel
over his shock at her; Emma was used to scaring people, but Cal
had only just become capable of it. This was what she'd feared
for Eric in his first years in San Francisco, that one day he'd
come home like this: hollow, wasted, doomed.

"Please come in, Cal. Thank you for coming." She answered
Howard's inquiring look with a tilt of the head: *Come back later.*

More flustered than she'd anticipated, she made directly for
her stash. "Would you like to smoke a joint?"

"No, thanks," Cal said.

She nodded. "Yes, I hear you have other tastes."

There was something in this that riled Cal, though Emma
had meant no harm. "Yeah, well, we all medicate our own way."

She looked at him sideways, critically. "And what are you
medicating?"

"A terminal illness, same as you."

"Your medicine is hastening your end."

"Is that such a bad thing?" Cal asked, surprising himself.
He'd never thought about AIDS; it was simply the way he would
die—someday, some other day, a day that wasn't today, and

therefore didn't have to be thought about. This was the first time he realized that all this time he hadn't minded the knowledge that he would die young, maybe soon. "I'm enjoying what's left of my life, anyway."

"Are you? Enjoying it?"

He shrugged. The helplessness that had washed over him in the bar was gone, the brisk walk up to the hotel burning off some of the frustration he'd felt. "I feel pretty good most of the time." He considered this the truth. That the moments of unparalleled delight were fewer and farther between and the efforts to attain them were ever more Herculean was not something he would yet see.

She fired up her joint and held the hit, squinting at him, using the time to think. Exhaling, she coughed violently, and Cal stood there with the helpless bewilderment of someone in the presence of the sick, feeling they should do something and at a loss to think what. "You all right?" he asked as the coughing fit subsided, and she nodded, holding up a hand in a "give me a moment" gesture.

"I hate the coughing," she said finally. "I hate it when Eric sees me coughing. It's very hard on the family when someone dies." She thought back on what Eric said about being the last one left. "Harder on the survivors than the one who dies."

Cal leapt ahead to finish her thought. "So Gina asked you to find me."

"No, Carol asked me to find you," she said, watching his face and not disappointed by the surprise she saw there. "Gina went to Carol and told her you had HIV and that you'd disappeared. They're both very worried about you."

"My mom's probably worried some of her right-wing helmet-haired bitch friends will find out her son has AIDS—a matching bookend for the daughter who had the abortion."

"No, she's worried about you." Emma thought a moment, weed sending her mind down the garden path. "It's funny, really—I think this is the first time in her life that her religion is something more to her than something to foist on other people."

"Well, I've got my own religion, just like you do," he said, pointing at the pipe. "Pleasure."

Emma wanted to retort but reconsidered. What would she do without weed, she asked herself. She'd be mad from sleep deprivation, wasted from nausea, probably dead already of depression. Who was she to judge Cal? And yet, look at him. "Your religion is killing you," she said finally.

"I'm going to die anyway. You're not going to tell me 'there's so much to live for' and all that shit, are you? You're smarter than that."

Emma winced. They were so alike right now, Cal and Eric, so lost and so sure there was no hope. She felt the same pain for Cal she felt for Eric, as if he, too, was her son.

There had to be something she could do, she thought with sudden rage, *something that would shatter this certainty they had, this smug passivity. What* was *the point?* she wondered. What was the point of doing all she could for Eric, Howard, Cal, all these children, if all her death made them do was to lie down and die, too?

Her rage overwhelmed her, and she made an impulsive decision. She picked up the heavy chair she'd been sitting in; it was no effort because she'd refused to wonder if she could or not. Rage precludes such thoughts and makes such acts possible. She lifted it above her head, and before its weight could unbalance her she threw it at the window, smashing the pane. The chair and the atomized bits of safety glass went plummeting to Powell Street below, and bitter cold wet air came rushing in.

She turned to a horrified Cal, looking to him like some incensed goddess. "Do you hear that? Can you feel that? Smell that?"

She went to the window and listened to the noise below. "Muthafucka!" a homeless man yelled. "Muthafucka put a chair through the window!" She laughed. Even at this late hour the act was causing a commotion.

"Hear that? That's life. I'm losing it and you're throwing it away. I'm going to die and Howard's going to die. Eric's not, and you know what? You're not either. I can tell. You're too full of something. Don't ask me what. Maybe just luck. You're going to live, Cal. You *wish* you were going to die, because that makes all this, all this shit you're doing *OK*. But I won't let you. Any of you. I'll come back from the fucking *dead* and *make* you all live."

Cal stood rooted to the spot, unable to speak, to think. Half of Emma's words had been nonsense to him, more for herself than him, and yet... Then he heard a riot of footsteps coming down the hall, pounding on the door, the pass of the electronic key in the lock, men coming in and making for him and Emma stretching a hand out, some power in her, in this tableau, freezing them, too something about her celestial calm making them believe her improbable story about an accident, and Cal's wild drug-addled eyes mistaken for the ordinary terror any ordinary person would feel in such a situation. Then he realized that Emma was being packed up and moved to another suite (anyone paying this much money on a timely basis for this long is asked few questions), and he can go. He has to go.

He came out on the street and saw the chair lying smashed in the middle of the street, the only thing to prove it wasn't all a dream. He started walking up Geary toward home when he heard a voice, *There he is, the one who threw the chair, he made that sick lady crazy, he did it he did it.*

"I didn't," he said out loud, walking faster. "I didn't do it." He wasn't the only person walking down the street talking to himself, but he wasn't talking to himself, he was talking back to them, to anyone who could hear them, defending himself. "I didn't do it," he repeated all the way home. "I didn't."

CHAPTER FIVE
BENEFACTOR

Cal's route from his mother's house to Albertson's took him through Old Southwest Reno's leafier side streets. He left her house on Arlington and got onto Plumas, a parallel side street, as quickly as he could. He felt exposed to too many eyes on Arlington, too many passing cars, too many dour glances. He turned left on Mount Rose Street, passing the famous Redfield mansion, where a rich old crackpot had died with his fortune in bags of silver dollars. Crazier than Cal, no doubt, but you're only crazy when you can no longer afford to be "eccentric."

He'd only been back in Reno a month, but certain things had already struck him. San Francisco had been bad for him in many ways, but the simplest one would never have occurred to him until now: That city was dark and gray most of the time, whereas Reno's location in the high desert provided a bounty of sunshine. He was sure he hadn't seen the sun in years; of course, this wasn't true since even in San Francisco the sun shone sometimes. Nevertheless, he already recognized that he'd been suffering from an absence of light. He'd taken up September sunbathing with a passion, sprawled out in Carol's backyard, trying to ignore what he could hear the neighbors saying about him, what people said about him in the supermarket, on the streets, everywhere he went: There he is, the speed freak, Crystal Cal, the Freak of Van Ness Avenue.

This was the second time in his life he'd come home, fleeing a life he no longer wanted. *Well, that wasn't exactly true, was it?* Cal reminded himself—reminded himself because if he didn't, *they* would. There was no longer any opportunity to lie, even to himself; every thought was exposed to this glittering hard fall sunlight for *them* to judge. No, this time he'd *had* to come home—it was home or the nuthouse or drug rehab (again).

He got to Albertson's and went in with his head down. What he hated most was walking in somewhere. *They know*— everything that was on the radio about him in San Francisco had been passed on to civic-minded citizens in Reno so they could watch out for him. Nobody ever said anything, of course, but that was part of the sentence they'd passed on him—that he never know, really, what was real and what wasn't. Whether he'd ever been talked about on the radio, denounced by his neighbors, made infamous, notorious, recognizable as a public menace (but not such a menace he could be arrested for it). Whether any of the voices, the faces, that had seemed so real, were anything other than his own demons. Whether it would ever be safe to call himself crazy and leave it at that, and it wasn't, was it?—because you never knew, it had all been so real. There was no way to be sure, was there, whether any of it had really happened outside his own head? You had to say no, it hadn't, but at the same time you also had to hold onto a reserve of paranoia, *just in case you were right after all.* Because *that* was what would really break you, wasn't it, if you resolved to believe it wasn't true, and it turned out you were right?—it was, it had all happened after all, but how could you ever know for sure…?

The Terror had begun that night as he fled Emma's hotel room. That was the night *they* broke out, no longer confined to home's near environs, the street below him and the apartment above. Now they were everywhere, and legion. At the baths, they were there. Not moments after he slammed his hit, he could hear an angry voice: *I saw him, he shot up, he's HIV-positive and he's here to* infect *us.* How could someone have seen him do it, unless they were peeking over the wall? Bathhouse "rooms" were in truth nothing other than cubicles with doors, so in theory there were five people who could have seen him do it. And was Cal in any position to denounce them for spying, when clearly they were doing a public service by catching him at his disgusting dangerous habit? And then he'd hear the voice of authority responding to the accuser, presumably an employee of the baths, coolly informing the enraged man that the police would be called. Cal would freeze—should he run? But he'd have to check out; the cops would get him on the street. He would bolt out of his room to try and confront his accuser, see confirmation of what he'd heard in the disapproving looks on the faces of the towel-clad men in the halls. Yet except for that clue, everything else looked normal, and so Cal would beat a retreat back to his room, shutting the door, turning off the lights, tense as a suspension bridge cable, waiting for the cops to come, for the confrontation, which never came. Hours later he would realize it had been a hallucination; Jesus Christ, most everybody at the fucking bathhouse was HIV-positive and after a certain hour of the night most everybody was spun out, too, for God's sake. Then he'd sheepishly pack up and go home, having never even gotten laid.

He would hear the neighbors upstairs when he slammed at home; somehow they were able to see and hear what he was doing. Were they dangling a camera down out their window to look in his window? He tacked blankets up over the windows. But they still heard him, were still talking about him—did they have infrared film? Had they drilled a hole in the ceiling, a tiny, tiny hole through which some high-tech camera was watching him? He got on a chair and examined the ceiling microscopically for microscopic clues. There was this heavy metal radio station that had a call-in show that specialized in gleefully savage evisceratory humor, and he knew the upstairs neighbors had called him in, he was the butt of jokes all over the Bay Area, a running gag on this station—but every time he dialed the station in on his stereo, the joke was over, because every time *they* could see him doing it, they had a hot line to the radio station and warned them when he was listening, and if he ever caught them they couldn't fuck with his head anymore, he could have them evicted, sue the station, if only, if only, he could catch them at it...

He would take his hit to the dirty bookstore and pay five bucks for a "preview booth," where he could watch a movie and have about an hour's wank time. But they could see him shooting up in there, too, see what it was in the film that made him at least close to hard, and he heard them talking outside his door: *So he likes to get fucked, does he? Fuckin' loves it. Well when he comes outside, we'll get him, take him down the alley, fuckin' gang-bang him—he'll love that.* Cal felt a mix of lust and horror at the thought—there was something so exciting about it, even though he knew in reality it would probably mean his death. But what he was looking for now was something *more*, still something more, even more than slamming could give him. A man in every hole, all the time, that would give him no opportunity to think, would free him from the burden of consciousness, would gather him back up into the Rapture, that thoughtless wave of pleasure shooting up had first given him but gave him no longer. Every thought was pain now; there was nothing but pain and fear—unless you stopped doing speed. But crashing was unendurable. Unthinkable. The greatest horror of all. In fear, in the Terror, there was something to react to, to flee from; but when you crashed there was this awful *nothing*, this postnuclear wasteland in your head. Beyond existential anomie, it was the horror of finding yourself completely alone in the world, a world where nobody loved you *and* nobody hated you because you hardly existed, didn't matter. It was an emptiness, a hollowness, a sadness so deep and conclusive it precluded tears, for how could you cry over the awfulness of it all when the awfulness was the norm? It was Hell, in short. Cal had never ever thought that Hell would be the price of the Rapture. You could feel the Terror, or face that emptiness—and the Terror was better, because a world where you were constantly pursued and tortured by demons was better than a world where there were no demons, no angels, no God, no nothing: a Hiroshima of the psyche. The nuclear metaphor is no exaggeration: All the centers of Cal's brain responsible for generating bright spots and happy thoughts had been incinerated, vaporized.

Cal knew this. He would go to the library and do research; the speed gave him focus as long as there was something to focus on. It was when there was nothing to focus on, or even just not enough, that his mind provided its own sensory input. He knew how crystal burned out his dopamine production centers; he knew this dopamine depletion led to a state that mimicked paranoid schizophrenia; he knew that research indicated that the "voices" many schizophrenics heard were actually subtle modulations emanating from their own voice boxes, which is why they always sounded like they were coming from another room (a scientist had discovered that opening your jaw as wide as it would go would block the voices as long as the patient could hold this position). He knew all this, and he couldn't stop.

He had enough sense left not to go around telling people that he was being spied on, laughed at, talked about—as long as he couldn't prove it, it would prove only that he was paranoid, and if he did that, they'd put him in the nuthouse where he couldn't get high anymore.

He knew from watching Luke's life what awaited him when there was nothing left to sell. He would live on the street, and he would sell his body. He knew this was coming, knew he needed to get a pager so that he could put an escort ad in the gay rag, but every time he had the money to do it, drugs came first. He met Luke's friend Casey, who was wanted by the cops for murder. Seems a young boy had come to town, 16 years old, fresh as a daisy and twice as sweet, and Casey had befriended him— actual friendship on the streets is a remarkable rarity, a testament to the special nature of this new boy. Then seems this boy, who'd never done speed and didn't want to, went to a hotel room with this old man who tied him up, shot him up, and fucked him for days, leaving him mentally shattered and most likely infected with HIV. Casey got a gun, and when he saw this man, a regular on Polk Street, he walked up to him and shot him in the head. If the police found him, he'd go to jail, maybe get the death penalty, but knowing the facts of the case, they weren't looking too hard, and as long as Casey kept a low profile he'd probably get away with it. That was what was left of life when your demons called the shots; those were the kind of men who preyed on the desperate. The demons that lived only in Cal's head now would be his very real physical companions, his deadly partners in his necessary transactions, when he ended up on the street, too.

Luke had been over one day when they'd heard a commotion in the street. They'd looked down to see a bunch of Mexicans kicking someone on the sidewalk, then running away, laughing. "I should call the cops," Cal said.

"I know those guys," Luke said. "They're chiba dealers, and he's someone's customer who didn't pay up. Leave it." It hadn't taken long in Luke's company to realize that the Mexicans who walked up and down O'Farrell, making eye contact and grabbing their crotches, weren't interested in blow jobs—the crotch grab was a old signal meaning *drugs for sale*, even though these days dealers kept their balloons in their mouths (for easy swallowing if arrested) rather than in their baskets.

He had an argument with Luke later that day—nothing remarkable. Seems all they did was argue now. Cal said something stupid; Luke told him how stupid he was; Cal nursed his wounds in hurt silence, which only made Luke madder; something mean came out of Cal's mouth and Luke would leave. Only this time, instead of just leaving, Luke nearly kicked in Cal's thin front door—not to get back in, just to take his rage out on something. Luke never touched Cal; he was too smart for that. Drug charges in San Francisco were one thing, assault charges quite another. Even in his blackest rage, Luke could still calculate what sort of revenge was allowed.

Cal stood in his apartment terrified as the door splintered. His adrenal glands pumped out even more flight-or-fight chemicals into his system than the meth had already triggered, and for Cal the response was always flight. He *knew* where Luke was going, didn't he, going to get those chiba dealers to kick down his door and kick him to death. He ran out of his house, down Van Ness at five o'clock in the afternoon, rush hour, thinking someone, surely someone, would see the terror on his face and stop him and ask, "What's wrong, are you OK?" But anyone who might have had that compassion was stopped by someone who said, *Don't you listen to the radio. That's Crystal Cal, Stay away from him. He just shot up, he's dangerous, he's crazy.* Cal could hear the boots thundering down Van Ness behind him, Luke and his connections grinning like the horsemen of Cal's apocalypse, and there was only one thing to do: Run, run!

At Van Ness station, he found an ambulance picking up a drunk who'd fallen down the stairs. Cal begged the paramedics, "Help me." They took him to the hospital where they put a shot of Ativan into his ass, and after a while Luke and the chiba dealers were no longer in the hallway outside the emergency room, demanding his head on a plate, or they'd tear the fucking place down. Very early in the morning, Cal woke up on a gurney and walked back out into the world, still quiet inside his head and out, and walked home with no jacket in the freezing-cold, windy mist. They were talking about him upstairs when he got home—they never rested—they laughed at him for being such a fool.

There was only one thing to do, and that was get all the speed out of the house—all of it. Then he'd be safe. When the cops came there'd be no evidence. He had two quarters left, and he almost threw them down the toilet, but then thought, *That's silly.* So he got out his soup spoon and mixed up the biggest hit he'd ever done, stuck it in his arm and went back to his bed to rush. But however much he did now, it didn't matter, the Rapture factory was burned down, and there was no rush. Instead he heard them shouting upstairs, *He did it, he shot it all up, he's ready, let's go down and fuck him till he DIES.* And he could hear their steps on the back stairs, right next to his apartment, hear them running down to get him. He ran to the door, to make sure it was bolted, waited for the door from the stairs to the hall to open, but it never did. *Ha ha ha, you asshole, do you really think we'd fuck your diseased butthole?* came the cold metallic voice through the ceiling. Cal went back to his bed and lay there, heart pounding, too high to be embarrassed or dismayed or relieved or anything other than watchful, ever watchful, for the next time they came caroming down the stairs, just in case this time they really meant it.

It was an outreach worker at the needle exchange who got him into rehab. October was a college student who volunteered at the program, which set up each night at a different place in town to let addicts exchange dirty needles for clean ones, no questions asked. If you only had a few and didn't start any shit, she'd usually give you a few more than you brought in, along with free tie-offs, antibiotic cream, alcohol wipes, cookers, bleach, condoms, lube—pretty much anything that constituted harm reduction. It was October who'd slipped a brochure for Emerson House into Cal's brown paper bag, circling the part about the residence they ran for HIV-positive addicts. *How did she know?* Cal thought, then realized, *Yes, the radio, she's heard about me on the radio.*

She hadn't done it maliciously, Cal knew; October always smiled at you no matter how fucked up you were, no matter whether you were too nervous to even look her in the eye and never knew if she was smiling or not—somehow you always knew she was. He couldn't say why this seemed like a ray of hope to him; the abstraction of "rehab" had always been a possibility but had also always been a joke on the circuit, a place for people who couldn't handle their drugs, the losers. (How they'd laughed at white-trash speed freaks who were stupid enough to believe bugs were crawling on them or that the devil was under the couch; Cal was too smart to believe in such foolishness, but now his intelligence had betrayed him, created demons he *could* believe in, taken the fear of others' judgment he'd had all his life and turned that into the devil under his couch.) But it was obvious now to Cal that he was *already* a loser, *couldn't* handle his drugs, and there was no way he could stop on his own: he knew that now. And yet he had to stop, didn't he? Didn't he? *No, of course not,* said the one voice in his head that never spoke aloud, that wrote its words on the water of his subconscious for him to read as if they were his own, words that said, *You just need to make some more money, you just need to get hooked up with a source who's got Xanax you can take when you get too high, you just need to take a few days off, you just need to do anything you have to do other than stop.*

Nevertheless, he asked October anyway the next time she saw him, and she smiled and said, "Emerson House is great, Cal. That's where I went."

"You? You?" Cal asked twice, disbelieving.

"I was worse off than you are now, let me tell you."

He couldn't believe it. She was young and pretty; her skin glowed with health, not heroin. Moreover, she was *happy*. Cal listened to her story with growing astonishment, heard how she'd turned tricks on Geary for crack and gotten regularly beat up by her pimp and the johns, how she'd been through jail's revolving door, how she'd slept in Dumpsters to keep warm, and on and on. And yet here she was, living proof of this amazing fact: that Hell was a territory you could *leave*.

He blurted out his own desperation, careful never to assert that he was being spied on—as if she didn't know from looking at him, the fatigue and terror on his face. She hugged him, and he cried for the first time in a very long time, because it had been so long since someone had cared, since he'd even remembered there might be one person in the whole world who didn't despise him the way he'd come to despise himself.

The first few days in Emerson House, he slept. The days before that had been a whirlwind, selling what little furniture he had left, throwing away the porno tapes and drug paraphernalia, going through the usual useless motions of trying to get his deposit back on his apartment, taking the TB test necessary before he could get into Emerson House. The strangest thing of all was that upstairs all was quiet—nobody had a bad word to say about him, and on the street people no longer glared at him. If everyone knew what he'd been doing, then they all knew he was going into rehab, too. He could have crowed with triumph—that'll shut the fuckers up! (Because it *was* all real, it had all been *too* real to have been a hallucination, but it didn't matter now because it was over.)

The next few days, he cried all the time for no reason; it would just come on him—he'd let out a sigh and that would be all it would take to trigger sobs. It astonished him how freely the tears came, as if speed had been a dam and the stream of ordinary pains of everyday life—which should have brought a frown or a sigh or a curse each day for so many days—had backed up, unfelt. And Cal had always thought these pains had been eliminated in the wash of pleasure slamming had given him, but they'd only been postponed, stored in a reservoir until now, the dam cracking as the speed left his system. Annoyances and minor frustrations and all life's little daily sadnesses had swirled and eddied together over time in that reservoir to become this, this astonishingly swift and heavy cataract of tears that just flowed and flowed without even any object or thought attached to them; Cal merely stood there above himself, watching himself being swept away as he cried and cried and never knew what for.

After he'd eaten and slept like a teenager for a week, the fatigue was over. Then came the sadness, the emptiness, the cosmic loneliness that comes from realizing how thoroughly you've disconnected yourself from your own humanity. This was a fact that wasn't in any of the recovery pamphlets: as emotional capacity returns to the addict, it's the capacity for pain that returns long before the capacity for pleasure.

Still, there were pleasures in life again. Everyone in Emerson House had a job of some sort, and as low man on the totem pole Cal got the job nobody else wanted: dishwasher. The thing of it was, this was the job he liked best, and when it came time to cycle him off to another task, he asked to stay, and since nobody else wanted the job, they let him (eventually the counselors would put a stop to this, the idea being that residents *should* be assigned jobs they don't want). There was one simple reason he liked the job: In the kitchen, and nowhere else in the house, there was a radio. Cal had forgotten how much he loved music, never knew how much it had meant to him until it, like all other normal pleasures, had left his life. As his energy returned, he could shake his booty to the amusement of the other residents, even when it wasn't his turn to choose the station. (And yet still there was the silent voice, whispering words to fall into the water of his sub-conscious, willing him to forget every bad thing that had happened and remember, remember, remember the Rapture, what was this silly little pleasure compared to that...)

Most of the day was spent in classes of some kind, designed to help the addict, but most days Cal couldn't help but feel that so many classes defeated the point, the point being to occupy most all one's time so as to leave little time for thinking about drugs, but when all you did all day was talk about drugs... (And he'd lie on the bed as he had when Gina had taken care of him, and he would dream, to shatter the boredom of life in a facility you could leave only once a week, chaperoned, for a trip to Walgreens, but instead of dreaming of the pipe he dreamed of the point, and the humdrum days and prayers and phrases memorized through repetition fell away. Like a monk in his cell, he lay in bed and dreamed not of virtue but of vice, dreamed of the day he could slam again, and he could someday; he just had to get his shit together for a while and then, repaired, he could return to the bosom of the Rapture...)

He'd been in residence for four weeks, and things were starting to make sense to him. Things in the 12-step materials they gave him, things other addicts said about their experience, resonated with him, gave him the blessed realization he wasn't the only one who'd ever felt these things, who'd ever heard voices and seen things and felt like a fool afterward. A man came in to speak whose story was basically Cal's own: the fundamentalist upbringing, the sex-and-drug marathons, and the blankets over the windows, and Cal had asked him afterward, "You shot up, you *know*," putting an emphasis on the word that condensed everything the other man did, indeed, know. "How in the world do you just *walk away* from that much pleasure?"

"Maybe you need to ask yourself why you need that much pleasure—why ordinary pleasure isn't enough for you."

This struck Cal with particular force. (And yet, what were ordinary pleasures compared to the Rapture, if you could have *that* who'd *want* the ordinary...) Yet this voice was losing power; he was learning to *hear* that voice's rationalizations out loud and therefore contradict them out loud, taking their power.

When he'd entered Emerson House, he hadn't just entered a rehab center but also AIDS, Inc. He was HIV-positive, and there were a vast array of services available, as Eric had discovered when Howard had gotten sick. Only unlike Eric, Cal hadn't needed to fight for them, probably because he hadn't entered the system through the San Francisco AIDS Foundation. He was put on these new miracle medications, "protease inhibitors," which had just been on the cover of *Time* and heralded the end of the worst of AIDS (in America, anyway). He'd been signed up for MediCal, for Social Security Disability (his T-cells having been under 200 for some time, qualifying him as an AIDS patient), for everything available to give dying people comfort. He'd thought all this to be infinite kindness until the day someone at Emerson House heard him say he was depressed and tried to hustle him from the detox unit to the Triple Diagnosis unit, one floor down, where clients had HIV, substance abuse problems, *and* mental problems unrelated to drugs. "I'm not crazy," Cal said firmly, "at least not when I'm off speed. And I'm *not* going in with the mental patients!" Unfortunately, one of the mental patients heard this exchange and complained, and everyone in detox was treated to a consciousness-raising about TDs, who were not to be called crazy mental patients, even though they were. Cal smiled slightly, but only slightly—the counselors had eagle eyes for smirks and other nonverbal insults. Still, it was an eye opener to him to realize that the more problems he could be diagnosed with, the more money there was in him for Emerson House to get out of the city and county of San Francisco. All for a good cause, sure, sure, *if* you weren't just being hustled into a more lucrative diagnostic category, put in where you didn't belong.

It made him feel good to see this—not because he wanted to think less of Emerson House or its employees but because it was a clear realization, a use of his long-dormant cognitive faculties, yet also a street-smart realization of what the game was, and that was a new kind of smarts for him. Was it worth what he'd paid to get this new kind of smarts? *Didn't matter* was the next street-smart realization. *Shit went down, didn't it? What did you get out of it?* For many addicts, life becomes a purely transactional activity, and this way of seeing life endures long after the drugs are gone, when they acknowledge that the hard truths they have learned had to be scored through experience—a deal had to be made to get that knowledge, didn't it?

The day the worst happened was the day Cal got a letter from Social Security. Turned out that since he'd essentially had an AIDS diagnosis since the last time he'd gone to the free clinic (a visit he'd only made in an attempt to get a prescription for Xanax), his SSDI was retroactive for five months (unlike many of the other residents, he'd worked all his life and paid into the system and therefore got the more lucrative SSDI instead of the subsistence-level SSI). And since he'd signed up for direct deposit, he now had $6,000 in the bank.

Cal cried as he read the letter. These days he usually knew why he was crying, but not today. Maybe he was crying with relief, that the poverty he'd accepted as his inevitable lifelong destiny wasn't to be, maybe he was crying with disappointment because he could hear the voice again, so recently silenced, the voice reminding him that he never had a drug problem, did he, just a financial problem. and now he had it, so much money, enough for so many hits, so many escorts, so much rapture, now after he'd all but accepted it was never to be again...

Three days later he was out of Emerson House. He checked into a weekly room in the Tenderloin, called his most reliable connection and scored an eight-ball, bought a few new points from someone outside needle exchange, and paged Luke.

He did his hit while he waited for Luke to come over, he couldn't wait. It was going to feel so good, he knew it would; it had been so long, weeks and weeks, and all the dopamine centers had had plenty of time to rebuild, he was sure, and he did his hit and lay down on the bed and the Rapture did come, but only for a few minutes, because after a few minutes he could hear them out on the street, his upstairs neighbors—they had found him! Eddy Street was always noisy. People were always screaming and fighting, and even when you weren't on speed, there was plenty enough to hear out there to frighten you, and how little it took now for every shout Cal heard to be a call for his blood. His heart hammered in terror as he waited for Luke to come, and he prayed he wouldn't be alone when they came running up the stairs to get him.

A night came that broke him finally and completely. He'd done his hit and started hearing the voices upstairs; somehow his upstairs neighbors from the old apartment building had taken up positions above him in this fleabag weekly. They were ragging on him like they always did when he surprised himself by saying, "Yeah yeah, you're going to come down stairs and rape me and kill me ho hum." He almost laughed; his own terrors had become so predictable as to be boring, his clever mind's boredom had finally trumped its norepinephrine response.

Actually, the voices said, *we have something a little different planned for you tonight, Cal. There's someone up here you know.*

Cal waited, his full attention as always on this frequency in his head. Nothing came.

Say something, why don't you?

Another pause. *I don't have anything to say to that motherfucker.*

Cal's blood froze. "No," he said aloud. "No way."

Yes way, Cal, came the voice again, not one of the familiar voices that were only distinguishable as male and female. This was indisputably Luke's voice, coming through the ceiling. *I've been up here all along, with them. Who do you think told them all about you?*

"No. Luke wouldn't do that."

Why not, Cal? asked one of the other voices.

"Luke doesn't lie. He's never lied to me. Whatever else he's done, he's never lied to me."

I HAVEN'T DONE ANYTHING TO YOU, YOU FUCKING PIECE OF SHIT. YOU'RE THE ONE WHO USED ME TO SHOOT YOU UP. I GOT AIDS STICKING MYSELF WITH YOUR FUCKING DIRTY NEEDLE.

"No. Oh, no. Oh, my God." This circle of persecution and rebuttal had been Cal's life for so long; the voices had condemned him for collecting disability while shooting drugs, for getting fucked without a rubber even when it was another HIV-positive person who did it, for just being an all around fuck-up. They knew everything about him, the worst, all of it, and yet always he could argue with them; always he could find some way to say, "I'm only hurting myself, I'm only killing myself, I have the right to do that." Now that was gone. The horror that had come already was nothing compared to the unimaginable guilt he felt now. Not Luke, anyone but Luke, if I infected anyone let it not be Luke.

He thought to run for the door, to run upstairs before Luke could get away, he had to know, he *had to know*. But as always they were one step ahead of him. *He'll be out the fire escape before you get here*, they said. *We all will. If we're even here!* they laughed gleefully.

"I have to know."

And you don't, do you? Luke's cold, scornful voice came through. The voices had never sounded human; they had always had a metallic ring that could only carry one emotion: anger. There had always been two of them, a young man and a young woman, occasionally other young men but always the same voice. But not now; this was *distinctly* Luke's voice. Cal had heard, and he had believed, and yet, and yet, he'd never *seen* them; they never *had* run down the stairs and broken down his door; he could never be sure they were real; he *had to assume* it was all in his head. But this...Luke's voice, so real, so full of the rage and hatred it could carry when he was flinging insults at Cal...

"It can't be real," he insisted aloud, even though they could read his emotions on his face, even though they already knew what he was thinking, he had to say it.

Can't it? asked the girl. *You'll never know, will you, Cal? That's your punishment for what you've done to Luke—YOU'LL NEVER KNOW.* And then an awful silence, where a human being might have laughed maniacally, but the voices never laughed.

Cal ran out of his room, ran down the streets, saw the looks on every face, every one knew, it was on the radio, everyone knew who he was and what he'd done. The voices were a mob now, a mob reporting his every move to the radio station so everyone would know which way he was going. He got to Geary and slowed down—mustn't run, or the cops would suspect something. He was a white boy still reasonably kept, and that if nothing else had kept him out of jail so far. The cacophony of voices faded somewhat as he crossed Divisadero, up over the hill past Kaiser, on out into "the other Chinatown" of the avenues, now reduced to the occasional shout of "faggot" from a passing car—a shout that even now reminded him of another such shout long ago.

At a certain point he realized he had to turn right, get over to Lombard. It was the usual clammy, damp summer in San Francisco, but Cal didn't feel the cold; the speed and his motion kept him anesthetized. Blind flight had turned into a goal, and the thought of the goal brought him peace. The air got even colder as he approached the Golden Gate Bridge, the voices quieter. *He won't do it*, the girl said from down the block. *He's a chickenshit.*

As he passed a phone booth, Cal realized there was one thing he needed to do. They had worried about him when he'd gone down the rabbit hole, and it was only fair to give them closure.

"I have a collect call from Cal, will you accept the charges?"

"Yes," Carol said automatically, too surprised to register anything else.

"Hi, Mom."

"Cal…"

"I don't want to bother you, or cause you any more trouble. I just called to say goodbye."

"Where are you going?"

"I'm ending it. It's the only way."

Carol's mind glided over all the things one could, should, was expected to say, and yet none of them came to her lips. "Where are you?"

"Golden Gate Bridge. Kinda cliché, I know." Before *they* could say it.

"Cal, you don't have to do that."

"I do. I can't go back to rehab, I can't go back there and sit there and talk about drugs all day with all these other drug addicts when all we really wanna do is get high and fuck each other—when all *I* really wanna do," he corrected himself before the voices could correct him.

"You can come back here."

"What?"

"You can come back here. You can get on a plane tomorrow morning and come back here. You can come back here and get yourself straight."

The words rang like bells each time Carol said them. He remembered the way he'd felt when October had directed him toward rehab: This idea that Hell was a place you could leave, if you really wanted to. He should hang up, he should jump, it was best for everyone, the conspiracy against him would be revealed, and *they'd* be punished: Carol wouldn't have to worry, and he'd never have to face Gina... He waited to see what the voices would say, and to his astonishment they were silent, perhaps as startled as he was. Leave San Francisco, leave it all, burn your bridges behind you instead of jumping off one.

"I'm going to go to the airport and buy you a ticket right now. You can't buy a ticket over the phone for someone else. You have to do it in person," she said, as if reminding herself of that fact. "You do have ID still, don't you?"

"Yeah...yeah, I do."

"Call me back in...an hour and a half. And I'll tell you what flight you're on. Can you do that?"

"Yeah. Yes." All his life he'd felt like he had to deflect his mother's brisk, cold efficiency; now it had become his shield. Suddenly he had a way out, another chance he didn't deserve. He had to get back to his room and pack what little he had and call his mother and get to the airport somehow—*how? Beg enough change for the bus to the airport?* No, he had a bag of new points; he could hawk them on Eddy Street for a few bucks.

"I'll see you tomorrow. Call me back."

Cal started to cry. "Thank you. I don't deserve it...."

Carol's voice softened. "Just come home, Cal. It's time."

Later Carol realized she'd unconsciously made that decision long ago— that if Cal ever called, she'd tell him to come home.

All that remained was for him to call, and now he had.

She called Gina and left a message on her machine to fill her in on developments. Gina's concern over Cal had faded significantly since she'd discovered that he'd lied to her and used her for money for drugs. But then Carol thought a most pagan thought, *She's a Scorpio and they are not the forgiving kind.*

She went out the door without her purse, went back for it, drove to the airport. If she had consciously picked one word to describe her mental state, *resolved* would have been be the best. It was time at last to take action.

She got onto Plumb Lane before she allowed herself to cry. She never, ever would have admitted to anyone the selfish thought in her mind right now, that she was so glad there would be someone else in the house at night, a man around the house to do the things she had to ask a neighbor or pay a stranger to do, and she was so selfishly glad her son was coming home so that she could be useful again, so that maybe somehow, finally, she could have a family.

Just across the street and over one house, Eric was burrowed into the basement bunker that had once been his teenage playroom. He probably wouldn't have heard Carol's car pull out even if he hadn't been engrossed in his latest occupation, seeing how big a hit he could pull on his new bong, even if the television hadn't been pumping CNN's brisk, stern tones into his THC-attenuated ears. Eric was proud of his ability to pull a room-filling cloud of smoke into his lungs; it was one of the last physical capacities he still retained from his previous life.

The sharp cough that hit him at the end of his exhalation required a swig of fruit nectar, which simultaneously lubricated his throat and quenched his sweet tooth. Shortly thereafter there was a feeling in the pit of his stomach that might or might not be hunger, but that he always took to be, because it was a good reason to get up and check the fridge.

He found himself huffing and puffing at the top of the stairs he'd once bounded up without any detectable increase in heart rate, but while part of this was due to the weed, most of it was due to the 40 extra pounds he was carrying around these days.

Maybe more, now—it was 40 the last time he'd weighed himself, but like many fat people Eric had taken to wearing sweats and other elastic-banded bottoms, which enabled him to remain oblivious to any further waistline expansion.

He'd made it out of the house today, a big expedition to the store to stock up. This happened about twice a week—he could have gone less often and loaded up, since Emma's fridge and extra freezer and capacious cabinets could have held a pirate's bounty of Pepperidge Farm cookies, Ben and Jerry's ice cream, Entenmann's cakes, potato chips, Wheat Thins (a healthy alternative, Eric convinced himself), etc., but he limited himself on each trip to a carry basket of crap snacks, all too conscious of the hideousness of a big fat guy bellying up to the checkout with a shopping cart full of hydrogenated sugar. Now he stared into the refrigerator as if into a crystal ball, as if it could provide answers to all of life's more troubling questions.

At length he decided on variety, some guacamole and tortilla chips along with several beers—several to avoid another trip upstairs; he'd thought of using the little fridge downstairs he'd stored Cokes in as a youngster, but then he'd never get above ground and there had to be some limit. Beer had become a valuable accessory to pot and in truth was responsible for most of his bloated appearance. Hard liquor was sickening to him, wine was what he and Howard had enjoyed so much, so now he drank beer and ale, the good kinds: Sam Adams or Sierra Nevada Pale Ale or Henry Weinhard, thick and delicious and far more fattening than the weak industrial piss beers that came in cases the size of foot lockers. There were days when weed was indisputably not enough, because weed had an unpleasant tendency to stimulate your central nervous system, and when Eric became too excited or agitated he could hear whatever sensible thing Howard or Emma would have said, and that was when he would weep, when he would bawl; that was when he would curl up in a ball on the floor, fully aware that there was no sense in the world anymore, that there was no love, no life but the life inside this unbreakable globe of pain and loss. Beer made sure he didn't weep as much as he would have otherwise.

Downstairs he flopped back into the easy chair and tried to

decide where to put everything; the little table next to the chair was cluttered with marijuana paraphernalia, the *TV Guide*, empty juice cans and beer bottles, so he wedged the chips between his gut and the arm of the chair and put the guacamole on his belly. A thought flitted through his mind: A picture of Howard hilariously preparing Eric for a holiday visit to Howard's family, his description of his Uncle Roger's "shelf": "this great promontory built up over geologic ages out of prime rib and butterfat, whereupon Uncle Roger as you will see will rest his wine glass as if upon a shelf he carries around with him for this purpose." Eric had nearly driven off the road laughing then, and he laughed for a moment now, but the very act froze him, guilt and shame overwhelming him at the idea that he would dare to laugh at anything ever again.

CNN was detailing the skull-crushingly boring election of 1996, an election that proved the bankruptcy of the two-party system, since it allowed an unpopular president to win reelection because his opponent had trudged dutifully to the top of the ranks of his party, and whether the American people liked him or not, it was "his turn" to be president. The only thing the American people disliked more than their current president was a bitter-looking old man who thought the rest of the nation should put their own hopes and fears aside and vote for him because it was "his turn." By this early September evening, the election was already pretty much a wrap and CNN was desperately trying to find some tidbit of interest to pluck off the picked-over bones of this dead story.

He and Howard had rarely watched TV; Howard had even had this routine where he played the Professor, a supercilious bow-tied intellectual, whose official line on the subject was "I don't own a television. Well, I do, but I leave it in the closet under a blanket and only take it out when there's something very, *very* good on PBS." Eric watched TV all the time now, or at least had it on all the time. His mind would, of course, wander far and long from whatever was on the set, only to be pulled back home by either some keyword that triggered his return to attentiveness or some particularly loathsome commercial that would make him shout at the TV. He and Howard hadn't been against TV; they'd just been too busy doing other things, dinner with friends, a concert, a reading, or something at the theater Eric had been obliged to review. (He'd come to loathe gay theater, little of which was worth a tinker's damn but only, as he put it in a column, "an excuse for middle class fags to see naked boys onstage without the terror of being seen coming out of the Campus Theater.") They'd had a *life*, Eric reflected now with some amazement during an accidental moment of clarity, a moment he hastened to end with another swig of beer and another bong hit.

The television was always on, partly for company but partly for another reason. Eric had grown terrified of silence. Silence was the sound of hospitals, the sound of Howard resting fitfully, the sound of the absence of living things. SILENCE=DEATH, the stickers had promised, and now Eric knew it to be true.

This is what Eric could not think of, could not stay sober long enough to confront. Howard and Emma were dead, first Emma and six months later Howard. Emma died and Eric was busy; there was the estate to see to and things to settle, and of course there was Howard, who needed him more every day, and like so many others, Eric buried his grief in work, but then Howard was dead and there was nobody to hold, to cry with, to love. There was grief and only grief and nothing and no one to make it better. And because of that, grief became impossible. The magnitude of it was of such width, such depth, it could never be crossed; the more you tried to cross it the deeper into its depth you went, and you couldn't see up when you were in it, only down, so you could never be sure there was an up, that there was really anything other than further down. Cal had thought when he slammed that he was banishing pain, pain that was never to return; Eric knew when he ate and drank and smoked that he was only postponing pain, until "someday," that unimaginable day when just being alive didn't hurt so bad that letting yourself feel the horror of it even for a second would kill you on the spot.

Cruelest of all had been the arrival of these new pills, pills that could have saved Howard's life as they were saving so many others, pills that for Howard had arrived like the governor's call a minute too late, and that made it even worse, the guilty feeling Eric shared with every survivor, that surely there had been *something* he could have done, some little secret he could have discovered that would have kept Howard alive a little longer, just long enough to make all the difference in the world.

I have no stirring deathbed scenes for you. Emma and Howard both died well, which is to say they died having accepted their unexpectedly early absence from the lives they'd loved, and they were both able to look back and say, "It wasn't wasted. I did what I set out to do, and I'm not sorry." When the time came they each opted for assisted suicide rather than wait for the demeaning and gruesome "natural" end. Once upon a time helping someone die had galvanized Eric, shattered his shell and launched him into the wider world, but not this time. Within six months of each other, the two pillars of his life died, and now he understood Patrick and Ron's retreat, or Anne Rice's move back to New Orleans, because when you love someone and they die you are alone, nobody can take away the horror of the wrongness of their absence. Life goes on around you as if nothing has happened, and yet to you nothing happens anymore. You don't go on; you're dead, too, only you're still feeling the pain of dying without dying's release.

One of Howard's favorite movies had been *Terminator 2*, and they'd watched it again and again in his last days. Howard's favorite part had been when Sarah Connor carves the words NO FATE into a picnic table—"No fate but what we make, the future isn't set." Even as his own fate was sealed more irrevocably with each lost T-cell, each lost pound, each lost memory, Howard was optimistic, if not for himself then for the ones he was leaving behind. But what Eric remembered from that film was the way the shotgun blasts would punch a hole right through the bad Terminator, the way they'd seal up before Robert Patrick would put on that grimly resolute face and come after you again. That was how he felt now, as if something had blown a hole right through the center of his being, but a hole that wouldn't seal itself up, a hole that was there because what was there was gone.

The very core of his being had been blown out of him with a shotgun blast, and when you feel that way you begin to live in a parallel universe that only slightly and occasionally crosses paths with the one everyone else lives in.

To feel deeply, to love fully, is to ensure your own destruction; the only alternative is to skate lightly over life's surface, holding fast to no one. Break that surface, dive deeply, life fully and give your heart, and you *will* drown someday. Feel nothing or feel too much, it will probably kill you, and then you will have to make yourself live again, somehow, if you can.

Eric knew this. He knew that he would have to live again someday. This was necessary but not yet possible. Since it was not possible, then, there was only this, anesthesia and time and waiting for something, some cosmic benefactor, some deus ex machina that was now the only power that could make things right.

While Cal was home, Carol cooked and cleaned and moved the water around the yard and everything else involved in running a house. But with Cal gone for a moment, she felt she could take a rest. She knew it was silly not to rest whenever she needed it, but at the same time some part of her felt she needed to set an example for her son, that somehow by plunging into each day's tasks she could show him how sheer doggedness could sometimes get you through each day no matter how dreary.

How he'd cried when he'd come back, how they'd both cried, how they'd cursed Cal Senior and their wasted lives. As she sat down in the living room now, she thought back to those days, thought of the day she'd sat here in the dark wondering what terrible thoughts Emma Hamilton was putting into her son's head, when in reality all the terrible thoughts had come from here, hadn't they…?

The blinds on the street weren't closed now; in fact, all the drapes and shades were wide open, letting in the dazzling slanty October light. This had been mandated by her therapist, who'd stubbornly refused her Prozac etc. and put her on light therapy, exercise and a modified diet. Gina's book and Cal Senior's death had led to years of depression and isolation, and the same money that had enabled Cal to spiral downward into drugs had left her free to fall as well. Her religion had been no comfort to her, not in its previous form at any rate; comfort would have been available at the price of denouncing her children, and however much she might have railed at them in her heart (especially Gina), she stubbornly refused to rail at them aloud to others—or let others do the railing. Initially, it had amazed her how few of "their" friends called or came around anymore after Cal Senior's death, until she realized he had been a tool in their cause and little more, and she nothing but the symbol of his conformity to their rules. In those first days she sat in the dark by herself for hours and ruminated much on the nature of Christian fellowship.

It had taken months of therapy for her to see why she was so incoherently angry; Dr. Gladish never would have said it *for* her, even though he'd seen it right away, she knew now. It had dawned on her one morning in church, as the minister railed against gay marriage. She listened to the words the minister and the proposition campaign manager spoke from the pulpit: "This proposition is about *love*. Marriage is about the *love* between a man and a woman."

Carol stood up and asked the campaign manager, "If marriage is about love and you don't think gay people should get married, aren't you implying that gay people are incapable of love?"

He looked at her. She heard the whispers, knew they were talking about her gay son and abortion-inducing daughter, but she didn't care. She wanted an answer. "Not *Christian* love," he answered in a tone that assumed the matter was therefore settled.

She sat down thinking, *This is a church of hate. All this talk of love, love, love, and it's all a lie; it's all hate.* How all these years all they'd ever talked about was whom they hated—women who had abortions, illegal immigrants, homosexuals, anybody powerless. *All my life that's what I've been worshiping—I've been worshiping hate. All these people want is someone to look down on, to hate, to blame.*

Carol didn't sit down. She had another question. "I want to ask you about something else in this brochure," she said, referring to a strictly informational and nonpolitical pamphlet the church had printed for its parishioners, purely to inform them of the moral danger inherent in granting equal protection against discrimination in employment and housing to gay people—a brochure that in no way constituted political involvement on the nonprofit church's part, despite an upcoming November ballot measure that, if it passed, would grant such protections. People around her huffed and sighed; suddenly it was clear to them that Carol and Gina were peas in a pod. Craziness was catching, wasn't it?

"This sentence that says tolerating homosexuality will destroy the family. Well, *whose* family, exactly? If a gay person gets tolerated, and you get divorced, how is that his fault? How can you blame *him* for what *you* did wrong in your marriage?"

She looked around and realized she'd been silently excommunicated. *Fine*, she thought, her radiant anger finding a focus in the people around her. "It's been my experience that people destroy their *own* families because they care less about the people in those families than they do about what people in *other* families think about them. It's been *my experience* that people can talk about *love* till they're blue in the face but when they're trying to *hurt* someone at the same time, it's still *hate.*"

She got up and walked out and never went back. A thought crossed her mind, the thought of Christian forgiveness. *Do I forgive Cal Senior for this life? Do I forgive Gina for this life?* It wasn't her natural instinct to do so, and yet she thought, *Why not? I forgive everyone, I hate no one, I blame no one.*

She went to a different church now, a little tacky and a little too hippie-ish for her liking, what with the fluorescent lights in the drop ceiling and the pastor with a guitar and the daisies on the altar, but the love there, however inelegantly expressed, was real, and that more than compensated.

She picked up the phone and called Gina. This was another thing she didn't like to do with Cal around. She and the girl had reconciled at last. Cal's disappearance had provided the flimsy excuse both of them had needed, but Gina had been to the house once since Cal had come home. That had been a scene Carol never wanted to see again: Cal on the couch crying, Gina standing there like one of God's more cantankerous archangels, her words cutting through him like whips through butter—"How could you! You lied to me, you used me, you made me think you were dying—all so you could *shoot up.*" And Cal taking it, the look on his face telling her what was in his mind: *This is life, life is pain. I have no defense. I've done these things, and there is no mercy and no forgiveness. This is my punishment: to stay alive and feel all this pain I never felt, all the pain I caused others to feel instead of myself.*

After Gina had left, Carol had tried to comfort Cal. "I don't know if I can do it," he'd sobbed. "I don't know if I can do it." She knew what he meant, for she'd wondered the same thing for herself: *Can I start over, can I go through all this...shit that is ordinary life. Can I get through these days of pain and regret and sorrow and loneliness and boredom and lust and frustration with no sign that anything will ever be different from the way it is right now?*

"I got it!" Gina enthused at the other end of the line. "I got the job!"

"Of course you did," Carol said practically. "You're a writer and you applied for a job in a bookstore. How could they say no? I mean, congratulations," she appended, and they both laughed. Gina was aware that a good deal of Carol's work with her therapist consisted of learning to be positive, to say nice things and not be so hard and brittle.

"I didn't tell them about the book, actually. And that was years ago, Mom. Nobody remembers it anymore. I'm nobody now," she said breezily, as if having become nobody again were the best thing that had ever happened.

"Well, we should go out to lunch and celebrate." She wanted to invite Gina over for dinner to celebrate, but she reminded herself it wasn't her place to screw up the good news by bringing Cal into this moment. "I'm proud of you."

"Thanks, Mom. I appreciate that." It was a formal game, these statements, almost like a liturgy: Call and response, thank you, you're welcome, glad to do it. They'd never had an emotional relationship, and the easiest way for both to begin one was within the framework of polite manners that came naturally to neither of them.

Gina had needed this job, not for the money but because her own days were like Carol's had been, long and aimless and hard to fill—and worst of all, lonely. It had been hard for Carol to bite her lip when Gina laid into Cal's drug use; after all, the girl had been stoned for how many years now, passing the time inside a pink cloud all because she couldn't think of an idea for another book. "Well, it's time for us all to start living again," she said, sufficiently elliptical to get her message across to her bright daughter without causing any trouble.

She was proud of Cal, too, though she couldn't tell him the way she could tell Gina. Cal had given up speed and come home because he'd been scared and ashamed, defeated in short, and Dr. Gladish had warned her that drug addicts are extremely manipulative people, and if she'd ever expressed how glad she was to have him home, to haul the trash and wash the car and stack the firewood and to keep her company and help her feel safe at night in the house...well, he might have felt a little too secure in his position in the house and thought a little tweaking might go over all right—and then where would they all be?

Her view out the living room window encompassed the Hamilton house, and that was a sight that brought her some discomfort. She'd promised Emma she'd do what she could for Eric, and she'd tried, and she kept trying. When Eric had moved home from San Francisco alone, she'd been over with food, with what comfort she could give him, invited him to dinner again and again (before Cal came back), and he'd thanked her, taken her gifts of pie and casserole, declined her invitations with a smile so weak and faint it stunned her. *This was Eric Hamilton*, her memory firmly told her. *Remember how much you resented his golden sunny life force, and now look at this shadow.* From her experience with Gina, she recognized the smell of prime-grade marijuana when Eric opened the door, and she knew he was doing what Gina had been doing, if at least with more excuse than she had. All the same, she made a habit of delivering a pie every week or two, and calling (and getting the machine) and leaving a dinner invitation that might never be accepted. On her last message, she'd left the news that Cal was back, that he'd had "some problems," as Eric already knew, and was home for "a while." She wondered if Cal's return would make it more or less likely that Eric would ever accept her invitation, or if by this time Cal's existence didn't really matter to Eric one way or another.

What would the neighbors think? That question had plagued Carol for years, until her own tiny epiphany that day in church. She didn't care anymore, not much anyway, but she still wondered out of habit. Hers was a quiet house, her and Cal's comings and goings restricted to daylight hours—the sort of schedule the aged would follow. Some neighbors had subtly enquired about Cal: "How long is he staying with you?" Carol was still religious enough to consider answering this question a penance that she deserved for having formerly trumpeted her son's Stanford MBA and his brilliant career in finance. The answer she gave was honest enough for a court of law: that Cal had experienced some financial setbacks and had come home to regroup. It was the best answer she could have given to discourage further prying; other people's monetary situations were of conversational interest only when they had plenty of it, or had plenty of it and lost it all spectacularly.

A respectably maintained exterior in a house or a person can mask all manner of darkness and turmoil. But there was no calm and quiet within Cal; that the war within him had no visible collateral damage in no way diminished the unseen damage it had caused. The voices were still with him, his certainty that all the neighbors knew his past, his shame—he could hear them in the warm nights when he had to sleep with the window open. He knew they could hear him, so he argued with them, only loudly enough that they could hear with their supersensitive spy equipment, never loudly enough for Carol to hear. But he only argued when they lied about him, when they said he fucked innocent young HIV-negative guys and infected them. These were the things he heard that filled him with terror, because they were lies, and yet who would believe him? What credibility did the speed slammer have? "Who?" he would demand. "Who did

I fuck? Bring him here. Knock on my door. I have the right to confront my accuser. I have the right." But nobody ever knocked on Carol's door, any more than they'd ever knocked on his own in San Francisco. Sometimes he would have a moment of peace, usually after a few glasses of wine with his mother, and he'd think, *I'm crazy, I'm permanently crazy, I haven't done speed in months and still I'm crazy.*

The reconstruction of his life took place bit by bit, and none of it would have happened without Carol's help. First, she'd loaned him the money to buy a car (payments to be made out of his disability checks; his own credit had been ruined by his more imaginative schemes to raise money for drugs). He hadn't had a car since he'd been at Stanford, and the freedom it gave him brought him the first faint stirrings of natural pleasure he'd had in many years besides what music had given him during his brief stint in rehab. Then there had been the computer she'd bought, allegedly for herself. Cal was supposed to teach her how to use it, but it seemed Carol never had time to learn, and while the fiction was maintained by the computer's placement in Carol's home office (formerly Gina's room), Cal was the one who used it the most. An AOL account allowed him to talk with other gay men for the first time in a long time— after all, his exchanges with men the last few years had been little more than whatever small talk was necessary to get to bed with them. AOL's gay Reno room was kind of sad: mostly bored teenagers and middle-aged closet cases, but one kid had put him on to IRC, where he'd found a more sophisticated group. IRC made him laugh; he'd gone into rooms and announced his beginner status, would anyone help him figure this out? Some of the more alpha teenagers snootily implied he should have been born, as they were, knowing it all already, but he found himself making Net buddies among the seasoned hands who were kind and patient enough to show him the ropes. It was good to talk to people, real people not ghosts in his head, even if it was only through a box.

The bars in Reno were pretty much the only way to meet other gay guys, and as far as Cal was concerned, the bars were out of the question. A 24-hour town with 24-hour bars was a meth-tropolis, and Cal knew it would take only one offer for him to say yes, to dive down the rabbit hole again, that there were the voices he could hear and the voice he couldn't, the one that whispered all the things he wanted to hear about the rush and the Rapture and the feeling of a man inside him.

But he knew it couldn't be. It was too late. He had taken a different path when he'd come home—there was no way he could shoot up and come home to Carol without her knowing, without her feeling his tension and terror and seeing his inability to sit still, the way he'd been when he'd first come home. *Consequences* were no longer something he could discard as something to be dealt with tomorrow because now the consequence would be homelessness: Carol had made that clear.

But this was a battle he had to wage most every day. There were so many unfilled hours, so many long achy stretches of nothing in a day, and the more his strength returned to him, the harder it got to bear the idleness. The lust for the Rapture would sneak up on him, the voice would remind him there was no need for a prescription to obtain points in Nevada; there were always people hanging around the Citifare bus depot who could, for a price, score him what he wanted…it felt so good to imagine getting high, so often he gave into the fantasy, a fantasy where everything went right. The drugs were good and the sex was hot and lasted all night…but then the other voices would return; they *knew* what he was thinking, probably had heat sensors or some ultrasensitive sound equipment that could hear his heart race the way it did when he dreamed of the Rapture. *He's in there dreaming about it! You know he's going to do it again—it's all he thinks about.* And just as it did during the real thing, the Terror would banish the Rapture, the guilt and the fear would come pouring in just as powerfully as the pleasure had, both just as real as if he'd actually done it. It was as if the drug had carved such deep grooves in his head that even imagining it powerfully was enough to trigger the whole cycle.

Cal had eschewed recovery; quite simply he couldn't imagine life without some kind of medication. Carol drank wine in the evenings, and Cal joined her in a glass or two, sometimes more when Carol would give vent to the anger built up in her, the anger at her husband and her God and her life—and her son, who flinched but bore the lash as stoically from her as he resisted it from the voices. She would listen patiently while Cal talked about Luke, how he wasn't a bad person, how he was so smart and had so much going for him, how if only there hadn't been all the drugs, somehow something might have been different between them...Carol thought, *Without the drugs you never would have met him,* but she kept her peace from time to time.

There was something purgative about these nights, two voices raised in a chorus of pain, often ending in tears and hugs and two people going to bed stunned by their own grief and sleeping the sleep of the just, for once. And of course, recovery meant surrendering everything, not just speed but booze and pot and everything, and to Cal this was unthinkable. *I can do this,* he thought. *I just can't do speed.* Many people in recovery will insist that total abstinence is the only way, because it's true of most people, because if they ever allowed themselves to think there might be another way, they'd try it, and they would fail just as they had before. But many people who are not in recovery will tell you it happens sometimes, that a person gets off the drug that's killing them and still has a drink or a toke and doesn't explode. It's possible if they can develop a perfect horror of that one drug that will stay with them at all times, no matter how fucked up they get on something else.

It was the afternoons and early evenings that dragged the most. Cal and Carol had always been morning people, and one positive benefit to Carol of Cal's return had been his ability to assist her with her investments. She drew income off what Cal Senior had left but hadn't sold a share of anything; Cal looked at her portfolio and told her she needed to get out of some of the allegedly "blue chip" stocks in which her husband had left the bulk of his assets. "But my money's safe there," Carol protested, and Cal had to tell her that no, it wasn't; the world was changing, and corporate hugeness was not only no guarantee of financial stability but was in fact the opposite. However fucked up he'd been in San Francisco, he'd seen the new economy starting to blossom and was able to steer Carol in new directions. Carol hesitated; her entire generation had been drilled out of financial risk-taking, but

Cal persisted, insisted, that at this point the biggest risk was sitting still. Carol knew the drugs were still working on Cal, but when he talked about stocks and money she could see a *focus* in him so different from how he looked when he was idle, a clarity and self-confidence that led her to operate on instinct, to take a risk on her son and turn over a substantial part of her money to him to reinvest (in her name only, of course, with her approval required for every transaction; Dr. Gladish's warning about drug addicts was not falling on deaf ears).

Now they had some excitement in their lives as the stock market began its multi-year rampage. They were up by six A.M., and Cal had finished off his triple mocha by half past six when the market opened, both of them glued to CNBC, Cal in the living room and Carol still in bed. Like millions of other Americans at this time, things that had never mattered to Carol, such as how the prime rate affected the markets and the way to calculate a P/E ratio, were suddenly as important as knowing how to drive. Each earnings season became a critical time in their lives; they tried to interpret the sonorous ambiguities of Alan Greenspan as if he were the oracle at Delphi; they both developed crushes on Joe Kernan, so cute *and* so smart, my goodness.

There were celebration days, when a stock rose by some incredible factor on the slightest of good news, and they sold out, Carol doubling or a few times even tripling her money. And there were grim days, when some sure thing flamed out and thousands of dollars vaporized when large investors lost all confidence in a concern, even if only for a moment, confidence never to be regained because there were other fish to fry. But this was the '90s boom, and between Cal's diligent research and the pure luck of having had money to invest in such times, they saw Carol's net worth move from comfortable to cushy.

So life was a little better each day, a little more tolerable. There was never a perfect day; the markets closed at 1:30, and there were days when Cal wished, even more ardently than he'd wished for speed, for a magic wand that could transport him every afternoon from three to five in the blink of an eye, edit those longest hours right out of the day. Even better, Gina actually came over for Thanksgiving, and was civil to Cal at a dinner that reminded all of them all too well of other tense dinners with Cal Senior. But all the same, if forgiveness was not forthcoming, at least truce had been declared; love did not reign supreme, but manners had taken over a respectable regency.

Then Christmas Eve came, and an E-mail that destroyed every bit of Cal's carefully, painfully, painstakingly built equilibrium. Normally he'd delete anything from a Hotmail address unread, more spam, but the subject line caught his eye: "hey cal its luke." Disbelievingly he opened it:

hey its me.......guess where I am. call me.

Cal looked at the phone number, recognizing the Reno prefix. *Luke was here—in Reno!* He practically stumbled down the stairs to the kitchen where Carol was finishing off some pies. He picked up the phone and dialed.

"Luke? It's Cal."

"Hey, man," Luke's lazy smile came over the phone and warmed Cal's bones. "How's it going?"

"Great, great. Where are you?"

"Here in town, staying with this guy I met in the city. Hey, we need to get out of here. His roommate's done too much partying, and I was wondering if you wanted to get together."

"Right now?"

"Yeah, man, this guy's got all kindsa shit. We'll have a good time. Maybe you could take the roommate off our hands—know what I mean?"

Cal knew. The familiar feeling gripped his bowels, dread and excitement, everything he wanted so close—to get high, to see Luke... Then he looked over at his mother, whose face he couldn't see as she kept working. He realized he'd said Luke's name out loud. She knew whom he'd be meeting, she knew what he'd be doing. Tomorrow was Christmas, there would be a roast. Tonight was the night Gina was going to come over, and they were going to open presents and have champagne. If he left now there would be no way he could come home for days...well, ever.

Carol had heard Luke's name and she'd frozen. Everything was about to be wiped away; she was going to have to start all over. But what startled her the most was the calm that came over her, almost as if she had her own voice inside that said, *You've done all you can, and if he goes now, you have to let him go. You have to be strong enough to have the locks changed the minute he walks out the door. If this drug, if this boy, are strong enough to take him out that door on this of all days, there is no hope, there is nothing on God's earth that would ever be enough to save him from it.* She'd never felt such peace in her life.

"I can't," he stumbled. "I can't right now. My sister's coming over, it's...we're..." He could feel it, the twisted snarl that turned Luke's beautiful face into a monster mask when you were saying something that made him despise you. "I can't," he finally said. "But listen," he said desperately, "how about tomorrow? We could meet in the afternoon. I could show you my car," he added stupidly.

"Sure," Luke muttered. "Sure, call me tomorrow." And hung up.

Cal didn't know what to say to his mother; she'd heard it all, could draw her own conclusions. Instead, he went back up to his room, to his bed, and cried. "I wanted it," he said to them, the Committee of voices, appointed to monitor and condemn him. "You know I wanted it. I couldn't do it. I just couldn't do it to her after all she's done for me. I'd be a monster if I did." *They* had nothing to say; he'd done the right thing, but *they* never applauded, only criticized, and the most he could hope for from them in his most exemplary moments was silence.

Luke would understand, wouldn't he? He'd have to understand he couldn't just walk out on his family on Christmas Eve to get loaded. He'd have to. He'd just have to.

When he'd first come back to town, there had been days when Cal had been sure he'd had a psychic link with Luke—that among all the other voices he could still hear Luke's, the only one in his fantasia that had ever been distinctly attached to a real human being. Amongst all the metallic static chatter in his head, he could hear Luke's voice, fighting to come through from hundreds of miles away, an act of magic that proved to Cal that there had been love there, some form of intimacy however twisted, and that love continued strong enough to bridge physical obstacles.

There were days later on when he'd flush with embarrassment at the thought that he'd really believed Luke was speaking to him over the mountains. These were much the same days that he'd wonder what he'd been doing with this kid, why he'd chased off the other guys he'd met on speed who'd wanted him, who'd wanted to fuck him, maybe even love him as much as anyone on speed can love, all rejected so he in his turn could chase Luke, who despised him and wouldn't touch him. But then he'd remember other nights, alone with Luke in his apartment, Luke spinning out some story so entrancing that even Cal's frantically darting mind would wheel and turn toward it and focus, relax, and suddenly the city night was not terrifying and ugly but beautiful, magical—there was peace in Cal's head, and maybe it was only the dopamine undaunted at last by the epinephrine, but in those moments he felt loved.

So it was not easy that day to turn away from Luke, who for all his cruelty had also been kind, who had smiled at Cal as well as laughed at him. And Cal had hoped with all his heart that Luke would forgive him, that they would spend some part of Christmas day together. And he called the house where Luke was staying, and left a message, and waited, and hoped, and the day passed.

Carol had been relieved when Cal hadn't left, and she was unruffled by his explanation that he needed to see Luke. Did she mind if he went out for a while on Christmas Day? "No, not at all. Last night was the family night, and you're free to do what you want today." She knew with all her heart that something had changed, that the boy had lost some of his grip over Cal and that this was a sign that the drugs, too, had lost some of theirs. She heard Cal leave a message for Luke—*Who isn't home on Christmas morning?* she thought. *It's not like he's in church, is it?*

She watched Cal as the day passed, fidgeting and watching the clock and doing his level best to make conversation. Finally, five o'clock came. "Do you want some dinner?" she asked, and that was when he broke down in torrents of tears. Luke hadn't called, wasn't going to call. Yesterday Cal would have been of some use to him but not today, and when Cal wasn't of use, he was nothing and nobody, nobody, nothing. Carol held him and consoled him as best he could; she had no sympathy for the cause of Cal's distress, but she could divorce the cause from the effect, and she pitied his pain with all her heart.

They split a bottle of wine and ate some roast beef, and Cal went to bed. It was five o'clock, but it was dark enough—why not? In such moments of emotional anguish, there can be a good deal of comfort in turning off the lights and getting into bed. But he tossed and turned. The more he thought, the more agitated he got, until finally he couldn't rest with his rage. He got up and called the house where Luke was staying, getting the machine, but he didn't care. He knew Luke was there, could hear him. "Thanks for ruining my Christmas, mean faggot," he said, and hung up. It was a reference to a story Luke had told him, about a guy who had picked him up on Christmas Day, done all Luke's drugs, sucked his dick, and then refused to pay him. The man had been stupid enough to do this in his own home, and Luke returned that night with a can of spray paint and wrote "MERRY CHRISTMAS, CHEAP FAGGOT" on the john's door. Cal hung up taking an angry injured person's black satisfaction in knowing that he could wound as deeply as he'd been wounded.

Half an hour later the phone rang and he bolted for it. "Check your E-mail," Luke croaked and hung up. Cal's blood froze. There was something terrible awaiting him, but he had to see it, had to know. Carol had luckily also gone to bed early and had slept through the ring. He booted up the computer and checked his mail.

> You are a fucking idiot if you think i'd want to spend my Christmas with you Cal. I can see thru you like saran wrap and your about as thin you fucking crankster. You had your chance to see me and you didnt want it now suffer and dont blame me. Go cry on your momma you fucking bitch and dont come crying to me.

Cal couldn't breathe. There was something in Luke's words that made a mockery of his attempts to convince his mother of Luke's redeeming qualities. There was something so hateful in this note, it crushed Cal like a bug. All these months he'd held onto the notion that somehow, someday, when he was cleaned up, he could see Luke again and make it all right, that he'd spend time with him without speed and it would be...wonderful. But here he was, dry as a bone for three months now, and this was what he got. This was what Luke really thought of him—despised him with all his heart—*all* his heart, all of it. Until that moment he hadn't realized how much he'd held out the hope that he and Luke were special, that there was a man who loved him at least a little.

There is a feeling that comes over some people, if you can even call it a feeling. More, it is a suspension of feeling, a state of cold shock, in which the emotions are so brutalized they simply stop working. There is only a voice, your own voice, telling you that at last, you've reached the end of the road. You've now felt all the pain there is to feel in the world, and the news is, there's nothing else to feel *but* pain. Not for you. Not ever. It's not the voice of self-pity, of misery; it's the voice of someone who's solved an obvious mathematical problem, so obvious there isn't even the joy of discovery in it. That's all it is—clear logic, there on paper: either you stay, where there's nothing but pain, or you leave.

This is not the peace that came over Carol, but it is peace of a kind, a sort of black nirvana. You are unchained from the wheel of life; you no longer need to try. The wheel spins, as fast or as slow, with or without you, so you're free to go. So you go to the medicine cabinet and take every pill you can find, and tomorrow there will be a tomorrow, but not for you, and that will be fine. So let go of the wheel; there is nothing but pain to be gained from holding on, so let go.

A sympathetic doctor had given Cal some sedatives to help him sleep, fairly mild ones, but he'd just refilled his prescription so he had a full bottle, and he opened it and poured the pills in his mouth and filled the cup with water and swallowed them. The calm voice of inevitability reminded him that it was very important that this not be misinterpreted as a cry for help—if you don't take enough pills, you don't die, and then they put you in the mental hospital, which would mean the pain wouldn't be over, would be worse. So he opened a bottle of wine and drank that, too, slugging it back. It was important, that part; the pills themselves might not be enough, but with the booze it was more of a lock.

His first emotion since reading the E-mail came now, a twinge of guilt—if he stayed here, Carol would have to find him in the morning. Well, he'd just taken the pills and drank the wine, it would be a while before it hit him; there was time enough to find somewhere to die. He put on his clothes and his coat (the point of pills was to die peacefully; no point in being cold in the mean time) and took his car keys and wallet and left the house.

He drove to Reno's small bathhouse, an unobtrusive two-story building that used to have a sign outside that had said JEFF'S GYM until too many out-of-town visitors tried to come in for a workout. Now it was unmarked, but Cal knew where it was. He had his choice of a six-hour or 24-hour room and he had just enough money for the latter—he was concerned that at the end of six hours they might open his room if he hadn't checked out and he might still be alive, and then they'd pump his stomach and then off to the mental hospital.

He looked at his watch. It was still early, only eight o'clock. He undressed and lay down on the thin mattress and thought, *This time there really is no tomorrow,* and this thought was of such comfort to him that he fell asleep.

Cal woke up. He woke up in the daze of the freshly aroused, that momentary puzzlement in which certain questions are asked automatically—what time is it? Or, if the surroundings are unfamiliar, where am I? Facts that had waited for him to wake up presented themselves in order: *You're at the baths, you've had a good rest.* Then he looked at the watch he hadn't bothered to take off: It was 11:30 in the morning. He'd slept for almost 16 hours. That was when another fact took its turn: *You're supposed to be dead.*

He sat up, not at all groggy, only slightly dull of faculty. He took off his watch and went downstairs through the deserted halls, some cheesy pop station pumping DJ enthusiasm through the speakers to an empty house. He took a shower, and that's when he thought, *I'm alive.*

Surely the records are full of those in the same situation who fell to their knees at this instant and thanked the Lord for another chance, but Cal was not one of them. His emotions were still blunted, not even so much from the remaining medications in his system as from a second shock nearly as remarkable in its way as last night's. For last night he had allowed himself to let go of the wheel, and he had let go, and yet here he was anyway. As if the decision was not entirely his after all.

He dressed and checked out. Overnight the Sierra weather had gone from still and cold to blustery and snowy. His car was piled high with snow and driving was a slow, treacherous affair. Some part of his mind noted the irony of the fact that he was driving carefully.

He got home and found Carol digging her own car out. The calm she'd felt on Christmas Eve had to her surprise remained with her when she'd woken up this morning and found Cal gone. She looked in his eyes and, satisfied he wasn't high, handed him the shovel. "Would you mind?"

"Sure," was all he said, relieved to be asked no questions. "Do you want me to go to the store for you?"

"No, I need to get out of the house today."

Cal only nodded and took up the shoveling. When Carol left he went inside and made himself an espresso; he'd gotten a machine soon after returning, since once again he'd found himself unable to get going in the mornings without caffeine. He took his coffee back up to his bedroom and sat down in a chair where he could look out the window at the snow.

He didn't think much; more, he wondered what to think. *All my life has been pain. All my life I've been trying to end it, drugging and fucking without rubbers and now going about it more directly. And I'm still here. Why? Why me? Why save me?*

It had been a long time since Cal had thought about God. God had never been a being for him, a presence, only a tool in the hands of men to beat other men with. God says this, and

God says that. Do as God says, or God will punish you—well, *we* will, but in His name and that makes it OK. Cal had now done most everything these men had said God said not to do. And if God had wished to punish him, he'd made it easy for Him last night. He had done a thing so certain to end in death only God could have saved him. And here he was, still alive.

Why?

The snowstorm meant little to Eric; he was well-supplied with weed and food, and as long as the power (and the cable TV) didn't go out he'd be fine. His basement room was warm and toasty because it was next to the furnace, and days like this were the best, really. It was the sunny days that made you feel guilty about not frolicking and gallivanting and participating in life. On days like this you were supposed to stay home, off the roads; Eric was only doing his civic duty today, doing for once what he was supposed to be doing, what he could tell himself was the right thing to do.

At noon he was on his second beer, alcoholic balm just now smoothing the troubled waters of his brain. Once he'd sworn not to drink till four, then three, then noon—then fuck it, whatever. He let out a rich frothy belch and took a spin around the dial.

His brain stirred sluggishly at the sound of a voice on the television, the voice he hated more than that of any other human being on the face of the planet, that of a crusty old codger responsible for the voice-overs on most every beer and truck commercial made. As the old coot growled manfully that a certain SUV came "nicely equipped," Eric reached for his micro-cassette recorder.

"Nicely equipped," he muttered into the machine. "Isn't it pathetic, the things that sell trucks to men? Can they really be so blind to the subtext of these commercials? I mean, it's bad enough some poor sap thinks he'll be a tough motherfucker because he buys some jacked-up hunk of fiberglass. Now they're subliminally telling him he's buying a big dick, too. I mean, come on! 'Nicely equipped'! What else the fuck is that supposed to mean! Well, it's our fault. I mean, us in the media. We made so much fun of how they looked in their minivans that, what do you know, it *mattered* to them that we thought they looked uncool! So they sold their safe, economical minivans and started buying these car-crushing, road-hogging, gas-guzzling behemoths. And it's our fault because we mocked them into it!"

In his mind he heard the audience's laughter. One of his more pleasant stoned fantasies, the one he indulged in more and more often, was that he would someday be the host of his own television show—"*Spy* magazine meets the *Economist*" was how he put it in his imaginary press interviews. He'd get to go on the sort of outrageous tangents only angry fat men on the radio were allowed to do these days, but when people evolved, watch out for Eric Hamilton! "And why are those guys so angry? They're always fat and angry," Eric raged into the tape recorder without a segue from his truck commercial. "What are they stuffing down? What makes them so mad that they have this platform to air all that rage? And that's *still not enough*—they still go home and stuff the leftover rage back down their gullets with a couple buckets of KFC!" An impartial observer would have noticed and pointed out that while Eric's own girth was nowhere resembling that of the typical right-wing talk show host, he was gaining ground on them steadily.

The tape recorder was essential; the tape recorder, after all, made all the difference between insane ranting and rehearsal. Someday this show would be real; someday he'd have an audience. People would listen to him, and he'd change things, damn it.

"You know, Emma and Howard, in their last days, they used to talk about this book that *every single one of you* should read. If I was as rich as Oprah, I'd put a copy under every seat in this hall." [*Laughter*] "It's called *Shikasta*, and the author is Doris Lessing. She's also written some very perceptive things about how people should be educated to resist the messages we get from government and advertising, but we'll talk about that on some other show. But there's something in this book, a question, a question we all need to ask ourselves, and we don't. It's very simple: 'What are we for?' In other words, why are we here? What are we here to do? I'm here to do this show. I'm here to…"

He trailed off. Excited, he'd stood up, pacing through the

discarded clothes and old newspapers and other detritus on the floor. There was a full-length mirror on the inside of the door to the walk-in closet, a mirror he never looked in because the closet was usually shut. But today it was open; during one of yesterday's diatribes he'd had to rummage through a box in that closet for some piece of evidence to justify his point, and he'd left the door open. Now he looked at himself in that mirror and froze. Memories returned, memories against which the booze and the pot had built a Maginot Line, a line now just as effective as the original had been in its time.

Howard had come with him to visit Emma several times, back in the good days. They'd stayed upstairs in the real bedroom, but once Howard had heard about Eric's secret boy cavern, he'd not only had to see it, he'd gotten carried away. The two of them used to stand in front of this mirror, Howard's arms around Eric's then-ripped torso, his lips against Eric's ear, their eyes meeting in the mirror. "All the days you must have been down here alone, looking at your own beautiful young body in the mirror, whacking off from across the room, splooging so hard you could hit the mirror from 50 paces away." Eric had laughed, tried to break free then, but Howard's grip was always stronger than you expected and he pulled Eric's shirt up and off him. "Touching yourself here...and here...and here..." And then the mirror forgotten as Eric slipped enough in Howard's arms to come around and embrace him in turn, for the two of them to fall to their knees, to do it all right there, on hands and knees, while looking at each other in this mirror...

Eric used to think death was the Truck that came to hit you. But the real Truck was grief. But unlike death, when you see its headlights, you can slow its approach for a while. Food will delay the impact a little, weed and booze a little longer, opiates the longest. But someday the Truck will hit you, no matter what you do. And no matter how you stretch the time between first catching sight of the Truck and impact, the moment of impact will always come at full speed—the moment that kills you sooner or later.

Eric looked in the mirror and saw Howard. The memory he had blunted with a thousand blunts was suddenly fresh and terrible, the irrefutable knowledge as to what Eric had been for was clear: he had been for loving Howard, and now Howard was gone. Therefore, so was what Eric had been for.

Eric looked in the mirror and saw a fat young man, whose weight made him look older. The memory of the vibrant laughing stud in the mirror showed him how far he'd fallen. Nobody would ever give a television show to a fat, deranged faggot mumbling to himself in his basement. He wasn't rehearsing for anything, preparing for anything, waiting for anything. His life was over, this life was nothing. This was what people did who were only waiting for the end.

What are you for? some part of himself asked him mockingly. *What are you for now?*

He dressed himself and went out to the street-side mailbox; he hadn't collected the mail in days, and he felt the urge to do something, anything, that was normal. He'd set his beer on the kitchen counter, unfinished but unwilling to pour it down the sink. That was so dramatic, wasn't it? But it didn't mean anything, did it, when there was plenty more in the fridge? Something more substantial would be required as a token of his desire to return to living.

At the mailbox he looked up at Cal's window, something he did from time to time since he'd heard of Cal's return. He'd never thought about why, but then lately he'd been making sure he couldn't think of much. Always before there'd been nothing to see, but this time there was a figure backlit in the window, the slim figure of Cal. Another memory came to him now: of Cal on the chair in Eric's room, reaching for a book.

Cal saw Eric come out to the mailbox, and thought of that day, too, and remembered with shame the hope he'd had that Eric would someday come home a beer-bloated frat boy who'd therefore have no power over Cal's soul. Clearly, Eric was now what Cal had wished him to be back then; the down jacket could hide the bulk, but Eric's face told the story like the tip of the iceberg.

"All my life I've been afraid," Cal said to himself, thinking of another day when Eric had kissed him in the park, and so many other days since, days spent fleeing in terror from things that weren't even there. *What am I afraid of?*

He raised his hand in greeting, almost lowered it quickly but left it up, willed it to stay up, and waved slightly at Eric.

Eric looked up and saw the wave, recalled Carol's constant invitations to dinner, remembered what she'd said about Cal having had "some problems." *A benefactor, a hand from above,* he thought absurdly.

He looked as hard as he could, till he was sure he was looking Cal in the eyes. And he was; Cal was looking him in the eyes, too, and didn't blink. And then Eric lifted his hand and waved back.

CHAPTER SIX
PINK CLOUD

As he had on all his better days since his childhood, Eric woke up early this brisk March morning. As he had done for a few years now, he reached over and grabbed the clicker and turned on the TV. The morning news was mercifully uneventful enough that he could get up and go to the kitchen and turn on another TV. He made his morning coffee, grinding the beans and making it the way Howard had always insisted was the *only* way, and smiled as the news reported an unexpected snowstorm on its way. *Cal will be happy about that*, he thought.

He went back to bed with his cup of coffee until the caffeine had sufficiently agitated him to the point where he could throw the covers back and dash into his gym clothes; like most large old houses, this one had a few rooms that never got entirely warm, and Eric's was one of them. He could have gone back to living in the warm basement, but the thought gave him shudders that trumped the shivers he got upstairs.

He threw a jacket on over his sweatshirt, holding in some of the heat he would be losing off his legs. Eric wore shorts to the gym every day, rain or shine; he was proud of his legs, the one part of his body that even in his most bloated days had still held some allure. It had been Cal who'd gotten him out of elastic-banded sweat shorts and into baggy cargo shorts. "The gym is full of hot men and you don't want them seeing you looking hopelessly unfashionable, do you?" Cal had asked. Eric had laughed, pretending not to care about such things, but they'd gone to Old Navy, and Eric had gotten properly equipped à la mode.

In the car he decided what today's workout would be—chest and abs, that was a good one, not hard like legs or boring like back. Recently, he'd realized that he was plateauing on his bench press, that to be able to push it a little harder he'd have to start asking someone at the gym for a spot. But he'd been putting that off for some time now. He just wasn't ready to talk to a stranger, to ask a stranger for help. He couldn't, or wouldn't, put it any more clearly than that, but there it was.

He did the best he could on the bench, knowing it could have been better but refusing to let that nagging voice spoil his still reasonably good sets. Then it was upstairs to the treadmills, where he put on his headphones and set the machine at a steep incline. He'd tried running the way he had in younger, thinner days, but it had been murder on his lower back and knees. Walking was the best he could manage at this weight and endurance. The music was courtesy of Cal, who'd discovered the joys of downloaded music and was pressing his favorite mixes on Eric for use at the gym. Cal had pretty much decided that anything that made him dance in his chair or drive too fast was also suitable for the treadmill, and Eric couldn't disagree. Cal's taste these days tended toward trippy electronic music. "Trance," he called it. "Music for people on X," Eric had initially dismissed it.

"Yes, but if the music is good enough, you don't need the drug. The music is the drug," Cal countered, and Eric couldn't argue. There was something dreamily uplifting about the music, a spacey vibe to the lyrics that helped this music transcend the usual "feel it, feel it" bleats of most dance tunes. In truth, this sort of music wasn't entirely foreign to him; during his long pot haze one of his favorite records had been The Orb's *Adventures Beyond the Ultraworld*, which although more ambient than Cal's selections had certainly enhanced Eric's stoned rhapsodies.

It was funny to think that the same sort of music could be put to such a different use now, Eric thought as he pushed the incline on the treadmill up to 11%. He'd been back at the gym now for...well, back seriously this time only for a few months, after having laid off for a while last year. When he'd originally started working out again, a few months after he and Cal had reconnected, things had gone really well. He'd been sick of pot, sick of being fat and tired all the time, sick of wallowing in his grief and pain. He couldn't pin a reason on it, but he could pin a time—one day, with a Little Debbie snack cake halfway to his mouth, he suddenly thought, *I don't want this.* "This" being not just what he held in his hand, but this life, well, this nonlife was what it was. In this he was extremely fortunate; like any addict he'd come to think of a day without his drug of choice with terror and panic, and had always made sure to hoard plenty of strategic sugar reserves. To all of a sudden have a switch just flick in his head, to all of a sudden just have had *enough*, was perhaps a tribute to Eric's essentially nonaddictive personality.

He'd been embarrassed to sign up at the gym, so sure he could read the employees' minds—another fat guy handing us his money for a membership he'll never use. This may or may not have crossed their minds, but Eric's imagination had been left idle and was now the devil's workshop. When he'd gone into the locker room to change, he'd been mortified to see himself in a full-length mirror (after that he'd started suiting up at home). He'd been even more horrified to get on the scale and see the awful number: 2 4 0. He'd gone through his first workout in a daze, shocked that he'd let himself go so badly, flagellating himself at dinner with Carol and Cal that night, until with laser-like precision Carol had cut his self-pity away by saying in her wintriest voice, "Oh, so now that you're doing something about it, now's the time to kick yourself?" He had to laugh at that, and since at his core he was still the Eric they'd once known, the self-pity and remorse were gone as soon as they'd come.

Some things didn't surprise him at the gym and some things did. Of course, the weights he was capable of lifting on his bench press and his squat had both fallen dramatically; he was prepared for that. What he wasn't prepared for was the way he almost fell over when he tried to do a squat—it took him a minute to realize that what his body remembered as his center of gravity was no longer there, thanks to his big belly. And what really shocked him was how differently he was treated as a fat person. At any gym he'd ever been at, Eric had always been one of the young princes, the ones some envy, or emulate, or use as an excuse not to try: *It's too hard. I could never look like that.* He'd always preferred mixed gyms to San Francisco's distinctly gay gyms (there is no such thing as a completely straight gym). But even in mixed gyms he'd been able to pick up vibes from both the gay boys and the bi-curious types. Now there wasn't a vibe coming his way, no longer was he a sailor on the gym's sexual currents (*More like the Flying Dutchman,* he thought morosely). Instead, he was *not there,* a nonentity, a fact that hit home one day when he was walking toward a good-looking, pretty obviously gay guy, who looked at him glassily, looked away, and then, as he passed Eric, rather dreamily put his hand on his own stomach and patted its flat surface reassuringly. It took Eric a moment to feel the punch in that pat, to realize that to this man, he was *not a person*; it was perfectly all right for him to treat Eric like no more than a funhouse mirror, as if Eric couldn't *see* the man's abstracted horror that he might ever have a tummy like Eric's, as if Eric wasn't even a person whose feelings might be hurt, or even matter. Before, Eric had always been the object of desire, and having he saw now rather naïvely always believed most people were just nice, because they'd always been nice to *him*. Eric was stunned to discover how differently they could treat you when you no longer had anything they wanted.

The mix he was listening to now had taken a curious route to his CD player. It had begun as a radio show in London featuring DJ Paul Van Dyk, which someone had recorded and turned into an MP3 on their computer, which in turn Cal had downloaded and burned onto the CD Eric was listening to now on a treadmill in Reno, Nevada. Had it not been for the Internet,

Eric reflected, his mind free to wander while his body worked on automatic pilot, he never would have heard of Paul Van Dyk, a purveyor of a musical style outside America's dominant pop culture. Eric wouldn't yet be so bold as to say there was an article in this, but he knew the signs of imminent creativity, the reflection triggered by a fascinating phenomenon, the magnitude of which only he and a few others had yet grasped. It had been a long time since he'd written anything, even thought of writing anything, but along with the weight he was losing around his middle, it seemed to him he was also losing some of the weight in his head as well, feeling lighter and more agile all around, and while he wasn't yet ready to sit at the computer and face the blank screen, he noted thoughts beneath the surface being stirred, linking up, forming into concepts that when the right time came might become words on the screen as easily as they once had.

Around 20 minutes into his cardio, Eric's energy flagged a bit. *I had a good weight workout,* he thought. *I could lay off at 20. You could,* he reminded himself angrily, *and you could stay FAT, too.*

No, he said, digging deeper for what had to be found whether it was there or not, not this time. Instead of quitting, he jacked the incline up even further, swinging wildly as his legs pumped him up hill (he never held onto the handlebars, that would have defeated the purpose of the incline, which was to increase the stress on your legs and ass and back and refine your balance). He knew some people laughed at him when he was in this final stage on the treadmill, the fat man huffing and puffing and swinging his arms and *willing* himself to the top of this hill that was a landmark only in his mind. But he also knew that it was working.

When he'd started back at the gym the first time, about a year ago now, it had been easy, the weight had fallen off him two, three pounds a week until he'd lost 15 pounds—not enough to say he wasn't overweight anymore, but enough to keep him rolling at the gym and off the sweets and weed at home. But then he'd hit a plateau; his metabolism had adjusted and the weight wasn't coming off so fast, then not at all. He got frustrated, started snacking again, complained bitterly to Cal, stopped going.

But a few months ago something had changed, something that caused him to make a commitment to this goal the way he hadn't really before, something that had happened in a conversation with his new friend Cal Hewitt.

Cal was awake and still in bed while Eric was mounting his assault on the treadmill. He'd recently moved into his own small apartment, no small step emotionally or financially. He hadn't known how much disposable income he'd had on disability until rent began disposing of it for him. But it had been necessary: *How can I go back into the world and hold up my head? Who's going to be my friend when I say, "I live with my mother?"* Sure, he could work the disability angle, but one look at him and people would know that he wasn't so disabled he needed his mommy to take care of him.

It had been scary, moving out. *They* were around again, watching him to see what he'd do. The seductive silent voice told him, *You have your own place now. There's no mom to see you coming home glassy eyed and terrified. No one will know, do it, do it, do it.* He drank more wine than he should have, more than he could really afford (Carol had passed on her own newly sophisticated taste in wine to Cal, so the cheap stuff was now out of the question). Alcohol shut *them* up, shut the other voice up, too. But you couldn't drink all the time, he knew, especially when all you had was a part-time job and plenty of spare time on your hands. What he *could* do was go snowboarding, and that he was now doing as often as he could afford to.

He'd been boarding the previous day, and he was stiff and sore as hell and pretty sure his nose was broken. He had the morning news on and had seen the snow report, but it was of little consequence since Cal had the distinct feeling his season was over. Yesterday had only been his eighth trip to Mount Rose, and it had been going pretty well; in fact, his last run had been the first time he'd stayed vertical all the way down from the top of Ponderosa, the bunny-slope lift. But he had to admit now, as he gingerly touched his nose, he'd probably gotten—unbelievable for him—a little *too* confident on that last run, which was probably why he'd caught an edge and ended up in a face plant on the icy surface. He'd sat there stunned, wiping his bloody nose, until some kind soul sent the ski patrol up on a snowmobile to bring him down the hill and administer first aid. A few people had grinned at him as they pulled up to the lodge, an acknowledgment that getting banged up was a part of this sport that Cal had so perversely decided was the one for him, and he gave them game smiles and a rueful thumbs-up.

The ski patrol dude had been a hunk and hadn't flinched or altered his kind demeanor a whit when Cal had revealed he was HIV-positive. There was a biohazard bag in the first-aid room, and Cal's bloody napkins went in there with everyone else's.

This late-season injury in itself might not have been enough to deter any further trips up the hill, but there was also the matter of his car. At the end of his last two trips from the valley floor to Mount Rose's 8,000-foot base, he'd parked his car in the lot and been panicked to see smoke belching from under the hood. There was no question it was smoke and not some mysterious high altitude condensation thing; he could smell it in the car. He'd opened the hood and stared down at a mass of stuff he could interpret no better than he could tea leaves. At first he'd thought, *Should I call Triple A? Should I just get back in the car and roll it down the hill to the garage?* But instead he experienced an emotional process that had become more and more familiar to him recently, a strange alchemical process wherein his rage, so long directed at himself, was being magically redirected against obstacles in his way. *NO*, he shouted inside his head, *I WON'T*. I'm here and if all I can do is roll downhill, I might as well do that *after* I have a good time. Nobody who had ever seen Crystal Cal running down Van Ness Avenue in terror would have recognized the broken-nosed man doggedly shepherding his barely operational car back down the hill yesterday.

Everything had changed the morning he'd woken up in the baths. For weeks afterward he'd gone through the motions of life: going to the store for Carol, moving wood, getting his car fixed. And yet the essential part of himself lay stunned on the floor of his mind, staring at the sky, unable to take in what had happened. It was as if he *had* died and were watching the world in that way people say they experience in the moment nearest to death, as if he was above the scene, powerless to do anything but observe and yet impassive about what he observed. But in that kind of moment, if it's really as described, you're only there a moment before you're either sucked back into your body or sucked away to whatever comes next; whereas Cal spent weeks in this frame of mind.

Eventually (after one of their nightly bottles of wine) he told Carol; she was after all his only friend, and he had to tell someone. She surprised him by neither weeping nor screaming nor recommending institutionalization. "Well, I hope you got it out of your system," she said, but then she hugged him as well.

He was standing in the checkout line at Albertson's one day when it struck him that if he was after all alive, he might as well, in the words of Dorothy Parker, live. He smiled as he recalled an old Smiths song as well as better days with Gina— that song about what you do when you decide you want to live, how did it go? He couldn't remember; speed had punched random holes in his memory that often left him groping for a word that should have been obvious. Still, the fact that he *could* stand in Albertson's and smile was in itself a miracle. Something or someone *had* died that night; there was no denying it. The voices in his head had faded significantly; they tended now to come only when he was under stress, or when he made his morning coffee too strong. He kicked himself over that last one—*Stupid, stupid, of course you hear voices when you're drinking a triple espresso. You think speed is that much different from caffeine as far as your fucking head is concerned?* He scaled back his caffeine intake, and the demons in his head had fuel for far fewer scheduled flights.

He'd also started walking around Virginia Lake, unaware how Eric had enjoyed jogging around it ten years earlier. Only hardy souls took this walk in January, die-hard runners (including the occasional studly college boy whom Cal would cruise as furtively as he could) or old people who either disdained the softness of mall walking or were too restless early in the morning to be able to wait for the mall to open. Sitting in front of the TV all morning watching CNBC had become an unwholesome activity, and moreover, both he and Carol were sick of the stress that such constant market-watching causes. He discovered that just a few brisk laps around the lake seemed to calm him down for the rest of the day. When he'd been young, the tennis he'd played so aggressively had never made him happy the way Eric's physical endeavors had satisfied him; it had burned off a measure of stress but, he was realizing now, he'd probably had faulty wiring in his brain's reward centers all his life and happiness was just always going to be harder for him than for other people.

Now, however, he was discovering that his laps cleared his head wonderfully, not just of demons but of all the bleating, skittering, rattling frets and worries. And one particularly cold morning when he'd had to pick his pace up just to stay warm, a particularly absurd thought hit him, and he nearly said aloud, "I tried to kill myself because a homeless hustling heroin addict didn't like me." There are people in the world who have stayed on the straight and narrow all their lives, and to some of them it is incomprehensible how anyone else might have a problem doing so; had Cal made this statement to one of them, they would have reacted with contempt and disdain for anyone with less steel than themselves (they would never ascribe any part of their lives' fortune to luck). But most of us, on the other hand, have not taken such an orderly march through life, heroic enough to hack away all obstacles mental and emotional with an unbreakable sword of confidence. Most of us could probably make a statement just as absurd as Cal's, if we looked back on our lives and thought about it.

It was a milestone for Cal to see things this way. It meant that he was at a remove now from that state of mind; it was a state of mind that now existed as part of his past and not his present. It meant that on some level he was at least beginning to prepare for the possibility of a life where his continued existence had some potential appeal. Only if you have lived with an utter blackness in your head can you appreciate what a giant step that is.

The soul needs a steady intake of hope the way the body needs a steady intake of water; hope is the fluid that keeps possibilities alive and moving in the soul, that flushes out the poisons of doubt and dismay. Cal was not yet ready to be grateful that he was still alive, had not found enough joy in that life for that, but the fact that he was alive despite his best efforts, which surely meant *something* might be different *someday*, was enough to give him his first deep draught of that essential fluid.

It was at one of their lunches that Eric and Cal both had their tiny epiphanies. After the event that they'd come to refer to as "the wave," Eric had finally accepted one of Carol's dinner offers. The first night's conversation had been general and light, avoiding all subjects that might cause pain to anyone.

These dinners became a weekly event, and after a few of them, Eric and Cal had both realized they hadn't been to the movies in a long time—"Yeah, let's go. That would be great." Lunch accompanied the movie; neither man delved into painful subjects, but at least they each referred to them and acknowledged each other's admissions with nods rather than prying questions. Cal confessed his suicide attempt, and Eric confessed his basement megalomania. Then formalities started getting ignored whenever Eric would pop over to Cal's to help Cal and Carol with some manly household task, and Carol would then repay him by sending Cal over with whatever Carol was cooking in large batches that day. These were the days when life started seeming possible again for all three of them.

At this particular lunch, they'd had plenty to talk about. "You're bursting with something," Cal said as they stood in line at Port of Subs.

Eric smiled. "I got the job. At the bookstore."

"Yay," Cal smiled back. "Good old Gina. But I guess when you told them you were an important writer, they were glad to have you."

"Actually, I didn't tell them. I figured if the name didn't ring a bell, I wasn't such a very important writer after all."

"That's funny, did you know that's what Gina did there? Never mentioned her book?"

"Yeah, I do now. She asked me if I said I was a writer and I said no."

"Why?"

Eric shrugged, but his lips were pursed. "Well, I'm not, am I? When's the last time I wrote a word? I *was* a writer, but so what? God, when I was younger, I always hated those old fuds who'd get a doctorate in creative writing, then write *one* novel about someone with a doctorate in creative writing who's writing a novel about someone with a doctorate in creative writing, and they'd get a modicum of praise in a 'New and Noteworthy' blurb in the *Times* and that was it. They spent the rest of their lives coasting on that one book. And I said, 'I'll *never* be one of them. *Never.*'"

"He'll pass on the hot peppers," Cal said to the sandwich counter man, and Eric laughed.

"You know what I'm saying, though?"

Cal nodded. "Sure." He smiled. "I didn't tell Hopes I had an MBA, and they hired me, too."

Eric broke into a wide sunny smile. "All right! Cal, that's great!"

The job in question was a little part-time contract employee job at Hopes House, the HIV services organization in Reno, a job to which he'd taken a very circuitous route. As he began to reassemble the broken pieces in his head, as terror faded and boredom took its place, Cal realized how very lonely he was. No doubt his days on speed had been bad for him, but there was also no doubt that any time he'd been lonely in San Francisco, he could just get laid. Take out the devastating impact of shooting speed, and Cal had been doing what many gay men (and more often these days young straight people) do: He'd taken up sex as his hobby, if you think of a hobby as that thing you can always do when you're alone and bored. This hobby wasn't available in Reno; he could get online here, but the pickings were slim—even slimmer because he mentioned in his profile that he was HIV-positive. Partly because *they* were watching his every move, even if only from a distance now, but also partly because he did feel compelled to tell guys, and it was easier to put his status up front to weed out the ones it bothered enough they wouldn't even talk to him.

One day Cal had seen a listing in the local weekly for an HIV-positive support group meeting at St. Mary's. *My own kind*, he thought, realizing for the first time what he'd really lost in leaving S.F., where at least as an HIV-er he was in the majority. He went to the hospital and was directed to the meeting room, where he sat for half an hour waiting for someone, anyone, to show up. No group, no group leader, nobody showed up. Cal sat in the meeting room and looked out over the city and thought, *I'm the only HIV-positive person in this city.*

That couldn't be, and he knew it. Grilling people online, he discovered that there was a clinic in town for HIV-ers, and he called them. They referred him to their social services arm, where maybe he could find a support group. Being an arm of AIDS, Inc., they immediately did an intake to get him into the system: "We don't have any support groups right now, but we do have a client services arm. We have a food pantry, and we hire our clients to staff it. Would you be interested in a job? You'd be a contract employee, and it wouldn't mess with your Social Security." Two weeks later, having gone through interviews and training, Cal had the job.

"Yeah, it's not much, $8 an hour working in the food pantry, filling client orders. There's just one problem, though. Guess who I work with?"

Eric winked. "Your friend Harry? Why is that a problem?"

Cal sighed as they sat down with their sandwiches. "Well, I'll tell you." Eric already knew about Harry, whom Cal had known in S.F. Cal had discovered on his introduction to the pantry that Harry had come home to Reno as Cal had, and he'd been delighted. Harry was one of the party buds he'd had while he was still smoking crystal, before he'd gone to shooting it and the near-total isolation that involved. They'd never fucked, but they'd hooked each other up with connections, gotten each other high back when times had been good enough they'd felt they could afford to share. Now Harry was here, handsome, clever and poor, and Cal had been delighted to find a friend (and maybe more, he fervently hoped now, lonely in more ways than one) who was poz *and* who'd been through what he'd been through with speed.

"The problem is," Cal said now, "I just found out his speed freakage is still current."

"Are you sure?"

"Listen, when I'm around that shit, I can *feel* it. Especially when the person in question is so high he's vibrating like a fucking tuning fork."

Eric laughed, then sobered. "Can I ask you something?"

"Sure."

"Were you tempted? I mean, to do it with him? Speed, I mean. Well, and the other!"

"Well, yeah. I told you about the Committee, right?" Eric nodded. "Well, part of me thought, what could the Committee say if me and another poz guy got high and fucked? Nothing, nothing at all. But see the problem is I've got this tendency lately to start thinking about consequences, and I thought, well, what would happen if I did? I just got this job, so in addition to the Committee there are *real, actual* people watching my behavior! And you know Mom would know, and I've managed to get a fraction of her respect by getting my shit together a little, and it's only very recently Gina's started talking to me again without sounding like a corrections officer, and then there's you…"

"Me? You think I would judge you for that?"

"No, I don't think you'd *judge* me, but…well, I wouldn't be much of a friend if I was off chasing my high all the time, not thinking about anything but my own nut. Would I?" Cal asked, looking Eric in the eye.

Eric swallowed and looked away. "Well, I'm glad our friendship means that much to you."

Cal looked away as well and started in on his sandwich. Finally he said, "You know, this is going to sound really stupid. I mean, Mom laughed at me when I said it, but you know, I just wasn't prepared for how *hard* this would be—I mean, living. After I tried to kill myself I thought, OK, maybe I'm ready to live now. I'll do the right things, and everything will follow, you know? But it *doesn't* happen that way! At least, not as fast as I thought it would. I mean, I have to admit, when I met Harry I was so psyched. I thought, cool, he's poz and he's been through speed, and why didn't I ever fuck around with him when I knew him in S.F.? And then we started talking about all this shit we wanted to do, like he wanted to learn to snowboard, and to be honest I thought that sounded pretty fun—and hot." At Eric's raised eyebrow Cal said, "I know, that's for boys."

"Yeah," Eric nodded, "very cute boys!"

Cal laughed. "Don't think that's not part of why I wanted to learn! There's something about a guy in goggles and a beanie that just turns me on—I can't help it!" They both laughed and Cal went on. "But I could never go up there to the slopes by myself. I'd look like a fool. And *he's* not going to have any disposable income anytime soon for something like that. And that's too scary, I guess—I mean, doing something new all by yourself. I'm not scared of cracking my head open or anything. I mean, if I was ever afraid for my physical health, I never would have stuck a needle in my arm, you know? Isn't that funny, that I'm more afraid of someone laughing at me than I am of smashing my skull?"

"I know what you mean, about it being hard," Eric offered. "When I started going back to the gym, it was so easy to lose weight. And then it just stopped. But I guess what happened was it stopped being easy—it got *hard*, and I wasn't ready for that. All my life my body's been my friend, and now it's my enemy. And I have to admit, Cal, I haven't been in a while. I guess I'm afraid, too. I'm afraid I'll go back and redouble my efforts and work as *hard as fuck*, and it won't matter. I'm getting older, my metabolism is slowing down, my joints hurt…" He trailed off, realizing how lame they sounded out loud, these arguments he'd been using to convince himself it was OK to just give up. Cal was not the only one who had a voice that wrote on the water of the subconscious, pointing toward the easy way out.

Cal nodded. "You had a pink cloud."

"What?"

"That's a phrase they use in rehab. Some people, when they get off drugs, it's hard from the first day. It's just agony to be away from your beloved. But other people, at first, maybe for a few weeks or even months, they just feel great—it's so great to be off that shit, everything is better. But sooner or later that pink cloud you're on blows apart, and you have to face life the same way everyone else does. And it sucks, and it makes you want drugs, and you're amazed because you thought you'd had an easy cure. But it was just the pink cloud."

Eric sighed. "That's what happened to me." He guiltily grabbed a roll of tummy fat. "And it's coming back on me again. That's why I wanted to go to Port of Subs: something healthy for lunch." Eric eyed two teenage boys at the counter, who'd probably run over from Reno High to get their lunch. "Don't you wish you could be that young again, feel as good as you did back then, still thinking the world was your oyster?"

Cal shook his head. "No. But you feel that way because you were happy back then. I wasn't. I mean, it's crazy, but this is the closest I've come to being happy my whole life." He laughed. "I'm 32 years old, I live with my mother, I'm on disability, and this is the best my life has ever been." Then he scowled. "But it's *not enough*. Maybe...no, no maybe: there's *definitely* something wrong with me, but I guess I just...well, obviously the reason I did so much speed was because it made life *great*. I felt *great*. And I guess I still think it should feel great. Somehow. Like feeling OK, which I guess I do now? It's not enough."

Eric bit his lip as he thought about that. "You know, my whole life's been a pink cloud. I've always had it easy. Everything's always come easy to me. Things *were* great for me. I mean, I had to work, but I always knew that the work would pay off, and it always did." Cal nodded, thinking of a younger, sunnier Eric sitting on his bed announcing that he was going to be a writer. "Anything I set my mind to, I achieved. And it's only now I see it was because I never really had to do anything overwhelmingly difficult..." This wasn't true, of course, but in this moment it was true to Eric, and it had to be said that in the struggle against his weight he had found a battle he was for the first time in his life afraid he might not win.

"Listen," he said impulsively. "Here's a crazy idea. If I were to go back to the gym, would you go with me? Not all the time, just sometimes? And I'll go with you a few times to the slopes. Because, maybe if we try together, we can try harder, but at the same time it won't be as hard, you know what I'm saying?"

Cal blinked. Suddenly it seemed as if things *could* be easy, or at least easier. It just hadn't occurred to him that he had a friend in Eric, and friends did things together. They supported each other and encouraged each other, right? Cal looked back at the ruin that had been his life so far and realized that with the exception of Gina, he'd never had a real friend. "Yeah, I do, actually. That would be...that would be wonderful."

Eric extended his hand. "It's a deal, then? We'll really do this?"

Cal took it and shook it. "It's a deal."

On a busy winter weekend, Mount Rose had a festival atmosphere that reminded Eric rather happily and Cal rather uneasily of a concert or a street fair. But the difference was, once you'd been flagged through the parking lot and stood in line for an hour for rental equipment, you emerged not into more noise and more people, but less. Maybe it was the thin oxygen at 8,000 feet, or the dampening effect on the snow, or just the vast amount of space in which noise could get lost, but there was a *calm* on the slopes that surprised them both. They rode up the lift for the first time as part a group class that taught them little more than how to fall down, which is what they spent their day doing, watching other people whoosh by them and therefore proving that it was indeed possible to remain vertical on a surface that started moving under you every time you got on it. "You know something?" Eric whispered to Cal, watching more practiced boarders go by. "There are a *lot* of fat guys on snowboards. I fit right in!"

Cal laughed. "Well, they say snowboard boys are all stoners, and you know what *that* does to a waistline."

Eric chuckled, but the truth was, he felt better. He'd thought he'd be the only tubby guy on a mountainside carpeted with people in tight one-piece ski suits, but a good number of the boarders were "big guys" like himself. They spent a few more hours falling down and picking each other up—or trying to; the attempt usually led to both of them on the ground. When both their sets of buns and knees and elbows were too sore to go on, they returned their rented boards and boots and drove back down the mountain.

Cal sat in the passenger seat as his musical choice hummed out of the stereo. It was Junk Project's "Composure," a track off a Paul Oakenfold mix CD. There was something about it that was so appropriate for a ride down the mountain, a serene shimmer that matched both the white cliffs and the internal wavelengths of both Eric and Cal.

"That was awesome," Eric said, and Cal nodded. He felt *giddy*. He felt…high. But not the agitated high of speed or the disconnected high of pot. Like most addicts, Cal had become accustomed to monitoring his own emotional temperature, ever alert to what raised it to a warm, comfortable level. Had it been vigorous exercise at a high altitude? Had it been Eric's company? Both Eric and Cal had been pleased with each other for being game for another try. Like most novice snowboarders, they'd been victim to the body's natural desire to stop itself from moving swiftly downhill, and while their continued labor against this natural terror had not resulted in any measurable external success, Cal was still well aware that he had been terrified, and with reason, but had done the terrifying thing anyway, again and again. And he had to admit that had Eric not been there, had he not hauled him up here to fall and hurt himself alongside him, he probably would have given up after the first run. Well, maybe not—Harry was a chip on his shoulder now; he had pleasantly bitter fantasies about going into work and showing off his sexy snowboarder boyfriend to a spun-out Harry, as if to say, "You may be all talk but I'm not." But no matter; today it had been the positive of Eric's presence rather than the negative of Harry's absence that had driven him. At this point, Harry didn't even cross his mind.

Summing up all the day had brought him, Cal was astonished to find himself feeling something that could only be called *peace*. Was this what Luke had felt on heroin? If so, no wonder he never wanted to get off it, no wonder ordinary life seemed so impossible. And yet he had this feeling, and he wasn't on anything. What did that mean...?

Eric had been amazed as well by the snowboarding experience. All those young athletic years in Reno, so close to the slopes, and he'd never gone skiing or snowboarding or anything. *I've missed out!* But he hadn't felt old on the mountain, or fat, or anything—put everyone into the baggy microfiber jackets that were de rigueur for snowboarders, and the only thing that mattered was your sense of balance. Snowboarding, Eric realized, was like horseback riding, a sport where even fat people could be graceful. *If I'd never made this pact with Cal, I never would have known how wonderful this feeling is...* It occurred to him that boarders must have such a reputation as stoners, because how else could you feel as good as he did now the rest of the time? And yet for him, it decreased his cravings for weed: *All I have to do to feel like this is come up here*, he thought.

"So we should do this again?" he offered.

"Definitely," Cal agreed. "You're off Thursdays, aren't you?"

"Yeah."

"Maybe we should try a weekday next time. A few fewer people to run into, you know?"

Eric laughed. He hadn't minded the crowds at all, but he knew they irritated Cal. "Sure. That sounds like a plan." Boarding was a drug that had plainly hooked both of them.

Cal fulfilled his part of the bargain as well by accompanying Eric to the gym. He'd never been in a gym in his life, and yet he didn't feel the fear he'd felt snowboarding the first time—in retrospect he supposed it was because he knew that in Eric he had a guide familiar with the territory. Cal delved into the arcane language of the gym, learning the difference between a fast twitch and a slow twitch muscle, the best weight loads for pyramid sets, how to keep a shoulder width stance and bent knees at all times without thinking about it, how to keep your back out of it when you did curls.

One day as he was returning to the bench from the bathroom,

someone asked Cal for a spot. "Umm...I don't know what that is," Cal admitted sheepishly, and the man had sort of laughed and waved him off with a "No problem, buddy," gesture.

"Eric, someone just asked me to spot him, and I have no idea what he was talking about."

Eric laughed. "Oh shit, I'm sorry. I should have taught you that first off. Part of your gym etiquette lessons, like wiping off the bench. And also a good way to strike up a conversation with a guy you like," he grinned. "It's what we do when we're benching, when I ask you to grab the bar when I can't do anymore. I just forgot to tell you what it was called."

"So when you want to do just a little more than you can on your own, and I'm not here, that's when you ask for a spot?" Cal asked.

"*Or* when you want to hit on someone," Eric grinned, although he himself still hadn't asked anyone here for a spot.

"Like that guy over there."

"What?"

"See that guy over by the Smith machine? He's been checking you out."

"No way." Eric looked in that direction as subtly as he could. "He's pretty hot."

"So your point is?"

"Cal, I'm a big old tub of guts. Maybe I went to school with him or something, maybe he just recognizes me or thinks he does."

"Eric. He's like *21*."

Eric laughed. "All the more reason he couldn't be looking at me."

"You're underrating yourself."

"No, I'm being realistic."

Cal shrugged. "You're better-looking than you think."

Eric turned to him. "What do you mean?"

"Well, let's be blunt. You've got those legs of yours."

Eric smiled. "Yeah, they've never let me down."

"And that smile. You've still got those bright eyes and that smile, and a little weight on a guy with your frame isn't the end of the world."

Eric flushed. "Thanks, Cal. Thank you. You're looking pretty good yourself." He said it out of politeness but, as he really looked at Cal in his gym clothes for the first time, suddenly realized it was true. Eric was still fighting the voice that wrote on water, the same voice that told him it was OK not to do squats because of his knees, but he had to do them now because Cal had discovered that squats were the best conditioning for boarding, and he'd become hell-bent on getting good at it. Cal would never be stacked, but his legs were definitely thicker, his calves a little riper, his thighs meatier. Cal was, Eric realized with a swallow, *more* beautiful now than he'd been as a teenager.

Cal wanted to deflect this praise as eagerly as Eric had deflected his, but he knew that would sound like he was playing a game, fishing for compliments, sounding Eric out, and that would have defeated his purpose in convincing Eric that he was still a very attractive man. That purpose, Cal told himself not quite as sternly as he'd once told himself he was not gay, was *not* because he still wanted Eric, but because Eric was his *friend* and he was good-looking. So he simply said, "Thank you, Eric," and nothing more.

"We need to go over there," Cal said, indicating the Smith machine. "If your knees are bothering you, we should try the Smith for our squats. How convenient that we have to go over there now just as that cute boy is finishing up."

"Cal," Eric chided softly, but he grinned and followed his friend across the gym floor.

Eric's shift at the bookstore coincided with Gina's twice a week. Saturdays were busy, but Mondays were practically dead, and they had plenty of time to drink coffee and bullshit.

Eric loved working in the bookstore. The forward-looking owner had knocked down the wall into the next storefront in the strip mall and installed a café, which she'd realized was already becoming an indispensable part of a successful bookstore, and half of Eric's time was spent doing bookstore work and the other half he spent once again pulling coffees—which was the experience on his résumé (such as it was) that had gotten him the job.

He'd watch people sit in the café writing in notebooks, some of them clearly college students working on papers, but some of them clearly writing for the love of it.

"So Cal tells me you're working on something," Gina said, watching Eric watch a young man with a laptop. Eric turned, embarrassed as if Gina had read his mind, and in a way she had. Two writers, two keen observers, and neither one likely to miss a pang in another so familiar to themselves.

"I might be," he shrugged, wiping the counter. "Just some ideas I'm kicking around. About this new music," he indicated the stereo, currently playing a Jan Johnston song.

Gina wrinkled her nose; her own taste still tended toward nonmechanically generated music. "What's so special about it?"

"Well, it's dance music, but at the same time it's dance music for the head. If you listen to the lyrics, they're about emotions, the good and the bad, and most dance music is hell-bent on keeping you up and manic. It's music for raves, but like Cal says, the best of it is a replacement for drugs; you trip on the music even if you're not on drugs. I just...I don't know yet. There's an ethereal quality to some of it. And you know how when you hear most dance music? You know when you hear it that it's meant to be played in a club, on giant speakers, with at least a thousand other people pressing in on you; you know when you hear it anywhere else it sounds *wrong*. But trance, you can listen to it all by yourself, because what's a more solitary state than a trance? Whether you're alone or not, it's music for that solitary state in your head. And it's crazy, you know, that a country like Britain can have songs like this at the top of the charts, and we'll never hear them on the radio here." Eric finished, surprising himself. He'd thought idly about this for a while but had never sat down and made any notes, had never before just now tried to put his speculations into words. After having gone so long without writing, without saying anything to the world, what surprised him was that he did after all have something to say.

Gina wrinkled her nose. "No, all we get are the Backstreet Boys and that tripe."

Eric laughed. "Right, and why? Why doesn't music this

good—even you have to admit it's better than Whitney Houston and all the other shit in the Top 40—why doesn't it get airplay here? I don't know. I've never written about music, so I don't have the words for it yet. I may never. Maybe I can just write about the mechanics of how so many songs that suck get on the radio and the really cool ones never do." He shrugged. "It's just an idea. It might not pan out."

"At least it's an idea," Gina said. "I haven't had one of those in years. I'm the Fran Lebowitz of the confessional autobiography set."

"Would you rather be some Elizabeth Wurtzel type, gloaming onto your own misery and treasuring the importance of your own every statement, immortalizing each moment of navel gazing angst in 'luminous' prose?"

"Bah," Gina said, making a sour face. "No, but it would be better than never writing anything ever again. Wouldn't it?"

"Well…" Eric said, and they both laughed.

The bell on the door rang, and they turned to see Cal come in. "Hey, baby!" Gina said with affection and delight. Gina's relations with Cal had been improving steadily over the last few months, but this was the first time Eric had seen her so friendly.

"Hey, Cal," Eric said, automatically starting Cal's double mocha. "We need to get you fired up. Gina needs an idea."

"I'm jealous," she said. "Eric's got an idea," she said with mock petulance. "Where's mine, damn it?"

"The perils of the youthful autobiography," Eric cautioned her too late. "Afterward, all you have to write about is what it's like to be famous."

"You could write my life story for me," Cal said. "We could call it *I Hear the Refrigerator Singing.*"

"What?" Gina asked.

"Oh, when I was really, really high? But before I got completely insane, I would stick my head out the window, trying to hear where these voices were coming from, singing my name: 'CAL-vin HEW-itt, CAL-vin HEW-itt.' Finally I figured out it was the refrigerator motor, going *WHEE-dle, WHEE-dle.*"

Gina bent over laughing. "I shouldn't laugh. That's terrible."

Cal smiled. He was feeling pretty "on" today, having just come back from Mount Rose where he had managed a run that had lasted an epic 30 feet before he'd succumbed to panic and fallen. He hadn't heard his sister laugh in a while so he went on.

"Do you know the four kinds of tweakers? There are four, you know. There are the talk tweakers—blah blah blah—won't shut up to save the day. Then there are the project tweakers— 'I took apart your VCR!' Then there are the dance tweakers— won't get off the dance floor and everything sounds GREAT. Then there are the sex tweakers. That was me. No explanation needed there. Thanks," he said, taking his mocha from Eric.

Gina was bent over laughing. "Oh, no, this is too much."

"I got a lot of material, let me tell you. Hey, what's the difference between a junkie and a tweaker? A junkie will steal your wallet; a tweaker will steal your wallet and help you look for it."

"Oh, stop, it hurts," Gina begged. "You're killing me."

"At least you can laugh at it," Eric said. "I mean, it sounds like it was so horrible, and yet you're laughing."

"Well, there was a lot of absurdity as well as a lot of awfulness. There really is a book in it. Too bad I'm not a writer."

Gina looked up and this time it was Eric's turn to read her mind, with a flush of pleasure. "You should," he blurted. "Both of you, together."

"You think?" Gina asked Eric. "You wanna?" she asked Cal.

Cal looked at his sister's face, all lit up. No, he didn't want to, not really—he wanted to forget it ever happened, wipe away the memory. But he owed Gina, didn't he? Owed her money as well as pain, and how could he ever repay the money? "Well, we could sit down together and I could tell you the whole story. I've never really done that. And then we could see, you know, just how much material there is..."

And while the idea of reliving it all did sound awful, a light had gone on in Cal's head as well. Ever since the night of his suicide attempt, there had been a question mark in his head; that *Why?* had refused to fade or die. *Why am I still here?* Maybe this was it, this book, or at least the attempt at it, and what that attempt could do for Gina...

Gina's eyes were blank. The wheels were turning, and it was

Eric's turn to be jealous. But even as he was jealous, he was happy for her, happy for Cal, for all of them.

Irrationally, a moment from his past returned unbidden: the night he and his first friends in San Francisco had stood outside the Great American Music Hall and he'd nearly cried because he wasn't alone anymore. *The wheel turns*, he thought. *Here I am again.* Only this time was better, these were no friends who'd blink uncomprehendingly in the face of death and sorrow, never having known either; this time the friends and the happiness were for real and for good—he knew it, he knew it.

That night Eric went home, and for the first time since Howard had given it to him, he took the ring off his left hand. It was not an impulsive thing; he'd known this moment had been coming for some time. And that when it came, he'd know when. It wouldn't be a matter of asking himself, *Now or later?*

For the longest time, the memory of Howard had been nothing but pain; all the more so because their relationship had caused him so little pain and so much joy when Howard was alive. For the longest time, laughter, pleasure, sex, had all seemed like blasphemy; Eric was still celibate, had been for three or four years now since Howard's death. There had been so many things he wouldn't do, foods he wouldn't eat, places he wouldn't go, because they were associated with Howard and the very thought of them without him was agony, was sin.

Worst were the unexpected moments: those were the ones that really kicked you in the ass. For escape one night he'd rented *The Crow*, thinking it would just be a fun flick. But at the end when the grieving hero's beloved returns from the dead, if only for a moment, Eric lost it, blubbered like a baby, because he knew it was a lie, that when they're dead, they're dead; they're gone, and they don't come back, no how, not ever, not even for a moment.

The pain had faded more in the short time since he'd made friends with the Hewitts than in all that time alone in his basement, drunk and stoned and gorged. The memories of Howard were becoming pleasant memories, to be brought out, unwrapped and shared with his friends, as evidence that someone so wonderful, something so wonderful, *had* been real and he could prove it. He no longer felt like having sex would be "cheating" on Howard, wondered now if he was still celibate because he just felt too fat to get laid, but he knew that wasn't all of it—with Howard he'd learned what sex could be like when it was complete, when heart and mind and crotch were all linked each to the others. As he heard the plaints of the store's other employees, including Gina, about their incomplete relationships, the games people played instead of just connecting, he realized that he'd been so terribly lucky to have had what he had with Howard at all, that only God's own favorite could have been allowed to keep something so good as that forever—and that he no longer had any desire for the sort of relationship that was anything less, that he'd rather be alone the rest of his life than settle for less.

Taking off the ring was just one of a series of things that would have meant nothing to anybody else. First had come the night where he'd made Brussels sprouts the way Howard had, sautéing them in butter until they were exquisitely squishy. Then had come the night he'd watched *Aliens* again, a movie he and Howard used to love to watch stoned. And now this night, when he took the ring off, the ring he knew was telling the world he was married, unavailable, off the market. Maybe it was Cal telling him about that cute college boy checking him out; maybe it was the joy he'd gotten from seeing Gina get restarted with Cal; maybe it was something else that made it time to do it.

He looked in the mirror and was amazed at his own calm. "Yeah," he said, examining himself sideways and ruthlessly, "I'm still fat. But not as fat. Somehow someday somebody might find me attractive again. You never know." He thought back now with mild surprise at how enraged he'd been when he'd plateaued last time, how his greatest enemy had become the tape measure he would wrap around his belly every morning to register what he called his FP, the fattest point on his body. He'd conditioned himself now to measure it only once a week, and to look back critically on the previous week when it hadn't moved or moved back up a quarter inch and ponder, *What did I eat?*

How hard did I work at the gym? What did I do wrong that I can correct?

He was feeling stronger, healthier, more daring, and on some level he knew that he might dare to fall in love again, even though there was danger in that, too. There was always danger in having people in your life—people died on you, that's what they did, and then you died a little, too, but if you didn't die with them, sooner or later you had to find some more people who might also die on you and, if they did, put you right back in that quandary where you couldn't stand to ever be again. He went to bed and resolved to himself, *Tomorrow at the gym I'm going to ask someone for a spot.*

After his suicide attempt, Cal had started accompanying his mother to church on Sundays. Not that he'd gotten religion or anything, he hastened to tell Carol and himself, but certainly his experience had left him wondering about a good many things, and as he knew that this church was nothing like the church of his childhood, he was willing to give it a try.

His mind often wandered during the service, as many people's do, as perhaps they're intended to do if they wander in the right direction. He'd been afraid the first time, of course; for purposes of the book he and Gina were now outlining, he called it "*Body Snatchers* syndrome," the nagging fear that someone would stand up, point a finger at him, and make that horrible accusatory noise. But nobody knew who he was; he had no reputation that had followed him from San Francisco; there had never been a radio station devoted to his destruction; none of that had been real—but he wondered if he might not always fear in some corner of his mind that someday all that had seemed so real would be proven real after all. And which would be worse, the mad irrational delusion or the truth?

The pastor was a good speaker, the sort of minister who kept up with biblical scholarship and passed on interesting tidbits about what scholars were now saying Jesus *really* said. And the talk of love really was just that, not a smoke screen for smug hate. Cal doubted he'd ever really believe Jesus Christ was the son of God; the demagogues of his youth had made sure of that.

But the point of church for him was to give him a place where it was safe to at least think about it, to wonder if he was alive because there was a God of some kind after all and He had some reason for keeping Cal Hewitt around.

The mountains were a place like that for him now. He'd gone up several times with gritted teeth, resolved to conquer this difficult and occasionally painful sport, and had left each time spent, albeit a little closer to success. But finally one day, he couldn't say what it was, but it all came together—he picked the right music for his drive up the hill: Dead Can Dance's "The Serpent's Egg." The peak of Mount Rose was wreathed in a mist worthy of Cecil B. DeMille; the slopes were fairly empty. He forked out the $29 for an hour with a personal instructor and got Mikey this time, who was close to Cal's age and taught him more in an hour than the young boys he'd gotten before had given him all winter. Mikey was Master, and Cal was Kwai Chang Caine, and he laughed and had a hell of a good time, and that was probably why he was able to relax and do garlands on both heel and toe edge. After his lesson, Cal wanted a solitary turn at applying his new knowledge. He rode the chairlift back up alone and noticed the mountain's silence for the first time. *You could become serene just being here*, he thought. There was *something* up there that was so calming; he couldn't explain it because, like Eric, he'd never been a devotee of silence, but this was a different quality of silence…all he knew is that up here, there was no Committee of voices, they had never been heard from on any of his visits—you could be fanciful and call them demons and say we were too close to God up here, or ascribe it to the lack of sin in what he did up here, or you could just take that snowboy approach and smile dreamily and say, "Hey, whatever, man. It feels good, don't it?" And that's just what he did.

One Sunday morning a family came into the pew in front of where Cal and his mother were seated. Cal's heart stopped. There were two parents and two children, a boy and a girl. The boy was about 14 years old, and he was a dead ringer for Luke. It took all Cal's inner resources not to stare at the back of the boy's neck through the entire service—not that he didn't want to, but he was afraid someone would think he was a sexual predator. But the truth was, there was no room for lust in his heart when he saw this boy; the astonishment he felt at the similarity was too powerful to leave room for that. The boy had Luke's glossy hair, but cut in a style popular with teens; he had Luke's almost feline features, right down to the slight points on the tips of his ears, and, as any 14-year-old boy would, he had that amazingly soft, glowing skin—the skin that Luke owed now to heroin, not youth.

If only, Cal thought, his mind reeling. He thought of Luke's stories of abuse and abandonment, how he'd left home not long after the age this boy was now. *Where was this boy going?* he wondered. When it came time to get on their knees and pray, he looked at the parents; they were softly pudgy and careworn, but when they prayed, Cal saw not the fervent tension of the people in his own childhood church, but rather an emotional vulnerability that was almost shameful of Cal, of anybody but God, to watch. And yet he had to, had to know if this boy would be all right. And of course, it also passed through his mind how different his own life might have been had he been raised in a church like this, where the middle-aged gay couple was smiled on tenderly as they assisted with the service.

Where was Luke now? On a Sunday morning? Was he safe and warm in the house of one of the wealthy older men who loved the way they could take him out to dinner, so attractive and well-mannered, and then take him home where he'd do unspeakable things to them but never steal the silver? Or was it one of those weekends where things didn't work out, the kind of weekends on which Luke used to call on Cal for shelter and a loan to get his hit, a loan Luke would pay back with a financial honesty and farsightedness that always astonished Cal in a street person.

"You don't love me," Luke had snarled at him once, in the last days. "You can't love anyone." Cal had flinched and would have cried, if he had not been on speed and wanted to argue, but he had said nothing. Now, in this pew, looking at this boy as if God had given him a chance to see Luke again without heartbreak, without the fog of drugs, Cal forgave himself and said,

No, I didn't love you, Luke. I didn't have it in me. I wanted you to love me, with all the childish selfish need I had. But I wanted to be your friend, I did everything I could for you, and I didn't ask you for anything except what I didn't deserve: your love. I couldn't get your love because I didn't have any to give. Maybe someday I will. Maybe someday I'll meet someone, and I'll be able to give and not just take.

And when he stood up to sing, or at least mouth the words he didn't know the tune to, there was peace in his heart.

Carol's mind wandered as well as she prayed, oblivious to the family Cal was observing so minutely. She thanked God for bringing her son back to church, if only to visit. She thanked God for giving her a new church. She thought about Jim, the man she'd started seeing, whom she'd met here one Sunday when she'd come without Cal, and wondered when she'd tell her children about him. That was a big step in her mind; she'd been seeing Jim for several weeks now. (Cal's move to his own place had been partly motivated by his own desire for a social life free of complicated explanations, but it had certainly uncomplicated Carol's explanations as well.) She tried to tell herself it wasn't serious, no matter how much she thought about him when she wasn't with him. He was divorced, but that didn't bother her; things like that weren't important anymore. You tried, you failed, you picked up the pieces and went on. God knows if she hadn't outlived Cal Senior, she'd have divorced him by now. Jim was an engineer, obviously steady; he'd been employed by the same company for 20 years. After he'd finished putting his children through college,he and his wife had stared at each other when the kids were gone and realized an amicable divorce wasn't a bad thing. Now he was free and lonely.

Carol had watched him closely; she knew the ways of men and had stood back in her mind with folded arms for longer than her heart had desired, waiting to see what he would do in all the little situations that meant so much, not the manners he presented to her (any dolt could hold open a door) but to others—when they went out to dinner, how did he treat waiters?

Car parkers? The little people? How did he drive, cautiously or arrogantly? More importantly, how did he react at the sight of a beautiful much younger woman? Carol looked good for her age: she was still trim,and her face was less lined now that she frowned less. Her hair needed chemical assistance, but she forked out at the salon to make sure it looked natural. All the same, most men with Jim's still-athletic body, his plump income now free of attainder with his kids out of college and a no-fault divorce, would choose a wife younger than Carol. Still, it was becoming apparent to her that amazingly enough, Jim preferred a woman closer to his own age, albeit one who was as active and vibrant as himself.

She stole a look at Cal, curious to know how church was affecting him, wondering if he was here out of bored duty or if there really was something else pulling him in. She saw him looking at the Luke-alike but recognized that the look in his eyes was not puerile lust, but that somehow or another this inarguably beautiful young boy was giving him some kind of food for thought. She looked away, feeling slightly ashamed to have peeked.

Dear Lord, she prayed, *thank you for returning my family to me. Thank you for introducing me to Jim. Please let things stay like this for a while. I know these things go in waves, that it'll all turn to shit again someday, but damn it, it's our turn to be happy. Just let it be like this for a little longer. Amen.*

Ever since he'd signed the papers on his own apartment, Cal had both looked forward to and dreaded his first night out. Like any young person leaving the nest, his thoughts turned to the infinite possibilities available to the parentally unsupervised, but unlike other young people, some of those possibilities filled Cal with a bubbling ambivalent soup of desire and fear. There had been two things he couldn't do in Carol's house—get laid and do drugs. Now he could do either one and who would know? *They* would, of course; they were always there to watch his every movement. But if *they* really were only in his head, he could get high, couldn't he? Get high and fuck all night and who'd know? His new place was a duplex with thick walls—he could probably scream bloody murder and nobody would know. There was nothing to stop him.

Well, there was, actually. The thought of the infinite consequences that could befall him, probably would befall him even if they'd never befall anybody else, kept his lust for drugs at bay. It wasn't the same in Reno, Nevada, as it was in San Francisco; certainly drugs were as prevalent here as there, but it wasn't likely the cops would bundle him off to the hospital for a shot of Ativan as they'd done in S.F. No, get busted with speed in this town and it would be jail, and he got so paranoid on speed, he was bound to end up looking suspicious and attract the cops' attention, and if he was in jail he'd lose his job and thus his apartment, and if he was in jail for drugs, Carol wouldn't take him back in. Consequences that he had once ignored—sure, they were washed away along with all life's other minor concerns in the cataract of bliss that descended on him when he used to shoot up—those consequences were now themselves the stuff of the cataract, each thing that could go wrong (and his long spell of speed paranoia had given him a finely honed sense of everything that could go wrong) tumbling down and bringing with it the next thing that would go wrong. In the end it wasn't that he didn't want to get high, it was just that he was afraid to.

And afraid, too, to go out to the bars, to even try and get laid. Not because he wasn't good-looking enough; exercise and a generally healthy lifestyle had restored much of the youthful bloom to his cheeks, Cal being one of those lucky men, by nature slim and lithe, who keep their boyish looks beyond their usual expiration date. He was afraid to go to the bars quite simply because he knew they were full of speed and he would meet someone on speed and he would go home with that guy and they would get loaded and the cataract would begin. There was also the fact that not once in his life had Cal ever had sex without one drug or another; even his boring loss of virginity to the "nice man" had been accompanied by a joint. He couldn't imagine how excruciatingly boring sex would have to be without speed, but he knew it would have to be boring, could be nothing like the endless bouts of psychosexual combat that seemed to go deeper and darker as the hours went by, finally touching the very core of your being in the process. How could sex without speed be anything like that?

And yet here he was on a Friday night, getting ready to go out at last, alone. Conflicting desires continued to rage in Cal even as he showered and had a cup of coffee—some stimulant being necessary if he had to stay up until at least eleven before even walking out the door. *I should have asked Eric to go with me,* he thought now, kicking himself for not having thought of it earlier. *He would have gone, and if I'd have been with him, I'd have been safe—no way I would have ditched him for some tweak boy.* And yet at the same time some part of him also realized that if he'd gone with Eric, he would have had to leave with Eric, which would mean going home without sex for sure. And that was part of the problem, part of what was driving him out of the house after all his steadfast stolid resistance to the idea—the fact that he was as horny as fuck and if he jacked off one more time, he was going to cut it off rather than go through the motions again. *But will I be horny enough to have sex without speed? And even if I go home with someone who doesn't look high, what if he offers it? And then what about my being HIV-positive? I have to tell anyone I go home with*—they *would kill me if I didn't.* He knew guys he'd met at work, clients who said they didn't disclose their status but just had safe sex, and that was all they felt compelled to do. *Yeah,* Cal thought grimly now, *they can do that because they don't have a fucking Committee shrieking in their heads every time they even think of something remotely dodgy.* The voices were no longer his constant companions, but under stress—like now—they could be heard. *He's going out,* he heard the neighbors saying. *He's HIV-positive and he's a speed freak and he's going out to the bars.* "It's not illegal to go out for a drink," Cal muttered, kicking himself. He'd broken himself of the habit of talking back to the voices, but under duress he could find himself slipping, compelled to say something *out loud* to refute their argument.

Because there was one more overwhelming argument for

going out, and that was simply because he was afraid to. He was well aware of the transformation he was undergoing on the slopes of Mount Rose every time he went snowboarding: at first he had been afraid to go at all, then he had felt the natural human terror of standing on a board that was sliding downhill underneath you, out of your control. Then he had conquered that and found himself with a block against making toe-side turns; something about being dragged down the mountain backwards he resisted. Then he had conquered that and then there had been the fear of going too fast, of losing control, of being hit by another rider or hitting someone else on slopes that could at times resemble rush hour in L.A. But each fear had gone down to defeat, each one to his surprise but each one to a little less surprise, a little more satisfaction, a little more certainty that the next one would go down, too. He'd started reading the snowboarding magazines and had been introduced to an idea that had migrated to this sport from its precursors, surfing and skateboarding—the idea of progression, that you were never finished getting better, and yet each time you got better, that was the victory over that part of yourself that had been unwilling, uncertain, afraid you couldn't do it. It was the idea that you were competing against yourself, the keystone of skateboarding and snowboarding and other sports that could be not just individual but solitary.

Cal was in his 30s, and he would never be a halfpipe champion, but he knew now he could beat fear down, and if he could do it on the slopes, maybe, just maybe, he could do it in the valley, too. There were few things left on the hill he was afraid of now, but so many in the valley, and more than anything now, his fear of going out was holding him back, preventing him from resuming normal human relations. (*Beginning them, actually,* he thought, since he'd never had them before.) So tonight he would go, and even if he came home alone, at least he would have done it, broken through another wall of fear.

He drove down to Visions because he knew his paranoia wouldn't let him get drunk and drive, and if he didn't get drunk his judgment wouldn't be suspended and he wouldn't do speed.

Well, he would be less likely to do speed. Hopefully. *But what if I see someone I knew on the circuit? In Reno? I doubt it. And would I really be more afraid to see one of them because they had speed, or because I'd have to explain how the hell I'd ended up here? And I'd have to, wouldn't I, tell the whole truth, every word...?* In this whorl of fears and doubts he entered the bar.

Visions was the biggest gay bar in Reno, but at eleven on a Friday night it was deserted. Reno being a 24-hour town, nobody shows up at the bars much before midnight, unlike in California where the two A.M. closing time of bars encourages reasonably early arrivals. But Cal had gotten ready, let his eyes glaze over the television for a while, registering nothing he was seeing, and finally the caffeine triggered his impatience and he thought, *Fuck, I'll just go now.*

He stood on the edge of the dance floor with his drink, having strategically placed himself. He had decided not to be a wallflower, because that would defeat the whole purpose of conquering fear; nobody would talk to him, and he might as well have stayed home. Yet, standing by the dance floor, he could have something to watch (the self-absorbed dancers) without having to worry about being watched in return as he would back in the main part of the bar where the bulk of the cruising took place.

As he stood there an attractive young man came up to him. "Not very busy yet, huh?"

"No," Cal said, relieved that someone had done the hard part and talked to him first. He made small talk with the guy for a minute or so until he realized with a sickeningly familiar dreadlust that the boy was on speed. He could see it in the glaze of his eyes, in the pupils, and then of course there was the occasional drainage sniffle. *I can't, I can't, I want it, I can't.* SO EASY to walk out of here with this boy, get loaded and fuck, and then, but then, then what...

He walked away after having shown sufficient polite disinterest. He knew he should be feeling a surge of triumph: *The first time in my life I walked away from speed.* But instead he felt a sick shame, a sense of defeat, a yearning and a rage and a frustration as his black-winged demon flapped its wings inside its cage and screeched madly, so close to its supper and now so far. *It isn't fair*, it raged. *They are all high and having a good time, and why aren't I? That boy is so cute, you could fuck all night. It's not fair, I want it, I want it...*

Cal had not mastered his demon, but he had learned how to bargain with it, and he knew another drink would placate it, dull the blunt edges of its need. He got another Absolut Citron and made a strategic retreat to a banquette against the wall by the pool table—pool being another bar activity to keep your eyes busy. One of the players struck up a friendly conversation with him after asking Cal to move out of his shot, and sat down after he lost to chat with Cal.

"You're really hot," the guy said.

"Thanks. You're pretty hot yourself."

"What do you get into?"

"Everything, basically. Pretty anal. I mean, I like oral sex but, you know, it's just foreplay."

"I bet you have a nice smooth ass. I bet it's good fuckin'"

"Well, I know you have a nice ass, because I've seen it bent over the pool table. And it looks like good eatin'." The other guy laughed and Cal started to relax. *So this is how normal people do it*, he thought. *It's not so hard...*

"So you live by yourself?"

"Yeah," Cal said hesitantly, realizing that they were entering final negotiations and it was time for "the Talk." "But before we go anywhere, there's something I need to tell you. I'm HIV-positive."

"Oh. I'm sorry to hear that. How's your health?"

"It's fine, I'm doing good."

"Cool, cool," the guy said, taking a pull on his beer and looking around the bar, nodding his head to the music as if nothing untoward had just happened.

"So you still want to go?" Cal asked.

"Well, I don't know, I'm negative, you know, and I don't know if I should fuck someone who's positive."

Irritation flickered into life in Cal. "But you were about to go home with me and have anal sex before I told you I was HIV-positive."

"Yeah, and thanks for telling me. That's really straight up of you," he said with a smug insincerity that turned up the flame on Cal's rage. "That's great that you're honest."

"And if I hadn't been, we would be on our way to fuck right now," Cal said, unable to look the other guy in the eye for fear of punching him between them. "So since I was honest with you, you're going to be careful and avoid me, and end up going home with someone who maybe is positive but doesn't know it. Or does know it and just won't tell you."

"That's not the kind of thing someone wouldn't tell you," the guy announced smugly.

"How do you know? How do you know how many guys you've gone home with who haven't told you? If they don't tell you, how would you ever know?"

Cal got up and walked out of the bar. This was how people protected themselves, he realized: They refused to think or talk about "It." As long as nobody mentioned "It," everything was fine. It wasn't being HIV-positive that had blown his chance of getting laid; it was being honest about it.

He went home feeling shame and rage and frustration, wishing with all his heart, now that it was safe to do so, that he'd gone home with the tweaker boy. Nobody on drugs cared about safe sex, why should he? He wished with all his heart that life could be the way it was the first time he'd slammed and nothing and nobody in the world mattered at all. He beat off in a rage, allowing himself to dream of the point and the Rapture, but after he came and fell into bed, the alcohol hitting him harder than he'd thought it would, he was relieved. *I did it, I went out, and I didn't do it, I didn't get high. And I could have.* But still enraged at the pleasure denied him, it wasn't until the next morning that he looked at his accomplishment, looked at the fear he'd beaten, and nodded his head grimly, as if another bloody battle in an endless war had been won.

He'd gone up the hill the next day and had his smashup and ended his season. In retrospect, he knew he probably shouldn't have gone hung over and pissed off with an unreliable car, but boarding had been the only thing that could blot out the previous night's unpleasantness, the thing that more and more to him seemed to be the one thing that could just be *enjoyed*, a simple guiltless pleasure.

He watched cartoons all day and only got out of bed in the late afternoon because he was going to meet Eric when he got off work.

"What happened to your nose?" Eric asked when Cal got to the bookstore, regarding Cal's black and blue face and the Band-Aid on his nose.

"Broke it yesterday," Cal said nonchalantly, feeling like a tough guy.

Eric peered at it. "Ow. Does it hurt when I do *this*?" he said, feigning a palm strike.

"Don't even," Cal said. "And all I can score for it is aspirin. What I wouldn't give for a Percodan right now. You ready to go?"

Eric was nearly finished shutting up the store. "I need to go to the bank, drop off the deposit. Do you mind?"

"No, not at all."

"It's downtown, can you give me a ride?"

"I didn't drive. It was too nice out to drive."

Eric nodded. "I didn't drive either." It was nearly April and he could tell; the sun wasn't in his eyes all the time when he was driving, it wasn't dark when he closed the store this Sunday afternoon.

"It *is* nice out," Cal said. "Let's take the long way." Eric assented. They both already knew the "long way" involved taking Keystone down to the river and then hooking back along it; it was a much nicer walk than the dreary 4th Street corridor.

"So how's the book going?" Eric asked as they walked.

"It's hell," Cal admitted, and Eric looked at him with concern. "I never wanted to do it, but Gina needs it."

"Don't you think you need it, too? I mean, it can be cathartic to write about these things, you know. Gets 'em out of your system."

"Or just brings them back to the surface again." Cal couldn't ever explain to Eric what it was like reliving those times, how at the same time it caused him untold grief and pain at the same time it brought the black-winged beast out of its slumber, how even remembering the worst and craziest times could still make him *want it*, the needle and the rush. "I guess this is part of my punishment," Cal said. "Maybe if I suffer enough, it'll be enough. I'll cancel out the suffering I avoided all that time, the suffering I caused. Then maybe I might get to be happy."

Eric felt something welling inside him. Cal's gritty fatalism had touched him, his grim expectation of more "punishment" to come, his mights and maybes when he spoke of happiness. He looked at his friend and thought, *He deserves better, he's a good person. There's so much good in him, and these are just words. They sound hollow, I can't say them.* He looked at Cal and felt a familiar sensation, an old sensation—the same feeling he'd had ten years earlier, looking at Cal standing on his chair. What had Eric seen in Cal so many years ago as he reached for a book, head up, but beauty in motion, a sense of possibility, something in flight he yearned to reach out and grab as if he could take flight with it. But this Cal was different, physically, Eric realized: a few pounds heavier from their workouts, thicker in the shoulders and chest, but still with that waist you could put your hands around. And the look on his face now…it wasn't just the broken nose and the accompanying black eyes, but the set of his face that was different. There was something denser about Cal's soul as well as his body, denser and darker and more solid, less evanescent than it had been back then. Once it had been Cal's fragility, the willowy quality of his body and soul, that had attracted Eric, but this was different—it was almost as if he was recalling his initial attraction to one person, even as he looked now at a very different person.

Eric was different himself, too. The pain of love had once been a feeling to be embraced, enjoyed as a new experience; arrows shot through his heart were tidings of joy. Now he knew otherwise: Love someone and they will die on you. Cal was HIV-positive; yes today he was healthy and aglow but what about tomorrow, when the pills stopped working or their side effects killed him off? Could he really stand to go through the agony of loss again? He had been horrified to learn his own capacity for grief, for pain. *I would rather die than be that alone again*, he thought. *But if you don't risk love, then aren't you that alone for the rest of your life anyway, only without either the pain of loss or the consolation of love while life lasts?*

No, he told himself, shaking his head. *Don't get all analytical, and most of all don't ruin it.* They were so close to Wingfield Park now, the site of that fatal fateful kiss so many years ago—how many? A thousand? It felt like it. *Besides*, the snarling voice in his head told him, *You're not what you used to be. You're still too fat, too fat by far to be loved.*

Cal turned and looked at Eric and thought, *Now, how did this happen?* The look on Eric's face just as he looked away and shook his head was unmistakable and impossible at the same time. Cal looked away; they kept walking in silence. The look of love—that's what it had been, he was sure.

And yet. There had been so many days, things, he'd seen things that hadn't been there—people standing vigil on the rooftops across the vistas from his apartment building, so many people required to keep watch on him, people who'd never been there, voices shouting words that had never been spoken, an army of persecutors so real and not real at all, nights spent running in terror up and down Van Ness looking into people's faces, seeing their disapproval as one said to another, *He's disgusting, he won't stop shooting up.* Cal had learned in those days, learned from those days, that never again could he trust the evidence of his senses. If he turned and saw Eric looking at him like that, wasn't that a hallucination, wasn't it?

But hadn't those visions always been of what he'd always been afraid he'd see? Had they ever, even once, been of what he'd *wanted* to see? And even as he asked the question, he knew he wanted to see this. He wanted it and he'd always wanted it, and for so long he'd forgotten because forgetting had been the only way, and now all of a sudden maybe it wasn't.

This is insane, he thought. *This is really crazy, crazier than dreaming up the Committee.* Ten years ago Eric had been attracted to him, and Cal had run away, and they'd just been kids, really. So much had happened, so much to both of them since then. They weren't the same people; it was crazy to think you could go back like that, back to where it all started, only this time do it right, make it right, start all over again...

But there had been a reason Cal had become a drug addict, the same reason he had become an investment banker: he was a single-minded individual who had seen a single thing that could make it all right—the money and power he could have had that he thought would have protected him, the drug he did that mantled him in an armor of pleasure against all the pain of life. When the desire for a single thing took root in him, it was there until bitter experience poisoned those roots. And his desire for Eric, now, was not being poisoned but watered; hadn't he always looked for guys who looked like Eric, who felt like he imagined Eric would feel?

There was only one way to find out if he'd really seen what he thought he'd seen. *Do I dare?* He asked himself. *This is more than just waving at someone, you know.* And then something took hold of him, some inheritance of his mother's surely, that said to him in ringing tones, *Well, are you nobody? You have a job. You have your own place. You're not bad-looking when your face is in one piece. You're just a gay guy and so is he. And so you make a pass at him, so what? So he doesn't want it. You'll live.* And the voice of another mother might have been there, too, reminding him, *Like it or not, you'll live.*

"Eric," he said, stopping, and Eric turned and saw the decision in his eyes and waited, but not for long because Cal closed his eyes and kissed him on the lips, softly, just once, just for a moment, then backed away to see what he had wrought.

"Oh, God, Cal," Eric responded, relieved and terrified, and kissed him back, in front of God and everyone who might have cared or noticed if they hadn't been busy with their own business, so oblivious to most everything in front of their noses including two men kissing in a park.

Even in these moments, when we hold our breath in

amazement, our minds work on. The process of turning chemicals into words is suspended for a delicious moment and we're free from, if not the burden of consciousness, at least the burden of carrying that burden by ourselves. They say there are always two, the lover and the loved, that what goes on in one mind is not what goes on in the other's, but in a process of magic or grace or coincidence; in that moment there was one feeling in both their minds, one word that came to both their minds to sum it up:

Finally.

CHAPTER SEVEN
FORGIVING DAVID LEAVITT

Cal sat in the air-conditioned kitchen and tried to decide just how much he hated summer. "Let me count the ways," he muttered; talking to himself was one habit from his days on speed that had remained with him. First and foremost there was the fact that there was no snowboarding in summer— although he could have gone to Mount Hood in Oregon, had he and Eric not just spent all their available funds on the trip to Paris from which they'd returned a few weeks ago. Cal hadn't been wild about spending what money he had on a trip to Europe, but Eric had been so obviously mad about the idea that Cal had consented and shelved his own plan. That was the kind of thing you had to do in a relationship, he kept reminding himself. Probably most other people had figured that out by the age of 34, but since this was his first relationship, he had to try harder to think of these things.

Secondly, there were the wildfires that the drought had brought to northern California, fires whose smoke the jet stream brought right into the valley that held Reno. He watched Eric mowing the lawn, an incongruous sight in shorts, shoes and surgical mask. It had been 12 years since he'd first stepped into this house, and a critical analysis of

Eric then versus Eric now was unavoidable at the moment, given that his partner was wearing about as much on both occasions. Eric was hairier now, both front and back, although a few months ago he'd gone and gotten his back waxed one day. When Cal had seen the results at bedtime he'd said, "What did you do?"

"I got a wax," Eric said sheepishly. "You know, 'it really does look better with the hair gone' and all that?" he quoted an ad for electrolysis.

"Does it?" Cal asked in his Carol voice. "How often do you look at your own back?" On some occasions—i.e. when the lash was on someone else's back—Eric appreciated the clean cuts it could make, even as it gave him new insight into how difficult it must have been for Cal growing up with that lash on his own back. But that day it was aimed at him, and it stung more than the *rip-rip* of the cloths wrenching follicles from flesh.

"I thought you'd be pleased."

"I like you hairy," Cal said, looking away. Eric flushed, knowing that this Cal shared with his mother, too, this rare willingness to put themselves out there and express a desire, to let someone else know what pleased them.

"It grows back," Eric attempted, then realized that wasn't the right thing to say. "I'm sorry."

Cal looked up and smiled. "Wax your chest and I'll kill you."

As he watched Eric now, he noted with satisfaction that all the shorn hair was back. As it had grown, he'd reminded himself to pay attention to it, brush the little hairs with the back of his hand the way he knew made Eric suck in his breath. That was another thing you had to do in a relationship, Cal knew—keep the man sexually stimulated, don't let him get bored. But so far that hadn't been a problem.

Eric was tan and his skin had a healthy sheen of sweat— and sunscreen; that had been Carol's doing. She'd known how Emma felt about the sun and felt it her duty to carry on her work on Eric, showing him so many gruesome pictures of skin cancer that he'd caved in just to get some relief. His body was fit again; his work at the gym had paid off. Cal watched with satisfaction as the slight pad of fat around Eric's belly button bounced from side to side as he crossed the lawn. While Eric had escaped the chrysalis of fat he'd wrapped himself in years ago, the deep cuts in his abs he'd had in his youth had not returned. He knew he could get them back, if he and Cal stopped living as well as they did now, eating good food and drinking good wine (as they'd done with gusto in Paris), but that wasn't likely to happen. Still, he was watching himself now; the little pillow that Cal had come to love as much as Howard had was not, repeat *not*, to be allowed to blossom into a settee. Cal respected this willfulness in Eric and still went with him to the gym—as much now, he admitted to himself, to make clear to the others in the gym his claim on his no longer invisible mate as to maintain his own fitness.

Cal was enjoying this moment. The air-conditioning was a pleasant improvement to Emma's old house, and an unlikely source had paid for this new comfort. Howard's essays, which in their time had been considered rather politically incorrect, had suddenly been rehabilitated; his ideas on gay culture as the ultimate global homogenizer were suddenly of interest even to gay people, whose leaders no longer felt the need to suppress ideas like Howard's for fear that "they," the malevolent right wing, would use any dissent to their own benefit. (Indeed, this tendency to suppress internal dissent in the gay community had been one of the threads of Howard's argument against "homo-monoculturalism.") A university press had offered to reprint Howard's collected works, and as his heir, Eric was the beneficiary of the $30,000 advance, which had been the money that had made the trip to Paris more than just Eric's dream.

Cal had his own income; he still worked part-time and had his disability, and to his enormous surprise the book he and Gina had written was going to be published. It hadn't been easy, any of it—reliving it, talking about it— especially admitting the venal loveless thoughts that had gone through his mind when he'd been scamming Gina, but he'd known the Committee was listening when he talked to her, they would always be there, and the moment he lied they'd awaken, shouting their accusations and their rage at him in their zeal to destroy him in the eyes of the world. He had to be honest because the price of lying was to go mad again.

It hadn't been easy reading what Gina had written and telling her, "No, that's not it. That's not how it was, that's not how it felt." He wasn't the wordsmith, didn't know what to do to make it sound *right, true.* Gina had been insecure enough when they'd started, the book being her first project in years, without Cal telling her she wasn't doing it right. *Fights, pouting, drama,* Cal thought. *Thank God it's over. But it was good, or good enough at least.* Sometimes nagging doubts ate at him— these people in publishing, they remember her name and can trade on it, that's all: it's just a brand-name game. Eric ranted and raved about the business, constantly telling Cal, "It doesn't matter what's in the box of cereal, what matters is the box. That's all they give a shit about. They'll say, 'Here's a book about a gay guy in San Francisco.' So they'll try and convince people it's like *Tales of the City,* because that's the only other book they know of about a gay guy in San Francisco—And hey, that book sold a shitload of copies, so who gives a shit if this one is really anything like it or not?"

Cal knew in these moments that Eric was venting his own frustration, not realizing how his words made Cal wonder about his own cereal, whether it really mattered whether it was good or not, whether he'd ever know. Cal couldn't know he was feeling what every creator feels at the end of any project: *Does this suck? I don't think so, but I can't be sure. Oh, God, don't let it suck.*

The only way to know for sure, from someone who wasn't Gina, or Eric, both of whom were empathic that their book didn't suck, was to wait. "Publishing," Eric intoned one day on a roll, "is the last Stone Age industry. Do you know, they put books out faster *250 years ago* than they do now? Samuel Richardson could finish *Clarissa*"—they both smiled at that reference—"and go downstairs to his print shop and start cranking out books."

"So why do I have to wait a whole fucking year for my book to come out?" Cal asked.

"No good reason. Because publishing is slow, and it likes to be slow. For God's sake, they take the whole week off for Groundhog Day. They need a committee to decide where to go to lunch six months from now..." Cal smiled; he enjoyed Eric expounding in what they'd come to call his "TV star mode," named after the basement fantasies Eric had confessed to Cal.

Cal hated waiting. *Yeah, yeah,* he said to the dim memory of the Committee and what it would say—they were looking for the sort of immediate gratification that got him into a mess in the first place. *Actually, that was more like something Carol would say,* he thought with a smile. And whether the book was any good or not, whether anybody would ever cheer it, or damn it, whether he'd ever have enough money to feel like Eric wasn't pulling the lion's share of their financial weight, one thing he already knew: Since the book had been finished, the voices were gone, all gone, and not just when he was on Mount Rose or when he and Eric lingered in a nice restaurant over a couple bottles of wine. The silence in his head was golden.

When Eric came back in, the stereo would come back on, another accommodation Cal made to Eric. But where Eric had come to dread silence, Cal had come to treasure it, couldn't get enough of it. Fortunately, it was a big house and there was plenty of room for both of them to have their way at once when necessary. And room enough for Cal to begin in secret a project that was probably futile and pointless and which nonetheless he could not resist.

Eric pushed the manual lawn mower across the grass, lost in thought. He liked mowing the lawn; the rattle of the mower's blades rising and falling with his own efforts had a rhythm he enjoyed. Emma hadn't liked motorized lawn mowers— "Is the poor grass really so strong you need a machine to cut it down, dear?" she'd asked adolescent Eric, who'd complained about the extra work involved in doing it by hand. Certainly, on a smoky day like today he could relate to Emma's ardent desire to reduce air pollution, and he himself had come to enjoy the absence of noise pollution that came with using the push mower.

He liked the opportunity to get a little color, too, and at his age he felt silly slicking himself up to lie in the sun. The insecurities of middle age were encroaching on Eric's sunny confidence, insecurities that led him to worry about being too pale, too fat, too hairy—exactly to whom he would be these things was not specifiable; all he knew was that when he went on Gay.com to chat, the banner ads made it clear what it was to be gay, to be approved of—thin, tan, young, hairless. And all the erudite wit Howard had arrayed against this absolutist regime was no match for Eric's own unease about his fading beauty. *So call it shallow,* he thought with a grimace as he mowed, *I don't want some kid calling me "sir" anytime soon. I don't want the guys in the gym to stop looking at me again the way they did when I was fat. I don't want to dry up and blow away, and I won't, I won't.*

Eric had recently realized that the great danger of aging is acceptance, especially in a small town, especially when you're all settled into your life, for life. So you're married; so you can't screw around, and your spouse isn't going anywhere. So what the hell if you get fat and let yourself go? So you've got your job. It pays the bills and buys you some entertainment and anesthetic. What the hell if you don't learn anything new— let that roll of fat grow around your brain, too.

"I don't want to be like that," Eric had said to Cal in favor of the trip to Paris. "And now that we have Howard's money, we don't have to—we can keep moving, changing, growing, learning, *doing!*"

Cal agreed with Eric in principle; he'd already decided that now that all the drama was over, it wasn't such a bad thing that his whole life had been in flux, that he'd never settled in as an investment banker (or as a drug addict for that matter), and as a consequence he was still younger than most people his age, still ready for what life threw at him and ready to pick up stakes and go—though he hadn't mentioned this last part to Eric yet, who seemed for all his talk to be as awfully comfortable in Emma's house as he was. He still called it Emma's because Eric didn't like it when he called it Eric's, but Cal had a hard time appropriating someone else's property into this new organism that used words like "ours." Eric knew that, which was why he'd called it "Howard's money" when proposing the trip, knowing that made it feel to Cal as if they were both the beneficiary of someone else's largesse.

But however comfortable he might have looked to Cal, Eric was craving change. He knew it, he knew now what had prompted him to be so adamant about the trip. After Cal and Gina had gotten full swing into writing their book, Eric had started one of his own, a memoir about his mother. It had been inspirational, being around other people who were being creative—he'd forgotten that even writers can't work in a vacuum. And his mother had certainly had an early life, pre-Eric, that was worth recounting. *Post-Eric, too,* he thought with a wry smile, recalling of his mother arrayed in battle against Carol Hewitt—what, 20 years ago now?

And yet as he worked on it, something nagged at him, something new in himself. One morning he'd sat at the computer, blocked. He had his notes, his materials, his outline, and a self-imposed five pages a day to produce, and all the grit that he'd developed writing on deadline that enabled him to write whether he was inspired or not, but nothing was coming out. He knew there were advantages to getting older, one of which was coming to know your own emotional terrain, and he knew this wasn't ordinary writer's fear of the blank page, or run of the mill sloth, or anything else that could be overcome through sheer grit.

He confessed to Cal that he was blocked, and didn't know why. "You know," Cal said, "I've thought about why we can both write and not get jealous of each other. It's because I'm writing about myself, and you always write about other people. And maybe I'm asking for trouble by suggesting it, but maybe it's time you wrote about yourself."

The block in Eric's head was suddenly clear, its shape and texture and weight. "You're right," he nodded. "I've always written about what other people have done. But you know what the problem is? I'm not that interesting. I haven't done anything worth writing about."

"Like I have, besides being a fucking drug addict. You've been in ACT UP, been on presidential campaigns..."

"Right, and I've written about all that, and those were all about *other people.* What have *I* done that's so interesting?"

"Well, what do you want to do?"

"I don't know. Something new, something different—with you!" he appended hastily lest Cal think he was hinting about a breakup. "But something..." He let it drop and Cal, wanting to comfort him but not knowing where to lead the conversation, let it drop, too.

Not long after that, Eric had come to him pumped up with the plan for the trip to Paris. "I've never been there. I can write it off as research on the book about Emma. It'll be fun." Cal had thought of his snowboard, looked into Eric's bright eyes, and said yes.

Now as Eric put the mower away and wiped his brow, he thought, *I know now what I want to do. I know now what would interest me, might even make me interesting.* The road ahead would have been so clear, if not for one thought: *What will Cal say when I tell him?*

So it had been settled, and for once to Cal it seemed the time between deciding they were going to go and actually going had flown by. The vagaries of air travel pricing had them flying into London and taking the Eurostar through the Chunnel. New sensations kept both of them distracted—the dreariness of the landscape along the train tracks, both from the airport into London and from Waterloo station to the Chunnel. The English having chosen autonomy over progress, the train moved at a leisurely pace on ancient tracks until it hit the tunnel, when Cal could feel the train starting to pull G's.

As the train came out on the other side, the announcements, which had formerly been made in English then French, were now first made in French. Cal had a funny feeling of having come through on the other side of the world rather than just the other side of the water.

The train now ripped up the landscape as it made its optimal speed. "Auntie Em," Eric said as they watched the trees go past as if swept by a hurricane.

Cal smiled, misinterpreting Eric's meaning. "We're not in Kansas anymore, are we?" Eric thought to correct him but then decided, *That's true, too.*

Eric's college French served them well at the train station, when they needed to get a cab to take them to their cheap little hotel off Rue de Rivoli. At the hotel, the attractive young cab driver smiled at Cal and winked at Eric in such a manner that neither was aware of the attention bestowed on the other. They dumped their luggage, freshened up, and went for a walk, the fatigue of travel banished as it so often is by the pleasant shock of the new.

A quick trip down the Rue Saint Paul and they were on the Quai des Celestins and on the Seine, where tourist gravity pulled them toward Notre Dame.

"So this is what they mean by the light in Paris," Cal noted, glad that "they" were better at painterly prose than he was so that he could simply refer to them rather than try his own hand at it.

"Suddenly, Henry James makes sense," Eric said, and Cal laughed.

"Yeah, at long last."

At Notre Dame, Eric realized that the city was aware of the special quality of its light, and had recently done it justice. In a program possible only in a socialistic state, every building in the city had been cleaned for the millennium celebration. They could still see behind some scaffolding where bits of the cathedral retained grime—in itself almost an artistic statement, the shadow left to accent the light of the restored facades. Cal and Eric had been well prepared by their tour book readings to keep their wallets in their front pockets around the cathedral as it had become the holy citadel of pickpockets.

Inside the cathedral was a sight that struck Cal with its oddness. Mass was in full swing, even though the silent solemn worshipers were surrounded by a turbulent throng of tourists; occasionally a stern but surprisingly polite man in a jacket would remind tourists to keep their traps shut. *How could you have such a private communion with God,* he wondered, *when you were being watched like some curiosity from another era?* It didn't fail to occur to him that he himself had spent more than enough time feeling watched in his most private moments. "Let's go," he said to Eric, who having been raised without religion was glad to go.

Everyone spoke English. Well, there were always a few old people who pulled a sour face and would point at the cash register rather than speak to you, even if they were in the heart of the tourist district and had probably absorbed more English by osmosis than most students of the language had in years of school. Eric and Cal were both hungry but in no mood yet for a sit down dinner; they ordered sandwiches out of the case from a stand near Notre Dame, a roll with tomatoes, cheese and mayo.

They'd intended to just wolf it down as they left the Ile de la Cité but as they took their first bites of the roll they stopped and looked at each other. "The bread," Eric said first. It was so flavorful, so unlike anything he'd ever had.

"The mayo," Cal added, which was clearly freshly made with a hint of dill.

"The tomatoes," they said at the same time and laughed.

"Emma grew tomatoes like this. Almost as good as this, may she forgive me from above."

"She was here, remember? You think she didn't know these were better?"

Eric had read about French food—not just the Michelin star restaurant food, but the whole French approach to it, the stringent regulations, the ornate grading of the butters, the legendary bread. But he never imagined that some shoveable snack would be up to those standards as well. Maybe it wasn't— maybe *this* was low-grade food in France.

"No wonder they hate McDonald's," Cal noted as they leaned on the wall and ate their sandwiches over the river, watching the flat bottomed tour boats hum up and down.

At first, along the walk towards the Pompidou, Eric had

tried to make note of little places he wanted to come back and check out, perfect little cafés and exquisite candy shops, the legendary Berthillon ice-cream store where there was always a line out the door. But there was just too much, there was something around every corner to take the place in his mind of what he'd just seen.

They'd been walking around for four hours before Eric looked at his watch and realized it was nine o'clock. Cal was astonished; yes, it was summer, but it was so *light* for nine at night! They got back to the hotel around ten, at which time the June sun was just setting.

Their room was small but convenient; they'd paid extra for their own bathroom. Eric took a shower as Cal, already cleaned up, opened the French doors over the Rue Saint Paul. The sound of cities was altered here; there were more little scooters, raucous live music rose up from a local bar without anyone sticking their head out to complain, even though it was well nigh on midnight by now. And of course, there were the strands of conversation in French that echoed in the narrow street and bounced around their room.

They made love with the lights off but the French doors still open on the warm night. The thought that they might be watched occurred to Cal and yet strangely provoked no fear; he had already realized this was a city of pleasure where even cardinals probably lingered over aperitifs. Though he couldn't know, of course, he thought he knew that even if someone *did* see them, they'd shrug and look away; sex here wasn't like it was at home, it wasn't something people felt bad about, it wasn't...well, fucked up. The laughter and the arguments and the singing that rose up from the street seemed only to fuel their sexual fire; it was as if they needed to do justice to the cascade of life washing over them.

They went to the Louvre, which was closed thanks to a museum guards' strike. Eric was disappointed but perversely pleased that something so French had been the reason he'd been denied access; Cal was relieved as all he'd really wanted to see were the pyramids.

Men looked at them, women looked at them. There was no

hard aggressive edge to it as there was in cities at home; it was more a courtly game. An eyebrow raised ever so slightly, a supercilious gaze that deigned to recognize an equal, the occasional smile and glance backwards that signaled a promotion. They crossed a pedestrian bridge near the Louvre with flat benches along the middle like road stripes at home. On one of them a beautiful young man was sprawled, legs open across either side of the bench, head propped up with one hand, long-lashed eyes that were indisputably closed until, as if through some psychic gift, he opened them just as Cal and Eric were looking up from his crotch to his face. His eyes had a bored, sultry, seemingly impassively evaluating yet simultaneously seductive quality that by now both men knew was more show than anything; nonetheless after they passed him Eric looked at Cal to see if he'd been jealous and smiled to see Cal's eyebrows wiggling at him.

Both men understood what Emma had meant when she had talked about that look in Parisian eyes, that look that said, of course life is about pleasure—beautiful buildings and beautiful people and marvelous food. Every little thing *should* be this good, *n'est-ce pas?* They took a bus to the Eiffel Tower, and that was when Cal realized, really felt in his bones, *I'm here, I'm here. I'm in Paris, France. I never knew I ever wanted to be here and now I never want to leave.*

A thought began to buzz in Eric's head like a fly he kept swatting: *Don't be ridiculous—a writer in Paris, how clichéd.* He thought of the old buffalos on Clinton's press bus, hooing and hawing about the good old days—Paris before the War, Paris after the War, blah Blah BLAH—And yet...

He and Cal split up one afternoon; Eric had finagled a meeting with a French agent, less for any serious purpose than to get the tax write-off on the trip. He took the Metro to the 9th arrondissement and walked down twisty streets to the woman's building. He buzzed himself in with the code he'd given her and found himself in a courtyard, where he stood lost and confused for all of three seconds before a bustling concierge emerged and inquired as to his business. His meeting was surprisingly pleasant;

both parties knew it was a formality, a favor called in by a mutual acquaintance, and yet the agent was in no hurry to get him out. In fact, she seemed rather interested in his book on Emma, especially when he talked about her time in Paris and how she'd left for his sake. But afterward he wondered, *Did that go as well as I thought. Would she really be interested, or was it all politesse?* The creative part of him, allied with the ambitious part, wanted so much to believe it, wanted to walk on a cloud on his way back up the hill, where he was to meet Cal at the Anvers Metro before they scaled Montmartre to Sacré Coeur. He'd come to spot a realtor's window from half a block away, with its orderly block of cards advertising properties for sale or rent. Over the last few days he'd also become agile in converting dollars to francs and vice versa in his head, and while he and Cal had looked at several of these windows out of idle curiosity, this was the first time Eric had seriously stopped and taken the measure of his capacity for paying Parisian rents. To his surprise, they weren't that bad, nothing like London or San Francisco. In Paris, it seemed, people of all economic circumstances could actually live *in the city.*

I could do it, he thought. This morning, taking the metro with the people on their way to work, walking down the little streets as neighbors said *bonjour,* watching the little green machines scour the sidewalks, he already felt like he lived here. It was as if the die had been cast; he was already here.

Cal hadn't picked up any French before their trip, partly out of laziness (Eric knew enough) and partly out of fear (I'll get a vowel wrong and they'll laugh at me). He'd relaxed on discovering the prevalence of English, but today was his first time out alone and he was nervous. Not of anything tangible— years of residence in New York and San Francisco had given him an easy facility with public transport systems, and he knew when and where he was to meet Eric and how to get there, he had plenty of little green *cartes* for the subway stuffed in his pocket, and plenty of time to get there.

He knew what he was afraid of, in the concrete—his first

conversation with a French person. In the abstract, though, he knew it was something else, just a wall of fear, the same wall he'd felt when he'd first gotten on a snowboard and the ground under his feet started moving; the wall he'd felt trying to master toe turns, trying to overcome the instinctive terror of being dragged downhill backwards; the wall he'd felt trying to psych himself up for his first little jump; the wall he'd felt trying to psych himself up for his first 180, then his first 180 with a grab—which was as far as he'd gotten in two years of boarding, but was nevertheless satisfied with. In the course of reading the snowboarding mags, watching Bluetorch TV, and talking to his instructors and the acquaintances he'd struck up on the slopes, Cal had been introduced to the idea of progression, the knowledge that each step you take is a major victory, though at the same time you never allow yourself to rest on those laurels. And it wasn't about you versus anybody else; it was about you versus your own limits, your own fears. On his best days on the slopes, Cal could remember how far he'd come more than he dwelt on how far he had to go.

Without a doubt the grit he'd learned on the board was cross-pollinating; the fear he had banished on the hill had by osmosis been banished down in the valley as well. Fear itself, etc., he reminded himself as he went into a café. *"Un café, s'il vous plaît,"* he said at the counter, and the man nodded and went to work pulling Cal's espresso (cheaper when ordered standing at the bar than it was when ordered sitting at a table, probably designed as a labor-saving device for the counterman). No laughter, no eyebrow, and Cal realized he'd crossed another wall of fear, a wall that was gone now, forever. He paid with the attractive franc coins, left a proper tip, knocked back the heady brew, said *"Merci,"* and departed into the bright morning.

"Bonjour," he now said breezily to the newspaper man at the Anvers Metro as he paid for his *International Herald Tribune.* *"Merci,"* he added with a smile, thinking of an episode of *Dexter's Laboratory* where Dexter shouts *"Omelette du fromage!"* as his inexplicably correct answer to everything,

and feeling his own sudden giddy urge to speak his handful of French words to anyone who would listen.

Now, sitting in their kitchen back home, Cal gently extricated himself from his reverie. Memories of Paris now filled his single-minded imagination as drugs once had, leaving little else of sufficient interest to engage his mind as completely or as satisfactorily. He checked Eric's progress on the lawn and estimated he had another half-hour to go to finish up. There was just time to squeeze in a lesson, he thought, and he headed up to Emma's old room, which now being his and Gina's workspace was respected by Eric as off limits. Inside he put on headphones and pressed play on the CD player, which picked up where it had stopped.

Cal listened keenly and repeated, *"J'ai besoin d'une ordonnance. Je prends habituellement Septra."*

When Eric finished the lawn he looked for Cal downstairs. He didn't find him there, so he checked outside to see if Cal's car was parked in the driveway. He saw it and stopped looking, figuring Cal was upstairs. He took a shower (alone—he'd looked for Cal so they could have done it together), flopped onto the couch, and idly spun the dial. News from France on CNN perked him up—nothing remarkable, just the usual political financial scandal. Still, there was Paris on TV.

Eric's foolish desire had coalesced on his return. More than anything, a visual in his head prompted him, egged him on: He saw himself ending up like a character in one of those old *New Yorker* stories from the '50s. He would be the little man in a little town who'd been to Paris once and spent the rest of his life miserable, sighing and dreaming. The kind of story *they* wrote, he thought bitterly, the ones with their grants and their fellowships and their residencies, snug and secure and self-satisfied, taking little slices of human agony and pinning them to corkboard as if they were butterflies. Divorced from human struggle and human pain and human desire, plumply above all that, looking down to tweeze out someone else's misery and coat it with "luminous prose." Wasn't that literature, wasn't that art, the unhappy ending? Weren't happy endings for middlebrows who still hoped to find some happiness themselves, who hadn't fetishized suffering as a higher form of existence? Eric had risen and fallen, and he was glad now for his fall, glad that he hadn't ended up on some fucking pedestal somewhere, divorced from any desire other than the desire to solidify one's position in the literary firmament.

Recently, Eric had read David Leavitt's story, "The Term Paper Artist." He had been aware of Leavitt's fall from literary grace after a plagiarism scandal. While Eric hadn't been happy about it, he'd recalled the author's pompous, self-important statements at the height of his fame; how Leavitt had referred to Europe as "the continent" when he'd been living in Italy. Most importantly, Eric remembered reading *Family Dancing* as a young writer and thinking, *I'll never make it if* this *is what they want, if* this *is literature.* "The Term Paper Artist" had shocked him; it was like something written by a different person—the sense of humor, the plainspoken admission of guilt, the ribald tales of the coin in which college boys paid for the term papers the story's narrator, coincidentally also named David Leavitt, wrote for them... Eric forgave David Leavitt everything after reading that story, and more, he forgave himself for his own fall. *You can start over,* he told himself. *All over. You don't have to do what you used to do, what people expect you to do.*

Eric loved this house, loved his memories of it, and he wanted to leave, wanted to start all over. *I want to be happy; I want to live. I don't care if it's cliché to be a writer in Paris. I don't care if it's cliché to be happy. I want it.*

A summer storm threatened, and the temperature plummeted as the clouds rolled over the Sierras. Impulsively, Eric dressed for a run around Virginia Lake.

He'd been glad when he'd been able to start running again. Some things were different; he wore knee braces now and drove to the lake rather than running there and back. What hadn't changed was the feeling he got somewhere around the end of the second lap, the easing of the sharp edges in his mind, the sooth-ing rhythm of his own breathing.

Life with Cal was different than it had been with Howard, with any other man. For Howard, sex had been an art, like being a geisha, and he'd approached it with almost as much formality, Eric saw now. For Cal, sex was creative in the way exploding stars are creative. Cal had introduced Eric to rough sex, slowly, almost fearfully, as if Eric might recoil at the idea of treating a lover other than tenderly. Eric had found dark places in himself, a black satisfaction in attacking Cal's body that had surprised him. "I'm sorry," he'd say when he thought he'd gone too far, and Cal would say, "For what?" Some nights Eric looked forward to their sex with a mixture of excitement and dread that he'd never had in his youth.

There were sharp edges between them outside of bed some-times, too. Like the first time they'd had ice cream after coming back from Paris. "It's not very good," Eric remarked. "It used to be better."

"It's not as good as Berthillon, that's why," Cal said.

"No, it's not. But I guess we'll just have to forget how good that was."

"I don't want to forget," Cal snapped, immediately regret-ting it and taking Eric's hand. "Sorry." Cal had been afraid that he'd just revealed his secret desire, but Eric couldn't know that. Eric didn't want to forget, either, but what could they do? He could afford to go to Paris, but what about Cal? What would Cal do there? How could he ask his partner to just pick up stakes and go?

It hurt, as he ran around the lake. Not in his back, or in his knees, but in his heart. It hurt because he was so sure he would have to choose, Cal or Paris, Cal or Paris, seemed to be the choice from left foot to right foot. And he knew he would choose Cal and not regret it; he knew he would dream of Paris all his life and wriggle under the pin through his heart that this unfulfilled desire would cause. There were things in Paris that had been unforgettably beautiful, and none of them compared to Cal on his back with his legs in the air, looking up at Eric, reaching out to him, waiting for him to pin Cal to the bed, but not as a specimen, not an abstraction, but to join him to his other half, and if Eric had to be pinned in turn, so be it. It was worth it; he'd never have it any other way.

Cal came downstairs and saw that Eric was gone. The positive ions in the air before the rainstorm made him agitated so he got in his car and went for a drive. He wanted something magnificent, something thunderous, he wanted to get on the freeway and cut loose. He picked a Radio 1 Essential Mix he'd downloaded off Napster, *Oakenfold at Space in Ibiza, Part 1*.

DJ Pete Tong gave the intro as Cal pulled out and took Plumb down to the freeway. As he accelerated to merge into traffic, the first song ripped wide open, keyboards like bells ringing and bees buzzing. Cal shifted and moved into the fast lane. He knew what happiness was now, what joy was; it wasn't the Rapture, but it lasted longer and the punishment for feeling it wasn't Hell. There was a cost, though—there is no paradise attained without pain. Turning his face away from the Rapture, for good, would never have been possible without Eric in his life. To turn away from something towards nothing, in the hope that somehow, someday there'd be something...he thanked God he hadn't had to be strong enough for that.

He had Eric, and something with Eric that he thought impossible for him, for two people, a private communion most people never get, a few get with God, and the happiest few have with each other. He'd found joy in sex without drugs, he'd found sweet silence in the presence of another, all the things he'd been offered once long ago and had run from in terror were his now, at last.

In Paris there had been a feeling in him, an astonishment that people *could* live for pleasure without it costing them their souls—it was what Parisians did every day. He hadn't been wrong, after all; everything *should* feel good, every moment of every day should be fully satisfying. He'd just gone about it the wrong way, that was all.

The tears ran down Cal's face as his car threaded up into the mountains, this was how he'd wanted to feel all his life, and he loved Eric, and he loved Paris, and he would have it all, he would. *I won't choose, I won't have to, I know it in my heart.* Here was another wall of fear and hesitation to knock down, as he thought of what Eric would say when Cal came home today and brazenly and finally announced that somehow, some way, they were moving to Paris.